Citizen/Alien

by

H.C. Whittaker

Grosvenor House
Publishing Limited

This book is published by
Grosvenor House Publishing Ltd
Link House
140 The Broadway, Tolworth, Surrey, KT6 7HT.
www.grosvenorhousepublishing.co.uk

A CIP record for this book
is available from the British Library

ISBN 978-1-78623-174-1

To The Dreamers
The Believers
And Mark

CONTENTS

INTRODUCTION

To Collection

It is another beautiful sunny day in Nassau. It is made more beautiful because my granddaughter Kiera is here to share it with me. We are sitting on the terrace at my beach house. The gentle breeze is swaying the palm fronds, and the ocean waves are lapping almost noiselessly at the shoreline. We talk, we laugh, we sing, and I marvel at the miracle, or series of miracles, that have brought us together in this paradise. These hard-won miracles that delivered me from financial ruin, depression, and loneliness in to the light are the basis for this book.

"Here's the church

And here's the steeple,

Open the doors

And all the people." Kiera is laughing.

And all the people indeed. And where was I, and what was I doing at four years of age?

The first story - THE INNOCENTS - is the first in this series of sixteen stories that chronicle my fifty years, stretching thousands of miles, and seemingly many lives.

This memoir begins by telling of the experiences of an unwanted child, born to American parents in the Canadian city of Vancouver, British Columbia. This child's experiences as she grows, and ages, lead us through North America, Europe, Asia, South America, and finally the Bahamas.

It took fifty years to banish the demons planted in the mind of the innocent child that this author was. Fifty years for her to accept the fact that she, as much as anyone, deserved respect, love, and to live a life free of fear.

"Never let them break your spirit," her grandmother often admonished her. The spirit faltered often, yet it did for her what all the King's horses and all the Kings men were unable to do for Humpty Dumpty; it never failed her entirely. Through trial and error, she finally became a whole person.

My little Kiera is dancing in the sun. Dancing and as happy as all children everywhere ought to be free to be. My desire is that this memoir will enlighten, and encourage compassion, empathy, and understanding.

Weather I shall turn out to be the hero of my own life, or weather that station will be held by anybody else, these pages must show.

Charles Dickens novel

David Copperfield

THE INNOCENTS

CHAPTER 1

Grandma Malone (Grand) was the sort of grandma that appears in children's books, at least physically. She wasn't very tall, and her figure was, well, round I guess you'd say. She called her form a (borderline figure). She dressed mostly in black, a classy, versatile color she told us, one that goes anywhere and with anything and when she went out the last thing she'd do before opening the front door was to pick up her little black hat from the hall table, and standing in front of the mirror she would tip the little hat a bit further to the left.

"Cockily," she would say with a wink. "You want people to know you have spunk dear, and that way they won't be as inclined to walk all over you." Proud of having designed and made everything she had on, including the little hat, she would grab her cane, (she would likely have made that as well if she had had the time) and off she would go, with at least one of her seven grand-children trailing behind. This was Friday night after all, and when we were small, (small being younger than fifteen, by which time most children are too busy for such things) we took turns accompanying her on her shopping trips.

We loved those Friday nights. They were the high points of our week. I'll admit to being happy when my three older cousins decided they were too old or busy (to help Grand shop) and I came in to my own, so to speak, at the age of eight.

It must have been close to six o'clock by the time I got home from school, changed, and Grand was finally ready to set out. In my mind's eye it's always rather dark, and definitely always raining.

I guess it sounds strange, but I remember feeling particularly cozy walking along beside Grand in the wet, dark evening clutching tight to the handle of my huge umbrella.

We always took the bus downtown, and people being kinder and gentler then, always made room for the little old lady and the child to sit together. After we finished shopping for sewing material and choosing a half pound of candy for each family member, (everyone had their favorite kind) we, each grabbing a handle of the brown paper shopping bag, headed straight for the Woolworths lunch counter.

Hot tea and fish and chips, and unless she had been suffering from a bit of heartburn, lemon in her tea. At the end of the meal, her work-worn hands searched the cracked, and peeling black leather change purse for just the right change, and she said with a wink: "Here, you leave this extra for the lady, because she treated us special."

On the way out the door she would slip me a quarter, coincidentally just the right amount for the little booth that took four pictures all in a row once you adjusted the stool, pulled the curtain, and deposited the quarter in the slot. Grand never did join me.

"No darling. I don't look good enough for a picture to be taken." Yet she looked awfully special to me.

She must have been very special to the many people she clothed, fed and housed as well. For as I grew I came to realize that the bits of material she had purchased, and I never saw again, had been used to ("Make some adjustments in a garment that is just right for so and so.") The friend who stayed over a night or two, and we never saw again, who left with a "Nice bagged lunch so you won't have to bother to stop to eat." A man, young, and his very young wife and baby who one day knocked on the door of the old Victorian looking for a room to rent, who stayed two weeks, and were sent away with more than when they had arrived, and a thank you for being such good company. "You don't owe me a thing. Just do for someone when you can someday."

Well I guess in the strictest sense of the word all of these people were homeless, but to Grand they were "Just people who need a little help sorting things out."

Grand always told mum that she was setting a bad example for my brother and sister, by her treatment of me. She never did stop however, and it was (us and her). Somehow I wasn't one of them but Grand often told me that someday I'd be glad, happy to be me, to be different.

When mum was pregnant with my sister she had me memorize my dad's work number just in case she fell ill and needed him to come home. I was twenty-two months old when my sister came along. Grand told me that I should have been sent to school early. Mum held me back however, until my sister was ready for first grade. I was eight and one half years old by then.

"She's tiny, no bigger than Laura. Why should I bother to send her before I have to?"

"She won't be with her own age group. She's being held back when she, if anything ought to be put ahead."

Mum even dressed us alike; she loved the attention she received when people approached to comment on (the twins).

"You have no right to undercut a child's potential, and individuality" Grand always said. "Never allow anyone to break your spirit, or tell you what you can, or cannot accomplish darling. You must believe in yourself" Grand always said.

Of course there were always people who had the power to hold you back, no matter how hard you worked, and how positive you were.

I was ten years old when Grand bought us a house to live in. My worst memory during the years of all the evictions was one particular motel. We three children and mum had arrived late at night in a cab and entering the room, I ran straight for the bathroom and closed the door before turning on the light. Spiders, I remember the spiders. Large and black, they covered the walls, shower curtain, tub, toilet, everything. Within minutes we found ourselves in a cab again, on our way to Grand's.

I was five when we took our first cab ride to nowhere. At the time I was afflicted with the nervous habit of blinking. Grand told me that she couldn't count the number of times I blinked per minute. I shook too, and would burst into tears for no apparent reason.

Mum was always telling me that I was a wicked child, and that the devil was going to come along one night while I was sleeping and carry me off. Sometimes when I was sitting across from her at the kitchen table she would look up, and pretending to see something behind my shoulder would make faces, and laugh and pretend she could actually see Lucifer, as she called the entity, and at the time, being small, I had believed her.

The day before dad left I remember sitting at the dining room table, and he and I building the most beautiful house of Lego blocks. They had been arguing all day, but that was usual. Now just as I placed the last block on the wonderful dream house we had built, he raised his hand and smashed the dream apart. I began to cry, and he told me not to be a baby, and more words went between them, and was you're nothing meant for me? And he got up and left the table and she laughed maliciously. I was five years old.

The next morning before sun up I heard someone moving about and got out of bed. I found dad walking to the front door, and he told me to stand at the living room window and watch for his car. He was just going to the store. It seemed an awfully long time, and the sun was up, and his car never returned.

Looking out of my bedroom window I liked to watch the duplex that sat across the side street. I knew that if I stood long enough the smiling lady would come out and wave to me. I must have made a sad little picture, crying and waving, my little face framed in the dirty window pane.

One day mum got very busy. She bathed us all and even washed our long matted hair, and dressed us in our best dress. We were having company she said. Years later I would be told that the company had been a social worker. After the social worker left I was not permitted to look out of my bedroom window, and the blind was pulled down tight and tacked in place. That was the last I would see of my friend, the smiling lady.

I had another friend however, a friend I didn't think anyone would take away. She was so kind to all the children who visited her, and sometimes she would look right at me and speak. Sometimes she even said my name. I knew she cared about me. Then one day a man came and unplugged the television set and carried it out the front door, and with it my friend Betty White. That afternoon we rode away in a taxi, and I wondered if Betty White felt badly because she couldn't say hello to me anymore, or if the smiling lady had seen my hand waving out the side of the closed blind.

Dad reappeared not too long afterward, and we moved from the motel to one of the most expensive hotels in the city. Initially, we had room service, and ate dinner in the lovely hotel dining room every night. However, as the weeks wore on our dining experiences became more and more humble, until finally we found ourselves eating in all night greasy spoons. The best of the worst was frequented by drunks, and shabby elderly people. One old lady in particular always wandered over to our booth, to, she said "Admire the beautiful children." She smelled of urine, and had the odd habit of putting ketchup into a mug of hot water and then she broke the crackers up and stuffed them in with the ketchup. Fortunately, we were too young at the time to realize the full horror of what was happening.

Eventually we found ourselves back at Grand's. The Salvation Army brought us a big box a few days before Christmas. Laura began to cry that there must not be a Santa. I told her that he had to have helpers deliver early because he was so busy. The lady looked sad and told mum that she was lucky to have a girl like me. I was seven that year.

Another rented house and I was allowed to attend the school across the lane, but only for a few months. We all came down with the measles. "You had to go to school, didn't you? You had to bring this home to the others." The chicken pox came next. I was covered with what felt like millions of mosquito bites, and burning blisters. I was left alone in a dark bedroom and told to be quiet. I lay listening, and when it sounded as though everyone was in the other part of the house, too weak to walk, I crawled on hands and knees to the telephone in the hall and called Grand. I remember my thirst, terrible thirst, and when I asked for water mum told me that if I nagged her for it I would not get it. "Patience is a virtue and wicked people are supposed to suffer."

It seems as though Grand stayed for days. She brought calamine lotion to smooth over my burning itching skin, gave me all the water I wanted to drink, and fed me chicken soup.

Well Grand bought the house for us to live in, and dad went away again to work. Laura and I began day classes at the convent school. Mum often threatened to send me there to live permanently. I guess the only thing that had prevented her from doing so was her sorry financial state. She didn't like it when I called Grand for help. Like the time she grabbed Laura by her hair and jabbing her knee in Laura's back forced her face into the wall. I pulled her away, and Laura escaped.

That evening mum ordered me into the den to listen to her make a phone call. She called my best friend's mum and told her that I was a wicked child, a child who had raised her hand to her mother. As she hung the receiver back in its cradle she turned to me, and with a sneer said: "Now let's see how many friends you have."

My friendships remained intact. The adults we came in contact with must have at least sensed the neglect and abuse we suffered. They were kind, though none were either able or willing to try and free us from our nightmare.

When I was ten years old Grand gave me an alarm clock. Now I could wake myself and the others, pack our school lunches, and braid my sister's hair, praying all the while that they would hurry and not be late for class. I would catch it if they were. The Mother Superior stood watch every morning, then went from room to room to check for late arrivals.

The Mother Superior had problems of her own. She was young and beautiful, and very lively. She would gather the long skirts of her ugly black habit up in one hand and delight in playing soccer with the boys at lunch time. She could play hop scotch, and skipped double Dutch better than anyone we knew. However she cried a lot. As we girls grew older we realized that her crying times coincided with the unannounced and abrupt departure of a handsome priest. There were two over the years, and the crying episodes were followed by her taking little vacations. Sometimes she took quite a few vacations until the crying stopped. Years later we found out that she left the Order (ironically named the Sisters of Mercy) and because of doing so was disowned by her family. The good news was that she married an ex-priest, who, quite happily became a city bus driver.

Most Saturdays I carried a big green bag of dirty clothes to Grand's to wash them in her old ringer washer, and spent time visiting with Grand while they dried in the sun. Rainy days were laundry mat days. We had a new model washer and dryer in our kitchen but were never allowed to use them. Mum claimed the noise gave her a headache.

Sundays I left at eight a.m. for the ice rink. I had my quarter, enough to get in and buy a candy bar those days, and water from the fountain was free. I made sure to stay all day, and prayed all the way home. Yes, I prayed as I walked that neither sibling had done anything to enrage mom that day. I was now held totally responsible for their behaviors. They had learned, as Grand had predicted, to disrespect me. They now blackmailed me, particularly Laura, by threatening to misbehave. They might accuse me of swearing, or saying something about mom, anything to get something from me, though I had little to give.

I once asked them why they wanted to see me hurt, when I had always defended and cared for them, and Laura answered that I was supposed to look after them, and give them what they wanted because I was the oldest. "And besides, they like us best." Everything I did was belittled, whether academic, athletic or simply wanting to be left alone. I once asked the whole family seated together why they did not leave me alone if they did not like me. I never did get an answer, and was too young at the time to make any sense of them on my own.

A kind British lady who taught elocution at our school three times a week asked me to join her drama club. "You will need ten cents three times a week, and we will meet after school for one hour. All those dimes will add up and help us pay for transport to the spring competition." I was thrilled. I ran home that day as fast as my legs would carry me. I kept thinking, "I am not a nothing, I am not a nothing." And I somehow convinced myself that mum and dad would be real happy to hear this about me.

"Oh my God" Mum laughed. "We would have to hide in the last row of the auditorium in the dark. Look at her. Would we claim to own that?" Dad would go along with her if they were having a friendly period.

"The others were not asked to join were they? Who do you think you are?"

"We were the greatest singers, and your mum was the most beautiful entertainer I ever saw. Did you know that? You think you can compete with her?" Their laughter followed me to my room. I was ten years old. I should have known better.

That spring dad started a little league ball club for my brother. He had been turned down when he tried out for others. "You run like you've got a piano tied to your ass" he told him. My sister got a camera, walking doll, and those new style shoes they called squashed heels.

Jack did get a shiny new three speed bike, judo lessons, a new ski jacket, and skates. I did ask how he could do so much for one, and deny me a dime three times a week. "He deserves the best; he's going to be a great man someday, you watch. Christ, you'd better be nice to him so that he'll talk to you." They were given wonderful presents that year. Transistor radios, a walking doll for Laura, a camera, I will never forget that year. On Christmas morning I tore the wrapping from a small china perfume atomizer, it was empty.

I did not say anything; all of my concentration was centered on holding back my tears. "You keep your nose in books. We couldn't see that you needed anything. You're not like the others".

I began sleepwalking shortly after this Christmas. I shared a bedroom with Laura, and mum noticing the window open one morning, and the floor soaked with rain commented, "you will give dear little Laura a cold. We really should send you to the convent. The nuns will give you penance to do, and perhaps put you in a cloister where you won't be allowed to talk to anyone. You'll spend your life in prayer, and have a chance to save your black soul." On another occasion I sleepwalked into the den, picked up the telephone receiver, and began talking to the dial tone.

One evening as we sat watching television, I happened to glance up and saw tongues of fire reflected through the piano window. The neighbor's roof had caught fire. I froze in fear, afraid to utter a sound. I would be chastised for disturbing mum with the bad news. It had happened before. That was the day President Kennedy was assassinated.

It was a dreary, rainy day. The Mother Superior came running into our class crying, something we had seen her do many times. This day however, we were marched over to the church for an impromptu mass, and then sent home for the day.

I entered the house by the kitchen door. Mum appeared suddenly in the doorway leading to the hall. I immediately told her the news, and she scolded: "Why would you burst in here with such awful news? You are wicked. I had a lovely day planned, and you have ruined my day." I walked to Grand's.

This time I kept quiet. I heard the fire trucks approaching, sirens blaring. Next morning we found out that the kids next door had been playing with matches and ignited a tree. The flames then shot up to the roof. Our little neighbor had been injured, though not by the fire. Her alcoholic father had beaten her as punishment.

I knew about alcoholics. Once while we were staying at Grand's between evictions, mum's brother burst through the door one evening. I was about six at the time. Finding no-one downstairs, he began to throw things, curse, and finally hollered that he was going to kill whomever he found in the house. We heard thuds as he bounced from wall to banister and back, as he made his way up the stairs. For a moment there was dead silence, then suddenly he burst through the door. I looked round the room. Mum was backed against a kitchen cupboard, eyes wide, frozen in fear. My brother and sister, he a toddler, stood holding on to one another crying uncontrollably and a couple of cousins had fled and were hiding under a bed.

This scene has replayed itself so often in my memory. I did not hide. I remember my feeling of anger as though it were yesterday. I hollered to him to go ahead and kill us. No one could quiet me.

It was David and Goliath and David won. Uncle fell to his knees in front of me, and taking my hands in his, quietly apologized. Then standing, he slowly turned, and made his way down the stairs.

I would grow to know many more tyrants.

One of the most frightening, vicious people I have ever known was a fellow grade school student I nicknamed (Nazi boy). Good grades were rewarded every summer with a trip to the Berlin Wall. He was every teacher's nightmare, occasionally tyrannizing the class by launching into long, frenzied speeches proclaiming the superiority of the Aryan race. Shouting and pounding his fists on his desk, his face would turn beet red, as he lamented the end of the second world war before all undesirables had been exterminated. The teacher would order him to drag his desk out into the hall, and tell him that he was not going to join the rest of the class until he apologized for the disturbance. Days would pass, and his parents would intervene, apologizing for him taking class time, yet never for the wicked remarks.

The war had ended six or seven years before his birth, and so he had been trained to hate. He was no more than a robot, an anti-Semite, an anti-everyone, with no mind of his own: Whose family had immigrated to North America after the war and took advantage of the democratic right to voice an opinion-by voicing the opinion that most, or at least half of us had no right to exist. He attended church with his parents every Sunday morning, and as I stared at the back of his closely shorn head, from a pew a few rows back, the dichotomy of hatred for most of the human race, and their claims of Christianity always confounded me.

The little girl who sat in the first seat in the first row of our class was particularly vulnerable to Nazi boy's claims that the imperfect should be eliminated. She was fourteen and in second grade. Her size was that of a six year old, and her face, that of someone older than her years. Her little fingers were curled and misshapen, and her nails deformed. And when Nazi boy frightened her, the little hand reached in to the pocket of her uniform and drew out a Kleenex, then silently crying she wiped her eyes.

Bev was a kind sweet soul, and her presence taught more about compassion and hope, than Nazi boy's tirades were capable of converting us to hatred. In fact they had the opposite effect. He was by far the most unhappy, miserable child among us.

I was in my late teens, and happening upon a concert in the park I stopped to watch the amateur musical competition taking place at the outdoor theatre. Within moments of finding a place the little one appeared. Dancing, playing her accordion, smiling happily, free I thought of the burdens German boy carried. Her parents, now quite aged, sat front row center, supportive, and proud as always.

My friends' parents attended parent teacher nights. They hugged their children and told them how proud they were of them, and had long talks with the teacher. These were the children that were favored by most teachers, and who were the most successful. These were the children who had school supplies, and who did not have to risk a sharp rap on the knuckles with a metal edged ruler for writing on both sides of their paper, or letting their pencil go dull for fear of sharpening it away and being left with nothing. I always wanted to ask the teachers who disliked the disadvantaged children if they blamed us. Didn't they realize we wanted nice things, necessities? These were questions only I could hear.

Silent screams of indignation, anger, and so intense that sometimes I thought my eyes were going to pop out of my head, if my skull didn't burst. The nuns claimed to have taken a vow of poverty when they joined the order. They seemed to be very proud of this. I wanted to know if choosing poverty rather than having it chosen for you because you were small and helpless, brought you closer to Gods?

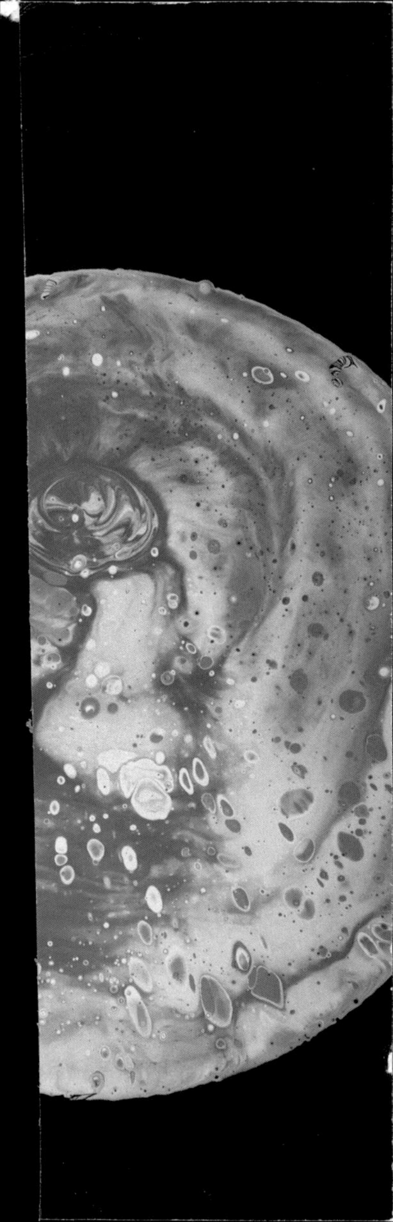

From a distance the world
looks blue and green,
and the snow-capped
mountains white.
From a distance the ocean
meets the stream,
nd the eagle takes to flight.

From a distance, there is
harmony,
and it echoes through the
land.
's the voice of hope, it's the
voice of peace,
t's the voice of every man.

From a distance we all have
enough,
and no one is in need.
And there are no guns, no
bombs, and no disease,
no hungry mouths to feed.

From a distance we are
instruments
narching in a common band.
Playing songs of hope,
playing songs of peace.
They're the songs of every
man.

Oh, God is watching us, God
is watching.

Christmas Peace

treehouse
community and faith

CHAPTER 2

Grand's kitchen was often a place of refuge. I never think of her but what the image of her brandishing a big mixing spoon as she talked and hopped up and down between stove and kitchen chair doesn't appear in my mind's eye. On one such chilly autumn night I sat with Grand talking when uncle's two daughters arrived home.

The eldest of the two was sly and manipulative. Overweight, with mousy brown hair, she did not speak but squealed, high pitched, yet monotone. Her sister Erin, younger by only ten months than Terra was slight, blonde, and popular with the boys. Both were nervous, and while Terra overloaded on sweets, Erin always appeared to be sitting on a chair of nails.

Out of the blue this particular evening Erin, usually the most pleasant of the two said: "Let's evaluate Hedy. I say she's quiet because she's a conceited snob."

"No" Terra said. "I think she is what Aunt Ellen always says she is. A wimp who just listens, and no matter how nasty we are doesn't defend herself." She followed this with her signature high pitched giggle, and bit into another doughnut, while all the time complaining about her weight.

"Well at least you know you're nasty." Grand told Terra. "Now what are you going to do about it?"

"Eat some more" Erin remarked. And the battle, another of their daily battles was on. Grand referred to them and my sister as (the fighting cocks) and attributed their behavior to a dominant Irish gene. Whatever the cause, they spent a great deal of time with mum, who complained that I irritated her because she (couldn't get a rise out of me) as she put it.

"Don't let anyone control your mood dear" Grand had told me often. Put downs, of which there were many, were an invitation to fight. Hurt feelings were the stuff of wimps, and placid is what I was dubbed.

While I could move out of the way of nasty people there was one day of the year that I could not escape. Ash Wednesday. The first thing in the morning the nuns marched us over to the church. At one point during the mass the priest dipped his thumb in a bowl full of ashes, and we moved single file past him stopping to put our forehead in the way of his big dirty thumb so that he could smear the sign of the cross across it, in big dirty ash. We were forbidden to remove this mark for the remainder of the day. We were admonished against removing it even to walk home after school. Walking through the Protestant neighborhood had never been pleasant in the school uniform that the neighborhood kids referred to as our monkey suits. But with a big black mark across your head?

I believed that God expected me to be smart enough to protect myself. Therefore by fifth grade I decided to wipe the big ugly smudge away before walking home. Out of sight of the school, forehead clear, I made my way home by the usual route. That of ducking down alley-ways, and through yards to escape the kids who would holler cat licker, cat licker, and throw rocks my way.

The following morning Nazi boy told me he had seen me wipe my face and then reported me to the nun. My hands red and sore from the beating with the metal edged ruler, I spent the remainder of the day in the corner of the room, my face pressed to the wall.

Fifteen years later I would encounter Randy, who told me that our school years had been the worst years of his life. The nuns and clergy had harassed him by telling him repeatedly that if he did not convince his father to convert to Catholicism, his father would never enter the pearly gates of heaven. His father was Jewish. A Russian immigrant who had spent his life laboring as a maintenance man, while a good portion of his hard-earned money had gone to support these so-called Christians. Most painful to Randy were the memories he had of causing his father to cry. The guilt he was unable to overcome preyed upon his mind and heart and led to a prolonged period of depression.

I recall dad being home only twice on Christmas day. Pre-occupied with her unhappy life, Christmas was a particularly depressing time of year for mum. She took the bus downtown Christmas Eve, to buy what little she could afford to put under the tree for us. Most often we did not have a tree, but went to Grand's for Christmas dinner. The night before Christmas was chosen, because of the last minute sales. She returned home late and alone she wrapped the little things she had taken so many hours to select at the dime store. She wrapped with bits of paper that had not been torn, when ripped from last year's presents.

Creeping to the foot of my bed, I listened as she wrapped and cried quietly. Barely five feet tall, she seemed to me to be simply an aging child. One could not help but feel sorry for her at times like these, despite her sometimes cruel behavior. The ten cent perfume, the scarf she said would bring out the green of my eyes, or compliment the gold of my hair, I remember these things with tears of my own.

I was ten the last time I visited Santa. I had been made to go for the benefit of the younger ones. I told him that there was no point in any of us believing. Poor sad-eyed Santa. His compassionate kind eyes, peeking out from between the inches deep synthetic white hair, wished me well and I beat a path to the nearest exit.

The grandchildren who lived with Grand full time were allowed to put a tree up in the entrance hall, and decorate it. Grand did not pay any attention to the tree, and if I happened into the kitchen while she prepared the turkey dinner alone, I often found her crying. Perhaps that was her reason for wishing to be alone.

Christmas and Easter season the nuns ordered us to go door to door selling cards. Grand paid our tuition, but it was never enough. Parents were expected to do extra work to raise money as well. Bingo, bake sales, and flea markets all needed volunteer labor and donations. This put tremendous financial pressure on many of the families. Some of which were so large, they were given a tuition discount for two or more children.

We were instructed to wear our school uniforms while canvassing the neighborhood. The nuns wanted it to be obvious that we represented the school. The curses, and doors slammed in our faces were points we were racking up in heaven. Christ, we were told was suffering right along with us. Now this was a fine idea if you were one who believed that misery liked company, otherwise it was not much comfort. Personally I did not feel one bit comforted, or comfortable, with the idea of all that suffering.

I couldn't see how people could get away with dictating how we spent our free time. We dare not refuse the sanctimonious nuns and priests, therefore the burden of moving the merchandise was placed squarely on the shoulders of the parents. Most parents did not want their children going door to door (begging) yet most could ill-afford to buy up all of these unnecessary things.

Cat licker, cat licker, I run as fast as I can: I am crying and praying that I don't trip and fall or drop my books before I reach home. I was fourteen years old before I found the courage to ask the leader of the ignorant neighborhood group (he standing alone at the time) what he thought of me forming a group of my own. Yes I said I thought we might punish him for living in a particular house, or attending a particular school. He told me that was crazy, and of course it was, which was my point. Then I asked him if he had chosen to be born into a Protestant family. "Of course not.

You can't choose who you're born to." No of course not. An odd confused expression crossed his face, and as he turned to run away he directed a few obscenities at me. After this the stones he threw never came quite as close to hitting me as they used to.

Grand told us to be true to ourselves, because the nasty behavior of others was their problem. She used to say that sticks and stones could break your bones, but names could never hurt you. Of course they could hurt, but her message was not to let them. "Consider the source, consider the source darling." Though her eyes would tear up sometimes, and she would tell me that ignorance bred fear, fear fuelled hatred, and that eventually everyone was cheated by irrational thinking.

Grand's mother's family had emigrated from Austria through Ellis Island and though Grand's mum had married a French immigrant, the children were raised with their mothers' cultural traditions. One day the teacher asked our class to report to her the next morning on our ethnicity. Both mum and Grand told me that you trace your heritage through your mother's side. The following morning I reported this to my teacher, only to be told that I was crazy. Oh well, we ate chicken soup to cure our colds, felt guilty eating pork, and were told all about the Day of Atonement every year. All of this while attending the Catholic school. This was all very confusing, until one evening I overheard a conversation between Grand and one of her sisters.

I was fifteen the year Grand took me on a trip to California. "Well we just followed mother's traditions; they did not even speak about religion."

Then Grand, "Well father would have sent us to that Baptist church remember, where they forbade you to cut your hair."

They both laughed, and then Grand's voice broke a bit, and she said "Mother just wanted to protect us. Well, we marry Catholics, and are we any better off? I was never really accepted in that church, no matter how hard I worked for them. They aren't much better off in some places either. Look at all the fuss over Kennedy, because he is a Catholic running for President. Now this one is asking questions. She does not feel that she belongs anywhere. The men in our family never drank or raised their hand to a woman either. No good comes of denying your own. Poor mother, we have been subjected to bigotry anyway, and have to feel guilty to boot." then as they both began to cry a little, I slipped off to bed, and cried myself to sleep.

My happier memories are of Grand seated in her big wicker armchair on her front porch. Spring and autumn evenings were spent this way, listening to stories of her past. Tell me a story, Grand, is all we had to say, and laughing she would ask if we had yet heard this one or that, and once we found one we had not heard yet we settled down to listen.

Grand was only ten years old, and her mother sick in bed after giving birth called Grand in the middle of the night and told her to go out and kill a chicken and make chicken soup. After graduation from school Grand worked as a teacher, nurse, dressmaker, and designer. The story about the period spent working in a sweat shop best illustrates the kind of woman Grand was.

The sweat shop inhabited a dingy, dirty, shabby old building. It warehoused human beings paid by the piece, and worked until they could not see straight by the end of the day. The worker was given a ticket for each piece of work completed, the ticket placed in the worker's drawer at their work station. At the close of the day the worker turned in their tickets, and collected their pay. Grand found it odd that the woman that sat to her right never raised her head to acknowledge her, not even to say good morning. After finding her tickets short day after day upon her return from lunch, she realized the reason for the woman's odd behavior. She always returned from her break sooner than everyone else as well.

The workers were not allowed to take their tickets from the drawer until the end of the day. Now on the tenth day Grand returned from lunch, and turning to the silent one said: "Here, you obviously need these more than I". Handing the woman all of her tickets she stood and walked out. Grand never looked back. The following morning, dressed in her best street clothes, and carrying a carpet bag full of samples of her work, set out. Walking door to door in the wealthiest neighborhood of the city, she canvassed for customers. Within a short time she had more work than hours of the day to complete it. Pride, motivation, and an unwillingness to be beaten down, had changed her life for the better. "Friends called me reckless for walking away from what they considered the security of the sweat shop, but you know darling there is never any security in being a door mat."

When we were in the early elementary grades Friday nights were spent with mum. After school we boarded a bus for downtown with her. We referred to it as going shopping, though looking is a more accurate way to describe our forays through the dime stores. The old wooden floors had been worn white over the decades, by people such as us. People with not much money to spend, women mostly, wandering the aisles, looking at the pretty inexpensive things. Perhaps they bought a ten cent perfume for a little girl, such as me.

Or a ring for twenty cents, your very own birthstone, set in a cheap tin band. And for twenty five cents you entered that little booth, pulled the curtain, and had four black and white pictures taken in a row. Mum never would have her picture taken with me either.

Stores closed at six o'clock those days on Friday nights, and after browsing with mum we would make our way to the coffee shop up the street. There we sat in a booth, and mum would teach us how to order our meal, and use the cutlery in a proper manner. Yes we had to sit up straight and mind all the proscribed table manners.

It was on these occasions that mum listened to what we had to say, and the conversations never deteriorated and dwelt on the anger she felt toward dad, as it did when we were at home.

I felt so sorry for him when she called him horrible names, and poked fun at his appearance. And sometimes when he had been subjected to her cruel assault for hours he would break down and cry sitting right there at the kitchen table. Then she would smile the mean ugly smile, just like the one she used when I cried.

She began to leave the house at around noon when he was home, returning very late, mostly after midnight. They had their own rooms on separate floors of the house, and had lived that way ever since I was about seven years old.

Dad made more money when he worked away, and he'd send all but what he needed to maintain himself in the lumber camps home to mum. She put it all away saying that she was keeping it for a rainy day, and then sending us to our Grand's to eat.

The first few weeks he was gone she would play the piano at midnight, and often in to the wee hours of the morning. When I complained that we needed to sleep so that we could go to school, she appeared at the end of my bed, and banging the iron footboard, began hollering. It happened more than once, and the tirade began with her spewing hateful thing about dad, and predictably progressed to her unhappiness about being a mother. It continued for hours and when sheer exhaustion and fatigue caused me to fall asleep in spite of her, she banged the iron footboard to awaken me.

She kept this up until she actually foamed at the mouth, and her hair, a thick dark mass popped out of her hair pins and flew wildly round her head. Framed in the light shining in from the dining room she took on the appearance of something not quite human, and very frightening.

On one such night as I looked at her she appeared to grow smaller, and smaller standing there. Her voice seemed to fade, as though she were floating further and further into the distance and I could no longer make out what she was saying.

Most nights like this I would simply block her out by saying my special prayer to God. It was a simple little prayer. I just asked him to please take me away, let me die in my sleep, if life for me were to continue this way. I imagined my ancestors up in heaven with God, and it seemed a wonderful place to be. I even imagined them smiling, and happy to see me.

Mum had refused counseling so often, and the few times she visited the therapist I remember overhearing her telling Grand how she believed she had outsmarted the psychologist. The sessions appeared to be some sort of game to her, something contrived for her amusement. Did she not realize how she hurt the innocents under her roof? Did she care?

It was all very frightening to me. She seemed to be two people. One told me that she wished that I had never been born, or that if I had died when I was an innocent baby my soul would have gone straight to heaven. The other spent hours curling our long hair. One Halloween eve she even made my sister and I little leprechaun costumes, to wear to our school party.

Early on during one of dad's absences the abuse was so bad that I struggled to the telephone, hanging on to door frames, and knocked down, crawling along the floor, all the while being kicked, yet managing to grab the telephone, crawl under the desk with it and call Grand for help. My clothing was torn, some hair pulled from my head, and I had teeth marks and bruises on my arms by the time help arrived in the person of my nervous cousin Erin.

She entered my room as mum, who had thrown me on to my bed was pounding me with her fists, and alternately tearing at my flesh with her long fingernails.

Erin, taller than mum, pulled her away from me, pushed mum out of the door and closing it sat down beside me, her arm around me. She talked to me until I was able to stop my convulsive crying.

I was about thirteen at this time, and slightly built, no match for the raging maniac, my mother.

The following morning I pulled my bed in front of my bedroom door, and throwing a few pathetic articles of clothing in a brown paper shopping bag, opened my bedroom window tossing the bag out, and following it clearing feet high rose bushes as I jumped. Landing safely I retrieved my bag, ran to Grand's barely stopping to cross street and never returned.

I don't recall any talk of children's rights back in the fifties. Rather, it was pounded into us by the clergy that one must honor thy father and mother, or face an eternity in hell, no exceptions. Mum always said that children were to be seen and not heard. A lot of women were not much better off. Parents, church, and eventually, their husbands controlled their lives. Grand said that it was not right. "People need interests, accomplishments, lives of their own. People are not property."

Mum visited Grand as usual, but I would usually make myself scarce when she was there. She always found something negative to say about my appearance and always repeated the claim that I had heard all of my short life: "I was so much lovelier than any of my children. This one of course couldn't be less like me. I can't believe she is even my daughter." Well neither could I.

I could overhear Grand telling her that children needed support, and encouragement, rather than condemnation. Sadly, Grand never got through to mum, nor did anyone else, including the parade of therapists.

Mum didn't care how she made people feel. I remember her often saying that she liked to "Get a rise out of people." I guess it made her feel powerful, in control, to cause others to lose control.

Well, being sent to school two years late caused me more pain than I've ever been able to effectively describe. Some of the children referred to me as retard because I was behind and the first day of school each year was always a devastating experience for me. As the teacher ran through the list of names on her roster she would ask each pupil their age and date of birth. I can still hear the laughter, and the whispers of retard, retard, when the teacher confirmed my age.

In the lower grades I was assigned a seat in the last row at the back of the class because of my height. One year I recognized this as a blessing, because of the holes in the soles of my regulation oxfords. These were very expensive, and parents were hounded unmercifully if they sent their children to class wearing anything else. And so, this particular year the soles of my shoes were reinforced with the cardboard cut from the back of a cheap writing tablet.

We were instructed to kneel during morning prayer. The teacher often wandered to the back of the room during our prayer; now if both soles were affected at least only she knew. Should only one sole be affected, I had only to cross one foot behind the other and no one was the wiser. This was good fortune.

The first year at the convent school was the worst. Our teacher that year was a young, fat, abusive nun. Because of her size she posed an even more intimidating figure, a fact I am sure she relished. I was handed an exercise one day, and smiled when I saw the big red A she had placed at the top of the page.

She said: "What are you so happy about? If you get less than an A you're retarded, you're older than the rest."

Just before Easter vacation she handed out papers, and instructed the class to make an Easter card for each parent. I raised my hand, and told her that my sister and I were each one paper short. She replied, "You don't even know where your father is. I'm not wasting paper." I told her that he worked out of town. That is what we had been told to say to explain all of his absences. Her face now beet red, this giant reached my desk in what appeared to be one long stride and accusing me of being sassy proceeded to beat my small hands with the metal edged ruler until they were numb. This was the year my sister failed.

The first half hour each morning was devoted to the study of religion. One morning when the giant asked Laura, "Who made you?" Laura replied, "The Devil?" She had suffered her share. Her reaction to the neglect and chaos surrounding us had been to become a bed wetter. Her escape quite often was to shut down. It was as though she entered a trance at times, not hearing or reacting to what was taking place around her. And poor little Jack bit the whole of his fingernails off, and began to smoke cigarettes by the age of eight.

Incredibly I was blamed for whatever mischief they got into, as mum claimed that the eldest child set the example. "They would never think of doing (whatever it was) themselves". This was an insult really, because it suggested they were incapable of independent thought. She absolved herself from any responsibility as well, by asserting that the eldest sibling rather than the parent was responsible for setting an example for children to live by. A secondary perk would have been that she had only to bother abusing one rather than two children at any given time. I was in my twenties when she told me why they had been favored. "They were not serious like you were. You were too serious, even as a baby you hardly ever smiled. They had such cute ways of manipulating us, and were so clever at getting away with things. They just seemed to deserve favoritism."

And one evening as I sat drinking tea with Grand mum entered the kitchen and said: "Remember my girlfriend Jean's mother? I was about the age Hedy is now when I realized that Jean had that certain something I can't quite put my finger on, that defect if you will, just enough to keep her from being attractive. Hedy is so much like Jean. Mother, aren't you going to say anything?"

And with tears in her eyes Grand responded: "I can think of a great many things to say to you. I won't however, because I don't believe anything I say will make any difference to you. It never has." Poor Grand.

I turned to movies for inspiration, and an escape into a fantasy world when I was not engrossed in a book. Audrey Hepburn, the idol of so many young girls my age became my role model. I worked very hard to improve my grooming, my walk, my speech, and did my best with the meager funds allotted me to put together a small, yet decent wardrobe. My attempts at self-improvement were met with disdain. I wanted to be the best that I could be, but was accused of either insecurity, or great conceit by mum and my older female cousins.

"I never chose motherhood. It just happened. I would have jeopardized my immortal soul by going against the dictates of the church." Mum was not shy about letting us know we were unwelcome intrusions, and although Laura and Jack enjoyed most favored status while I was under mum's roof, they left mum at the age of fourteen respectively. First to Grand, and then to dad.

Not long before I left Grand's, I approached the house one night and as I placed my foot on the first stair leading to the front door, I heard the crashing of dishes. Then it sounded like a piece of furniture had hit a wall, and my uncle's slurred profane language erupted. As sirens wailed in the distance, I ran next door and jumped down into what had been the basement of the house that had burned to the ground the previous summer. It was autumn now, and as I huddled in the corner of the ruins on this chilly night I looked to the stars. I made a wish, and prayed very hard that soon I would find a way to escape my awful existence. I had just left my best friend's home, and as I stood there listening to the sirens approach I saw Celeste and her family in my mind's eye. Oh how lucky she was.

The sirens stopped and I heard voices. The police had arrived, and were placing my uncle in their patrol car. The car drove away and I ran up the back steps and into the kitchen. I found Grand seated in the middle of the kitchen floor, on the only chair that remained in one piece. She was crying. Everything had been destroyed, including the corner chimney, now reduced to a pile of rubble, and many of the bricks scattered across the kitchen floor.

"It is not the material things that count. It is the human toll." I raised two self-centered, spoiled children, irresponsible people. One a violent drunk." She never pressed charges of course. She never had and back then the police were powerless to do more than keep him until he sobered up. When he returned he resumed painting the outside of the old house, a project he had been working on for as long as anyone could remember.

I returned years later to visit Grand, and there, perched half-way up the ladder in the same spot he had begun twenty years earlier, was uncle. The ladder was found in the same position the day he died. Electrical wiring was another on-going project. Thirty years of make work projects had cost Grand thousands of dollars, and produced nothing. They allowed her to make believe however, make believe that her son stayed around to help her. The fact that he was totally dependent had no-one fooled, not even him, we knew that much. The money had gone to keep the local tavern in business, and he and his hangers on in whiskey.

No-one wanted an education more than I, and yet the disparity in age, now very pronounced, between myself and my classmates, and the violent uncle who, now as he was aging and sick spent more and more time at home, was distracting. Unable to concentrate on my studies, I spent an increasing amount of time planning my escape.

One home room class provided the impetus I needed to put my plan into action. This particular morning the teacher asked each child to stand in turn, and tell the class what they planned to do when they graduated high school. When my turn came round I stood and told the class I wanted to become an archaeologist. Dead silence filled the room for what felt like an eternity, and then the laughter began. The teacher asked the class for quiet, and I continued. I talked of travel, exploring the world, an interest in other cultures, lost civilizations, and became lost for a few moments in my exciting plans for the future.

When I finished the teacher looked up from her desk blotter and told me that I had built a wonderful fantasy for myself, but that girls taught school, nursed, or got married. "Something normal," she said. The exercise continued, and as each child stood they confirmed for the group that they were willing to conform to the limitations that had been placed on them.

Yes, I was the only one who did not intend to be something normal. The last bell of the day finally rang, and I raced to my locker. I took everything home to Grand's: And late that evening I went out into the back yard, found the old iron drum, tossed all of my school supplies in to it and lit them on fire. I promised myself that someday I would get an education, which I did: but for now, this act was symbolic of my break with the past. I wanted to destroy my ugly existence. I wanted to escape.

I found a job at an A & W drive-in. They put me on split shift, and I walked the three miles each way twice a day to save the quarter bus fare. It was a lonely time. My friends were all in school, and we drifted apart. Now I spent my free time dreaming about my future. I did not know how I was going to accomplish my goals, nor when, but I knew that I could never give up. I was, I felt, pretty well all I had when it came right down to it. All of the adults in my life, including those who I believed cared for me had problems of their own.

The night before I left my Grand she came to my room to give me one last bit of advice. "Treat any child you have the way you would have wanted to have been treated darling. Never the way you were treated".

"A boy, Grand. Someday I'll have a son. A son like my favorite teacher Mrs. Thomas has. He came to the school to help her out when he had days off at high school. You can tell she is proud of him, and good to him: And you can tell he loves her back, Grand. It's the way it will be for me someday, Grand. So don't worry."

Dad. He was in town to visit us on the two week vacation he was able to get every six months, because he worked thousands of miles away. He picked me up at Grand's, and we took a taxi to the train station. I was proud of him. He looked good in his suit and dress hat. "First class." That's what he always said. He helped me find my seat in the coach, and placed my one big suitcase in the overhead.

"The train is your home while you're in it you know. Your way is all paid. You don't owe anybody anything. Just be confident. Be comfortable. Don't let anyone bother you, push you around."

The conductor began to shout "All aboard."

Dad took from his pocket an envelope, and handing it to me gave me a hug. His hands were worn, hard-worked, he had tears in his eyes. Glancing from his hands that held the envelope, to the tears in his eyes made my heart hurt. Yes, I remember thinking my heart hurts.

The train was pulling away from the station and I noticed that a few other people felt sad. I guessed leaving, even when you wanted to was sad, even when you knew that you would see your loved ones again.

I watched my reflection in the train window. I wasn't Audrey Hepburn but that was okay. There was already one Audrey Hepburn, and as Grand had told me; "There's only one you darling, and that makes you special."

"You're on your journey into the future, aren't you darling? You were always looking beyond what you had here. You cried so long and hard one evening when you were about eighteen months old and no-one could comfort you. Then your dad picked you up and carried you to the window, and asked you again what you wanted: And you looked up to the sky and said: “I want the moon.”

THE END

Heather Whittaker

THE STUDENT

My train pulled into the station late in the evening. It was a prairie city, and very cold in mid-winter. The people were very conservative, and viewed outsiders, especially those from my coastal city, famous for its hippie movement, liberal viewpoints, and laid-back lifestyle with suspicion.

I quickly found a job waitressing, and on my first day off paid a visit to the Board of Education. I had taken some of my hard-earned wages and dressed myself in a tailored suit, new winter coat, and all of the proper accessories. Yes I felt very good about myself when I opened the door to the education office, and walked up to the reception desk.

I gave the lady the information she asked for. Where did I live, work, where was I from. The answer to this last question caused her to stiffen her posture, and quickly snatching her half glasses from her nose, she pointed toward the door with her free hand and ordered me out.

As I opened my mouth to protest she angrily repeated her admonition for me to leave, adding "We don't want any damned hippies here. You had better go back to where you came from." I bolted for the door, and once on the sidewalk, I burst into tears. I was shocked, and frightened of protesting for fear that some government agency would force me to go back home. To what? I walked the city streets, and finally too cold and tired to do anything else, retreated to my room.

This bigotry regarding where I was from was new to me. It was all the more outrageous because I was within the same country. I kept waitressing, and one year later married a man of thirty-three, sixteen years my senior.

Having failed in my efforts to better myself, and quite poor, I married the much older man who had promised to protect and educate me. I was a new and hopeful bride, a resident of one of the most isolated places on the planet, a small mining town in the Territories. And within one year I gave birth to a beautiful, healthy baby boy. I named him after my favorite teacher's son, Clark.

Now my husband began to publically taunt me about my lack of education, but not before taking my cat to the local dump and shooting him. I spent every waking moment with my son never out of my sight. I loved my little one so very much, and would have sacrificed my own life for him had it been necessary.

I now spent the hours that John was at work keeping the perfect house. Mercifully, he was not at home much, and preferred the company of his drinking buddies.

Should I ask him what he would like for dinner he would tell me to fix whatever I liked, then sit down to the table and begin cursing because he wanted something else. If he asked for chicken, and I served it to him, he would then holler that it should have been steak, then when I told him that I was not a mind reader he beat me about the head, once splitting my lip, and blackening my eyes so that I could not venture out of the house for more than a week. I was much too ashamed.

With the sweep of his hand he laid the contents of the table on the floor, then kicked and cursed me as I worked to clean it up as ordered, and start over. This was my new life. I began to sleep very little, and exercised whenever I had time to spare. My five foot four inch one hundred and ten pound frame quickly shrank to eighty pounds. I developed pleurisy and strep throat.

A girlfriend took my son and cared for him. He was safe, and happy. Then one evening as I lay on the sofa barely able to draw water through a drinking straw, John returned home from the bar. Pouring himself a drink he laughingly commented, "Most people don't recover from a bout as bad as yours."

My only source of medical attention was a young nurse. We had become friends before my illness, and she was aware of the type of man my husband was. Advice and antibiotics was all she had to offer me. She told me I had an eating disorder, and that every time I was tempted to reject food, to put a picture of my son in my mind. I was to eat for him, if I could not do so for myself. I had to win. In a matter of weeks I was able to get up, and I began getting stronger.

I did not believe that I deserved to be abused, nor that the abuse was my fault. I was embarrassed that I was not capable of finding a way out. My grandmother had taught me that one person does not have the right to abuse another. So my problem was not ignorance, but isolation. I was but one of quite a few women in the small mining town who were in my position. We did not have an education, trade, or family to take us in. We believed that we were stuck, and feared not being able to care for our children financially on our own.

We did not have telephones, and the mail arrived every other day via a van. This same van carried people in and out of camp, and it was impossible for one to make arrangements to leave without the husband being alerted. There appeared to be no other way to handle the situation than to keep one's children safe, keep close to one's friends and as one friend had said: Make a plan. This was really the equivalent to being kidnapped, and having to be on alert to make a clean get-away. The getaway would take some time, but I had a plan.

Determined to educate myself I joined book clubs, and soon I was reading psychology, sociology, the classics, and many others. I actually read on every subject available to me, including articles and books dealing with spousal, and child abuse. Books had been my salvation as a child, and they were here for me now. These were my best friends, and I filled bookcases with my friends. I read my way out of depression, and I learned.

Knowledge is indeed power, and now I felt the power to tell John that I would expose him should he harm my son or me. The physical abuse trickled to very nearly nothing. Now the threats began. "I own you like the car or the house, every bit of food you put in your mouth is charity." Was that comment designed to cause me to begin to starve myself again? Starve myself in order to be more perfect. Starve to prove that I had control over something. If so it did not work. I had control of my thoughts.

"If you ever leave me I'll hunt you down and take your precious boy. You'll never see him again, and I won't molly coddle him either. I'll beat him into submission, he'll find out who his betters are." This was a sick man, though sick in such a cruel way. I had threatened to kill him while he slept, and only the fear of being separated from my son had kept me from carrying out my threat.

John had always told me that no court would award custody to a dumb, uneducated, bitch like me even if I were able to leave. He told me that the government would take my baby, and put him in a foster home. I found no books on the subject, and had no-one to consult. I found myself in the shower often, offering up the silent scream I had known as a child. The scream that had threatened to burst my skull open. And I prayed, I prayed to God to give me courage.

After four and one half years in the horrible mining camp, a place that I had come to believe was closer to hell than any fiery place mentioned in the bible, we finally left and moved to civilization. Now I worked whenever possible. I did everything. I babysat, clerked, earned secretarial, and cosmetology certificates among others, and worked full, and extra part-time jobs. Yes, I did everything but walk dogs, and all the while I raised my son, but I was not able to get enough money together to leave.

The lady my father had married shortly before Clark was born, was a kind and loving soul, a wonderful grandmother to my son, and the few times that I visited them my dad seemed to be happier than I would have ever believed possible.

She told me often not to wear my heart on my sleeve, but unfortunately failed to take her own advice. She remained with him, and two weeks before she died told me that she would as soon risk open heart surgery as risk a stroke, and be helpless and at his mercy. She had spent these last two weeks working to convince dad that a new will she had written was fair, in that my brother had received so much from dad she wished to leave my sister and I enough to leave our alcoholic husbands.

Sally never returned from the operating room: and the morning of her funeral he said, "It's mine, it's all mine". He had run to the lawyer that morning and failing to grant her dying wish had had her original will prepared for probate. Sally had not been a sophisticated woman and had hired a lawyer she found in a little office in a shopping mall to prepare a new will. Dad had had no trouble subsequently paying him off.

Three months later my sister and dad drove three hundred miles to show me the new car he had just purchased for her. And me, I said. But Laura informed me that I could not afford a new car. "They cost money to maintain. It would be a waste of money for dad to buy you a new car". Suddenly it was Christmas and I was eleven years old: And my sister and brother were opening expensive gifts, and I was pulling the paper from an empty perfume atomizer.

But it was not Christmas, and I was no longer eleven years old. Therefore I quietly asked about the money Sally had left Laura and me. Now his face turning its predictable shades of red, and his eyes cruel and cold he told me that he would buy me a car as well. I got the car, took it to the dealership at which it had been purchased, and found that it was not more than one-third paid for. According to the dealer, Laura's had been paid for in full the day it was driven off the lot. Now I made a deal with the salesman. Three thousand dollars, an old junker, and my new car was all his. I filed for divorce.

Now fifteen years after boarding a train and distancing myself from everyone, I ended up living in the same city as the family I ran from. I did not want to remain in the city my ex-husband was living and could afford to move no farther than three hundred miles away. My brother, whom I had not lived close to for over a decade, and his wife offered my son and me a place to stay until I found an apartment. Three weeks later, as I was packing my car to leave their home they asked me for two hundred and fifty dollars, to cover our food, they said.

I paid, and we drove away to make a new life for ourselves. I was only sorry that after all the years of hard work, and striving I was not able to put thousands of miles between myself and son, and these people. At twelve Clark was bound and determined to work for the summer. Well, he asked my brother for a job, and Jack was more than happy to hire him. Clark worked like a little beaver, day in day out, up early and very conscientious about being at the restaurant on time. Then on his final day of work he was presented with a backgammon set for his efforts. I told him as much as I thought appropriate to tell a child of twelve, and emphasized that it was nothing to do with him really. I believed that it was because he was my son, and my sister confirmed my suspicions when she said: "Fool me once, shame on you, fool me twice, shame on me. You're a wimp. It's your fault you keep getting sucked in by people who don't like you. We should have a pity party for you."

A therapist I had met told me that he believed that I allowed any contact with them out of a false sense of duty, or an irrational fear of some sort. Or did I not want to admit the truth about them? Was the truth too painful? He suggested I tell them how I felt. I did so, only to be charged with selfishness, and wanting to hurt their feelings.

I had no contact for a year, and then dad's new wife invited us for Christmas. As everyone sat at the table finishing their after dinner coffee dad said: "You should have been smart, and taken a trade like your sister did. She makes nothing but money. I don't suppose you'll ever do any good though." Mercifully my son was spending Christmas with his father's sister and her children three hundred miles away, and did not hear this. It always hurt him so to see me hurt. Now as I walked to the door, dad's wife said: "Every family has a looser and you just happen to be it, at least right now." And I concerned myself with not wanting to hurt their feelings. I must have been a bit crazy. Driving home I recalled my stepmother's advice, about not wearing my heart on my sleeve.

I asked relatives, farmers who loved Clark almost as much as their own children to be Clark's guardians, should anything happen to me, and I applied and was accepted at university. My plan had been successful. It was a plan I had not shared with a soul but my son. I was rejected five years earlier, as far as help with financing was concerned. I had approached the Finance Board and been told that it would be different if I were the head of the family. Under the circumstances however, I was advised to keep my two jobs. My husband now decided that it was he who deserved to further his education. Applied, quit work, and attended classes. I kept my two jobs.

I met my friend Anna while working at a low paying clerk's position. We sat across from each other at a large desk, and over the course of long days spent stuffing envelopes, filing and answering phones, I told her that I was starting university the following September. Our backgrounds were very similar, our childhoods, husbands, and siblings. We had both been working to better our lot in life, and neither of us could understand how we had become the black sheep in our families. She had an elderly aunt in her corner, and I had my Grand.

On Friday nights she liked to come to my apartment for dinner, and was happy to see my son. She wanted a son of her own. Despite her horrible marriage, she became pregnant, and when her little son was only three years she was diagnosed with cancer. "You are so lucky to have been able to watch your son grow up, and he will always be there for you, I can tell." She was right. "Oh if I had my health back I would not be afraid of anything. I would go, do, fight for what I want and need. Now you do it for both of us. No more victimhood. You will succeed. Prove to people that they don't have to be victims." She died not long after this conversation.

She fought for a year and a half to stay alive, to remain with her son. The last thing she did was spend what bit of money she could call her own, on a set of encyclopedias for her child. "I want him to be, to have more than I".

I had once asked her what the worst parts of her treatments were. "The children, they are innocent, and frightened. We are in a treatment room together, two, three, four children may be among us. Their little bodies hooked up to the machines makes me feel so sad. I hate their pain more than my own almost. If I live I want to do something for the children who suffer."

And so I lost my courageous, empathetic friend. The friend who listened and accepted me for who I was, as I had accepted her: and we told each other things we had not shared with anyone else. For one thing, though I was now thirty years old, the classroom setting at the university made me anxious. It caused flashbacks of my horrible school years as a child. I was once again older than many of the other students. I shared some of my school memories with Anna.

There were days when mum, having kept no food in the house would knock on the rear door of my classroom to deliver what was meant to be my lunch. She had stopped at the corner store on her way downtown, and collected a few items that were now handed me in a little brown bag. Twinkies, chocolate, milk, a candy bar. This was lunch. Taunted by the others as having been too retarded to remember to bring my lunch, I hesitantly opened the bag and removed the contents, knowing full well that the teacher was going to reprimand me for what I was eating.

For my tenth birthday party I was told that I could invite some school friends over. This was a shock to me, though I realized the intent behind the celebration. We were all instructed to sit quietly while mum played the piano, and sang with dad. I am sure this was my friends' first introduction to opera, and it was my first and last party. I had spent the afternoon wishing I were invisible.

Respect for others was not a part of my parents' repertoire. I was concerned about a fifth grade book report that had not been completed, and did not want my teacher to think less of me for it being turned in late. Dad told me that people were nothing but bone and hair, "nothing to worry about, don't you know that?" While mum said that this was a horrible thing to tell a child, she also referred to people as, "Someone else's mistake." They dehumanized others so that they would feel less intimidated by them. I knew that they considered us mistakes, and were intimidated by any small successes we may have had.

Dad attended only one Christmas concert at our school, and it was just as well. He burst into song while a carol was being performed by the children. Parents were offended, teachers shocked, and we were embarrassed to tears. The following year I was given the lead in the school play, and became so fearful of him attending that I began blanking out at rehearsals and forgetting my lines. I was replaced: and though heartbroken, I was relieved. I knew if the same thing happened this year as last, I was going to be well-hidden in the chorus, and could pretend that I was invisible.

My sister had wanted to learn the piano, and the aged little nun who taught music at the school offered her lessons after school for free. One afternoon I walked into the living room at home and there found mum threatening to slam the piano key cover on Laura's fingers. No-one was to touch her piano. Now the nun offered her own piano for practice. Mom would not allow this.

Decades had passed and during a trip north of the border to visit my son, I mentioned to dad how proud I was of Clark now working on his graduate degree. Old now and none the wiser, he leaned forward in his chair his eyes slits, his body tense, and told me I had better do the same or Clark would be, as he put it, "ahead of you". I said I certainly hoped so, and that I was very proud of him. Now he gave me the familiar look of dismay, followed by disgust, and said only, "you never could think very well".

In public he went out of his way to brag about our accomplishments. "Now tell me that I didn't do a great job with these kids." The voices ran through my head.

"She's a dreamer, she thinks she's so smart, says she's going to be something one day."

And dad, "Yeah, parents are supposed to mold kids, hell we own 'em. We can't control her thinking though; thinks she's better than us, can't break her, can we."

My favorite teacher had told me that dreams inspire us to set goals. I see her standing at the front of the class the day I gave an answer that differed from everyone else's. My answer was correct, and Mrs. Williams told me to remember that. "Always stick to your guns if you believe you are right, and remember, there is no such thing as can't." I repeated this phrase silently, and often. It became my mantra. All of the people who loved me from Grand to Ann had given me the same advice; I had been lucky to have them in my life. Memories of them and their belief in me had helped me overcome some of the most trying periods in my life.

Now I was a student again, and though not taunted by classmates, I had an administration to deal with. There were more adult students in the school during this period than there had ever been prior to the eighties. Many of us were divorced and single parents. Professors accused us of taking up seats that high school graduates might have occupied. We who had been working and paying taxes for fifteen, and twenty years apparently had no right to be here. One professor even went so far as to ask all those divorced and single parents to raise their hands. He then proceeded to tell us that in the school's opinion, we were there to collect benefits.

These were bursaries that those with dependents received. Though our incomes were less than we had realized while working, this was the accusation put forth. Some dropped out completely. Others downgraded their goals, to conform to what the arrogant professors had decided their futures would be. Looking to reduce their class sizes, and consequently their work loads, they had, I believe set an agenda structured so that most of us would simply disappear. I was not going to disappear, not any more.

During these years I could pick up a newspaper any day of the week, and turning to the editorial section, find at least one letter bemoaning what had become commonly referred to as the brain drain to parts south of the border. Well no wonder. While the United States was commending adults for returning to school, Canada was working to discourage as many of us as possible. With a healthy percentage of Canadian citizens fairly well educated, and few employment opportunities for these people, they needed a cheap labor pool.

I had had to tolerate the elitist attitudes of my professors, but when it came to my son being marginalized, had had enough. He walked in the door after school one afternoon, and told me that his teacher had told him that because of the fact that neither of his parents were professional people, the likelihood of him succeeding was almost nil.

Here was a child with an IQ of over one hundred and sixty, who had been asking questions of teachers for years, questions they had been unprepared to answer, and now he was being labeled, made part of an artificially contrived sub-group. Individualism, talent, effort, meant nothing. Who were these people who had appointed themselves gods, ready to dictate others' lives?

I asked him to consider some of the questions I was about to put to him: Does one have the right to live up to their potential, should they decide to do so? Someone in the teacher's ancestral line had to have become the first professional in the family, had they not? Does anyone have the right to put limitations on another human being? Are we programmed to continue through life like robots? Are we not responsible for our thoughts, and life choices?

The answers to these questions are obvious, and between us we agreed that people such as this teacher should be regarded as no more than challenges. Success being the best revenge, my son succeeded. And what of the other Children, those whose parents did not question, or did not care?

The first day of class one semester I entered the student finance office, and was informed that a new rule had been adopted over the summer. Single and divorced parents must now carry five courses, rather than three. Students without dependents were not affected however. I asked why I had not been notified so that I could have chosen the extra two courses. As things stood at this late date, the classes were already full. "0h you divorced and single people". This was all the answer I got from the advisor. Her title seemed rather ridiculous under the circumstances.

I ran to Social Services and asked to borrow money if need be so that I would not lose the whole semester. "You have to quit school if you want help." They offered me an office job at the local prison for five dollars and fifty cents an hour. People sitting next to me in that office were getting paid twice that for doing the same work. The first day on the job I was introduced as the woman from welfare. Yes, cheap labor. Why educate someone when you can force them to work for wages that barely allow for their survival.

The following semester I enrolled in school again, this time with a five course load. The young student living at home was entitled to the same amount of money as I. Day after day as I sat pouring over my books, I overheard them bragging about the new car, the ski vacation, or the trip to Hawaii they had just spent their new windfall on. Every semester I had to fight like a trooper to get my funding. Finally I transferred to a university from the college. I was assured by the university that half my credits would apply to my degree program. However after the first semester there I was advised that they were transferring one third of the credits. I had to redo all the others.

The rumors of a general goods and service tax circulated round the country, and the psychology professors I knew were delighted. I asked why anyone would want to pay even higher taxes. The answer: "Well those of us taking referrals will have a lot more clients. Stressed out people, we'll make a lot more money. Referrals from Social Services, it's a real perk."

From social worker, student advisor, to professor, there was not much more than hostility directed toward those they had been employed to assist. Now these supposed mental health professionals were relishing the fact that these people would be required to suffer all the more. Kinder and gentler nation? Happily I did not believe these fools represented the public at large. Sadly however I believe they represent the majority of the academics, and politicians there.

I wrote a short paper the summer semester of nineteen eighty four: The hypothesis of which was: The identity of the student in Canada. Single, divorced parents returning to institutions of higher learning, have a more difficult time maintaining good grades. Therefore, single divorced, parents are abusing the system by attending.

Singled out as an identifiable group because of their special circumstances, this supposition or conjecture has been stated a fact. To date however this hypothesis has not been used as a basis for further investigation. Simply stated as fact, it has not been used to prove or disprove the accusations.

The failure to disprove allows for tentative acceptance, and does not bother with a rival hypothesis. It therefore moves from observation "B" to inference "A". This hypothesis does not consider variables in circumstance, nor does it consider alternative explanations. Many factors contributing to these parents' inability to maintain as high a standard as their life experiences suggest that they should, have been overlooked.

The responsibility, care, and maintenance for those under their guardianship, the financial problems inherent to most of these individuals, as well as the time factor involved in maintaining a balance between home, and study, all contribute to a high level of stress. All of these variables are not part of the single student's experience. Therefore the external pressures present themselves in different forms, and to varying degrees as well. Because of these complexities, the so-called identifiable group has been poorly understood.

The Student Finance Board introduced a directive in nineteen eighty three stating that, single parents be required to maintain a five course load or lose recognition as a full time student. The single student is eligible for full time status with a three course load. It is a fact that the heavier the load, the sooner the student will complete the degree program. However it is reasonable to assume that this is the case for every student, whether single, or single parent.

The stigma attached to the single parent as a result of this bias, could over a period of time make observation "B" appear to be correct. Under duress, and therefore vulnerable, people are inclined to succumb to the expectations of others. Observation "B" then will have been used as a propagator. Taking into account the circumstances, and variance in life-style of each group, the relevant evidence suggests the hypothesis put forward here is far from correct.

I finally completed my studies despite the stigma, and bias and shortly before moving to New York I visited dad, who was now in the hospital. I had taken a psychologist friend along. His mild stroke had occurred three days after he had been accused of molesting a neighbor's child, though on the day we visited the hospital I was unaware of this charge. Now dad looked at my friend and asked HIM how my studies were coming along. My friend answered positively and dad replied: "Isn't that something? Hell she was always the dummy, you knew that didn't you."

And the dummy had tested in the top ten percent of the top one percent of the country for aptitude. To have shared this bit of news may have caused a legitimate stroke. I could not speak at any rate. I felt as though I had been kicked, and had barely enough strength to breathe.

We quickly made excuses to leave. Leaving the room, and walking down the corridors I recalled all the times when we were children, and had been told that dad was sick and in the hospital: all the nasty things said about children, and me always the nothing, the garbage, the dummy. As we reached the parking lot Gerry stopped, and looking into my eyes he brushed a wisp of hair from my forehead and said: "You know there has always been a sadness about you."

Three weeks before that hospital visit one of Gerry's friends had testified in an incest case. Frank had never made a secret of the fact that he was willing to testify for whichever side was able to offer him the highest compensation. Years earlier he had deserted a wife and children to, as he put it, explore his growth and potential. He had denied paternity when his second wife became pregnant, claiming he had had a vasectomy. Now married for a third time he claimed paternity and paid for an abortion. Now this ex-minister, turned psychologist, this weak and obviously unconscionable creature was selling himself as an expert on what was best for the families in question.

He testified that the father in this latest case deserved a second chance. "I told the court that I didn't think he'd molest again. No-one can be sure of course, but they may as well pay me as someone else." There was one little person who could be sure, and she would pay. The someone did not have a voice of course. She was after all, just another innocent.

I had spent my last year in school looking for employment. Those few prospects who answered my enquiries were indignant, and advised me that I was wasting their time applying for positions that had not yet been advertised. An American professor working in Canada had once confided in me that it was his opinion Canada defied one to succeed, rather than encouraged one. "It appears to be an obstacle course. It's as though they employ people to dare you to pass in spite of them. And if you quote me, well, just don't use my name." He was the only professor who had not been sucked body and soul into the bureaucratic bubble.

The professor of behavioral psychology is a prime example of the type of person I had been forced to deal with during my student days. I had been maintaining a B average in his class, and called him one day to ask if I might submit my final paper one day later than scheduled; I had to take my son to see a specialist because of a back problem. I offered to bring the professor a doctor's note. I offered to send the paper by courier. "Oh no, none of that is necessary, tomorrow is fine." Weeks later the final marks were posted, and to my horror I had been given a D.

"Your paper was a day late. It's not my fault you had other things to do, single parents". Single parents, or sick profs?

I felt I was the luckiest person in the world the day my plane taxied into LaGuardia airport. I felt lucky to be an American. I found employment just months prior to my grandmother's death. She was over one hundred years old when she passed away. The year prior to my move to New York, she had asked me to spend whatever it may cost to attend her funeral, on my son. She had asked me to promise her this. A practical woman, she knew the state of my finances, and more. "Funerals are for those left behind darling. They are an opportunity for the survivors to comfort each other. You don't owe it to them."

Then as she had when I was a child, she told a little story to illustrate her point. It was the story about the child walking in the woods on a cold wintery day, and encountering a snake in the grass. The snake promises to treat her differently than she expects, and she agrees to pick it up and carry it with her. Now feeling a sharp pain in her side, she asked the snake why he would hurt her after promising he would not: To which the snake replies, "You knew what I was when you picked me up". Unfortunately I would forget that lesson from time to time over the ensuing years, but that is another story.

Heather Whittaker

CITIZEN ALIEN

Spring had arrived and I was finally graduating from university. The auditorium was full to capacity, and although many if not most of the students were in debt, all were enthusiastic and hopeful about their futures. These years of struggle, sacrifice, and the financial burdens incurred were viewed as investments for the future. These students, many of whom were parents, believed they had invested in their children's futures as well as their own. I was one of these parents.

As a very young mother I had rocked my baby in my arms and dreamed of him graduating Harvard, as the Boston Pops lulled him to sleep. Well I was far from a Harvard graduate myself but this was my personal dream come true. The secret dream I had held on to for a lifetime. It should have been a wonderfully happy day.

"Do not expect to be any better off because you have graduated. Most of you will not be; in fact many will be worse off, student loans etc. ha, ha. Just be satisfied that you have accomplished this." This was the dean of the university who with his references to the economy and belt tightening, sounded more like a politician running for office than an academic presenting a convocation speech. I was sorry that I was in attendance and now I had to cross the stage and shake hands with this man to collect my degree. Well I would not have to trust them to mail it to me at any rate.

I had forged ahead in spite of those who told me that I was incapable of raising my son on my own, let alone attending university. I had succeeded in doing both and now it as time to leave. Being an American citizen I decided to move to New York City from Canada. America, and the American dream. Well, advertise and they will come. My son was beginning first year university in the fall, and I needed work, I needed hope, and there did not appear to be much of either to be found here. My ancestors had immigrated to New York through Ellis Island. While they had endured a long and uncomfortable boat trip, I looked forward to a quicker and easier journey thanks in part to them.

As my plane approached the island of Manhattan I got my first look at Lady Liberty. This was the wonderful experience described so often in novels, plays, and essays, and now it was mine.

This autumn found me living in a studio apartment on Madison Avenue, and Sixty Sixth Street in Manhattan. I thought it was wonderful. I found that if I stood in my bath tub to peep out of the window I had a lovely view of the apartments on Fifth Avenue across from Central Park. I loved their roof top gardens; and the trees in the park rose above these buildings providing a cavalcade of color. The breeze flowing through the open window felt crisp and fresh and smelled of autumn, and oh yes, I loved my new city.

My building was over one hundred years old. My room had ten foot ceilings, and old sash windows covered by lace curtains. I enjoyed the sound of the radiator clicking away, the people, and the traffic. Even the saxophone player making music somewhere down the Avenue contributed to my happiness. This city was one great big alive people machine, and I was right here in the middle of it.

I began work as a temporary a few days after arriving in New York. The first assignment was receptionist at a children's book publisher. I was offered a full time position but could not afford to accept. I had been what my grandmother termed financially embarrassed for far too long and needed more money. The people were very good to work with as was the case at the next assignment.

The collection agency placed me in their computer room. The boss offered me an advance on my wages saying that he understood how difficult it was to move to New York with its high cost of living, and start over. The receptionist demonstrated how to wear my shoulder bag New York style, strap over the head and across the chest. "Less likely to have it snatched from you, Heather."

At eight thirty every weekday morning the martial arts group gathered to practice beneath my office window, and throughout the day I would glance up and watch the traffic as it inched its way across the Brooklyn bridge in the distance. On occasion, rather than fight my way through the corner deli at lunch time I would walk to the hot dog vendor's cart a few doors down the street. I would order a fifty cent dog and be presented with a bun holding two dogs, and charged ninety cents; the vendor smiling all the while as though he were doing me a favor. Protesting did no good, it was that or nothing. Well lower Broadway was interesting, all of New York was exciting and interesting, and I had great plans for my son to visit.

I had been dating a Canadian psychologist for the past four years, and he was now interning at an institute in Manhattan. Bill's colleagues here had a much better attitude than that of their Canadian counterparts. These New Yorkers' appeared to respect perseverance and determination. They were not counting the number of degrees I held in order to determine me worthy of their company.

One of Bill's Canadian colleagues had been particularly obnoxious. I spent only Saturday evenings at Bill's back in Canada because my son was still at home, and Frank would choose these occasions to invite himself over pleading loneliness. He moaned constantly about the difficulty in finding a woman of his intellectual and educational equal. Completely ignoring my presence he described his fantasy woman. This lady should come equipped with long legs, long blonde hair, and a graduate psychology degree.

Apparently there was a shortage of super women out there capable of satisfying this bald-headed man, with the fringe of collar length grey hair, of average height, and impossibly thin frame. A short time after the last dinner from hell, he announced his impending marriage. Wife number three was approximately four foot ten, had hair one inch long all over her head and a bad attitude. We were invited to dinner at this newlyweds' home, and were treated to a few hours of complaints regarding her inability to lose thirty pounds, her hatred of her clients, and the wine we had taken was in her words nothing more than a cheap drunk.

Little miss sunshine worked for a large corporation counseling employees depressed about the new trend toward, downsizing, reorganizing, and early retirements; terms that have now become as common as bread and butter. To hear her tell it they were having self-esteem problems. Well, God bless them; I often wondered how many of these people had left her office, and proceeded directly to the nearest bridge. Frank and number three were matched very well. Arrogant and cold they claimed to have recently returned from a wonderful vacation in San Francisco where they had combined a trip to an abortion clinic with a honeymoon. Frank was upset about the five thousand dollar fine levied against him by the Psychological Association for having had an affair with a client. He even wrote a poem about the injustice of it all. I suggested to Bill later on that he advise Frank to keep his day job. Poet no, wimp absolutely.

All of this was behind me now, thank goodness, although in hindsight I cannot imagine why I had tolerated the company of these fools in the first place. Good job offers began to come my way, and I finally accepted a position with the City of New York. I was trained, presented with a certificate, and assigned to the borough of Manhattan as a Probation Officer.

Most of the probationers were either functionally illiterate or illiterate. We were required to read and explain the terms of the probation agreement to each person. The probationers were angry, anxious and often threatening. The frustration and embarrassment of not being able to read only heightened the tension. Occasionally a probationer would claim to have forgotten his glasses, only to sign the paper with an x before departing my office. Employment is one of the terms of probation. Now here was a challenge. A homeless, drug addicted, and often illiterate person sent out to find work; and the general population wonder how these people get caught in the revolving door of the criminal justice system. Interesting.

The probationers wanting to enter treatment programs were placed on waiting lists months long. The saddest part of the job for me was the sight of the little children who accompanied their parents to the waiting room. Babies in strollers were crammed into a huge dingy room, crowded with some of the worst people that society had to offer, their parents some of our biggest offenders.

The most outrageous aspect of the Probation Officer's job is that of assisting the illegal alien to obtain a green card. Remember, in order to avoid incarceration and remain on probation one had to be employed. These were isolated cases but no less ridiculous by being so. An airline ticket home and an authority provided to place the offender on the plane would have been far less expensive, and much safer for the tax payer.

One afternoon after the last probationer had left for the day, and I was clearing my desk, I thought of the lady who had sat next to me the day I took the written exam for this job. Sheets of paper were handed out and we were asked to write a short essay explaining why we were interested in this position. The lady began to fidget, and appeared to be nervous. I asked her if she was alright, and she told me that she had not expected to have to write a one hundred and fifty word essay with no preparation. This response prompted me to ask her what she did for a living.

"Oh I'm a teacher, but it's getting so dangerous to be a teacher I've decided to leave teaching." She was serious. I never saw her again. I had not asked what it was she taught, however it is a sure bet the kids were not required to hand in much written work to be corrected, if at all. Had she been hired she would have had the opportunity to become reacquainted with many of her former students. The blind was certainly leading the blind here.

A few probationers stand out from the crowd. The Lucchase crime family member was a real head-turner, he really did stand apart from our usual waiting room customers. Tony we will call him, had slicked back heavy black hair, expensive shades, shiny dark blue suit, and high gloss black dress shoes, nice pointy toes of course. Just like in the movies. Tony was very indignant. He told me that he was not used to waiting around with this kind of people, and that the system had wasted a whole day of his time. He had written a check for the twenty five thousand dollar fine levied against him before leaving court this morning. The construction job he'd done for the city of New York, two hundred and fifty thousand dollars of tax payers' money, had not been quite up to snuff as they say; faulty materials, that sort of thing. He asked me, "What's a business man to do?" I couldn't help laughing. Well he could sign his name. He was over one hundred thousand dollars ahead, and I did not see that he had much to complain about. Crime really did pay when you belonged to the right club.

One of the sad stories is that of the articulate, well mannered, and educated African American-man. Originally a poor kid from Georgia he had worked his way into a financial analyst's position on Wall Street. He now sat across the desk from me in tattered clothes, and teary eyes, the whites of which were as red as apples, asking to be sent to a drug rehab program. All I had to offer him was a subway ticket back to the Bronx, and a silent prayer. It was time to call in the next probationer.

Some days I would leave work and just walk for a couple of hours. You are supposed to feel afraid walking the streets of New York, however I was too busy exploring, and I imagine felt less vulnerable because of the work I was doing. I knew what to expect.

I passed by people huddled in doorways, and wrapped in rags. An old lady, her head stuck through a green plastic garbage bag worn as a rain coat. An old man stopped to read the front page of a paper on the news stand, ragged and shabby, perhaps too shabby to afford the twenty five cent copy. The twenty-something dressed in tattered clothes two sizes too big for his emaciated frame. He boarded the bus pale, weak, and the flesh that was exposed covered in sores. He was ten cents short of his fare, and as I jumped forward to offer him some change the driver hollered to him to get off. I was too late. The driver gave me an angry look and stepped on the gas.

This was the driver who would slam the door in your face if your foot was not touching the step when he decided to hit the gas pedal. The man who had slammed the door on my arm as I struggled to free myself as the bus pulled away from the curb. This was a crazy, and eventually I made the decision to walk rather than board his bus no matter how bad the weather.

I wished I'd had a camera with me one day down on Canal Street. I watched as a well-dressed man rummaged through the papers on the top of a trash can and finally having found what he had been looking for stood reading; while standing directly opposite this man on the other side of the can, an impoverished old man kept searching the can until he found something to eat. Neither acknowledged the presence of the other. I had never personally seen things like this before. It was a story right out of Dickens come to life before my eyes.

On Saturday nights Bill and I would walk over to the Fifty and First Street for dinner. One evening after crossing the street toward home I happened to glance back over my shoulder, and there sitting under our restaurant window was a little group of people huddled together shivering in the December cold. While in the window above them the smiling, happy diners sat sipping wine and obviously enjoying themselves as we had.

Everywhere I travelled in this city these were the sights I saw, on every block, on every corner, almost without exception. Among all the wonderful buildings, the libraries, museums, art galleries, parks, there appeared to be an astoundingly large number of disenfranchised people; particularly for the wealthy city of New York.

This city offered the best and the worst of everything. There were no grey areas, no, simply the yin and the yang, black and white. Nothing and no one was average.

In the early spring my friend Darlene died of cancer, leaving behind a three year old son. I walked over to St. Patrick's Cathedral thinking that this would be a quiet place to just be for a while. I was wrong. There was a wedding rehearsal in progress, and to my horror a gift shop. Tourists were milling about everywhere; yes even the church was a shock. Oh well, I decided that Darlene would have told me to be thankful that I was alive to see it all. From St. Patrick's I made my way to Central Park. Children were skating at the rink, laughing, happy, celebrating life; perhaps this was a better place to be today anyway.

When I returned to work on Monday morning I looked at the probationers who were throwing their lives away, and abusing their fellow citizens. I asked myself why I was spending my life, my time in such a place. When we lose someone close to us it forces us to face our own mortality.

Our supervisor, a woman who made it clear to everyone that she hated people - you can't be any more clear than coming right out and saying, "I hate people" - walked into the cubbyhole I shared with my partner. Bee placed her foot on the arm of a chair, took a few drags of her cigarette, threw the cigarette on the floor, removed her foot from the chair, ground her foot into the cigarette and informed us that she was sending us out on fact-finding missions. Fact-finding missions? Yes, we were to be sent to the Bronx, Harlem, all the lovely neighborhoods to validate the addresses of the probationers. This we were to accomplish unaccompanied and unarmed. Then in mid-sentence she suddenly turned to me and said, "You're from Canada?" Yes, I told her I was a dual citizen born in Canada, American parents. "Well give me you're tired, you're hungry, you're crazy; we have them here from everywhere."

My little partner was speechless, as were I would later learn all the other officers. "You, living with a psychologist on Madison

Avenue. Who do you think you are? You had better watch it, don't make any mistakes." My, the woman had an obvious inferiority complex, and used her position to victimize a select few in this most pathetic of kingdoms. Apparently she had been transferred from one borough to another until Manhattan was her last stop. Well this was a nice fresh borough, and she was starting all over again. There would be nowhere left for her to go but crazy, and many of us wondered if she was not half-way there already.

I was in the Interstate Division, and in communication with probation officers throughout the country. On one occasion I was talking with a P.O. in Broward county Florida when he asked me who my supervisor was. He had only recently moved to Florida from Brooklyn. I told him and he told me that he had worked under her in Brooklyn. He was an African American and had quit after countless attempts to have Bee stop taping racist notes to his office door were ignored. His and my experiences with her were virtually identical. The typical tyrant, she apparently needed a victim to feel whole. The gossip circulated that she had pull and that is why she was kept on at the department. If the tough New Yorkers couldn't take the abuse I wondered how long I would last. Not long, not long at all.

Problems at home do not help when you are miserable at work. There did not seem to be a refuge anywhere for me. Now I had to contend with something new from boyfriend. He told me that he had learned at this institute that no one else had the ability to hurt or affect you. Taken to the extreme of course this notion is thoroughly preposterous. He informed me that I was to be his guinea pig. He had decided to go out and experiment with what he called shame attacks. This meant, according to him going out and doing something which may cause him embarrassment. He had decided to go out and try to pick up dates in the subway stations.

"And my reaction should you get a date?"

"That is your problem. It's all how you interpret things, not my responsibility." Five of his fellows at the institute were involved in very shaky marriages. Perhaps their spouses were no better at interpretation than I. Imagine being told that should you be raped you had the option of feeling upset or writing it off to experience. So much for personal responsibility. As far as I could see this was a training course for psychos, and it was time I moved out. This exchange should not have surprised me. Two weeks earlier boyfriend had told me that his friend Frank had agreed that if a woman was physically abused it had likely been provoked by her. I wondered how well little miss sunshine was enjoying her marriage. Yes, definitely time to move out. Now I had a son I wanted to help, and I was trying to set a bit of money aside, and I had to contend with a psycho at work and at home.

The day arrived when I and a young African American were told that we were to be the test cases for the new address verification program. This young man had gone through college on a football scholarship. He worked his nine to five shift at the department Monday through Friday, and as a security guard from midnight to eight every morning. Now he and the single parent were going to be sent out to knock on the doors of crack houses.

I had not had any luck finding an affordable apartment in a safe neighborhood, and had not been able to find another job that paid as well as this one. I was frightened of remaining on the job, and frightened at home. I looked in the mirror one Saturday morning and decided that life was too short, and I was worth more than this.

The city was a mess of racism, bigotry, poverty and fear. Children passed through metal detectors on their way to class each day. Kids as young as ten years old were given guns and employed as drug dealers. They could not get an education unless they were able to attend private schools, this according to what I had read, and those I spoke with. So much for equality; these people did not start out equal, and mess up on their own. It had all been prearranged for them.

I had noticed that the conversations that took place all around me were always about one thing, and one thing only, money. Not social issues, family issues, not even politics, just money. This I learned was the great equalizer. Be smart, kind, helpful, compassionate, be anything, but baby be rich, and then it did not matter. How nasty, rude, disrespectful or insensitive you were, you had it made. Over the course of the next seven years I would realize that this attitude was not unique to New York city.

Well one cannot spend every day in the pits, it is not healthy, you'll go bananas. I decided to concentrate on what I could find that was positive. I walked miles before I slept each night. I saw everything there was to see, and when I ran out of energy I went to bed and counted blessings rather than sheep. My son, my friends whom I could always pick up the phone and talk to, and my health.

If New York was supposed to be the toughest place in the country to live I was confident that I had passed the test. One day I picked up and flew to Las Vegas. This little city in the Mojave desert was advertising itself as the new family-oriented Las Vegas. Sounded good; it was two thousand miles closer to my son, nice warm climate, friendly, relaxed atmosphere. Low crime rate, good job opportunities, affordable living. Wow was I naive.

This was a terrible mistake. Forget polite; don't worry about people thinking you are stupid should you smile too much. This I was advised by a well-meaning New Yorker. No this was dog eat dog, grapes of wrath Vegas style. Don't worry about a job not paying enough for you to give money away or save, you were lucky to earn enough to simply subsist on. There were no museums, big parks, or little ethnic cafes on nice side streets where you could sit and visit with friends either.

There were no busses or subways to ride. There were big hotels with personnel offices packed with job hunters. Most were desperate looking, and hoping to find work before they became homeless. When you located a bus stop you found that it would take you three hours to travel across town. You were lucky if you had not had to wait for an hour in one hundred plus degree heat before boarding the bus. Forget people watching. Most of those I saw I wished I had not. Little money pouches strapped to big bellies were the norm, as the glassy-eyed over-tired tourist sauntered from one casino to another, a cup of coins in one hand, and a drink in the other looking for the action. On their journey they of course had to maneuver their way around the paper boxes full of girly magazines, and once they cleared these there were the hawkers with leaflets at the ready to shove in their faces. If this was a family atmosphere it appeared to be arranged to accommodate the family from hell.

I had arrived so decided to make the best of it. My first interview for employment, I am told that it is not good enough for me to be carrying only my social security card around. "No, people forge those and your accent is different. You had better carry your U.S. passport." Well true I do not have a southern accent as many of these people did. A new acquaintance, a New Yorker told me that they did not like New Yorkers here. "It's who you know, not what you know here". That became obvious the day I called a man to repair the VCR and he asked me how to turn it on.

A positive attitude, good grooming and professionalism are very important assets; everyone I know would agree. However, this means nothing to your future success when you are confronted with a negative prospective employer. When you are judged by such things as your accent, country of origin, where you have recently moved from or the date of birth, stamped on your passport you have lost the contest before the competition even got under way.

In Las Vegas great emphasis is placed on the number of years you have spent on the planet. Looks don't count as much as who you know, and experience and education are of little consequence.

My first morning in Las Vegas I set out to find an apartment and a job. Although I had lived in what was considered to be the silk stocking area of Manhattan, we nevertheless had a man living in the next apartment who had a pit bull that never barked, and lots of people coming and going at all hours of the day and night. I did want to avoid a like experience if I could help it. I walked next door to my motel and bought a paper and a coffee. When I returned to my room I began calling the numbers listed in the adds. It appeared that there were lots of jobs. I made an appointment with an employment agency, then finding that there was not any public transportation to that area ended up taking a taxi.

Ten dollars, and a six minute taxi ride later I arrived at the office. Still it was an investment if it would land me a good job. Some investment. I was ushered to the back of the office by a grouchy young woman, and introduced to the woman in the cubbyhole. Cubbyhole woman wore a tight fitting polka dot dress two sizes too small for her Dolly Parton figure, loads of cheap jewelry, gobs of heavy makeup complete with false eyelashes, and what looked like one of Dolly's old wigs. This was the employment counselor. She offered me a chair and told me that she had a great job for me. I asked her if she would not like to read my resume. She then glanced at the resume, looked up and asked me what my qualifications were. Could she read? She offered me a receptionist position at five dollars an hour, nine months probationary period, culminating in a raise to six dollars. No benefits. Was I lucky or what? she asked me, then told me that these people were great to work for; she could swear to this because she sent people over there all the time to fill this position. Was I missing something? And more luck, how much could I stand in one day? "It's only sixty-five percent of your first month's wage for the agency referral." Someone was making money alright, and it was certainly not the people she was sending to this job. She urged me to hire on right away.

"These jobs really go fast." Apparently they were not going fast enough for her however, she was one pushy sales woman. I asked her if I might use her phone to call a taxi and she offered me a ride home. I promised to think about the job; actually I was sure that

I would never forget this experience. At any rate on the ride home she assured me that she was very successful in placing clients in good jobs. "After all" she said, "I've had the same clients for years, get them one job after another". Again, was I missing something? I was mortified, and yet I had retained my ability to think. Common sense told me that people being sent to one job after the other, and paying for the privilege was ridiculous. Yes, someone was making money and it was not the employees.

The following day Dolly called and left messages at my motel. I did not return the calls. She did catch me in my room a few nights later however. She invited me to dinner. Did I want to see one of the new hotels? I met her at the Excalibur, and over dinner she proceeded to tell me all of her personal problems. Everything you would not want to know, and never would have dreamed of asking. Her ex-husbands, boyfriends, and then the real shocker. She told me that she knew a man who loved sex, and was willing to pay good money to the right woman. Good God, had I walked onto the set of an X-rated movie without realizing it? This was surreal.

Thank goodness for the experience of having worked with a long list of people who were considered shocking by normal standards. My probation experience in New York had prepared me well. I told miss Dolly that I had decided to return to New York, and that was the end of that. I never saw her again, thank goodness. I learned a valuable lesson. Never let anyone know that you are alone in a strange city, and believe me this was a strange city.

I immediately joined a temporary agency and in the meantime I applied to none other than the Probation Department in Las Vegas. I made friends with the lady in the gift shop where I bought the morning paper. Debra told me that you need a connection to get even a gift shop job here. She had worked at Bally's Hotel and put in a good word for me there. I got the job at four twenty five an hour, four to midnight. Surely something better would turn up soon. This city was not cheap. I had not found one of those affordable apartments in a safe neighborhood yet, and therefore was renting by the week. One hundred and sixty five dollars a week. Maid service and bedding extra. What had I done? I cried myself to sleep every night, and prayed for courage.

The temporary jobs were not working out. Public transportation was worthless; you needed a car to get back and forth to most of the jobs. The Chamber of Commerce was obviously misinformed when they advised me of the wonderful Las Vegas transportation system. Well misinformed or something, you are invited to fill in the blank.

The temporary agency sent me to a strip hotel to work in the accounting department. The accounts manager asked to see my card.

"What card?"

"Your work card. We can't work ya'll without a work card".

Where was I, Russia?

As it turned out, one had to go downtown to a city office, be fingerprinted, have their picture taken, and spend eighteen dollars to be provided with a work card. Non-gaming for other than casino; for casino work you needed gaming. Gift shop where liquor is sold requires a card issued by the liquor control board, and where food is sold, a bag of chips is considered food, you needed a health card. For these last two you spent the eighteen dollars and spent an hour watching a film. By my calculations that adds up to seventy two dollars, and at one time I had all four cards. One should be flexible don't you know. It would have been logical and just as effective to have one card that fit all, but of course the revenue would not have been nearly as lucrative. The employer does not pay these fees, you do.

You are sent to the city office by your prospective employer to apply for these cards, and often you are not invited to an interview or offered an application form for a job without owning the card, or cards in the first place. Now we could all put our heads together and go bananas trying to find the logic here, but why bother? A friend once remarked that you cannot make sense of nonsense, therefore we may as well carry on for we have nuttier fish to fry.

On my days off from the Bally's job I went apartment and job hunting. One morning at six thirty I was standing on the strip waiting for a bus to take me down-town when I struck up a conversation with an elderly lady. The lady was on her way downtown to play bingo. Yes, at six thirty in the morning. Anyway I told her that I was feeling anxious, I had not yet found a decent place to live or a job. She said that a woman in her building needed a roommate to help with the rent. She took my phone number and name and told me that she would have the other lady call me.

I gave the number of the weekly I was moving into the following day. It was twenty dollars cheaper per week. The next morning I called a taxi. The driver popped the trunk and I loaded my own luggage. The ride was virtually across the street, took no more than two minutes and the driver asked for six dollars.

When I complained of the cost and his rude behavior, he told me to go back to L.A. L.A.? I told the desk clerk what had happened and he offered no response. I dragged my luggage up to my room, sat down on the edge of the bed and cried. I had never met so many really awful people in such a short period of time in my entire life. Actually I had never met as many awful people in all of my thirty-nine years put together.

Just then the phone rang. It was the lady who needed a roommate. We arranged to meet for lunch; she worked in a hotel just three minutes away as the shoe flies. I told her about the taxi driver, and the desk clerk. She told me that because hookers rent the weeklies. that they were likely assuming that I was a hooker and were treating me accordingly. Talk about jumping to conclusions. My, these people really were the dregs of society. This family-oriented city was closer to a Steven King novel than Disneyland, far closer. That afternoon I moved into her apartment. When I went back to the weekly to collect my bags I told the desk clerk that I was a Probation Officer from New York and did not believe that I would be comfortable in his establishment. He handed my rent deposit over very quickly.

At Bally's I made friends with a retired teacher from Montana. She was working there as I was until she found work teaching. She was fifty at the time, had two graduate degrees and was working for four twenty five an hour. We were in the same boat, and would give each other little pep talks which kept our spirits up. We worked extremely hard at being optimistic. One night after work she offered me a ride home, and when she dropped me off told me that I had moved into a bad neighborhood, a dangerous neighborhood. Well I certainly was in a mess, and not for the lack of a positive attitude and hard work either.

My experience should alert anyone to the fact that one does not have to be either lazy or stupid to find themselves in a desperate position in this country. No, all you really need to do if you are a woman is get involved with an abusive man and then proceed to move to big American cities where it is nearly impossible to simply survive without having a sizeable bank account.

My new roommate proved to be every bit as unusual as the majority of the people I have met in Las Vegas. Jean was up at three in the morning, although she did not start work, which was a ten minute walk away, until seven thirty. She had knee-length grey hair that she wore in a braid down her back. Although when the weather turned chilly in October she wrapped the braid around her neck for warmth rather than use a scarf.

No makeup, not even lipstick, jeans and tennis shoes were her usual attire, whether at home or office. On her days off she would work at her oil paintings, clean house, anything but venture out even for a walk. She had no relatives or friends that she communicated with, other than one of her ex-husbands, and the prostitute that lived downstairs.

The prostitute from Arkansas had apparently gained sixty pounds, and the extra weight had forced her into an early retirement before she was financially prepared. Therefore she had married a man who was dying of prostate cancer, and cared for him with the expectation of being left the sole heir to his will. This woman came upstairs occasionally to complain about her sorry state; and once stated that because black babies grow up to be just another nigger she thought it a good thing that their mortality rate is higher than whites. Drive-by shootings in the African American neighborhoods were another personal favorite; and yet she talked about being a good Christian. Unbelievable.

On her good days she liked to brag about the trailer home she owned back in Arkansas, and all the wealthy johns she had known. On my days off I was still looking for work, and now another apartment.

The summer months had been pure hell. Dressed for job interviews in heels, hose, and suit I walked miles dropping off resumes and trying to get interviews. In the end all I got were blistered feet, and swollen legs. It was beginning to sink in now. I would have to pay for a job, and pray that it was not a scam. I joined an agency that was going to charge me sixty-five percent of the first month's pay. They sent me to an interview at an optometrist's office. Dressed and groomed professionally and conservatively, I entered the building. I was shown to the Doctors office.

The first thing Dr. Eyes asked me was; "Do you sleep in your car?"

I had to ask him to repeat the question. I could not believe it.

He responded with, "Well, we have so many people moving here that you never know who is a transient."

To which I replied, "Do I look as though I sleep in my car?" No Answer. I continued. "If you had read the information on the application form it would be obvious to you that I have resided at the same address for the past six months. I am over-qualified for this position to begin with. However, had I have slept in my car and arrived looking this good for the interview you would have found yourself a talented and enthusiastic employee to say the least." That said, I suggested we not waste any more of our time, and I left. I have since wondered if a man in his mental state was not by this time sleeping in his own car.

My next employment interview was every bit as ridiculous, and discouraging as the encounter with Dr. Eyes had been. The position advertised was that of counselor at an outpatient clinic. I had stated my experience and qualifications by correspondence, and had been invited to fill out an application form and speak with the director. I entered the office, introduced myself, took a seat, and the lady said "Ya'll sound like Peter Jennings. Same accent." For the next ten minutes we discussed Mr. Jennings. I assured the lady that I had never met the man, although I am sure that had I known him she would have given me the job. A shame really. I offered to show her my American passport to prove that I was legally eligible to work. The lady however was not interested in anything other than my accent and I decided that rather than settle for providing her with her afternoon entertainment, to excuse myself and leave. Things must have been awfully slow at the treatment center that day.

By now it was time to check back with the Probation Department. After I had completed the oral and written exams, I had been informed that I was entered on their hiring list at number thirty seven. I had called every few months to check on my status and the answer was always the same, "we'll call you".

Now twelve months later I walked into the office and asked what number my name had climbed to on the list. "Number seventy four".

"Number seventy four? How does a person go down a list?" I asked. No answer. "I have spent the eighty-five dollar fee, and countless hours in time, and now when the application is about to expire I am twice as far down the list? When I applied in New York, and after acceptance, I was told when to report."

The woman at the counter turned her back toward me and said, "Well, ya'll, this isn't New York." No it sure as hell was not New York. I left the office after glancing around and noting that not one person there had the gumption to do more than sit with head bent, and eyes downcast. It might be interesting to know just how many new residents had spent eighty-five dollars applying for a job that they had no chance of getting.

I had submitted many applications to Caesars Palace during my first year as a Las Vegas resident. A year and a half later I knew someone well enough to place their name on the application as a reference, and was hired. My first day on the job I was asked by everyone I met there who it was that had gotten me the job. It is that common to be hired this way. I was working security and asked a co-worker and retired cop what he thought of the fiasco at the Probation Department.

He laughed and said "Oh, don't you know? When someone comes along who knows the right people, we call it juice; the Department slips his name in and the rest get bumped down." Well now I knew, and I also knew that the public has good reason to be concerned about the justice system in this city.

My third year as a Las Vegas resident and I am no farther ahead career-wise. Now I began sending resumes to the Commonwealth of Massachusetts. Of course by now the country is experiencing massive layoffs. California was hit especially hard. Military base closings, earthquakes, fires, floods, downsizing and reorganizing. The parade of people moving to Las Vegas had swelled to over six thousand a month. Most were from California. If you travelled the highway between Los Angeles and Las Vegas (dubbed the golden necklace) you would have witnessed the convoys of refugees rushing to set up house in the new promised land.

Many a vehicle was old and beat up, the owners' belongings tied to the sides and roof. Whole caravans of U-Hauls were all headed toward Vegas. It really was Grapes of Wrath nineties version. The homeless population would grow to ten thousand by 1994. The gangs followed, the hotel industry is rolling in clover, even building a roof over the main street downtown. The tax payers foot the bill for most of this enterprise while the city still has not come to terms with what to do with the homeless. To date there is not a city-owned shelter in Vegas.

Overcrowded schools, overcrowded prisons, and the hotel industry is continuing to advertise this city as the place to come to live and play. People were now sleeping on the sidewalks overnight waiting for personnel offices to open, hoping for the opportunity to apply for one of the many minimum wage jobs. Benefits after ninety days. Most new hires at many of the hotels are replaced when the ninety day period expires.

I was once advised by an employment counselor that there were too few jobs listed on the Vegas portion of my resume for me to be taken seriously. I commented that I had always understood that stability was important. "Well this is Vegas and the average job turnover per worker is three a year." Lovely family-oriented city.

I once spent three days as a temporary at the MGM Grand. The other temporary working with me was an immigrant from Germany. We compared notes and discovered that our pathetic employment histories in Vegas were virtually alike. At any rate, we were told to pull files. New hires we were told. Every new hire was being let go almost to the day that their ninety day period was due to expire, and they were due to qualify for benefits. These files represented hundreds of people being let go at the same time. Many had children to support. Well you have to keep the stockholders happy by ensuring a healthy profit margin. Cheap food and booze to lure the gamblers in so that they will lose their money to the establishment, and cheap labor. Expenses down, profits up. I never saw the German lady again. I do remember her telling me however, that her American dream had become her American nightmare.

It appeared to me that any treatment, of anyone, was alright as long as one could get away with it. There is no sense of shame here, and should one complain you will more than likely be told not to take things personally. I interpret this to mean that since everyone is treated like garbage, I have not been singled out. Of course I don't buy the notion that people treated like collective garbage feel any better than those who are singled out.

One day I stood at the checkout line in the neighborhood market. The man ahead of me was a well-groomed polite Hispanic with two small children. After the cashier totaled his order he handed her food stamps. This clerk, always surly and bad tempered began to complain loudly about having to cash the stamps. She made quite a production about verifying his identification. As the man left she continued to complain to the next person in line, which happened to be me.

I suggested to the foolish woman that the man may very well be a hard-working laborer, working for minimum wage as many laborers do in Vegas. She never answered me, and the next time I entered the store during her shift she told another clerk to serve me. She would not. "I hate that woman," she said. This was fine with me. At least I had made an impression. Perhaps she will think twice before she abuses any more customers. Somehow I doubt it though. In fact should she end up on food stamps I would wager that she will find a minority to blame. Hostile, intolerant and narrow minded, is the mood here.

I remember reading years ago that the worst thing that could happen to the United States would be the ending of the cold war. America without a foreign adversary would turn its hostility inward. This appears to be happening. Corporate America has abandoned loyalty to employee and country. Downsize, reorganize, and move overseas. Those left with no hope and nowhere to turn, are turning on each other. The politicians do not mind; divide and conquer after all weakens the collective voice of the people. The fastest growing industry in the country is the construction of prisons. In close competition for the number one position is the private security industry. Gated communities are popping up in record numbers all over the country. The latest gimmick on the market today is bullet-proof home siding. No wonder over two hundred thousand people every year are emigrating out of this country. Many are renouncing their citizenship.

They are being replaced by unskilled, and of course cheap labor. This keeps big business happy, the stockholders happy, the stockbrokers happy, for now. I suspect that if things do not change for the better soon however, that one day all of these happy people are going to wake up and find that the only people who can afford their products are afraid to leave their homes.

The manager of the check cashing business was interesting. My first day on the job he told me that the people to beware of were the blacks, and black government workers. "Well, black and female government workers; everyone knows they got their jobs through affirmative action, and they're stupid, and they don't care whether they pay their debts or not." Really?

"I once held a government position, and I am neither stupid nor dishonest." I did not stay here for more than a week. My grandmother had always told me that where there was no sense there was no feeling. Las Vegas was offering me a heavy dose of the reality of her words.

The answering service is a prime example of what life is like for the working poor in America. When I hired on, and again, I got the job through someone I knew; the owner told me that I was overqualified. I told her that while Vegas was decrying the fact that they did not have a better educated work force, those with more than a high school education were having a difficult time getting work. This while we are constantly told that one should be willing to take any job. So what was a person to do?

The owner told me her story. Her parents had built the service from nothing; call by call you might say. She had raised four children, and claimed that raising children in Las Vegas was just the same as raising them anywhere else. Over a very short period of time I would discover that this woman had never been anywhere else. She told me that I had to pay my dues to get a good job in Vegas. I asked if she had read my résumé. "Oh Vegas dues is what I mean."

Over the months that followed, her twenty year old son would be arrested for mugging seniors in hotel parking lots at gunpoint. Her nineteen year old unmarried daughter would give birth to a child, and she would divorce her alcoholic husband. Just the typical family? Mrs. Calls' eldest son managed the office for her. He delighted in walking through the office bragging to the employees about his vacation home at the lake, the boat, and various and sundry other material possessions he was acquiring. Every so often he would interrupt himself to holler "Speed, speed, remember half a penny a call, that's your raise." Ebenezer Scrooge could not have put on a better performance. At five dollars an hour the employees needed a raise alright. Those who were self-supporting needed food stamps to get by, and God help those who became ill; there certainly were no health care benefits.

It is wishful thinking to expect that one who has been at the bottom of the pack, and overcome adversity, is going to feel any particular empathy toward those occupying their old space. Personal experience has taught me that it is a rare bird who, after overcoming hardship, is willing to glance behind and offer a hand to a fellow human. The owners of this establishment were no exception. The workers here were a tough bunch.

No doubt life down here in the trenches had taken its toll. There was Miss Montana, a recovering alcoholic, and as crude a person as one could meet in an office setting. She did not have a tooth in her head. In any other first world country a worker of her lowly economic status would have been provided with teeth, or at least assisted in purchasing a set, something considered quite basic. Not here. It appeared that here one was allowed to flounder until they finally sunk. Low self-concept, and the accompanying behavior, eventually got her fired. She needed counseling, but of course could not afford that either.

Another lady, early sixties, had slept in her car at one point. On five dollars an hour she could ill-afford to have her lunch delivered, however this is what she did. Terribly overweight, and out of breath after walking from the door to her chair, she binged on food the way an alcoholic binges on liquor. This was her way of coping with her sorry existence. The other food binger had a beautiful daughter that she was trying to raise. She would be near tears attempting to work faster and faster for her half a penny raise. My, what a relief it was when sonny would hop through the office announcing that he was leaving early for the lake.

Twenty-something had quit university after attending two semesters. She constantly asked me to spell words for her, as did the others. Illinois and many of the other States' spelling and abbreviations had her stymied. Sadly, I do not believe she knew where most States were located. She and her good friend, the wife of the son now incarcerated were smoking so much marijuana I do not believe they knew where they were most of the time anyway.

Daughter-in-law, clad in cutoff jeans, her bare feet propped up on her work station, huge container of soda at the ready directed her calls to the rest of us. She was now free to whisper sweet nothings to hubby, who called collect from jail a dozen times a day.

At one point she told hubby not to worry, she kept her gun in her purse at all times. Another young lady who worked here was the daughter of Mrs. Calls' Pastor. Beautiful and intelligent, she should have been enrolled in university. Instead she worked as a Girl Friday for a Law firm, four twenty five an hour. Then part-time nights and weekends at the service. Any free time appeared to be spent worrying, and caring for her younger siblings.

One afternoon her father was asked by Mrs. Call to give a pep talk to the poor and pathetic. Alluding to the low morale, Mr. Pastor informed the employees that the boss had to keep wages low in order to stay competitive. He suggested that those unhappy with their lot should leave. I wondered how far they were going to get on the food stamps? "There are hundreds waiting to take your places, so count your blessings." The poor and pathetic were too intimidated to peep.

I asked for any suggestions as to how these paycheck to paycheck people were to leave, or were they in fact stuck? These people were too poor to even have bank accounts. You cannot cash a paycheck when your balance is zero. One of the reasons that check cashing services proliferate throughout this country. These services were not simply for the convenience of the gambler. Of course the hotels advertise on the local TV station that they will cash your paycheck, and this will make you eligible to win a prize. They are cashed in the casino cages, accurately predicting that those with little to lose will turn around and gamble, hoping for that one big break.

At any rate, the Minister's best advice to the disadvantaged was for them to read bible verses, and he was off. A few days later he packed his car, one of his four children, and left the state. Well he did take his own advice, he left.

There was one African American in the office. She had a smile and a kind word for everyone, and a wonderful sense of humor. She told me about her struggle to move away from a poor Mississippi town, and improve her situation in life. To be black, poor, and female in America was not a position to be envied. She had spent three thousand dollars at a Las Vegas school to learn to become a travel agent. This was done on credit, and now she was attempting to make payments out of her meager net income. She could not spell above a fifth grade level, her grammar was abysmal, and yet the school had taken her money and presented her with a certificate. One day I told her that I at least lived a few thousand miles closer to my son by residing in Vegas. She replied, "Oh Vegas isn't any closer to Calgary than New York, is it?" Yes they had taken her money, and presented her with a thoroughly useless piece of paper.

I got an atlas and pointed out her error. She was sad, then angry at having been led to believe she was qualified to do a job that she was not suited for. This was just another painful example of the way Vegas did business.

I did volunteer work in Las Vegas. The local PBS channel was happy to sign on as many volunteers as possible. One afternoon as I sat talking with the station manager an employee overhearing our conversation said angrily, "You know that we hire local university graduates." I had been enquiring about permanent employment. I stayed on, however I eventually left in disgust because of the callers who would call in during pledge drives to complain that there was too much, in their view, black programming. Their vocabularies obviously limited, they enjoyed using the 'N' word to voice their displeasure.

The Diabetic Association was an enlightening experience. Strictly volunteer, I was given a writing assignment for their newsletter. I worked hard on the assignment, and completed it ahead of schedule. I drove over to the director's office and she said, "Give it to my secretary; I'm busy." I did and left. I never did hear from the woman and let a few weeks pass before calling to ask if my work had been satisfactory. The answer, "Well yea, so I gave your number to other volunteer organizations." That was it. My phone had rang constantly. Since I was working, and volunteering at a nursing home I let it go at that. Crude and inconsiderate appeared to be the normal behavior here.

There was a sixty something man staying at the home. His wife originally from Britain, wished now that she had taken him back to her home country before his illness. She spent all day with him to ensure that he was fed. The elderly incapable of feeding themselves were often left sitting at the table until the meal was over. The table cleared, they were removed from the dining room, having eaten nothing. The residents were paying thirty five hundred a month for their care here. Only after their life savings were gone would they receive the Medicare benefits) this is unheard of in any of the other first world countries.

This home was eventually investigated when it came to the attention of the authorities that a social worker at the home was having some of the residents sign checks over to her. If a resident needed something as simple as a box of Kleenex, they were charged five dollars. This apparently was regular procedure, and perfectly legal theft. The day finally came when I decided to look for work out of State and I left my volunteer duties at the home, but not before someone remarked that we volunteers had nothing better to do anyway.

I had applied to the Massachusetts department that oversees senior care agencies in the State. At one point during my varied Vegas career I had cared for an Alzheimer's patient. I was told that once I arrived in Boston I would be sent out on interviews. Of course I flew to Boston, having been advised that there were positions to be filled. I arrived at the office of the director and was handed a stack of papers. These were listings of places to call for employment interviews. Apparently this was the gentleman's idea of sending one out to an employment interview. I could have made a great many long-distance calls for a lot less than this trip had cost me. All of the listings he had given me were dead ends. All were involved in budget cuts, and firing rather than hiring. His incompetence had cost me dearly. When I pointed this out to him and asked him why he had offered to send me on non-existent interviews, his reply was, "Why would you want to move to Boston?" Hardly the point nor his business.

I returned to Las Vegas and my job as Girl Friday, and housekeeper to a stock broker, as well as my temporary work. I had called the Department of Probation in Massachusetts, and they encouraged me to apply. I found a Massachusetts address. This was a boarding house, very nice, and when I returned to Vegas I asked if they would forward my mail from the Department to Vegas. I wanted to return to work in Boston.

"No problem" said the boarding house Owner. However I found out later on the few replies that

I received were thanks to the older lady who had managed to intercept my mail before the boarding house owner wrote 'return to sender' on it rather than forwarding it. I returned on the strength of a few encouraging replies only to be told that because it had been a bit more than three years since I had worked that position, and more than three years since I had graduated university, that I was not to be considered.

I talked with personnel agencies throughout the Boston-area and discovered that there were thousands of people in my position. Even CEOs willing to work for low wages just to be working, were being rejected. Many more talented people than I to be sure were having a difficult time. Most of us were about the same age. At forty I had joined what was now considered the over the hill gang. The future appeared to have no more to offer than a series of temporary jobs, low wages, and no benefits. It did not make me feel any better to be living in the home of a stockbroker with an attitude.

I had spent thousands of hard-earned dollars, and years of effort, only to be offered jobs that did not exist, and interviews that did not materialize. During this time I come across news articles, and television programs that bemoan the lack of a well-educated, motivated workforce.

While in Boston I met a lady who worked for the Department of Education. She had been in that office for seven years, and was yet classified as a temporary employee so that she did not qualify for benefits. She worked hard, and spent evenings and weekends working at a dress shop augmenting her income. Her husband had finally found a job after a three year search.

Most people in Boston were polite and helpful, yet ethnocentric. This I found to be an odd attitude for a city that plays host to thousands of visiting students from every corner of the globe. I decided to tour the Quincy home one Sunday. I sat on the bench outside the house waiting for the tour to begin. A tour guide happened to be standing there and I began talking to him. He was pleasant and the conversation only lasted about ten minutes. The tour over I began walking toward the gate; just then the guide commented to another that he thought Canadians were really funny. "I was up to Toronto once and everywhere you go they talk to each Other, even while waiting in line at a supermarket. Really weird, they have conversations with perfect strangers." I believe this man's comment speaks for itself, doesn't it?

The tour guide was representative of the local population. Most people here said no more than was absolutely necessary to conduct a business transaction. The ethnic communities were the most pleasant places to visit. There the people appeared to treat the customer the way they would like to be treated.

Back in Las Vegas I decided to work and save what I could without worrying whether the job offered me a future. No more flying across the country looking for something better. I had decided to look for work overseas.

In the meantime I accepted a job in the research department of a collection agency. They told me I would simply be checking, and locating numbers for the collectors. As it turned out I was forced to make calls myself. Many of the debtors were people thrown into debt because of medical bills, the direct result of living in a country that did not have a civilized health care system.

When interviewed I was offered medical benefits, six fifty an hour, and a raise after six months.

The big day arrived and thirteen of the new hires walked into our training class. As soon as we sat down we were handed temporary agency forms to complete. "Oh, we did not mention it at the interview, but you will be temps; no benefits, for an undetermined period of time. We're one big happy family here. Everyone has to really like and help each other. It's really peer hiring here; you will determine and be responsible for your co-worker going permanent or not." My, this was a company that respected its employees, wasn't it? I would learn that I was the only person in the room not raising a child, paying down a home mortgage or enrolled in university. I looked around the room; the others were upset, I was angry.

Well now, we were going to learn a new computer program and be responsible for the hiring of the staff. Yes people who work together need to get along with one another, and hopefully build good relationships over time. However a Personnel Department is responsible for the hiring of compatible staff members. This was a farce. This was designed to frighten the desperate, and these people appeared to be quite desperate. The better to control them. Personally, I find the notion of an employer offering to provide me with an instant happy family to be not only ridiculous, but insulting. I have a family, thank you and should I be dissatisfied with the family I am quite capable of choosing my own friends.

G.E. was the ultimate when it came to hypocritical hiring practices. They informed all of us that the reason they had opened their branch office in Las Vegas was because of the wonderfully skilled and educated population of the city. Please, even the most naive among us did not believe that claim. One fifty something lady asked why we were not paid accordingly, if in fact we were that sought after.

The reply was "You are being paid more than most Vegas companies pay their people to start, and besides this is a low wage town." How many highly regarded, well-educated populations do you know of that are classed as a low wage town? G.E. wanted it both ways, flatter them to keep them by telling them that you believe they are intelligent, and pay them less than what they are worth by blaming it on the city. It was insulting. Later in the week I opened the morning paper, and came across an interview with a G.E. representative. He told the reporter that he was having a terrible time finding employees, the population was so poorly educated. A line to fit every circumstance. Tiffany quality at Walmart prices was what this company was looking for. They wanted people who were capable of reasoning, however not too capable. This representative must have decided that his employees either could not afford to buy the paper or he simply did not care what they thought, as most were in no position to complain.

We were asked questions such as, what are your hobbies? How much time do you spend reading? When suddenly a first year university of Las Vegas student asked, very seriously, whether reading Christmas cards etc. counted. Well, this young man posed no threat to the company.

There were a number of trainers, each with their own method of training. Each stipulated a time line for work to be completed, and each stressed what they considered the most important area of the work. You would follow one procedure and a trainer would come along and after watching over your shoulder for a few minutes, order you to follow another, namely theirs. We had either some very confused trainers or trainers with definite ego problems. They had us checking each other's work, and told us we were to holler, yes holler, and reprimand our fellow worker should we find a problem. "You are each other's bosses."

One afternoon we were told not to bother bringing a lunch the following day. The company was going to cater the lunch for their new family. The following day just before noon a trainer came by and informed everyone that the company had decided to cancel the lunch. No explanation and no apology. "Ya'll just go out and just buy something I guess." I looked around at the shocked and disappointed faces, and the arrogant and tacky trainer with her battery operated Christmas tree earrings, and cowboy boots. I said to no one in particular that I thought this to be an inconsiderate, insensitive way to treat employees. Not one soul looked my way. I glanced at the clock, noon, I grabbed my bag, my coat and left. Merry Christmas.

My first day on this job I had eaten lunch and then announced that I liked to take a walk afterward. I always invited anyone to join me. No takers. Instead they were quite content to sit through their break and complain that their diets were not working. They claimed to be too tired to walk, and used their energy to gossip. While working quietly at my computer, this group was reprimanded for being noisy. They discussed everything from personal finances to their affairs. They called it sharing; I thought it tacky, and unprofessional. One woman even taunted me and told me that they would bring me out of what she termed my shell. Another nasty work environment.

At eleven o'clock in the evening of the day I left, one of these co-workers called my home to ask me why I had not told them I was leaving. That took gall; however these people had an inordinate amount of gall, except where it would have counted. I replied that I felt sorry for them. Which I did. I thanked him for calling, and wished them well. The fact that I lived in the home of a stockbroker had not endeared me to these people; I knew that and America brags that it is a classless society. Well, it is that; however not quite in the manner this term is intended to convey.

When living in a society of sheep you would do well to remain with your own flock. So much for individualism. When people operate on emotion rather than logic all sorts of nasty behaviors manifest.

I was sent to the new MGM Grand Hotel. One of at least a dozen temps, sent to the VIP department there. The hotel had recently opened and organization within the various departments was still taking place. Many of the temporaries regarded this as an opportunity to find full time permanent work. All were enthusiastically working at the tasks assigned them. I was an old hand by now and not at all surprised at what transpired. One temporary was a professional looking, thirty something with a B.A. in computer sciences who had been an office supervisor back east before her recent move to Las Vegas. She was spending her days here correcting the mistakes of some of the permanent staff, and training others on the computer. She asked for an application form, and was told that they were not hiring. We were working side by side at our terminals when a permanent staff member sat down at a desk close by and began making calls to friends, and even her sister, begging them to come in and apply for work. She then shouted across the room to other staff asking them to call people they knew, as the department was so short-handed.

The lady with the B.A. mentioned that she had been told that it was who, not what you knew in Las Vegas that would get you a decent job. Yes it was true, and to the exclusion of skill and talents and people are worried about the effects of affirmative action?

One of my friends was working in the gift shop of this hotel at this time. She told me that there were so many job postings on the bulletin board in her staff room that she could not count them all. I drove to the hiring office and asked the man standing at the desk for an application form, and a list of the postings.

He said abruptly, "Are you a chef?" No, I was not a chef. "Well then, there is no reason to waste an application form."

I related what my friend had told me. He just gave me a nasty look and turned away. Later I called my friend. She did not have the so-called juice to fix me up with a job. That was alright with me by this time anyway, really. This was the lady with two graduate degrees, still working the gift shops after four years in Las Vegas.

This was not a pleasant place to work as far as I could tell at any rate. I recall the afternoon a VIP manager walked into the office and asked for everyone's attention. He instructed those responsible for booking room reservations not to book the trash. "Sorry, but we are in business to make money and at this time of year anyone not able to carry a credit line of one hundred thousand, is just trash to us".

I wondered what Mr. and Mrs. America would think of being referred to as so much garbage, because they could not afford to wager the price of a home? Family oriented? I think not.

One morning I opened the paper and noticed an advertisement offering employment at a book store. The young person asked me one question when I called to enquire. "How old are you?" I asked her if an interest in the classics as well as contemporary literature would be considered an asset. She said, "I don't know nothing about classics, but I need to know your age if you want to apply." I thanked her and hung up. I had no reason to believe that she knew any more than she claimed. The latest stats for the Las Vegas area high school graduates stated that twenty five percent were functionally illiterate.

A receptionist position opened at the Dean Witter office and I asked Broker if he thought I might be considered for the job. The following day he informed me that the office manager had told him that he wanted someone younger. No-one in Las Vegas had to be concerned with a little thing like age discrimination. You see the equal opportunity office in Las Vegas was closing due to insufficient funding and ineffective management. The following month I attended a company function as the Broker's guest. A Broker approached me and said, "Well hi, old Heather." Everyone within ear-shot had a good laugh at my expense. Whoever coined the phrase, 'money does not buy class', definitely knew what they were talking about.

Indifference and apathy pervades this society, and yet people claim to be concerned over the general lack of common courtesy. The

Broker that caused the laughter with his remark is a big Howard Stern fan. I am hardly surprised. Apparently there are a few schools in the Eastern United States that have decided to hold classes to teach the children basic manners. Hopefully these children will return home and pass the information on to their parents.

Most of the gift shop customers were rude. One woman walked in one evening, picked up a paper, turned, and attempted to leave without paying. I called out to her and she angrily told me that she paid my wages. I imagine she had lost more money than she had wished that evening. I told her nicely that I was very happy to meet her, that on four dollars and twenty five cents an hour I could not afford to cover the price of her newspaper.

Yes there is a lot of rude out there parading around as individualism. The young husbands and boyfriends of some of the Dean Witter clerical staff are a good example. Picture if you will a lovely room decorated for a Christmas party. Cocktails are served before the five course sit-down dinner. Everyone is dressed very well etc., with the exception of the young men seated at this affair wearing their cowboy hats throughout the meal. I must sound like Miss Manners by now, but really, there does not appear to be anywhere to go in this country where people behave any better than spoiled five year old brats.

Trophy wives and girlfriends are big in Vegas with the moneyed crowd. I was not good at the trophy girlfriend position. Broker told me that I was too independent. I had started out as a girlfriend, and declined the offer of becoming a trophy wife. Now I was a trophy housekeeper, travel companion. Well that was alright. At least I was free to come and go as I pleased, and make plans to move. Looking back, I do not know how I stood the life. Horrible jobs, rude, and superficial people. I imagine I persevered however, because I never gave up hope.

Immigrants appear to be the undesirables of the nineties. Xenophobia is more prevalent than ever across America. Of course people will fear what they know nothing about. I found myself sitting next to a gentleman waiting as I was to take a tour of an historic site in Europe. We began talking, and he told me that he had been in Los Angeles for thirty some years. He ran his own business, and had raised a family, and became an American citizen. Yet he was treated as a foreigner, and ridiculed about his accent.

Moving to a foreign country requires a great deal of courage even when one speaks the language. Imagine having to learn the language while adjusting to the culture. It occurs to me however, that a country as ethnocentric as this, North versus South, East, West, is not the most likely place to be accepted. People who are not patriotic enough to accept their own native born are not going to be receptive to most others.

We are seeing a resurgence of blatant bigotry and racism and the media focus on the exceptionally successful immigrants when promoting American propaganda. Once in a while an immigrant will be the focus of a piece, and his or her success used to extol all that is wonderful about America. And while it is true there is much wonderful about this country, should not more credit be given to the individual? And when the American people are in effect told to look at the achievements of these people and asked in effect: Now why can't you do the same? The fact that many of these people arrived with a solid basic education, family background, sense of community, and values, things sorely lacking in many parts of this country, is not often enough taken into account. All men may be created equal in God's eyes; however the child born into abject poverty in the rural South, and the child born to the wealthy industrialist were not born with equal opportunities.

Well, Broker has purchased a home in Florida, and plans to fly between Las Vegas and Tallahassee for the odd week's break from the mean Metropolis. I have agreed to care for the home until I am sent overseas.

We will drive from Vegas to Florida, and I will see those Southern States that I have missed in my travels. I have read a great deal, and believe that I am prepared for what to expect. My friends advise me that I should not go; apparently they are not impressed by this area of the country.

As we drove out of the garish neon Metropolis, that violent, polluted, hot and angry city known as the adult Disneyland, and fun capitol of the world; I felt a sense of joy at leaving. This chapter was behind me now, and I was looking forward to teaching in Asia. For now however, I was prepared to concentrate on the trip south.

The trip was less than eventful until we reached Kansas. Broker wanted to visit all the towns he had lived in as a child, and there was a considerable number. The shabby little towns with their unpainted clapboard houses offered me an insight into this man.

Apparently Broker's grandpa had been a Die-hard Republican. He had hated F.D.R for forcing him to plant trees as wind breaks so that the top soil would not blow from his fields. This occurred during the depression, and the country was suffering a prolonged drought and economic deprivation. Therefore the President's order had made sense.

Grandpa had not appreciated being told what to do however, though it was for the good of the country as well as himself. This was and is traditional American thinking; a propensity for individualism practiced to an extreme, that borders on a disregard even for the good of one's own.

We drove through Missouri, Tennessee, Arkansas, Louisiana, Mississippi and Alabama before finally reaching Northern Florida. Before leaving Vegas I had read excerpts from a recently published book in the local paper. The book was titled White Trash Nation. I was now seeing First-hand what the author had been referring to in his book.

Stagnation, deterioration, and decay are words that fittingly describe the state of the cities and towns we passed through, and just as fittingly described are a reflection of their inhabitants. Much of this part of the nation had the appearance of what one assumes a third world country would look like. Abandoned, burned out buildings and garbage everywhere. It was commonplace to watch as people threw trash out of their moving vehicles. I had never seen as much road side trash in my life, nor as many unkempt, dirty, and crude people.

Everywhere we stopped to eat the female waitstaff referred to Broker as honey, darlin, sweetie or babe. They were an uncouth lot that did not smile much; whether this was due to their unfortunate circumstances or the fact that they were often missing a tooth or two, or both, I do not know.

I do know that if this was the new South I had heard about, I am very happy not to have seen the old. We read of urban decay daily; however the rural decay of the South was every bit as depressing. A hopeless place, and hopeless people.

Confederate flags hung from the rear windows of the ever-present pickup trucks. Men with greasy hair and wearing filthy army surplus clothes are a common sight in the South. They have their guns of course, mounted in the rear windows, and the unkempt, and usually overweight female companion, along for company.

Every so often we spotted a building that was not neglected and the same could be said for the odd person. We stopped in Mississippi because Broker wanted to check on the casino industry there. Amazingly in the midst of all of this poverty, great big casinos were establishing themselves. Broker was delighted, thinking of course of all the money to be made from the casino stock. I found this appalling. Those States willing to give the casino operators the biggest tax breaks were luring the casinos in the quickest.

They had a ready source of dirt cheap labor. And I could see the casinos offering, as they did in Las Vegas, to cash the checks of the poor and pathetic employees hoping that they would gamble what little they had away. So how would this impact on the locals I asked Broker? His reply was always the same when I asked this kind of question.

"You are small minded, you think like the little people. Peons worry about such things." Things like the neglected and abused children and spouses of people caught up in the gambling lifestyle. These concerns made me a peon. Well, Broker and all of his friends did consider themselves to be very patriotic. Hand over their hearts as the national anthem was sung at the ball games, and the declaration that this was the greatest country in the world. Although when I pressed for examples of greatness I always received the same reply, "We have made a lot of money."

I had told Broker before we left Vegas what I expected to find in the South. He had said that because I had never lived in the South I could not possibly know what it would be like. The gentle South is what he called it. To date I have not found anything I might refer to as gentle, however. On the drive here we stopped at a few historic mansions and took the tours. I walked out on the tour where the guide claimed that Hollywood had given slavery a bad rep. This woman looked as though she actually believed what she was saying, and was quite comfortable with it. Ignorance was bliss.

I remembered the day I had toured Louisa May Alcott's home in Concord Massachusetts and the tour guide who speculated that had the Alcotts realized the repercussions of banning slavery they may not have befriended John Brown. And the American tourist who rolled her eyes and shook her head in disgust when reference was made to the underground railroad; and the part that Canada played in helping slaves escape to the North.

We reached Carrabelle, Florida the first week of December. Unconscionable neglect was my first thought as we drove through the spot where, on either side of highway ninety eight this collection of dilapidated buildings was supposed to pass for a town. My first sight of a person was of the wannabe militia man. His gun mounted behind the confederate flag hanging in the cab of his pickup truck, the dirty unkempt hair, the filthy clothes; at least one article of clothing army surplus and with him the shabby overweight woman.

Broker's house was off on a service road three yards from the shore. I was horrified. Broker left for Vegas three days after installing me here. I had never owned a gun, and had always maintained that should the day arrive that I believed I needed one to protect myself I would make plans to leave the country. I had already made these plans, however I would have to purchase a gun to see me through the remainder of my time here.

My first night alone in this house and there was a knock on the door. It was one a.m. At this point I did not own a gun, nor had I a dog; I was frightened out of my wits. This was not a pleasant way to be wakened. The man was determined to come in and kept asking for my husband. I pretended that my husband was asleep, and hollered angrily at him. He suddenly bolted down the stairs. Three nights later the same thing happened. This time it was early evening and I was downstairs in the laundry room, which has its own entrance and is accessible only from the outside of the house. I heard the same squeak I had heard during the night on a number of occasions, and had never been able to determine where it was coming from. Now I knew. It was the rusty old bicycle the man was riding. I walked quickly to the stairs, and entrance to the main house. He approached me and demanded to see my husband. I said that we were entertaining company, told him to leave, and ran inside. Squeaky wheels was persistent and said something about money. I locked the door and called the police.

The police arrived and told me that the previous owner of this house had been a drug dealer. The man bothering me was likely looking for drugs. Broker had purchased the house sight unseen from a realtor. I asked the cop why the dealer had not been arrested. He hummed and hawed something about this being in the county's jurisdiction, not his. Then he told me that behind the trees on the other side of the road lived a lot of druggies in shanty houses, and rusted trailers. He promised to watch the house and left. It was the same story a few nights later, different cop.

Two weeks passed and I had to call the police again. This time another cop answered. This man was a real talker, and told me that he alone was really interested in cleaning up the town. He claimed to be from South Florida, and being an outsider here no one would listen to him. He liked blowing his own horn far too much to be taken seriously. I silently questioned why a great cop like this, barely fifty, had left a full-time position to become a part-time cop in Carrabelle; I would soon find out. Super cop said that his wife was lonely here, as the locals were not friendly to outsiders. He and his wife invited me to dinner one evening, and this would prove to be a dinner that I would never forget.

I entered their home and was immediately taken on a tour of all the pictures in their living room. Every picture but for two was of super cop in various poses wearing his uniform. He kept mentioning that he had told wifey how clean I looked, and that they bathed twice a day. I found this a bit odd, but said nothing. Now dinner was served at the kitchen counter. Three stools were placed on one side of the counter and I took a seat on one of them. Super cop and wifey, rather than take a seat stood across from me.

I had not eaten three bites of food when I noticed that the odd couple had gulped half of their dinners down already, and were emptying their plates into the trash, and clearing the table. They appeared to be nervous, and offered me a second glass of wine which I declined.

The conversation initiated by super cop revolved around guns. They wanted to show me their gun room; this in fact was their bedroom. They gave each other that look that passes between two people who have a certain understanding. At any rate, the guns, a veritable arsenal were kept on one side of the bed, a large fish tank on the other. As I attempted to leave after thanking him for showing me his collection, she tried to interest me in the fish, suggesting that I crawl across the bed to get a closer look. I walked from the room telling them that I had no interest in fish. I neglected to add that I knew a great deal more about people than they had assumed.

I agreed to have one coffee before I left, and after the coffee was poured they told me once again how clean they were and one and then the other left to take a shower and put fresh clothes on. I left my chair and made my way to the door, unimpressed with super cop's claim that he loved violence on television, maintaining that it was good for society. I was disgusted by his story of buying a trailer, and after discovering that it had been owned by a black family, ripped out carpets etc. He claimed that although it was clean he had visions of blacks sitting around eating chicken, and tossing the bones on the floor and furniture. Every sentence was punctuated with the use of the 'N' word. Just as I grabbed my purse and headed out the door this couple suggested that I stay over rather than go home alone. I thought not. I felt much more safe at home with a druggie banging on the door than I did in this house. All night when the conversation veered away from super cop's racial hatred, it refocused on the number of women that were enamored with him. Wifey stood smiling and nodding ascent as he told of taking her back after a year's separation, because he had not found as he put it, "anything better."

This was one sick couple, and it did not instill any confidence in me to know that this nut was out patrolling the road in front of my house. Two days later as I was packing to leave for the airport and a visit to Canada to visit my son, super cop knocked on the door. He was concerned that perhaps he and wifey had come on a bit strong, as he put it. I thanked him for an interesting evening, closed the door, and a few minutes later threw my bags into the car and headed for the airport.

I returned two weeks later to find the kitchen door hanging open but nothing missing. The next time however, the stereo and television would be stolen. When Broker reported the break-in the officer he spoke with did not even take the information down. Months later someone told Broker that now and then some kids break and enter.

"Nothing to worry about, everybody knows who it is." Oh good.

Meanwhile I am working to get my visa and accompanying paperwork through for the Korea job. In order to accomplish this I needed the use of a fax machine, and the services of the post office. The local real estate office assured me that they would accept my faxes and I agreed to pay the asking price for this service. My recruiter spent all one afternoon trying to get a fax through. In desperation the recruiter called me and told me that the person on this end kept picking up and cutting off the fax, even though she had called and told the lady that it was my fax coming through that very instant. I drove over to the office and asked why my fax was not being allowed to come through as agreed upon. The stony reply was, "I will pick up every time." This did not make sense; however, petty and mean-spirited people seldom do. Now I had to drive an hour and one half to a mail boxes etc. in Tallahassee to send and receive everything eventually.

The older man at the post office told Broker that he hated this place and everyone in it. He claimed to have been transferred here against his will. Yes, this would explain his nasty behavior alright. The older woman told Broker that she had lived here all of her life and was not used to foreigners. This would explain her nasty behavior. Now that we are clear on that score I realize why I get mean looks, and great sighs when I asked for service. The day the grumpy old man put one dollar forty on a forty cent post card to Canada was the last straw. I caught the mistake. I used the post office in the neighboring town thirty minutes away after this. At one point I had put a change of address in for Broker as he was away in Vegas most of the time. The older woman then insisted that all the mail had to go to Vegas, as she was not about to separate the mail by anything other than box number. My surname is different than Broker's of course. Broker had to open another box for me. He handed me the key. The new key did not work. I took it to the post office and the older woman told me that it probably was my old key from Vegas. I presume that she believes all people everywhere use postal boxes. I returned the next day praying that the polite young black man would be on duty. Sure enough he was.

I told him my problem, he checked a shelf, and came back saying, "Of course that key does not work; here are both the keys for that box." He shook his head and looked sorry. I decided that he was a far stronger person than I. How he could stand to work with those awful people was beyond me.

Broker told me never to complain at the post office. "We don't want anything to happen to our mail, do we?" No we sure did not. Well, accountability and responsibility were not in the vocabulary of these people. We had always been pleasant and friendly, therefore I can only attribute the behaviors of most of these people to extreme ignorance, and xenophobia. Citizen/Alien is the way I had always felt in this country; now Broker who had been born, raised, and served twenty years in the military was feeling it too. He is not here often, and is therefore less affected by the attitudes of the locals, although car repair, carpentry etc. is difficult to accomplish when the workers do not show up for work as promised. This does affect Broker.

I decided some time ago that the employees at the local IGA are all deaf. I came to this conclusion after repeated good mornings, and hellos were met with the local dirty look treatment.

I had told Broker that we would not be accepted here. Everyone is aware that the Southerner considers anyone outside the South a foreigner. Remember patriotic?

Broker's Stockbroker status was not going to endear us to the locals either, in this impoverished hamlet. One day as I was passing through the checkout at the grocery store the cashier said to a man behind me "Wow, a hunerd daller bill? I can't tell ya'll wens the last time I seen one of them."

One evening we stopped at the local gas station. We had been to Tallahassee and wanted to fill up before coming back to the house. It was ten p.m. Some local kids said, "Ya'll crazy? Everything closes here at ten. You can't get gas for at least twenty miles now. No, thirty miles and keep going."

The express lane fast food mart is an interesting place. You may be lucky and find the pleasant fifty something lady on duty alone. However if the other fifty something is around things change. She does not care to sell me anything at the listed sale price, and would rather charge me the original. I now drive down the road a bit where the people are polite and helpful. An oasis in this sea of prickly petty people.

One Sunday the Tallahassee paper ran an article regarding the sudden influx of people moving to Northern Florida. The general consensus is that they are moving here to escape crime-ridden cities, and get back to nature. Five thousand people within the last five years have moved to the Northern part of the State. One man had moved to the neighboring town fifteen years earlier, and was still considered a foreigner. He owns a business, pays taxes, and employs locals. He also has a very difficult time getting people to work. According to him it's "naw", or "yea", and they don't show up as promised. One woman, a lifer, explained that the locals do not want even the tourists here. "After all, I only had to hire two extra people, big deal." She runs a small convenience store. Apparently the extra jobs and income are not worth the effort and inconvenience of dealing with foreigners.

Another local wanted everything to stay the same. I believe that effort would be required if things were to remain the same without deteriorating. A coat of paint, knock down the burned-out buildings, refurbish the abandoned. Things do not stay the same without going to seed unless some effort is expended. How do these people claim to be proud of where they live? Stagnant and decaying, reflective of the local population.

Sir Winston Churchill said: “To improve is to change. To be perfect is to change often.” This quote would no doubt be lost on the locals. For one thing, Churchill was a foreigner and for another, it is obvious that improvement is not a goal, and perfection is out of the question. The next generation will be no more enlightened than the first. One day, as I was leaving my car three children aged twelve to thirteen asked me where a particular pizza place was. I told them that I was sorry I could not help them. “I am new here” I said.

One of these boys said: “Yea ya’ll, so am I,” as he walked away scratching his head. I bought my newspaper, got back into my car, and as I drove away handfuls of small rocks hit the windshield. They are learning their lessons well.

One would really have to stretch their imagination to believe that this is a gentle South. A man that Broker had met and tried to cultivate a friendship with claimed not to recognize him when their paths crossed a few weeks after Broker introduced himself, and told him which house he had purchased. The man lives the next lot over. The people across the road and down a few lots told Broker outright that they don’t like to get involved with new people.

The jury appears to be out on whether nature or nurture are responsible for our attitudes. However, whatever happened to conscience and an interior sense of right and wrong? How do you claim to be an individualistic society when you refuse to take personal responsibility for your own choices? I often wonder what the purpose, principals, and values of the people here are. Most living in the bible belt of the South claim to be Christians. Unkind and mean-spirited, would any of these people care to define the term ‘Christian’ for me? Super cop claimed to be a good Christian. Yes, believe it or not that is what he claimed when telling me that he and wifey had been unsuccessful in their attempts to adopt a child. All the while his conversation was peppered with the 'N' word.

Broker's former secretary married and moved to a rural area of Northern Florida. Her husband is a native of this part of the country. We paid them a visit and learned that they were very happy to have left Vegas. Yes, too many Mexicans, and Chinese there. They are happy here and proud of the fact that there are more churches per square mile in their area than anywhere else in the nation. Interesting.

A couple that I have been friendly with for some time visited me in Carrabelle. They want to leave the neon jungle of Las Vegas. We exchanged opinions about some of the characters there. Remember Redd Foxx the elderly black entertainer? He had his possessions and home confiscated by the IRS for payment of back taxes. Wayne Newton, the ten million dollar a year man managed to declare bankruptcy however, and although he owns a large estate complete with an Arabian horse breeding operation he is required to pay only a fraction of his debts, and his lifestyle has gone unaltered. We had a bit of a problem working out the idea of equality between these two situations.

In the seventies Ed Fike, a former Lieutenant Governor of Nevada was indicted on embezzlement charges. He owned a title company, and used the income from that business to purchase a run-down casino hotel. The title company finally went broke having financed the hotel operations. The locals, the Vegas oldies, of which Broker is one, claim that Mr. Fike was such a nice guy, and well-liked Lieutenant Governor that he spent no time in prison, and eventually moved to Hawaii. We wonder what would have happened to an ordinary citizen?

There is the doctor everyone in the medical community is certain killed his wife; and the dress store owner who, after bludgeoning his wife to death, fled his home and spent the night at his friend's, a doctor. The next morning they called police to report the wife lying dead at home. Neither of these men were ever charged, but then they knew the right people, didn't they?

Broker plays tennis with Joseph Cusumano, a known Mafia associate. They belong to the same tennis club. Apparently Mr. Cusumano kindly advises acquaintances that it is in their best interests not to show recognition, should they encounter him in a public place. The Vegas old timers have often told me that they preferred the mob-run Vegas to the present day arrangement. "Back then you knew who you were dealing with; these government officials are just puppets of the casino kings." I believe it and if Steve Wynn is correct in his assessment of Vegas representing the country we do have a problem. Of course it is obvious by now that I believe that as well.

A University of Southern Florida graduate student embroiled in a patent dispute with the university was incarcerated in a maximum security prison, then put to work on a chain gang. He took his own notes home. These were his documentations of his own work leading to his invention for treating waste water. This sounds more like the old Soviet Union than what the United States is supposed to be.

My visiting friends tell me that their eldest son has been trying for the past few years to immigrate into Canada. Medical care is of course of paramount concern in the United States. As Doreen said "If you are poor here you die." I remember the man who collapsed at a gaming table at Caesars Palace. Almost a half hour was wasted while the guards decided which hospital to send him to, and how the ambulance was to be paid for. Statistics have proven time and again that universal care is by far the most economical. Universal care is the most efficient; precious minutes are not lost which can mean the difference between life and death to a patient, while attendants scrounge around looking for money. Contrary to what the American pawns of the insurance industry tell you, Canadians do choose their own doctors, which is not the case in the United States. Depending on the company you are dealing with here, and the type of policy you own, this is what determines whether or not you choose your own doctor. I become irate when I watch the ads paid for by the insurance company propagandists in the United States. Liars and hypocrites the politicians, and insurance companies have an easy time convincing an uneducated public to fear the word 'social'. What sort of coverage does Bob Dole or any other politician enjoy? Socialized medicine paid for by you the tax payer. Apparently the rest of us do not deserve the same consideration.

Power to the people? I think not. It is said that knowledge is power; this being the case I see little in the way of power here. I met a cousin of Broker's who has a grandson that requires two kinds of medication to control a kidney disorder. His parents can only afford one prescription. Power? The father of four who is suffering diabetic symptoms, yet cannot afford a doctor's visit; power? I think not. However they pay the taxes demanded of them.

Everyone I am acquainted with in this country keeps a firearm in their home, including yours truly, just in case. The children of this country pass through metal detectors on their way to their classrooms. People are shot when they knock on a strangers' door asking for directions. Freedom?

Family values, ethics, morals, these are nothing more than words here. Actions speak louder than words, and should this country decide to become more people-friendly, the big boys stand to lose a lot of power, and a great deal of money. There is a relationship between the way people live, and the way people think. From what I have observed thus far, there is no indication that the majority of the population are spending an excess of time thinking.

Broker always tells me that you can't teach an old dog new trick. I believe, however, that people can change. Broker, for instance, just entered the kitchen to tell me that he has just tossed a horseshoe crab back into the ocean rather than keep it as a trophy. Now that is change. Perhaps one kind gesture or even one kind thought for the more helpless among us, would in time effect change for the better, benefiting all of us.

Heather Whittaker

THE HOGWON PEOPLE

Asia is enjoying an economic boom. Classified ads placed in North American newspapers are inviting native English speakers to apply for teaching positions. Good wages, free housing, and year-end bonuses are offered. The Hogwons of South Korea appear to be the desperate of all the Asian countries to attract teachers.

Hogwon is a Korean term meaning foreign language school. This appears to be a good opportunity for employment, at least for those who have been downsized, reorganized, or have not yet been able to establish a career.

Ever increasing numbers of North Americans forty years of age and older are finding few opportunities open to them in today's market. Those who have remained confident despite months and often years of rejections, are taking a chance on Asia. They are also competing with the recent university graduate for these Asian jobs. The fortunate succeed in finding a reputable school, while others merely survive the experience. This is one story of survival.

I needed a job. After spending months corresponding with a recruiter, and spending hundreds of dollars on texts, training manuals, and long distance calls, I was finally hired to work overseas. I boarded a plane one Sunday night in late February and left Tallahassee to begin my working adventure.

The recruiter had stressed the importance of this position. Now as my plane taxied down the runway and prepared for takeoff I ran through my list of qualifications. Child development, and learning behavior courses, as well as English as a second language course, had more than met the qualifications I had been told. However I would soon discover that I was far from prepared.

Age forty five. No problem, according to the recruiter. Age, travel, work experience, and life experience were all assets and complimented the university degree. "There will be twelve days of training, and orientation, specifically designed to prepare you to teach at our Hogwons. No other experience would prepare you for this anyway." This last sentence would be the most honest bit of information I would receive for the duration of my stay at the Hogwon.

"You will be met at the airport in Seoul, registered in a nice hotel, and take your meals at western style restaurants during the twelve day period, before being sent to Cheong Ju City. Do not worry, they are so happy to have you, and besides everything is stipulated in your contract, everything is guaranteed." Well as you and I know, nothing is ever guaranteed, and this was no exception.

One and a half hours after landing in Seoul I entered the greeting area of the airport. A young woman I will call Kim met me, and promptly informed me that this was the part of her job she hated most. Alright, she was having a bad day, was not quite professional, I would not take it personally. The next thing she said was that she was putting me on a bus immediately for Cheong Ju city. "You will begin teaching on the first." This was the twenty seventh of February. I had lost a day flying over, but twelve? What happened to the training course? The answer to that question was that someone would probably meet me at the Cheong Ju City bus depot. Obviously we were experiencing a breakdown in communication.

Although I had spent the previous night in Los Angeles, the flight to Seoul had been thirteen hours long, and now I was looking at a two and a half hour bus trip? According to Kim the relocation money that I was to receive upon my arrival was not available. I had been told by the recruiter not to pay to change U.S. currency into Korean Won, and now I was in the position of not being able to buy a doughnut, even if I had known how to ask for one.

I suggested that perhaps it would be a good idea for me to turn around and fly home. Now Kim asked me to wait while she made a quick call. Two minutes later she returned and informed me that she was taking me to a hotel in Seoul. The trip to the hotel took as long as the bus to Cheong Ju would have. No time saved here for the tired lady. I wondered who was coordinating the welcome of foreign teachers. On the bus from the airport I noted that the television program was an emergency response show called 119, our 911 reversed. I hoped it was not an omen.

I discovered later that the hotel I had checked into in Seoul was preparation for where I would stay in Cheong Ju. We left my bags in my room and made our way to what claimed to be an American restaurant. Up twenty four hours, and now too tired to eat I was ready to leave rather quickly.

I told Kim that I needed to shower and sleep. She replied that as far as she was concerned, the only good thing about meeting planes was the opportunity to practice her English on the foreigners. She hoped that I would not mind sitting for another hour or so. This truly was a harbinger of what was to come. I would learn very quickly that consideration, responsibility, and forethought were not on the menu.

Back at my hotel after the impromptu English lesson, Kim asked me what time I would like to be picked up the next morning. I said eleven, and she arrived at nine. My, I was happy that too hungry to sleep, who knows what would have transpired had I not been ready when she arrived. We taxied straight to the Seoul office. I asked if I might have a cup of coffee. One hour later the receptionist handed me a coffee and introduced me to the director.

Mr. Sung had earned his university degree in the United States, and spoke perfect English. He told me that I was replacing a very old man at the Cheong Ju school. I asked the old man's age. He said he did not know the age, only that he was much too fragile and quiet to handle the children. "Yes much too old and weak for teaching." Mr. sung then asked my age. I told him that my date of birth had not changed since I had been accepted for the position.

I reminded him that I had gone to a great deal of trouble and expense to reach Seoul.

I told him that if age was a factor in hiring it was a bit late. "Well you do not look your age so you should work out well." Amazing. It had never occurred to me that one could predict teaching ability simply by looking at a person. Things were getting more suspect each hour. Were things going to get much worse? You bet they were, much worse.

I asked for my relocation money. It was noon by this time, and I was hungry. Mr. sung handed me one fifth of the amount I was supposed to have received the previous night. He told me to walk around and see if I could find something to eat. It sounded like a challenge. He told me that I would get the rest of the money when I arrived in Cheong Ju. I found a KFC, forced down half of a partially cooked chicken burger, and headed back to the office. Along the way I stopped in a coffee shop that charged me the equivalent of four U.S. dollars for half a cup of coffee, no refills.

At one thirty I was told to board a bus. We were headed for the Olympic Plaza. We were to spend a few hours there, and an English festival was underway. There were children from Hogwons all over South Korea, competing for the grand prize of a trip to Disneyland. A little entertainment, I thought, may take my mind off of more pressing matters, such as food, sleep, and money, though somehow I did not think it likely.

Four o'clock, and I have found nothing to either eat or drink. Now someone pointed me toward a table stacked with newly arrived boxes, dozens of boxes. I stumbled over to the table as quickly as I could, and voila! mineral water, hundreds of bottles of mineral water. These were the refreshments. I remembered hearing somewhere that if one had not eaten in some time it was best to ease into it, but this was ridiculous.

Time dragged on. There were thousands of people in the auditorium, and hundreds of children competing. They were entering, leaving, back and forth, up and down. The children hollered, ran, jumped, fought. And in the midst of this chaos, they took the stage in quick succession to sing, "It's a small, small, world". I found myself sitting behind a couple that I had been speaking with earlier. They had advised me to "brace myself", for things had a habit of going from bad to worse. I watched as a child of about eight ran up behind the male teacher, and digging his fingers into the teacher's scalp, yanked a handful of hair. I could not believe what was happening. The teacher turned to the child and did no more than smile, his face reddening. Was being abused by the students without protest part of the job description?

I would learn the answer to this question within the week, and to my horror. At present however, just as I was beginning to believe that I had died and been sent to some sort of kid hell, I was ordered to board another bus.

It was now seven thirty at night and the couple of hours had finally come to a close. I found myself sitting beside Sandy, a teacher and future roommate. Behind us on the bus sat Mrs. Lowe, co-owner of the Cheong Ju school, and a bus load of kids singing "It's a small, small, world."

To take my mind off of my empty stomach I asked Sandy to tell me about the little old man that I had been hired to replace. I provided the Kleenex for Sandy to dry her tears, and eventually Sandy was able to quit laughing long enough to tell me. The fragile little old man was over six feet tall, forty-eight years old, and spent three or four hours each morning hiking on the mountain behind the apartment. Interestingly the little old man sounded more like Clint Eastwood than an elf.

Little old Ray had been asked to fly from Canada two months earlier, on a tourist visa. He had been assured by the school that though he did not have the minimum qualifications to teach, (a university degree) the school would handle everything once he arrived. Residence, and work visas would be taken care of.

They certainly had handled things. They placed him in a classroom long enough to get parents to quickly start enrolling kids, and paying tuition. Ray was not being let go because of age obviously. They had simply used him temporarily, and had never intended to keep him.

Sandy informed me that the school in Cheong Ju had only been open for two months. Two months? Ten years, ten years, the recruiter had assured me. Solid, a well-established school.

"Oh that's ten years in Europe", said Sandy. "The Korean franchise is only six months old and Cheong Ju school is a satellite of the main school." How wonderful. Everything so far had been misrepresented. How many more surprises were in store for me?

As the bus rolled along I noticed that there was a nasty aroma coming from somewhere. Sandy told me that the ice was melting with the spring thaw, and what we were smelling was the open sewage. I did not want to think about sewage just then, so asked Sandy for more information regarding the school.

Well, because Ray had flown in on one Day's notice he had paid the highest fare possible. The school had reimbursed him for only half. He was ordered to tell the kids and parents that he was an American, thereby denying his nationality.

The explanation for this was that the parents were hoping to send their kids to American universities and apparently wanted them to learn to speak with American accents. Let me see, Rhode Island, the Bronx, Texas, South Carolina, or perhaps Washington State. Which American accent? How stupid was this situation? Well part of the teaching process involved having the children listen to English-speaking tapes, the content of which were performed by instructors with British accents.

Dale, the director of the Cheong Ju school told me that I must never let on that I was born anywhere but in the United States. The birth place noted in my American passport is Canadian. One may attribute this attitude to bias in favor of Americans, but for the fact that he often sneeringly made reference to, "you Americans." As time progressed it became obvious that his was not about accents or nationality. No, Dale was an alcoholic who hated his job, and decided to take his frustrations out on the handful of foreigners he supervised. It did not take me long to discover that the English teachers at the other Hogwons, while misused were not subjected to the sort of treatment we had to endure. No, we had entered our own Hogwon hell.

There are approximately three hundred thousand people in Cheong Ju city. The area would accommodate fifty thousand comfortably. The night we arrived Sandy asked the owners of the school to take us to eat. There was nothing open but a small rather dirty Korean restaurant we were told, because of the lateness of the hour, ten p.m. Hard to imagine for a city of that size. This was my first visit to a Korean restaurant.

Ray, on one occasion, asked me as he scanned the restaurant, whether I would like to try some raw liver. He sat with his back propped against the wall, legs straight before him (all were seated on cushions on the floor as is the custom) and appeared to enjoy watching the people more than he enjoyed his meal. I glanced over my shoulder and yes, the man at the next table was preparing to let a large piece of raw liver slip down his throat. The conversation at our table now centered around the eating of dogs. An apparent delicacy, dog is eaten by the males of Korea during the hot spring and summer months. It is believed that eating dog meat keeps them cool. I have no idea what the females do to keep cool.

I was sorry that I did not enjoy the Korean restaurants. Life would have been much easier for me had I been able to accept the practice of spooning food from a communal bowl. I could not. I did not have the desire to poke my way through a dish of vegetable where other chopsticks had ventured before mine.

Mrs Lowe drew her chopsticks between her lips and then used them to turn the meat on the communal hot plate in the center of the table. I claimed to be a vegetarian, and declared the vegetables too spicy, which they were, and was left with a small bowl of rice.

After dinner that first night in Cheong Ju, I was dropped off at my hotel. It was well past midnight. As I lay there drifting off to sleep I recalled a remark made by talk show host Charles Grodin. He said he wondered why more people did not stay home. Right then I found myself wondering the same thing, although my reasons for leaving had been valid.

The next morning I went out in search of coffee, and got lost for about two hours. The signs on the buildings were quite naturally printed in Korean, the streets narrow and full of people, and I was very confused. With no orientation having taken place I did not even know how to use the pay phones. I wondered around feeling very lonely. I had travelled in many foreign countries, sometimes alone, but had never encountered anything to match this experience.

My face felt damp and I knew it was not raining. What next, a tear sliding down my cheek making its way toward my chin? Then suddenly, and as if by magic a young Korean woman appeared before me. Many Koreans wanting to practice their English will approach a foreigner, and attempt conversation.

Fortunately this young lady was one such person. She said, "Hello, how are you?"

"Not very well, I am lost" I said.

She led me to the little clothing store she ran for her parents, and I used her desk phone to call my future roommates. While I waited for my rescuers to arrive I told Chen that she was like a guardian angel. I explained that it was a good spirit that may appear out of nowhere to help one in need. My, I was in need.

Ray and twenty-something Brent picked me up. They had not suffered the misfortune of being left at a hotel and abandoned after their arrival. No they had been picked up three times a day and taken for meals, movies, and even spent three days in training for their new position when they arrived. Ray was occupying my room at the apartment. He needed a seat on a flight home, or another job. He refused to leave the apartment, and I as a result ended up staying at what was affectionately referred to by the locals, as the love hotel. It was one long week.

At first glance the room looked like the standard hotel room. However, upon further inspection I found that the tub had no shower curtain. The large drain in the bathroom floor was to take care of the water. I mentioned to Sandy that the room never did smell fresh, even after the maids had been in to clean.

"Oh I was in my room one day when the maids came in. She took that small plastic bowl that sits by the tub, remember that?"

"Yes".

"Well, she dipped the plastic bowl into the toilet bowl, and then threw the water on the floor. OOOH! Then she swept the water down the drain. I guess that's washing the floor."

It did not sound like a healthy practice, nor easy. Try sweeping a floor full of water down a drain with a two foot long pole, connected to a bunch of dried twigs. This would be your broom, of course.

The bath towels were the size of small hand towels. I was left one, and had to beg the front desk clerk for another every day. A bath mat was unnecessary. The bed was made up of mattress pad, and comforter. No sheets. I wanted to believe that they unzipped the cover on the comforter, and washed it between guests. Perhaps they had in my case. I found out later that I was the only teacher who had not been bitten by bed bugs while staying there.

I had never stayed at a hotel that offered me a tiny tube of toothpaste, good for one brushing, and a tiny tooth brush each evening when I collected my key from the front desk. On the dresser there were bottles of shampoo, cream rinse, combs, and brushes, all well used.

High heels clattered down the halls at all hours of the day and night. The sounds of men throwing up lasted until three and four a.m. It is no secret that the Korean men drink to get drunk. The fact was mentioned in our survival guide books; well, they were attaining their goals.

My first day at the school Dale sent me to observe Sandy teach for one hour. I then observed Ray for one hour. I returned to Dale's office and he told me that my training was now complete. Beginning tomorrow I would be given my own classes to teach.

Ray told Dale that he believed I would leave if I were not treated better. It was not his place to do so but I believed he was trying to help me. The co-owner's nephew was now assigned to take me for meals each day at his uncle's restaurant. They believed the restaurant was serving western food. The rasagne, that's lasagna to you, was actually macaroni soup, and each meal including breakfast was accompanied by a very tiny portion of thin green pea soup. Overall it was quite good, the best I had found thus far at any rate.

The two-storey restaurant was constructed of steel and glass, and designed to resemble a ship. Next door sat the log cabin coffee shop. It looked as though it had been relocated directly from Banff National Park. Uncle owned both of these establishments.

These two buildings were surrounded by the usual assortment of broken down, decaying shops, and homes. I sat in the sail and watched this strange world attend to its everyday affairs, as nephew practiced his English.

One evening I asked nephew to question the waiter about their hours, days off etc. It appeared to me that the staff worked seven days a week, and twelve, fourteen hour days. I had been right. It was hard to believe. The waiter added that he also lived an hour and a half away by bus. Since the custom was no tipping I was curious about the wages. The answer was approximately seven hundred dollars a month in U.S. dollar equivalent, gross. The wait staff did everything from waiting tables, to cleaning, to drying the dishes by hand. Nephew remarked that I should not concern myself with the staff. He told me that they were not high born like him. They were supposed to be treated poorly. I reasoned that nephew would be joining the Korean army soon, and that his attitude may well cause his lowly born comrades to educate him. He was to enter the army in a matter of months. The prospect terrified him, yet enrolment was mandatory.

In the Korean army anyone with as little as one day seniority was considered another's superior. It was accepted that a superior could abuse those under him without suffering any consequences. The junior officer was not permitted to defend himself. These claims were verified by Sandy's friend, a victim ten years earlier.

One of nephew's favorite duties as an employee of the school was taking new teachers for meals. The other was riding the school bus to supervise the children. Now this nineteen year old man was telling me that he believed himself to be in love with a ten year old girl. Too ignorant to realize what he was saying, he talked at length and appeared to be obsessed with the innocent. Music and American movies were his other though lesser obsessions. Brett Pete was his favorite actor. Brett Pete? I had only been away from home for one week; how had I missed a great guy like Brett Pete? Sandy eventually told me that Brad Pitt was the man of the hour. So food, little girls, actors, and music were nephew's life. Then one fateful night he began to use very naughty language while riding the school bus. The object of his affection had quit the school, he had turned his attention on the other girls and had them in tears. Then after threatening Sandy's life he was fired. It had been a very full week.

As I was about to enter my classroom on my first day of teaching, Dale approached me and told me not to worry. "Just smile a lot so the parents watching the closed circuit television will see that you are so happy to be with their children."

"Lesson plans, supplies?" I asked.

"Oh, just a guide line, you do not need them. Just play the nursery rhyme tapes."

These would be the British tapes, while at the same time I am supposed to be encouraging an American accent. Right.

"And do not be serious about the actual teaching. This is just a business."

How wonderful. I ended up sitting on the floor in jeans and sweatshirt, trying to have eight kids who would rather be bouncing each other off the walls sit still long enough to color an orange, orange. The money I had spent on texts, training, clothes? Forget about that, there is no dress code in hell.

In spite of the broken contract, and all the other irritations, I had decided to stay and do the best possible job with what I had to work with. Therefore I had asked Dale to please watch the monitor and correct me should he see anything he wanted changed.

Two weeks later Dale approached Jason, one of the other teachers, and complained to him that I was not planning my lessons properly. What? What lesson plan? No one followed a lesson plan; everyone flew by the seat of their pants.

None of us had the needed supplies. I entered Dale's office and politely asked why he had not come directly to me with his complaint.

He responded, "You have only been here two weeks. I did not complain to Ray directly until he had been here one month."

What sense did this make? It was so outrageous it was unbelievable, almost. Considering all else it was fitting in with every other nutty development. A few nights before this I had been approached by Dale after class, and told that a parent had complained of her child returning home with an assignment, and that one piece of fruit had been colored the wrong color. I had begun to laugh, thinking "well, if you are going to harass me find something a bit more substantial to throw my way. Do not give me petty nonsense to have to pretend to deal with". What a waste of time, and therefore life. This situation really was ridiculous.

Whenever Dale was approached and asked to clarify something regarding a student his response was always the same. "You do not understand Korean kids." Standard answer. He stereotyped us as Americans, and the children were all thrown together as being all the same because they shared a culture.

There was no consideration given to the fact that some had learning disabilities, just as children in every corner of the world are found to have on occasion.

Some of the children appeared to be neglected and arrived to class dirty. Others were extremely withdrawn, and yet others were undisciplined and rude. Most did not want to be there at all. The children were individuals and I was growing tired of Dale's simplistic reply to everything. I never have understood how people found it logical to blame the individual problems of children on the teacher. This man should not have been directing traffic let alone an English language school. But then he did tell me that this was not a school, but a business.

I wanted to ask Dale what had transpired between the time of his initial instructions, and their latest contradictions, a bad dream? He complained that the kids were not pronouncing their English words with American accents. I had been with them for all of two weeks by this time. They may have had a better opportunity to acquire an accent if they had not arrived to class with a knapsack full of candy, gum, and bags of potato chips however. The way things stood their mouths were full all of the time, and it looked like Halloween every day of the week. Munching away on all these goodies did not enhance pronunciation. A few of the boys were sent to class straight from their martial arts lesson, wearing their uniforms and wet with perspiration.

They were hyperactive and overtired, and refused their assignments by making paper airplanes out of them, after which they delighted in throwing them at the teacher. I asked Dale one afternoon what advice he could give me. "Oh I am not a teacher."

I asked if he had studied child development, psychology. "No, none of that is necessary to run this business."

This was the stereotypical cowboy school the training manuals warn one about. You entered the classroom each day never knowing what to expect from either student, or management. The only certainty you had was the knowledge that whatever happened next was bound to be something outrageous. The best I could hope for was to be allowed to function without being harassed, and of course to be paid for the aggravation.

The teachers at the Tae Jon school, one hour away and owned by the same people as Cheong Ju were not this fortunate. The month a new restaurant, art gallery, or coffee house was opened by the co-owners the teachers there would not be paid. The third time the pay did not arrive they simply refused to teach until paid. The Chungs were building a house of cards on the backs of the unsuspecting North Americans, and it would be only a matter of time before it would collapse.

We gave our students tags with their western names printed on them. Once they knew each other there was no reason for them to keep wearing them, though Dale insisted that my students wore theirs. I was also the only teacher required to take class attendance. The receptionist did this as the children entered the school.

Hollering at me in the presence of my students did not help to instill respect for me either.

My fellow teachers had advised me to put the trouble makers out of class for the duration of the period. This was the way they kept order. I was not permitted to do so however. He would send them back in almost immediately, and following behind them reprimand me in front of them of course.

The tone of his voice was enough; they did not have to understand English to realize what was happening.

"They are just babies, you do not understand Korean children."

In one instance, a baby almost my height and built like a sumo wrestler had nearly pulled my sweater off of my back, while at the same time another kicked me in the backside while the rest of the class stood watching and laughing at the show. Dale's solution? "Sing to them, it will soothe them." I could not picture myself breaking into song while being attacked by the students. It was well beyond anything I could imagine. At five foot four and one hundred and five pounds I felt a bit vulnerable.

The teachers found Dale's behavior toward me unusual, and Sandy decided that I was being singled out for special attention, but why? I knew why, but who would have believed me?

The night I moved into the apartment it had been Dale who transported me and my belongings to my new home. We placed my bags in the apartment and he offered to take me to dinner. I had been eating at this restaurant for one week, and since it was associated with the school I thought nothing of accepting the invitation. How naive can one be? Over dinner he told me that he had been watching me since my arrival, and that I had the body of a young girl. Oh no. Then he asked me if I had a boyfriend. Oh yes I said, and added that he would be visiting me in Korea. This was not true. Really all I had back in Florida was a stack of rejection letters from one time prospective employers, and a relationship that had deteriorated to a point where I had finally been reduced to nothing more than a glorified housekeeper. I was not about to discuss my personal life however, and certainly not with this man.

Wanting to change the subject I asked him what he had done before coming to the school. He told me that he had failed in the export business, and that Mr. Lowe, his old army buddy, had given him the position as school director.

He hated his present job he said, and wanted instead to become a recruiter for Hogwons, much more money in that. There was, he believed big money to be made as a recruiter. I believed that. The Hogwons after all were sprouting up all over South Korea like weeds after a spring rain. He had approached Jason and offered him commission for helping him get American connections. Jason had turned him down cold. He did not trust Dale. Smart young man, Jason.

Dale proceeded to tell me that he drank himself to sleep every night because of his loneliness. His wife and children lived in Seoul, and he spent only Saturday nights there. Now he claimed he was stuck in this crummy little city, living in one small room. This was more information than I wanted to know. I thanked him for dinner, and asked him to take me back to the apartment. I still had to unpack.

The following morning Dale arrived at the apartment ostensibly to see how I was doing. Unusual, according to my roommates. Brent asked Dale how he was, and glancing in my direction he told him he had had his best sleep in months and without a drink too, he stressed. Goodness, dinner and a half hour of conversation had accomplished a great deal. I began to feel very uncomfortable. From this point on I stayed away from his office, and him as much as possible, and that is when things began taking a turn for the worse. It is horrible to be harassed anywhere, any time, and when one feels as isolated as I did it is pure torture.

Toward the end of the second week Dale summoned me to his office and instructed me not to play the English tapes. These were manufactured in London, and were part of the course; in fact they were the only materials we had unless the photocopied pictures of fruit to be colored were considered, and the children were bored with these.

Again the parents were complaining that their children were not yet speaking with American accents, or so Dale claimed. They had been with me for all of two weeks. They appeared to expect an awful lot, or rather the impossible, from both me and the children. I told him that I had consulted with the other teachers and that they had confirmed for me that I was using their methods to teach, or cope, however one wished to view the situation. I asked him why he constantly contradicted his own instructions and he replied once again, "You are an American, you do not understand Koreans." I would be given this answer to absolutely everything until the day I unceremoniously left.

I devised little distractions to get the Children's attention. Hollering 'quiet!' as I wrote the word on the blackboard, and tossing a ball around were personal favorites. It got their attention and put a stop to their fighting at least for a short time. As the days progressed I began to understand that the children were refusing to speak English for fear of punishment should they make a mistake.

Our problems had little if anything to do with my teaching, or their abilities. Apparently at their regular schools they were not permitted to make more than one mistake. A second mistake was met with corporal punishment. When a child in middle school erred the punishment may mean kneeling in the school yard with arms raised above the head for an hour. The infraction may have been nothing more serious than wearing the wrong shade of socks to school. Wearing hair an inch or more too long was another mistake which was cause for punishment. According to recent reports these children are turning on one another to relieve their frustration. The result? A few suicides that have come to the public's attention. Their only escape from abuse. Reflecting upon my past, I understood them now, and I cared about how they felt.

They were testing me, and time and patience I believed would win them over. They began to settle down early in our third week together. I rewarded them with a hug and a smile when they deserved it. They showed their appreciation for me by offering me goodies from their Halloween sacks. We taught from three to five hours depending on the day of the week, with only enough time between classes to drink a quick glass of water. Patience under these circumstances was no small accomplishment.

Dale instructed us to write assessments of each child's progress in preparation for a parent teacher meeting. I handed my first set of assessments over and was belittled for my honesty. His face red, his voice raised, he laughed derisively and said, "Oh, you are so honest. Well, you will write the assessments with the tuition in mind. This is a business, not a real school".

Jason and Sandy had written their assessments honestly, hoping, they said, that their problem students would quit, and Dale had accepted these. I was not allowed this luxury.

I was to meet with the parents from one to three p.m. the day of the meetings. By one thirty the half dozen parents I had met with had all been complimentary. They were facing me smiling and nodding, and Dale had no choice but to translate honestly. At one forty five he informed me that he was leaving in a few minutes to meet a friend for a drink. Not surprising, and that he would not translate the remainder of my meetings for me. There was no one else capable of the job of translator. The owners of this English school did not speak one word of English. Fortunately parents began filing in again just as he was preparing to leave. All were very positive. Obviously their children had not been complaining about me at home. Even those two parents who had received the bit less than glowing reports which I had managed to get through were very kind, and appreciative.

I explained to the parents that because of the disorder in the class I was not as effective as a teacher as I wanted to be. One child, a little girl appeared to be weak and tired most of the time. the other child, a boy refused to cooperate. I told them that I believed the children had to assume some responsibility for their learning. One again this afternoon I was lucky. The parents of these two children spoke English well enough for us to be able to carry on our conversation without the assistance of the belligerent Dale.

The parents and children liked me well enough. I had the impression that they had been promised quick results, and given unrealistic expectations for their children when they had enrolled them at the school. Even a real English language school could not have sent little Korean children home initiating conversations in English, and speaking with American accents after only two weeks. Now who had sold these well-meaning, and unsuspecting parents this bill of goods?

These parents had left the meeting happy. The father of one of the problem children left me a note to say he hoped that I would continue as his son's teacher. This was not the scenario that Dale had hoped for. Using the parents alleged complaints of me as an excuse to continue his harassment was no longer remotely credible. I had happy students, happy parents, and healthy tuition pouring in. Dale would need to find another way to make my existence miserable. And he did exactly that.

Jason and I had been taken to Tae Jon to apply for our residency visas, Brent and Sandy to Seoul. We had been furnished with phoney addresses, and were supposedly working in Hogwons in these two cities. As far as immigration was concerned the Hogwon in Cheong Ju City did not exist.

Sandy asked Dale if this was a legal procedure, and Dale laughingly told her that of course it was not. "This is Korea. If we bothered to do things legally they would take too long."

That is right I thought, and you would also be paying taxes on this business. We were nothing more than a few English-speaking bodies shoved into classes for the sole purpose of extracting as much money from the most people, in the shortest amount of time possible.

We were made to leave our passports at the respective immigration offices. The English speaking officer told me that I would have mine back in ten day maximum, but that it normally took a shorter period of time. By the time two weeks had elapsed I became concerned. Dale now told me that the owners of the school would have to pay under the table to have my passport returned to me. "Don't worry I will handle everything." Now I really was worried.

I informed him that under international law one country cannot withhold the passport of a citizen of another country where no criminal behavior on the part of the foreigner had been alleged: and that it appeared to me that there was going to be a great deal of trouble caused by his insinuations regarding Korean immigration. I would communicate with the owners of the school immediately. Mrs. Chung could read English I had discovered. The following afternoon I was handed my passport and visa. Both had been date-stamped the day following my visit to immigration. What kind of fool would make their own Government appear to be dishonest in order to harass another person? It was a bit frightening.

Brent and Sandy began taking frequent dinner dates with Dale. They now told me that I should be more friendly with him.

"Go out of your way to visit with him" Brent said.

"Yes, he's lonely" Sandy told me one evening.

I asked them whether they had forgotten all of the mistreatment that I had been subjected to since arriving. "I am being treated like dirt, and it is alright? Would you appreciate being systematically hounded every day of your work week?"

"No, but if you just forgot about it and were nice to him because he is lonely (and trust us, he likes you) then things would be a lot more pleasant for you" Brent said.

"He always gives us what we want" said Sandy.

Well I was not that desperate. Apparently they were. They had a very low estimate of their own self-worth, that much was obvious and I had worked too hard throughout my life to achieve some sense of dignity to lose it now. There were four teachers at this school and if we had pulled together we may have been able to turn things around for the students, and ourselves. How wonderful was their situation when, in order to be treated anything akin to human they had to behave this way? They had allowed themselves to be marginalized and trivialized by a drunken tyrant. It really was sickening. Teachers and students were merely pawns to be manipulated for profit. I wondered how the general public both back home and in South Korea would view this mess.

Dale had Jason and I combine our late classes three evenings a week. Neither of us had been successful in getting these older students to speak. We planned our lessons together and they went well. Then one evening I noticed my three students and a new boy walk out of Dale's office, two minutes before our combined class was to begin. Dale told me to hold my class on my own this evening. Naturally I was not prepared for this. I had not been advised I was getting a new student either. Jason and I never were extended that courtesy, though Sandy was given a few days' notice, and Brent had not been asked to assess his students. This evening my class refused to do anything but play cards. After class I watched as they walked back into Dale's office. I had been set up to look bad, and the students robbed of an hour of learning.

Within days Dale demanded I turn over two passport pictures of myself to him. I asked for an explanation and never received an answer. The following morning he called the apartment, and instructed me to send the pictures with Brent who planned to leave for school much earlier. Again I asked why he needed these and he told me that he was sending them to the Department of Education in Cheong Ju city. Brent refused to comment when I asked him the reason for this. I was the only teacher at the school Dale had requested this of. Later that afternoon as I approached the door of the school I was met by Brent and Dale. They were unusually friendly, and Dale handed the pictures to me informing me that they were "no longer necessary". Was any of this necessary? Arrogant, his head always tilted back a bit, and his eyes cast down upon one, he gave the impression that he indeed felt himself superior. Yes that was Dale. I glanced over my shoulder as the two walked away, and decided they made a very unhealthy couple.

I called my friend in Florida and asked him to arrange to have a ticket waiting for me at the Seoul airport in one month's time. Dale had told me when it became clearly obvious that I was not interested in him, that there was an old Korean proverb, "The wood bug should stay in the wood tree." Well this bug was flying back to her own tree right after payday.

I wanted to believe that the British company responsible for selling the franchises were unaware of the manner in which the schools in Korea were being run. Perhaps, I decided, they have no idea. The future would prove me wrong in this respect. They are happy I now realize to simply sell their logo and run to the bank with the profits. But more about this later.

Brent was beginning to assume Dale's persona. He had even told me one morning that I did not understand Koreans. Offensive isn't it? I had to get along because I was sharing their apartment; therefore I never spoke of the school after the episode in which Brent and Sandy had suggested I be more friendly with my attacker. Brent told me about a bar where the foreigners gathered, and one evening with Jason along for company, I went along with Sandy and Brent. The Koreans had adopted this bar as a second home. Brent could now be found there any time he was not at the school.

What I found was a dingy large room where the reek of the filthy toilet permeated throughout. I wished then that I had remember Grandma's admonition to visit the bathroom before leaving home, because this was nasty. The stalls marked 'lady' were in the back, so that I had to past the filthy urinals to get to them.

Holding my nose I got there and found a hole in the floor. Now should a man decide to relieve himself, lady was stuck in there, unless lady got a kick out of walking by strange men in compromising positions. I am not an architect, but it occurred to me that these toilets had been designed backwards. Toilet paper and paper towels would have come in handy. Fortunately I carry a lot of Kleenex, due largely to the post-nasal drip I suffer as the result of living in a dusty polluted city.

The atmosphere was not pleasant, although I did meet some interesting people. One man, the only teacher at his Hogwon, had been given a room in his boss' apartment. He was required to go fishing with the boss and family on his vacation days. He did not fish, but the whole family had the opportunity to practice their English while working to catch dinner. Most of the foreigners were in Korea for one reason. They could not find work at home. Most had unhappy Hogwon stories to tell. Two girls from Ontario Canada had just been told that they were being sent to Seoul. However, they said that they had been told this almost every day since they began teaching. Two months had gone by. They could not order a telephone and were ready to pack at a moment's notice.

I paid a second visit to the bar two weeks after the first visit. The name of the place was 'The Bang and Beam'. The two Ontario girls were there, but this time they were sure they were leaving in the morning. The school they had been working in had quit paying their franchise fees. Now that they were all set up with official looking logos and materials they apparently saw no need to honor their contract. These two now had to be sent back to the franchising office in Seoul. Tina said they were making it very difficult for her to like Korea. I understood, believe me. It is not uncommon for the Korean Hogwons to operate this way, and there are hundreds of such cowboy schools throughout South Korea. The officials are not aware of many of them, and those in the know are paid to look the other way.

Brent believed that this way of doing business was alright. "They're just small entrepreneurs, they aren't hurting anyone."

"And the people brought over here and then tossed aside after spending their time and money?" I waited for a reply, but he simply shrugged and walked away. He seldom had an answer, though he had many off-the-wall opinions to offer.

Brent did tell me that I was too serious. "You have to go with the flow. For instance, when I was in Thailand, well the Thais find it acceptable for people to pick their noses in public, so I picked my nose when I felt like it. You see, you have to go along with mainstream society, adjust to the culture, embrace the norm in whatever place you are living."

Really. What were we, sheep? This was ridiculous, and taken to an extreme it could very well be dangerous. Look at Hitler's Germany for an example. I said all this and after a few seconds of silence between us he simply shrugged and walked away. I imagine he thought me a lost cause.

Whenever Brent was in an arrogant mood, which was most often his waking demeanor, or feeling belligerent his body language not only reflected this, but reflected his inner thoughts dramatically. Suddenly he would be sitting sideways on the chair, then he would throw his arm over the back, cross his legs, and immediately launch into a long and rambling oratory designed to educate all those within hearing of the ways of the world.

One morning as I sat having my coffee at the kitchen table Brent walked over, and sat down in a chair opposite me. Noting his body language, and hoping to distract him, I asked whether he had seen much of South Korea. But having already assumed the dreaded position, and with tongue darting between teeth and cheek for emphasis after each sentence, he proceeded to describe his first two weeks there.

Apparently these weeks were spent driving in the country side with one of the Hogwon owners and her family. He told me that he made a point of getting to know the "right people" when he moved to a place, and quickly. His tongue darting in and out of his left cheek, together with his right foot bouncing up and down, while he worked to force the appearance of nonchalance, was almost too much for any mere mortal to have to bear. Brent was a person who talked non-stop on his favorite subject, himself. Should one attempt to interject a comment his eyes would turn cold, and his sounding board of the moment would be met with a blank stare, as he waited for the unfortunate soul to stop speaking.

Brent was a chameleon. There was only one thing constant about him and this was his insistence upon growing a beard and moustache for one month every spring. He did this wherever he found himself, and seemingly without consulting the locals. The first day of the following month he shaved. Now what emerged was a baby face, not to be taken seriously by anyone other than himself, though even this was something to be marveled at to be sure.

While in Thailand, along with nose picking and drinking, he claimed that drinking was the thing to do there. He had found a friend really worth knowing. This friend was an older man from Los Angeles. Mr. L.A. was alleged to be in the business of selling REPOSESSED small yachts. These he imported from the United States, and sold to wealthy Thai residents. I told Brent that this enterprise sounded suspiciously similar to that well-known business of selling American vehicles over the Mexican border, after they had been repainted of course.

He replied, "Well yes, they were all fixed up and looked great, completely refurbished, and repainted. But I've never been to Mexico, just know about the yacht business."

It was obvious that he hoped the supposed importance of those he befriended would touch him, at least a bit. Tragically, one day it just might.

Roommate Sandy's self-absorption mirrored Brent's; however their similarities ended there. While Brent feigned interest in others, Sandy made no bones of not really caring a fig for anyone around her, and on occasion would say exactly that. At least she was honest. You knew better than to trust her from the outset, thereby saving yourself a lot of grief. She craved attention, and one day told me that the best thing about living in Korea was all the attention she got because there were so few foreigners in our area. She loved the locals staring at her wherever she went. The locals after all were not used to seeing full figured blondes walking around, and attention was easily had. Her shorter and considerably thinner boyfriend, a local Korean, only added to her excitement when they were out in public together. Sandy was up by noon every day, and certainly no later than one p.m. She would head straight to the fridge from her bedroom, grab the tub of ice cream from the freezer, a thirty two ounce bottle of coke, and proceed to have breakfast.

The boyfriend usually arrived in time to drive her to school, if not she hailed a taxi. The walk from apartment to school was twenty five minutes, and the sights along the way were interesting, however she would have none of it. Boyfriend spent most of his free time either at our apartment or the foreigners' bar. I found it a wee bit irritating to be wakened at two a.m. by the sounds of him and Sandy popping popcorn and chopping up vegetables outside my bedroom door. My room was directly off of the kitchen.

I had been the last to move in, and understandably was given the most inferior room. Sandy had been told when she and the others moved in (all men) that she was to do the cooking and cleaning. Mrs. Chung had a difficult time understanding that western women do not cater to men, simply because they are men. Ultimately Sandy managed to convince Mrs. Chung that each roommate was there independently, and therefore responsible for only themselves. Now the roomies had only to convince Sandy of the same thing. The way things evolved, we found ourselves cleaning and taking garbage out (hers included); sheer self-preservation, When I had met her she had told me that she did not trust people she considered too nice. Did doing the dishes make me look suspicious? I told her it was pure selfishness on my part, I just needed something to eat off of.

The apartment was always noisy. The speaker on the kitchen wall came on at all hours, day and night. This was an election year, and we were intruded upon with political messages. The security guards made announcements, and on a few occasions I sat and listened to a male and female guard fight. All of this was in Korean of course; we did not have controls and therefore could not turn it off or lower the volume. It was very loud, even with the sock stuck in behind the grill.

Peddlers shouted over megaphones, as they passed along in front of the shops behind the apartment complex. The shops were tiny broken-down shanty type structures, often equipped with living quarters in back. One shop was a video rental, where for a few thousand Won they would rent out pirated American videos. A man from the local dry cleaners tramped the halls of the apartment buildings in the early morning, advertising for customers in a voice that could have awakened the dead: and the child upstairs jumped up and down on the floor directly over my head, commencing each morning around six a.m. This was followed by piano practice which began precisely at seven. Friday and Saturday nights were particularly nasty. The local men stumbling home after their night out with the boys stopped often to relieve themselves of whatever had upset their stomachs, often directly under my window, and never out of ear-shot.

Making a long distance call was cause for concern. The telephone bills are broken down only by country. We were all on the same line. Who was supposed to pay what when the bill arrived? And Dale had told us to figure it out ourselves. It of course was all in Korean. The apartment service charges were comical. We paid elevator, elevator use, water, water use, maintenance, maintenance work. Apparently we were paying for the man to keep breathing, whether or not he did any work. I came to the conclusion that the monthly maintenance charges did not cover halls; the stairs, landings, walls, did not appear to have been cleaned since the building had been constructed. The grounds were full of papers, bottles, cans, and the garbage bins overflowed and spilled over the top, creating small mountains surrounding them.

Jason had spent only two weeks there before moving out. This left three roommates, which was the number stipulated in our contract. Two months after leaving he was still paying his portion of the user fees.

Sandy and Brent begged him to keep quiet about moving out because they feared a fourth person would be added. In effect Jason was paying to make life more comfortable for the rest of us. A contract Dale had informed us was only a guideline. “A contract means nothing in Korea”, he laughed.

Jason had been offered free room and board at the home of a university professor, in exchange for speaking English with the professor’s family. Now Sandy and Brent reasoned that because he was living for free he should pay some of their expenses. Frightening thinking. Jason paid rather than argue, or worse, they were very friendly with Dale.

I left the apartment early seven days a week. I enjoyed poking around the shops, and the one big department store. Crowds began gathering in the square at nine a.m., for the ten o’clock opening of the store. After breakfasting at a small coffee house around the corner I walked to the square and people watched. Sales clerks set sale tables up outside the doors facing the square, and when someone approached they would begin hawking their wares like a circus barker. Inside the store it was the same routine. Clerks were stationed at the entrance to each department, and stood shouting the sale of the day as the customers passed. The staff wore uniforms that reminded me of flight attendants. There must have been at least three clerks per customer, which sounds good to a North American used to having to hunt for help everywhere they shop. It was a bit overdone at times however, as one did not feel free to just browse. A clerk was usually hovering somewhere, like a body guard.

I enjoyed bartering, not something normally done in a department store; I found it a fairly common practice here. I replaced my travel alarm this way; it had been broken by students who literally wanted to know what made it tick. From thirty five, down to ten thousand Won, and voila! it was sold to the American. The clerk in the luggage store had an entirely unique approach to bartering. He simply rushed over to the customer shouting, "Two discount, two discount", and with calculator in hand pushed in one price and then another. The second was the biggest deal that you were going to get.

The foreigners believed that the little import store was kept stocked by an entrepreneur from one of our military bases. Shelves and floor were piled high with everything from cream cheese, (unrefrigerated) to hair spray. They may have sold more had they removed the American sticker price. Being charged the equivalent of four dollars U.S. for a sixty nine cent can of pears was a put off. I never saw or heard of a foreigner purchasing anything there, except for Sandy, though I am sure someone other than she had to have helped keep them in business.

Sandy was a merchant's dream. Her habits benefited other foreigners when she ran out of money before pay day, and began selling American goods half-price. I took advantage once myself, rationalizing that all the trash I had cleaned up in the apartment sort of equalized things between us. Most evenings I shut my bedroom door a little after nine. I had spent my day walking, teaching, and dodging cars, that for some inexplicable reason sped up when approaching a pedestrian. I mentioned this to Brent and he told me that this was the proper way to drive. Yes, he said he had watched a program about race car drivers, and it suggested speeding up rather than slowing down, so as not to lose control when approaching an obstacle you wanted to go around. I could not stand it. I felt duty bound to tell him that the narrow Cheong Ju streets did not resemble a race track in the least, and that people were not inanimate objects. This kook had an answer for everything. I came to believe that he thought any reply better than none; as long as he could hear the sound of his own voice, he felt secure.

Most nights Brent, Sandy and boyfriend were getting ready to leave for the bar at about the same time as I closed my door. They usually discussed the day's events at the school. The conversations included some sort of speculation regarding how long I would be able to put up with Dale's harassment. They really wanted me to befriend the man. They were very concerned about the possibility of being stuck with more classes, should I leave abruptly.

Now that I spent my days on the streets, and ate out, I had no reason to keep food at home. This should have been a relief to Sandy. Now she was not tempted to borrow, nor burdened with having to replace items at her convenience. I had removed the temptations of shampoo, soap etc. from the bathroom by the third week. I was beginning to feel like a squirrel with everything stashed away. Oh how I longed to be back in my own tree.

The hours I spent walking around the city taking in the sights, sounds, smells, were an adventure. This was national geographic, up close and personal. I had never before seen firsthand women carrying parcels on their heads, babies strapped to their backs. Women sat anywhere, and everywhere along the broken sidewalks shouting at passersby. I was offered goods I could not identify most of the time. Some had no more than a few loaves of bread, or a few sacks of nuts to sell. Others sat behind large plastic pans full of small sardine-like fish, turtles, and eels. All were swimming round, to the delight of the children passing by. They sold freshly-plucked chickens, vegetables, and grass. Grass?

One afternoon as I walked over the bridge toward the school I noticed a very elderly lady. As I watched she made her way along the river bank on hands and knees. She was pulling up blades of grass, and stuffing handfuls into the same kind of little sacks I had noted the vendors using. Now I recalled what appeared to be grass drenched in lemon juice served at the Korean restaurants. The fragile little lady glanced up at me. I turned my head and kept walking. I felt sad. One could imagine their own mother or grandmother, having to gather grass along a riverbank in order to survive.

Noise was my constant companion. Music blared from the little shops sandwiched together along the broken streets. In coffee houses, and restaurants people shouted as they carried on their conversations. Peddlers piped music through the speakers on their flatbed trucks, and push cart vendors hollered their way through the streets.

Motor scooters and bicycles used the sidewalks. Like the cars they would simply accelerate their speed and honk, to let you know that you were going to be mowed down if you did not move.

Negotiating my way down the always crowded sidewalks was a challenge. I was abruptly shoved out of the way by anyone wishing to pass. The locals often stopped dead in their tracks, without warning to speak to someone or look at something. It was the first time I had seen people rear-ended while on foot. The locals walked three abreast, and one had to hop out of the way, even if it meant stepping into traffic and it was not uncommon for a driver to honk as he drove his car up and over a curb to either park or circumvent traffic. And a local would drive even two blocks if at all possible; the ownership of a vehicle was considered a status symbol, the equivalent of which would be having one's children enrolled in as many extra-curricular activities as possible. It denoted wealth and status.

My first Sunday at the apartment I took a walk around my new neighborhood. We had been told that we were living in the Beverly Hills of Cheong Ju. Most large apartment complexes in South Korea are high rises, all look alike, and have large numbers painted down the sides of the outside walls. The construction of these buildings reminded me of pictures I had seen of multiple dwellings in Soviet bloc countries. I walked over to the little shop-lined street behind our building. Outside the market sat a newly butchered cow. The head sat by the entrance, while at a table off to one side two men worked over what was left of old moo. As I watched, a fashionably dressed woman looking as though she belonged in Beverly Hills California sauntered by, stopping now and then to squeeze the fruit set out nearby.

Finally I came upon a residential area of single family dwellings. The houses were of weathered wood or old brick, the thatched roofs repaired with pieces of tin, and sometimes heavy cardboard. Stray dogs, cats and children were running about the trash-strewn yards. Old people sat on their front stoops cleaning fish, vegetables, or starring off, lost in thought. The aged people and their homes looked as though they had seen their share of hardships. The apartment we lived in was visible from these mean little streets, yet a world away. Even here the music played loudly, but the expressions on the faces were sober, the smiles few. For an instant I had the sensation of walking through a studio backlot. This was surreal.

Brent was up and fixing himself breakfast when I returned. I told him how very sorry I felt for the people I had seen. He said, "Yeah, well it's their culture, they're happy." Had the poor old lady I had spotted on the river bank ever been asked if she were happy? Or is happiness not reserved for those whose very survival is not an hourly struggle?

Now Sandy emerged from her bedroom and suggested the best way to adjust to a new place was to ignore what went on around you. Gerbil mentality I thought, and left for another walk. While staying at the love hotel I had visited an outdoor Korean restaurant with Brent and Ray. We sat on small stools behind a green canvas hanging. While Brent and Ray ate I watched. Our cook picked up a pot and walked across the narrow brick road. Bending over and stooping down she poured the contents into the gutter. She returned, placed the pot on the burner, and as the steam rose from the pot she picked up two big filthy yellow rags, and wiped the inside of the pot.

The instant the cook laid the rags aside Brent happened to glance up. Seeing only the shinny pot he told me to look at how nice and clean she kept things. I had refused to eat as soon as we entered the place. I waited while he finished a plate of something I could not identify, but decided not to comment. As he happily munched away, I began to realize that this was a man who took everything at face value.

As he ate he told us that he eventually wanted to open his own Hogwon. He told us that Dale was a good person to know because he knew all the right people. Yes, dale had connections. I asked him how he could be sure of this, having known Dale for only a few short months. He replied that Dale had told him so, all on the q.t. of course. Of course. Now why was a man with such good connections not able to manage better for himself? This was a private thought. Once again I made no comment.

Brent went so far in his pursuit of proper connections as to offer, free of charge, English lessons to the school staff, and one of the owners. He spent six mornings a week, and his own money on teaching aids for this purpose. In the end there was not anything extra in his pay envelope, as he had expected. These people were dishonest in their business dealings, cunning and manipulative, and I cannot imagine how he believed he would benefit from a close association with them.

Brent came to know many of the people who frequented the foreigners' bar. One of these acquaintances, a Korean, had decided to open his own bar in town. Brent had not wanted to tell any foreigners about the new bar. He claimed we foreigners were too noisy, "too boisterous, they frighten the Koreans away." Really? They appeared to love to mingle with the foreigners at the B and B., in fact they sought them out to practice their English on.

Well, his claims did not make any sense. The day after the opening of the new bar, I asked Brent whether a large crowd had shown up. Ten people was the answer. Ten? I wondered, did Brent believe his new friend had opened his own bar so that he would have his very own place to drink? Or had he not intended to support himself with new enterprise? Well no one was going to be beating down Brent's door looking for a public relations consultant. The new bar was named after a soft drink company, very big, internationally known. They had hung a nice big logo too. I asked Brent how much he thought it had cost his friend to buy the rights to the name. I was certain that no one had made the effort. He said, "Well it's a small bar, why should they pay to use the name?" He said that a restaurant in Thailand had erected a sigh very similar to MacDonald's, and that MacDonald's had sued and won. Brent did not believe that this was fair of MacDonald's. I asked why? He told me that there was such a thing as big business ethics. What? I had no idea that there were such things as big business ethics and small business ethics. I have been running around this planet for some forty years believing that ethic, now this was quite a blow. Whoever had said that travel was educational, sure knew what they were talking about. Brent ended the conversation by telling me that this was Korea anyway, and that one did things illegally. It was the culture. Now had I not heard that from Dale?

I once asked Brent whether he preferred Korea over Thailand. He told me that he had no preferences. "I don't favor any place over another. I never question, just adapt. I meld with the local philosophies, and customs, and generally lose myself in the new environment. I become like the locals".

I tried to imagine reinventing myself wherever I went. Morals, values, likes, dislikes, ideals. Everything that contributes to the character and individuality of a human being would have to be altered. Apart from being a bit frightening, It made me tired just thinking about the effort involved.

I received a call from Florida one morning. My home had been burglarized, and television and stereo stolen. I hung up the phone and told my roommates the news. "Just plastic and glass," Brent said. "They probably thought they needed the things more than you do."

I said, "You know, when someone takes something that it took another time to earn, that someone is stealing more than the item, they are stealing the others time. Every minute of my time is a minute of my life." Well that is the way I see things, he obviously did not. This living arrangement was becoming very uncomfortable. We had been thrown together out of necessity, rather than choice. Jason and I were not able to enjoy our hour of preparation before classes without being subjected to lectures from the person without the personality, and the ever derisive comments from Dale.

At one of the Korean dinners (mandatory) hosted by the schools owners, I found myself sitting across from Brent. Sitting on cushions with your legs twisted to one side is uncomfortable over a long period of time. Brent complained loudly, and to our embarrassment made quite a show of his discomfort. I suggested he stretch his legs out in front of him under the table. I earned a lecture on Korean custom for my trouble. Brent informed me that Korean custom dictated he not stretch his legs while eating in the presence of an older person (meaning me). It would be rude he said. I reminded him that neither of us were Korean, and told him that I did not believe anyone would either notice or care how his legs were positioned. No, even a friendly comment or suggestion was met with a rude or nasty remark. Sad.

As I nibbled on the few vegetables I had placed on a side dish and ate my rice, I entertained myself by trying to figure out what made this man tick. I came to the conclusion that having to change his character often had begun to wear on his nerves. On the other had he may very well be just a run of the mill jerk who did not deserve any more consideration. I felt comfortable with this last theory: and now it was time to leave the restaurant. Mrs. Chung offered me a ride home, the rest were off to the foreigners' bar. Mrs. Chung's driver let her off at her stop first, and as she left the car she turned and handed me a small package of wafers.

Jason told me that he was no more comfortable with the school than I. He had been happy to leave the apartment, and was no more interested in the foreigners' bar than I. We spent many happy hours exploring the city, and visiting. My grandmother had always told me to keep my sense of humor, and Jason and I were fortunate to be able to laugh at all we had to put up with.

Sunday was our only day off. Actually Sunday was the only day off for many Koreans, if they were lucky. Clerks, wait staff, appeared to work seven days a week. One Sunday while sitting talking in a second-storey coffee house, Jason and I spotted a giant pepperoni stick strolling the sidewalk below. The pepperoni stick was handing out coupons to advertise the opening of a new Pizza Hut restaurant. We met there for lunch the following Sunday. Shiny clean, it had a real bathroom, paper towels, hand soap, real western food, everything. It was just like Christmas.

As we slipped into our booth we noticed all eyes upon us. This was true wherever we went. You did not have to be a big blonde to attract attention here. You just had to be a round eye, high nose, a foreigner. Cheong Ju was no tourist Mecca, not by a long shot. The guide book listed the local bus depot as the main attraction. Just as our meal arrived, the kids in the restaurant began approaching our table. The first few minutes were fun. The kids were cute, and wanted to listen to us speak English. They spoke to us a mile a minute, in Korean of course, and laughed at our inability to understand them. A few were able to ask our names, and pointed at objects, wanting to know the English word for everything.

Half-way through lunch we became annoyed. They had spent an hour with us by this time, and expected the adults in their group to have called them away long before this. However these children were allowed to run wild, as was the case at the school. When the Korean child was not at school or lessons he did just as he pleased. We joked that now we knew how a celebrity felt. We were operating at a deficit however, as we did not have any autographed pictures to hand out to signal the end of the interview.

The reaction to us was the same wherever we went. One of curiosity. We were odd-looking ducks with our high noses. The people were friendly, as on a walk to school one afternoon, I was approached by half a dozen children, and a few adults. The little ones shouted every English word they could think of. "Hello", "How are you?", "Merry Christmas", "Happy Easter", "You American?" When I replied the kids laughed and the adults ventured closed, wanting to touch me. Within seconds I was surrounded.

Jason and I arrived at the school by noon each day. The time before the others arrived would be the only quiet in a twenty four hour period. The arguing would start when Brent and Sandy came in. My particular favorite concerned the pronunciation of the letter z. Sandy said 'zee', Brent 'zed'. I, being from both the United States and Canada, Brent turned to me for support. I told him that it all depended where you were from, and what you had become accustomed to saying. I said 'zee'. He turned red in the face, and storming from the room told me to turn in my Canadian passport, and renounce my citizenship. A rather strong reaction to a trivial matter. He was open-minded only when it benefited him directly. A patriotic person does not deny their nationality simply because a soju-drinking boss orders them to, and Dale had ordered everyone to claim they were Americans even when that was not the case. He had only shrugged when I asked him if he found that insulting. After Brent left the room Sandy said, "You know I didn't want to say anything, but I think Brent is losing it. I have never even heard of the letter 'zed', have you?" Well I needed a good laugh.

Everyone had learned to expect these comments from Sandy. One evening Sandy told me that she could not understand why there was such concern about the friction between China and Taiwan: "They're so far away." I explained our close proximity to the two countries. She was also surprised to learn that China had not ALWAYS been a communist country. When Ray told her that he was from Vancouver she remarked, "I've always loved the State of Maine." Oh well, when I had met her she told me that she tended to be a little scatterbrained, she called it, sometimes. One frightening fact was that she had a degree from a well-known American university, an education degree at that. At least she knew who she was however, even if she did not know quite where she was. She had expected a five or six hour flight from the mid-west to Seoul, and was a bit put out that the travel agent had not informed her otherwise. She had never been out of the U.S. before this, and might have been living on the moon for all she knew, and I thought that she deserved some credit for getting here. Then one day she said that she had only taken the job because of the short hours, and good pay. "As long as I can sleep, eat, and play, it doesn't matter where I am". All the character traits of a cat.

Whenever Jason taught, the receptionist turned up the volume on his monitor for the benefit of his students' parents. Most were toddlers and their parents stayed in the foyer to watch the lesson. One child had cried, "Oh Ma, Oh Ma," and had remained huddled against the classroom door for over a week. She was only two, and screamed all through the hour, as Jason tried to teach. Dale refused to tell the mother to take the child home. The poor child suffered, the teacher suffered, but the money was flowing in. I voiced the opinion that this was a form of child abuse; the child was not emotionally ready for the class, and not even toilet trained. Again I was told that I did not understand Koreans. I understood abuse, I understood greed, and I understood that Dale was not a typical Korean, and that it was his countryman's misfortune that he claimed to represent them.

Jason tutored a small group of university students once a week who refused to discuss anything other than music and clothes.

They claimed to be too young to be concerned with politics, or social issues. At the same time the students happened to be demonstrating frequently. Their refusal to speak on certain issues did not make teaching English conversation very interesting, but it was obvious that a strict code of silence prevailed here.

The new students at our school were tossed into any class with room available. Age and level of English comprehension was not considered. We had seven year olds sitting beside twelve year olds, the younger speaking well, the older unable to do any of the work. This caused much of the friction in the classroom. The average child belonged to no less than three after-school clubs. Music, tae kwon do, and English classes were fairly standard, as were cadets and art classes. They were up at seven a.m., and not in bed until near midnight. They put in twelve, and fourteen hour days with no free time to be kids. Overly structured lives led to tired frustrated kids. They pled for me to take them out to the playground. "Teacher, teacher, outside, outside, please." Of course I was not permitted to do this, and the more I understood their lives, the more I grew to care for them. Often they were too tired to care about anything. When this was the case, they simply put their heads down on the table and went to sleep. Huddled in the corner of the room would be at least one sick child in a given day. Stomach problems were common. Some children would burst into tears for no apparent reason. They were pushed to the breaking point, and I was helpless. I could do nothing to help them.

Our students had been taught to read and write English at their regular schools. Their understanding of English grammar was more advanced than many of the English teachers in Korea. They were enrolled at the Hogwon to practice speaking, something most refused to do. When they were disinterested they liked to color. The class then took on the appearance of a social club. They did not then want any interference from me. They sat and visited in Korean, completely ignoring me when they chose to do so.

The students automatically separated themselves into groups. Girls sat at one end of the table, boys the other. As I walked around the table handing out work sheets, their little hands would pop up and grab the paper from me. They took from each other rather than wait their turn. They were very aggressive. Obviously part of the job description was going to have to be to teach some basic manners. Every child, no matter what their age behaved this way. Eventually they learned 'please', and 'thank you'. This required a great deal of effort and patience on teacher's part, but was, we believed, a big accomplishment.

None of the children were shocked or surprised when hit or kicked by another. Even hair pulling was commonplace. They were more shocked at my reaction to the abuse they inflicted upon one another than to the abuse itself. Some were dropped off at school an hour or more before class started. We had a glass partition between our office and the foyer, and the students hollered and banged on the glass for our attention. On rainy days they tore around the reception area. These were the first students of the day, and when the receptionist decided she could no longer put up with them Dale ordered me to start my classes twenty minutes early.

The European franchises spent twenty five minutes with a class of toddlers, ages two to five years. We kept them sixty minutes, the maximum length of time. Class length had been determined by developmental specialists employed by the parent company in Britain. Dale decided he knew more than the developers of the courses however. His motive was not optimum results it should be pointed out, but justification for the fee he was charging the parents. Any discussion regarding the attention span of a two year old in a controlled learning environment fell on deaf ears and while I was often told that I did not understand Koreans, I was certain of my understanding that a handful of people were living very well at the expense of naive parents, their children and a few harried, and one harassed teacher.

"Oh you are so honest aren't you, well this is not a school, it's a business." Dale was correct about that. Jason and I felt no dignity in our work.

I had inherited Ray's students, and one little girl had been very upset about losing him as a teacher after only two months. Twelve years old, she spoke English exceptionally well and told me that she would quit if I left. Her mother told me that she did not want another new teacher. Betsy was only seven, she spoke English very well and radiated warmth and intelligence. As soon as she completed one lesson she begged for more to do. She could decipher word puzzles in the blink of an eye, and had a wonderful sense of humor. Betsy rode my bus home, and when she hopped off at her stop she smiled and waved, and then skipped her way across the street to her apartment. Aware of all that went on around her, she never became involved, but rather amusedly observed everyone, and everything. Sadly, though I was succeeding as a teacher, it would soon be time to leave.

Pay day arrived and it was to be my last. The following day was a national holiday, and Jason and I spent all day wandering around the city. After lunch we stopped in a small park to listen to a political speech. We did not understand a word of what was said of course, but had a great time watching the reactions of the crowds. At one point our eyes left the speaker as we glanced round looking to see if we recognized anyone. We looked back toward the podium, and the speech continued though there was no-one standing there to accompany the voice. Then the candidate suddenly reappeared and joined his voice. He continued to mime as though nothing had happened. Apparently he had taken a short break, and allowed the tape to keep running to hold the audience's attention. It was hilarious, and all the more so because those around us appeared to take this weird turn of events in stride.

The following evening I packed my bags. Brent, Sandy and boyfriend were down at the foreigners' bar spending their hard-earned Won. I went to sleep early and woke at two a.m. to the sounds of popcorn popping, and veggies being chopped. I was up at dawn, and with only the sliver of light peeking through the crack in my bedroom door to see by, I turned on the flame under the kettle. My coffee tasted a bit odd. I lifted the lid of the kettle, and found a tea bag floating inside, the wrapper hanging from a string down the back of the pot. Fortunately it had not caught fire on the gas burner. Rude, insensitive people; well, I was not sorry to be leaving, not under the circumstances.

One advantage to these bar flies being up all night was that they would not be awake when I left. They very likely would not be up until I reached the Seoul airport. Jason arrived early and helped me carry my bags to the main street, where we hailed a taxi. We rode to the bus depot, a small television set was blaring the news. We ate our breakfast of sandwiches and coffee, and watched the crowd. Images of North Korean military forces entering the DMZ flashed across the screen. The faces in the crowd looked concerned, frightened, sad. I urged Jason to purchase an open ticket home, just in case. We never were sure what was going to happen next at the school, and now there were problems at the border. We hugged goodbye, and promised to keep in touch.

As I rode the bus to Seoul events of the past few months flashed through my mind. The roommates, and boyfriend playing cards outside my bedroom door at four a.m. Three a.m., Sandy blasting the television on, claiming she could not sleep. Well, I had not been able to enjoy my home. The school and Dale had been a nightmare, and I had explored the city many times over. The warning lights had flashed when the recruiter had told me that everything was guaranteed. I had not paid attention. I was too busy looking for an escape from my problems, and the possibility of finding a decent job. It's healthy to be open minded, but once again I had overdone it. A little skepticism would have served me well.

I walked into the Florida beach house exactly thirty hours after leaving Cheong Ju. It was my birthday, I was alone and I cried, cried for once again having failed at something I had worked so hard to accomplish. Well, perhaps this was where I was supposed to be, at least for a while to think things through. A week later I received a letter from Jason.

Sandy opened my bedroom door Sunday evening, and was shocked to find my room empty. One may wonder why she was entering my room in the first place. She called Jason, Brent down at the bar, and boyfriend. Boyfriend, our unofficial roommate, translated for Mrs. Chung. Apparently Mrs. Chung was very concerned about the reputation of the school, and the effect my disappearance would have on business. The following day Dale told everyone that he knew many people, and that he had found out that I was now working for a school in Seoul. He could not reveal his sources of information of course. However, if he decided to he could easily call immigration and have me deported. He said that if I had given notice, I would have been paid as usual.

"Although a contract means nothing in Korea." He continued to say that I did not understand Koreans because I was too logical. Was his comment that a contract meant nothing in Korea designed to reassure the teachers he had left? Brent was not concerned and said, "Dale sure knows all the right people, people in high places; he really is the person to know."

Jason inherited some of my students, and found that half of them had been told that I left due to illness, while Dale had told others that I had died. Perhaps that was just wishful thinking on his part. Dale has discovered that Jason does not live at the apartment, and will now add more roommates; remember, a contract means nothing in Korea. Dale told Jason that the user fees will be split five ways, and that this will save Jason money. Poor Jason, forced to pay a portion of others' living expenses to save money. Amazing, but true.

Another letter from Jason. The Tae Jon teachers were not paid again, and Mrs. Chung just opened two more businesses. The owners must have quit paying the franchise fees altogether and the teachers now must supply their own materials. Seoul is refusing their calls.

I sat down to read the Sunday paper, and an article jumped out at me. The caption declared; 'Baby Boomers Had Better Start Saving

Money For Retirement'. I should really send this to Brent. He informed me one Morning that forty-somethings should not be taking jobs Twenty-somethings could do. I had asked him how many forty-somethings he knew who were financially able to retire from the work force? Having worked all our adult lives and sacrificed to raise children, did we not deserve to be a part of society any longer? Frightening attitude, but not uncommon.

I have kept applying for overseas work. One young American school director called from Taiwan to interview me. He asked if I had worked with people of other races. Did he believe I had spent my forty plus years on another planet? I may well have for all he knew, as when I explained that I hailed from a cosmopolitan city in Canada, I realized he had no concept of what I was talking about. He kept stressing the importance of physical fitness where teaching children was concerned. I asked him whether the birth date on my passport had led him to assume I was less fit than any other applicant.

He continued the interview by demonstrating his knowledge of the history of Taiwanese cuisine, and the Japanese influence on Taiwan's culinary art. Then he informed me that I would have to purchase a moped to get around in Taiwan, because traffic was too dangerous to walk or jog as I do to stay in shape. Well that was the interview. I hung the phone up, and crossed this school off my list. The man sounded too much like Brent for comfort. A Chinese school director wanted to know if I was young and beautiful, a Japanese school hires only those under thirty five, and so on, and on, and on, and not one of these people were much interested in qualifications. All but the smugly ignorant kook in Taiwan offered me a position. As yet I have not accepted an offer. Most offer to sponsor a teacher and at the last minute suggest the teacher fly over on a tourist visa. We know better than to do that. Most are quite willing to have the teacher fly over with the promise they will be reimbursed for the fare, and sign a contract upon arrival. I know too many people who are now out of pocket, after having accepted an offer of that kind.

Another letter from Jason. Sandy was fired. No explanation really. Dale asked her to return for another year when her contract was up, and she had agreed. Sandy spent Christmas in the mid-west, and Dale called her there asking her to return two weeks early to cover for Brent while he was away on vacation. Sandy did as asked, returned on a tourist visa, not having had time to go through the proper channels. All was going to be taken care of by Dale in Korea. Well, in his unique way Dale took care of everything. When his pal Brent returned Dale told Sandy he no longer needed her, not enough students. Two more teachers were hired one week later.

Sharon was hired from another Cheong Ju school to replace me. Dale was adamant about looking after the immigration red tape. Sharon signed a one year contract. Airfare paid back to the U.S. upon completion of contract, no problem. Three weeks before the contract expired she was fired. Airfare will not be paid, because she was terminated before the contract expired. But a contract means nothing in Korea, right? No, not unless it is to the employer's advantage. Sharon was not paid for her last month's worked. The reason? "You were not a good teacher." Boyfriend went to the school to interpret, and Dale said: "Look, just to show that I am an honest person I will split her last month's wage between the other teachers." Sorry, we don't understand, but then perhaps we really are too logical to understand the Korean.

The school has become a revolving door for teachers, and most of the students have quit. Sharon was held at the Seoul airport for two and one half days in lieu of a five hundred thousand dollar fine. Apparently Dale had not taken care of the immigration business after all. Sharon had escaped a local school where she had been fondled by the director, and threatened with imprisonment if she complained. Apparently this director claimed to know all the right people. Mrs. Lowes' husband had attempted the same thing. I can't imagine how she managed to remain there as long as she did, except for the fact that she has a child to support at home.

Brent is now senior teacher there, and insists that no-one has access to making the coffee but him. He claims to know best how the Koreans like their coffee. Those few teachers presently on the payroll all plan to leave without notice. It's just as well, due to the fact Mr. Chung and Mrs. Chung filed for bankruptcy, and Mr. Chung is on the run, having made off with all the cash siphoned from the collapsed businesses. It is believed that Mr. Chung escaped to Canada, and Mrs. Chung left town with her two children and is now living with her sister.

I wrote the Head Office of the parent company. Based in London, they are known internationally throughout Europe, and now nationally in South Korea. I never did receive a reply. One would have to conclude that they are enjoying the financial rewards of their enterprise, and do not give a damn about the people used to fatten their bank account. That is not surprising; the same could be said for the British college that offered me a seat in their ESL course.

I had written, and called to be very sure that their claims of placing students after graduation would apply to me. I was interested in teaching in Europe. I had made it very clear that this was my reason for spending six weeks in England, and taking their very expensive (for me) course. I arrived and the day of orientation the instructor turned to me and said, "You know of course that unless you hold a European passport you cannot be placed after completing the course. Europe for the Europeans; you can always go to Asia: the Asians do not care who they hire." I am very sure that once there it was expected I would remain, and pay the tuition.

In fact this woman said, "Well you're here now, you may as well take the course." My how very generous. How very insulting. I could not quite place her accent, and told her as much. I had travelled all over Britain and her accent did not really fit anywhere. "Well, I'm from Quincy Massachusetts, but I've been here for twenty five years and I'm married to an Englishman so I'm secure. I'm even applying for British citizenship". Now nervous and turning red in the face, she ushered me from her office. I stayed in England for two weeks then, and met sympathetic British people who were appalled at the treatment I had received.

One gentleman even suggested I complain to their local citizen complaint board. Well I made the most of the visit, and having withdrawn from the course returned home.

I wrote the British consulate, and received an apology, and the promise that my complaint would be passed to the Education Minister. I received another apology, this time from someone connected to education, and again with the promise that my complaint would be passed to yet another department. There it ended. Interestingly I found that the Asians prefer North American teachers. We apparently are not the cast-offs the American woman with the identity problem would have had me believe us to be.

I do a lot of walking along the beach now, and have finally put the past behind.

"Hope," Grand had said. "Never give up hope."

I remember a day over twenty years ago when two friends and I talked of hope, and the future. We stood looking out my window watching our three children at play. There they were, one Caucasian, one East Indian, and one Chinese. The little East Indian girl's mother expressed our thoughts when she said: "Look how wonderful; they don't see their external differences, they relate on a deeper level." This was our hope for the future.

KEY LARGO

INTRODUCTION

Book 1

"A Wise Man Is Never Surprised"

Ellery Queen—The House Of Brass

Well I had finally arrived. I was about to land at Miami International Airport. Madeline, or Mad to her friends (our friendship goes back some twenty-five years) was waiting at the arrivals gate, and together we would drive to her vacation home in Key Largo. Charlie, her recently deceased husband of thirty years had inherited the home on the acre of beach from his parents, and for as long as I had known them, Mad and Charlie had spent at least part of their winters there. It was a concession Mad made to make Charlie happy, for she never had liked the place and now having decided to sell, was there in the middle of summer to tidy up last minute business.

This was my first trip to the Keys, my last opportunity to visit a place I had no real interest in, yet was curious about now that it was about to be disposed of. Mad needed the help, as anyone who has lost someone knows, it is a painful and difficult task, that of clearing out what remains of the material possessions of the loved one. As my plane taxied down the runway I recalled what few facts I knew about Key Largo.

1. Only living coral reef in North America.
2. Jet ski accidents killing so many people that they had been recently outlawed in eleven spots throughout the Keys, but not soon enough to save the lives of the three men who died over

a two day period a few weeks ago, not far from where Mad lived there.

3. Condos threatening to destroy what was left of the everglades, and the wetlands shrinking to accommodate more of the ugly, gaudy strip malls I had seen pictures of. The beaches were eroding due to the overbuilding of homes too close to the shore line, and the poor endangered Manatees were systematically cut to shreds by the propellers of pleasure boats at an alarming rate. Overall, the nature, the visual beauty and general health of the environment was being obliterated by greedy developers and shallow, uncaring individuals.

Mad had only recently sent me a clipping from a newspaper that referred to America as having become a lowbrow, crude, self-absorbed nation. Ill-mannered, poorly educated, an unhealthy society in both mind and body, scraping the bottom of the barrel. This last sentence Mad had underlined. She said that if to conform was to be doomed to mediocrity, then we were doomed indeed because in her opinion most of the nation had conformed to the mediocre and dumbed down accordingly.

James A. Michener, in his book "The Novel" claimed that it was the artist's task to "Provide society with a fresh and sometimes necessarily acid portrait of itself." Mad, a writer, was preparing to do just that, or so she had thought.

CHAPTER 1

The woods are lovely, dark and deep
But I have promises to keep
And miles to go before I sleep
And miles to go before I sleep

Robert Frost

I was one of the first to exit the plane having been fortunate enough to afford a first class ticket for my relatively short ride from New York. Another first for me. Was it worth the extra money? I don't believe I'd bother about the seating unless it was a very long trip. I had more leg room, our peanuts and beverage were served to us before the rest of the passengers were offered anything, but the passengers were no better dressed than those in coach; at least I didn't think so. Large stomachs hung over cheap slacks or shorts in many cases and rude demanding behaviors directed toward stressed-out flight attendants was the rule rather than the exception, but that was true everywhere I travelled now within the country.

There Mad stood, waiting patiently at the gate, Oxford shirt tucked into a pair of tailored summer slacks, plain tan loafers and a matching bag slung over her shoulder. Her short dark blonde hair layered to just below her ears, she looked not much older than she had twenty years earlier and certainly would never have been suspected of being a widow with two grown sons close to celebrating their thirtieth birthday.

The airport, one of the busiest in the country was jammed with travellers coming and going. Outside the terminal the vehicles were moving slowly, bumper to bumper making their way to and from the arrival gates. The heat was oppressive, the air heavy and humid, the exhaust fumes smelling worse than a cheap cigar. I was surprised by the number of people because it was the hottest time of year and traditionally what had always been known as off-season. I travel light, just the allotted two carry-on bags, a blessing in that we were able to make our way directly to Mad's car rather than wait at the baggage claim where people stood five deep at slowly moving baggage movers, anxiously waiting to spot their bags and hopefully grab them before someone else did.

We made our way out of the parking lot quickly and were on the freeway in a matter of minutes only to find ourselves caught up in a sea of slow moving, bumper to bumper vehicles. We passed through three toll booths before turning off onto US1 South Dixie Highway at Homestead, a little town devastated by a hurricane three years earlier. There was no denying the natural beauty of this area, home to eleven natural species of palms, and tropical isles connected by miles of causeways, the ocean sparkling blue green and so clear you can see the floor feet beneath the water's surface.

This seeming paradise functioned as a tourist and retirement area and I was told enjoyed Hawaiian-like weather for approximately eight months of the year.

Although the Miami airport is only Forty-five miles from Key Largo, the drive home took us almost two hours. At mile marker 103 we turned left off of the South Dixie Highway onto Snapper Avenue and made our way to the end of the street and through the gated stone-walled entrance to Mad's property. The drive was the length of a short New York City block and the two-storey home sat four yards from the water's edge.

It was a beautiful house. Every room was paneled in dark mahogany, doors, book cases, china cabinets, everything. Jalousie windows carried the tropical breezes through the house during the cooler months when air conditioning was not needed. Yes, everything was perfectly constructed, perfectly cared for, but as Mad said as she showed me round: "When you are alone, Hanna, the house might be big and beautiful, it might be a mansion for all of that, but it's not a home. I think this is true for someone who has spent their time in a house with family, not true for everyone necessarily. But when it's been an active house – well, with just me here now it is especially lonely. It was only a vacation place anyway and as you know I had never really wanted to keep it this long. The Keys have changed a great deal over the years. Charlie's parents would not recognize them and I am sure they would not be happy with the results of the changes. There are some good people working hard to recapture the old look and feel of the place, the romance that existed before the cheap t-shirt shops and ugly shoddy strip malls dotted the highway, but it is difficult to undo years of abuse and neglect. It's the same with people, isn't it? Yes I believe so."

Mad often asks a question and then answers it; It's her way of stating an opinion.

It was past midnight before we said goodnight. She gave me the master bedroom; she hadn't slept there since Charlie passed away. Achingly tired, I fell asleep to the sound of the waves washing the beach and the palm fronds rustling gently in the breeze.

CHAPTER 2

Tout Lasse,
Tout Casse,
Tout Passe,
Everything Palls,
Everything Breaks,
Everything Passes

I did not wake up the following morning until close to 8 a.m., and by that time Mad had been up for about 3 hours. She had always liked to wake early and watch the world come alive, is the way she puts it. After a quick shower, slipping into a pair of shorts and a t-shirt - the local dress code, I grabbed a coffee and headed out to see what Mad was up to. She was down by the entrance to the yard, just a few yards this side of the stone wall. To her right stood a huge traveller palm, an African import; its fanlike fronds arc out in a flat display, unusual and lovely as was everything I had seen here so far.

Yet it was terribly hot, mosquito-infested, uncultured and a very expensive place to live. These were my thoughts as I stood on the porch watching Mad, her machete poised ready to lay waste to a long length of palm frond. Self-cleaning in that they shed their dead fronds without any assistance; the coconut palms dropped fronds daily and these had to be cut into lengths no longer than 4 feet. The recycle collectors would not pick up anything that peeked too far over the rim of the garbage can.

Angry at her predicament, Mad gave vent to her feelings by swinging her machete. When finished with her chore she split a few coconuts (the trees rained coconuts) open for the squirrels to snack on and wet with perspiration returned to the house, showered and dressed. Rushing in to the kitchen in fresh shorts and t-shirt, she laughingly told me that she had exorcized her demons for that day at least.

"Hanna, I have always felt as though a stay longer than a few months in Key Largo would lull me into a sort of complacency. I cocoon here and it frightens me to think that I could easily sink into a rut and it would happen if I stayed here for a protracted period of time alone. It happened to the people next door, Emma and Jack. Oh, they're pleasant enough; actually they will help a neighbor any way they can, but they make a point of telling newcomers that they don't socialize."

I had looked out the bathroom window this very morning and spotted an elderly lady walking round her property, poking a foot here and there among a chaotic array of plants, placed here and there in a jungle filled with old boats of every size and description. Some were up on blocks; others had sat so long they had weeds, trees and fallen coconuts filling them. An old truck with a huge bed stood on blocks near the front gate and served as a giant planter. Everything was on blocks, stationary, trapped in a jungle of palms, gumbo limbo trees, and hills of coconuts. What did Emma feel when she wandered the property?

Charlie's parents met them and got to know them many years ago. Emma's sister Evelyn was her exact opposite according to Charlie. She and her husband visited here from Los Angeles about 20 years ago now. I'll never forget her. We invited Evelyn and George over for a drink one evening. She sat in her very loud dress and in her commanding voice commenced telling us how she and Georgie, as she called him, lived the good life on the West Coast.

"Oh we have with-it groups there. Out there it's a designer lifestyle."

Designer life style? I remember Charlie asking. "Yes, you know when one couple decides to move up, new, more expensive home, cars, all that jazz, well you have to go the whole hog, and that includes a new social group, of course. New friends to be seen with, people worthy of your new lifestyle. You don't make money and then hang around with people who can't keep up. You get used to nice things, expensive clothes, and all that and aren't about to be seen by your new friends with people who can't dress, if you know what I mean. Emma doesn't get it. She invited me to go along with her and a friend to a concert in Miami. She lives a few blocks away in a small rented house. Still working as a bookkeeper or something, and she's past 65. Oh, I told Emma it was out of the question. Her friend looks so funny, sooo short and too heavy, and you can tell by a glance that her clothes are what we used to call bargain basement. Clean and well put together, but cheap. Then she's Jewish to top it off, and we never have associated with people who were not one of us, so to speak".

"That is a horrible story".

"Yes, and it gets worse. Evelyn developed skin cancer. An ugly purplish spot the size of a quarter developed on her left forearm. She didn't seek treatment soon enough, I guess, and by the time she saw a doctor it was growing at an alarming rate. She said it must have been the result of leaving her left arm hanging out the window of her BIG Cadillac while driving round LA. Well, about 6 years before George died he paid the education and living expenses of a Korean woman and exacted the promise from her that in return, should anything happen to him, she would care for Evelyn. Then about a year after the Korean graduated with an education degree George dropped dead of a heart attack just months after they had moved into a new retirement condo in Hawaii. Evelyn was really alone now. Designer friends don't appear to be loyal when the going gets tough, and with the cancer Evelyn really did need someone, so now, in return for constant care and friendship the Korean was made sole heir to Evelyn's estate, estimated at ten million dollars. She died one year after George, with only her paid companion for comfort. She had managed to distance everyone else from her.

No-one really being good enough, she had even told a niece at one time that she did not believe in family. She said she did not want to be embarrassed by poor relations".

"They never had children?"

"No, unlike Emma and Jack who have three who visit often. Yet they've no designer friends, no friends at all".

"Ah, Mad "To live in hearts we leave behind is not to die." Scottish poet."

CHAPTER 3

"Happiness is like a butterfly,
The more you chase it,
The more it will elude you.
But if you turn your
attention to other things,
it comes and softly sits on your shoulder."

Nathaniel Hawthorne

"Mad, I haven't seen your tenant yet".

"Doris. No. She's away for two weeks and of course the rent check has bounced again. Charlie meant well. He thought that having someone here full-time would be a sort of security for the house. Car parked in the drive and all that. We were coming down less and less often as the boys grew older. We used to have to ring the realtor who found Doris and ask her to collect the rent and send it to us periodically. Now with Charlie gone it's take advantage of the widow time".

"You really think that?"

"Yes I'm certain of it. It's a new excuse every month; we share a mail box as you know, and the bills, it's unbelievable! Looks like 2 mailings a week from the same credit card companies looking for payments. Even a certified letter from the supermarket. I'm picking up her mail for one week now and it's seven inches high already. By the time she returns her next month's rent will be due. I see one of her men; she refers to them all as 'her men' is using this address as his now. Well, I listed the house this morning anyway. It isn't what it was when we started coming, too crowded, too tacky, just too, too, Hanna. And why come to the same place every year for a vacation? There are so many wonderful places in the world to visit."

"This bland sameness I could not live with for even 2 months out of every year, Mad. You know that. Yes, sell, bank the money and travel on the interest, at least for a year. I'll be honest with you; I walked around yesterday wondering how you could be happy staying here. Do you remember what someone - I can't recall who, once said about personality and place fitting together? It looks like a place to either come to die, or fry, Fry. That would be the drugs, alcohol, sun, or all three taking effect. I wasn't going to say much because I thought you had to find your own way, but this is no way. But now that you brought it up I'll be honest. I don't like the place. I'm retiring from teaching, you know. I know many of us are. New York is scrambling to hire teachers from abroad, Canada, wherever. Poor unsuspecting souls. Oh well, let them chalk it up to experience and what an experience they are in for. I'm going to tidy things up at home, sub-let my apartment and head for Europe for at least one year. I'm going to write, travel, and that's not a bad idea for you either. Blow off a little steam, get out of our ruts. Yes and be grateful that we are able to do so. Mark Twain said: "Twenty years from now, you will be more disappointed by the things you didn't do than by the ones you did do. So throw off the bowlines. Sail away from the safe harbor. Catch the trade winds in your sails. Explore. Dream. Discover".

"So let's get moving. Not the kind of moving Doris is doing, chasing happiness by running in circles, but let's head straight out to see new places, new people".

CHAPTER 4

"Find the truth by comparing the lies."

Leon Trotsky

I finally met the tenant Doris. No more than five feet tall, her feet larger than one would expect looking at her, were squeezed into tight flimsy sandals with 4 inch heels. Blonde and very fair skinned she nevertheless insisted upon lying on the beach for three and four hours at a time, claiming; "My men love women with a tan." Her skin was sunburned and dry looking and her face wrinkled from years of abuse. Yet I suspect she saw someone far different than we did when she looked in her mirror.

Mad introduced us and Doris immediately asked me if I wanted to take a walk. I did. She rushed into her apartment, the tiny studio suite that had once served as a guest quarters, and changed quickly into up-to-date and very expensive jogging clothes. We weren't two blocks from the house when she launched into a long diatribe of all her accomplishments. Degrees in nursing, psychology, and MBA, an important job, and she claimed a highly paid position at that as manager of an officer's club at a military base nearby. She advised me that if I did not drink, do drugs, lie in the sun then there was no point in me staying in Key Largo, as she claimed that was really all there was to do. Rock fever is what she called the condition most of the locals found themselves in. "If you can't lick 'em, join 'em; may as well have fun".

Only one hour's drive from Miami, she talked as though she was marooned on an island in the middle of the Atlantic. Life truly was in the mind. It appeared to be whatever this woman had convinced herself it must be.

When we returned from our walk, Mad told Doris that she had fed the stray and given it water. "The poor old thing you seem to have adopted while I was away came by whining; he was thirsty too".

Doris replied: "Well, it's just a stray" and walked into her apartment.

"She is insolent and pretentious, Mad, a real hard case. Arrested development". Mad said she knew it, and that in light of the fact that she was once again 2 weeks behind on the rent, it was becoming more than she wanted to tolerate any longer. We could deal with Doris later; for now, an old friend of Mad and Charlie was arriving from Chicago any minute, and we 3 were going out to dinner.

Bud walked through the door just as we finished dressing. Tall and lanky as was his identical twin Stan, whom I had grown to know and like much better than Bud over the years, at 70 he was every bit as gregarious, and raring to go as both brothers had been 20 years earlier when they owned and operated the Chicago Sports Club. Bud, always anxious to go, hustled us out the door and on the drive to the restaurant was told all about Doris. His response? "Well, people sure of their positions in life have no need for pretense. I'd get rid of her. We had to bar a few of the customers from the Saloon, you know, when we found ourselves feeling miserable because they were around. You women have a tough time with that however; I know you do. You're raised to be nurturing and to put up with too damn much crap if you ask me. I didn't raise Shirley and Sue that way. Always told them not to worry so much about being liked as being respected. And you know what? Both girls have great husbands and plenty of friends."

Yes, the girls had been lucky. Their mum had died when they were only 8 and 10 years of age, and Bud and Stan, who had never married, were both mother and father to Shirley and Sue. Stan hadn't married; we knew he had never intended to settle down with anyone in particular. So the girls were raised by two confident and well-heeled men, who brought people from every walk of life into their social circle. The electrician who had worked on the ceiling fan might find himself sitting beside the retired doctor at dinner; just one example out of many I could use to demonstrate the sort of men the brothers were. They had but one criteria for membership in their circle and that was respect.

Like most of the elderly in south Florida, the brothers were thousands of miles from family and old friends, and lived in beautiful homes or condominiums, in lovely neighborhoods behind locked gates, locked doors, security alarms set. They spent days pool side, thinking often of grandchildren who on many occasions were less familiar to them than the cashier at the local supermarket.

Mad and I had visited a couple of retirement communities just to see what they were like. Those considered to be the best of the lot were equipped with every convenience, even an undertaker, funeral parlor and chapel. A netherworld where children were unwelcome. I had the eerie feeling that once inside the gates there was no return. It was a sort of Oz for the aged, the Wizard, a large corporation promising everything: security, companionship, the social status derived from living in this expensive compound notwithstanding. A kind of river Styx between this world and the next.

The grandchildren would have no memories to tell their children of going to grandma or grandpa's house; Grand had to advise and obtain permission from the condo association before the children would be allowed in to visit. Now, when I hear people lament the state of the aged who are warehoused in institutions, I wonder at the state of mind of those who willingly closet themselves away from the rest of the world.

"As far as I know", Mad said: "The. US is the only country where, when a worker retires, he sees it as almost a duty to flee to an exotic locale. It's almost like a rite of passage, geriatric style."

"The women outnumber the men seven to One, I heard."

"Yes, and Hanna, the over fifty population is the group with the fastest growing percentage of aids sufferers. I watched a documentary about it. Terrible; lonely old people. It isn't real life here; it's a facade, the sun, sand, fun commercials we see on television. There is a big something missing here."

"Everyone is looking for perfection; well, many are. Like that couple you told me about who travelled the country from July to September looking for safe, affordable, and comfortable. Did they ever find it? It must be five years now".

"Six years, Hanna. Six years and they've just bought a home in the hills of Tennessee. The weather isn't perfection in the winter, but they finally gave up looking for the elusive earthly paradise.

"I've another friend, well, a friend of one of the boys really, who travels round Asia year after year, from one country to the next, teaching. He returns to the States every summer to visit his family for one month. Will he settle down? Where? A bartender in town who has worked all over the Bahamas, Caribbean, is now in Largo. Claims to be thinking about university one year soon he says. He's mid-thirties now. I suspect the wanderlust lifestyle has set in however. He isn't all that happy but can't quit what he calls the good life. All the advertisements say that this is the good life, so I imagine he thinks there is something yet to find here.

"Are rootless, lonely people ever happy? Man is a social creature after all. I get the impression that this part of the country is a sort of limbo for the lost confused souls among us to bide their time".

"You know, Mad, laid back doesn't begin to describe the atmosphere here. It's as though the days are a series of reruns. Like that old man next door, everyone is on neutral, just hanging out, moving slow; yes, just hanging out".

"Everyone living here, that is. My first week here I had a conversation with a cashier in that discount store. Nice lady from Haiti. I was the only customer, and she was friendly and just started a conversation with me out of the blue. What she had to say struck me as insightful. She had spent many an hour standing at her post watching and listening to the customers. "People, they buy, buy, buy to be happy." Then like the new dress, after one wearing, it is no longer a treat, an excitement and they must look for another thing to make them feel good. Because something is lacking within, you know. That is why I will not retire here. Sure it's an island, and island living I am used to, but this is a different kind of island. It is a place where one must consume. Things make you accepted here; it's not the person, only the outside person that counts. But these things do not make the people really happy. I see this. It's bad to be poor here. Not so good to have money either, maybe. Friendships and family cannot be replaced by things, no? No matter how expensive and beautiful, no matter the luxury, the owner is still lonely; Lonely heart. Well I sense you understand this. I sense this. She was right of course, Mad. It was odd; this encounter was odd in that I had been thinking these same things only moments earlier; artificial happiness. How's that for a phrase?

"I had seen an inordinate number of pet stores and clinics in my travels round here. You know when you take into account the fact that there are only 90 thousand year-round residents in all of the keys. The pets fulfill the need the Haitian cashier was talking about. I mean more so, to a greater extent than they would for people in more ordinary circumstances. Did I tell you about the elderly lady? Poor soul had the clerks held hostage the afternoon I wandered in to look around. She was telling them a very long and drawn out story about an exotic bird of some sort that had flown the coup and returned to her 6 months later. A sweet story as far as that but she didn't stop there. She wove the story together, and included her cat's rejection of the prodigal bird, and her dog's reaction to her cat's rejection, and suffice it to say, she was in looks and manner the epitome of the lonely, elderly, Key Largo lady.

"There are cats, strays so numerous here that a woman has set up a feline rescue mission. She told me that while there are 90 thousand residents here in the Keys, there are 400 thousand stray cats. I have a story to tell you about that, but not today; let's just watch the people and eat, drink and make merry."

CHAPTER 5

"Interests invariably separate man,
but the depraved always get along together."

Balzac

The restaurant and bar was what one would expect in a tropical paradise. One side of the building was open and allowed the sea breezes to cool the dinner crowd. The bar side was glassed in and air-conditioned, decorated with real palms and tropical flowers and advertised live entertainment. After we had finished our meal we wandered over to the bar and found a small table. As the waitress placed our drinks down in front of us I glanced up and spotted Doris heading into the lounge area. I had mentioned the man standing at the door to Bud, as we entered. He had looked so odd, standing as still as a cigar store Indian, Poker-faced, blank eyed and his complexion was far more ashen than tanned. Now, as Doris walked through the door she stopped in front of him, tilted her cheek up toward his mouth and he bent down, giving her cheek a peck without changing expression, or even blinking. His eyes remained fixed on the band that was setting up on the other side of the room. Long, unkempt greasy hair, and dirty sneakers; oversized grunge clothing, and peaked caps. So this was the entertainment.

Four young people stood at a high round table about two yards from where we were seated. They looked no more than seventeen or eighteen years of age. They were thin, pale and busy passing round what appeared to be marijuana cigarettes. Doris recognized us and wiggled over. Yes, she was still stuck in the old fifties Marilyn mode of walking, swinging the hips exaggeratedly to attract the attention of whatever man might be available. She told us that the man guarding the door was the owner and just then a thirty something in a black muscle shirt and shorts sauntered over and she introduced him as the bouncer. He launched into a series of ethnic jokes, none of which were funny unless, of course, you were a bigot, naturally. Then, glancing over to look at the kids and then an older man of approximately sixty, he began an incessant jabber about illegal drugs and their benefits. He told us that he was from Queens New York and sounded like someone who may have fit in an entry level position with perhaps the Gambino family. Running a hand through his coal black, greased back, thick head of hair he pointed to the sixty something. Mr. sixty looked like he could be anybody's grandpa. Thirty, forty pounds overweight, casual grey slacks, black loafers, and a light blue and white striped sports shirt. He wore his heavy iron grey hair cut fashionably short and I commented that he seemed to be looking for someone. He had been circling the bar for the past fifteen minutes. Tony, our bouncer began to laugh. Then he told us that grandpa was in fact busy WORKING.

"Working?"

"Ya, hey, last night he asks me for three hundred. So I tell em hey what? You can't do no business for yourself? C'mon. You want money you gotta get hustlin'. So tonight he looks like he's workin' the crowd okay. Know what I mean? Somebody musta loaned em sumpin to get em started. Little seed money and he's all set. I didn't have no three hundred on me last night, or I coulda made an investment. Know what I mean?"

So gramps was a drug dealer and Mr. bar owner was happy to hold his pose at the door, no doubt looking forward to his cut at the end of the evening. Tony excused himself and left to talk to a woman at the other side of the bar. This gave Doris the opportunity to tell us in a conspiratorial tone of voice: "He's so intelligent." Bud nearly dropped the glass he had raised half way to his mouth. Then Doris, raising her arm above her head, her hand bent parallel to the floor, said: “His IQ is up to here. I mean it. That’s why I like him. He’s so much smarter than the rest of us. There’s no way any of us can touch his brains.”

Oh, and God bless us all I thought.

A woman who looked to be about seventy years old sat at the bar. Perched on a stool and facing our table, she was alone, smiling and shaking her head back and forth. Her body weaved from side to side in an attempt to keep time to the music. Her hair was snow white and worn in a longish bob. Her glassy eyes were ringed in such dark circles she had the appearance of a raccoon. Every time she caught the eye of an unwary male a tight toothy grin spread across her mouth, giving her pale, unhealthy face the mask-like look of a corpse two days along in the process of rigor mortis.

Doris had pulled a chair up to our table by this time and had sat down. Her movements were jerky, her face flushed. The sun had succeeded only in making the pale skin blotchy in places not rouged. The masses of wrinkles round her eyes appeared deeper under the creasing and smudging eye shadow and mascara. The bright red lipstick applied to lips lined to make her mouth look fuller had smeared at the corners and caused her mouth to mirror that of a sad circus clown.

She might have glanced across the room and saw herself in less than 20 years a pathetic and lonely alcoholic. The more the woman with the raccoon eyes drank, the more aggressive she became. She eventually began to spin on her stool grabbing for any man who came within feet of her little perch. Finally, in a very loud voice she began to shout in order to be heard over the horrible band: “Hay! You had any in a while? You want some free sweetie?”

A conservatively dressed, quiet, rather shy woman of about forty entered the bar and stood at the far end as though waiting for someone.

"Oh look at her" Doris said. She works for me. I can't wait to see who she's with".

"Likely her husband; she looks married to me".

"Oh yea, she's married. Oh I love this; I can't wait to see who she's foolin around with".

Just then a nice looking man who appeared to be the woman's perfect match entered and stood by the quiet lady. Doris, crest-fallen, Exclaimed: "Well look at that. It is her husband. Guess I don't have anything on her after all."

Repulsed, we watched as Doris drifted, or weaved is more accurate, over to where the man and wife stood together, and kissed first one and then the other on the cheek.

"The Judas kiss," was Mad's reaction, and Bud said that it may be worse. "After all, Judas thought he was saving his own neck. This one's just downright nasty."

Doris returned to our table shortly after Bud made his observation. Waving to the bartender she ordered herself another drink of what was the most expensive brand of Scotch. "It's expensive but good, that's what I tell my men; I'm expensive, but good. I don't socialize with the people that I work with. They just aren't people that I want to socialize with, not educated ya know? My daddy was FBI. Did I ever tell you that, Mad? Well he was and anyhow when I finished school the FBI just begged me to join".

"And did you?" asked Bud.

"Well nooo, how could I do that? Hell, I'm from a small town in South Carolina; my friends all did drugs. So I said I cain't do that. I cain't turn in my friends".

Bud had asked the question tongue in cheek and now asked another. "Doris, where do people shop for clothes here? It looks like the mainland is the closest place for all-round shopping."

"Well now, Mad told me the other day she went to that factory outlet which is fine, don't get me wrong. That's fucking great for some, but I don't go to those places. I prefer quality. I buy when I travel. I don't want to look the same as everyone else. I guess it's okay for Mad while she's here."

Overconfidence belied her insecurity, jealousy. This pathetic creature owed the much younger and better looking Mad over half a month's rent by this time.

Bud asked us if we were ready to leave and offered Doris a ride.

"Don't tell me bout drinkin and drivin, now. You people who aren't used to drinkin can't control it. Ya just need to get used to drinkin more and then you'd be able to come out, drink and drive home. No problem. I can put away five, six, of these and drive home. You see what I'm tellin you? See, I'm used to drinkin and that's your problem, ya know; ya don't drink enough. Ya cain't go out and drink and have fun, and get yourself home. I like to be independent. I'm a regular here and three other bars, so I know about everybody. I'm gonna join 'em now. Bye."

"Birds of a feather flock together, my grandma used to say. What do you think, girls? Are all those birds we've left behind of a feather or what? God. Well, Mad, what else don't we know about your tenant from hell?"

"I'll tell you a couple of stories and then that's it. I can't stand to think about her much more tonight. I was hoping the house would sell before I had to evict. Well, We'll see".

"You know, it sounds crazy" Bud said over coffee when we arrived home, "but her assumption that we believe the claims regarding her education, etc. well, it's insulting. Insults the intelligence".

"Not if you realize that she isn't bright enough to know that everything about her belies her claims. She doesn't have the capacity to reason, really. Here's an example: One afternoon in the hot part of the day I was out wielding my machete and noticed Doris baking that white skin in the sun. So I told her about Charlie's friend and that California woman we talked about, Hanna, the one who died as a direct result of skin cancer. "That's just plain silly" she said. "Why ya'll just have to go and get the little spots burned off and there's no problem. That's all I'd do and I'd keep right on tannin. I won't change my lifestyle". But then Doris doesn't concern herself with DUI or seatbelts, or communicable diseases either. A few nights after I returned to list the house I became aware that she was guiding different men home from the bars, sometimes three and four a week. Very dangerous; transients, I'm sure. You never see the same car twice and I get up so early and notice these different men leaving her apartment first thing in the morning. There's no entrance connecting that suite with my house, but still. She told me that she couldn't understand why her husband wanted a divorce. She said: "We had such a great marriage, too. He had his friends, I had mine. We did what we wanted".

The entrance to the small apartment downstairs was set up like a mini liquor store. Bottles of every description were arranged against one wall. There was something to satisfy the tastes of those as diverse as the men she invited in to sample her hospitality. Two of the most expensive and ornate bottles of liquor were used as bookends.

"That first week I'd spent here alone and incidentally the first time meeting Doris, she asked me to go for a drink with her. I did, foolishly. She wanted to sit at the bar, and me never having sat at a bar, on a stool, a now unattached woman, I did, just to see how it felt. Horrible. Anyway she struck up a conversation with a guy much like that bouncer we met tonight. She must have drunk something earlier because she was getting a bit wobbly after only one drink. Well, the guy told her that he had been working with disabled children all day, as a volunteer at the school and Doris, my God, began running her fingers through the jungle of black hair on his arm and looking into his eyes said: “h, I just love disabled children. They’re my favorites”. I was mortified. Then she tipped the bartender thirty five percent. Hairy had left by this time and she was making a play for this twenty something that had poured her drink.

“So this is the clip, clip, clip of little heels on the pavement outside; Doris heading out around nine most nights to look for some excitement. Vampira, lady of the night; off to stalk and conquer. She’s her own victim, I’m afraid. Expensive hobby too, these bars. What was it Balzac said? “Money never loses the slightest opportunity for displaying its stupidity.””

CHAPTER 6

I believe there will always be wars, until perchance we all become so spiritual that by the evolution of our individual natures we will make war unnecessary. No matter what their differences, if great minds such as Jesus, Krishna, Buddha, Mohammed, sat together, they would never use the engines of science to try to destroy each other. Why must people feel it necessary to fight? The power of guns evokes no wisdom, nor has it ever accomplished lasting peace.

Paramahansa Yogananda - "The Devine Romance"

Light jazz played on the radio, and the beautiful palms swayed in the gentle breeze. It was a perfect morning. Then suddenly, at 6:30 a.m., the house was under siege. The plane, I was sure, must have touched the tops of the tall trees as it passed directly over the roof of the house. Once, twice, three times, back and forth, again and again, then out over the water and round to buzz the house again.

"Crazy, isn't it?" Mad asked. "I've called the FAA. The woman told me it happens here, some old guy re-living his glory days. That's a C47, old WWII plane. He doesn't give a damn for anyone I guess. Or perhaps his need to be recognized, get attention, you know, overrides any bit of consideration he might possess. I don't normally swear, but he's pissing me off, Hanna. You would think that they would be glad the war is over. Fifty-three years, over. Mad, I took a walk yesterday evening and passed by a modest house that was flying a banner. A satin banner hung on a large tree at the entrance to the front door. Bright purple lettering on a cream colored background proclaimed: 'Order of purple cross, combat wounded WWII'. I thought at the time that it screamed, 'Notice me! Respect me! See who I am! I'm somebody special!' Sad,

I thought. As sad as what I read the other day in the paper. Heston, the president, or spokesman, I call him the celebrity mouthpiece for the NRA, said he believes children should be taught to use guns to protect themselves. Beautiful isn't it? Children in this country being influenced that way? Glorifying war, killing. Pathetic. It's all so depressing. Violence for violence sake. I haven't paid to see a movie for years, an American movie at any rate, and neither have any of my friends. They're either violent or just plain stupid. Fighting, foul language, disrespectful kids".

"Most human quarrels arise from the fact that wise men and fools live side by side and each is so constituted as to see only one side of events or ideas and to pretend that the side he has seen is the only true, correct one."

"Yes, Balzac again, Hanna. True, isn't it? Everyone too lazy to talk to work things out. Sometimes war is forced upon one but I can't understand why these old men want to keep reliving what must have been a horror and disturbing everybody at this time of day, or any time. Oh, we don't even know who he is; and why the hell does he think we care about his flying ability? "Look at my accident the other day. I signal and I'm almost completely into the turn area between the divided highway and get hit. Just the right rear bumper, but still, obviously she was driving too fast and not paying attention to my car ahead of her or she would have had ample time to stop. I know that the older woman was driving and yet they, the daughter and her, insisted that it was the young twenty-something. Not that the mother said one word and refused to even look at me as well. The girl kept looking out into the distance when questioned about who was driving and just kept insisting that it was she. She trekked back and forth between mamma and me with first the insistence that she was the driver and then came over to the van to tell me that both our insurance policies would go up if we talked to the police."

"What?"

"Oh yes, dumb and dumber often believe that the rest of the world is operating at their level of stupidity. Remember, Hanna, it takes intelligence to recognize intelligence. Now they are threatening to blame me for the accident. The officer who wrote up the report even charged them. I don't know, though. When I called their insurer after speaking to mine and reported the accident, mamma's insurer told me that they hadn't even reported it yet and it had happened three hours earlier. I'm betting mamma has a whole lot of prior citations. I heard her tell the officer she was 62. The officer hadn't asked my age so I think she may be working on the same assumption that I am. But this happens all the time in south Florida.

"You'll start meeting the neighbors soon. Most of them are in their 80s and 90s and all of them drive. They don't signal; they tailgate and drive 20 miles below the speed limit, but they all drive. We keep reading about the accidents and near accidents. Even Ann Landers has written asking someone to put a stop to it, but it's all politics. The politicians want the votes and to hell with the rest of us. There is no mandatory driver's test, eye, hearing, and tests for drivers over a certain age here, you know".

The dichotomy of landscape, the tranquil appearing swaying palms, bright beautiful flowers, seemingly laid-back life style, and the reality of the place is unbelievable.

"I read your paper this morning. South Florida is in the top 10 regarding over-population, pollution, water concerns, crime, traffic congestion. Some paradise; Fool's paradise I'd say."

"It's one of the worst places to shop apparently, as well. I had wondered about that, although I hadn't said anything to you. Wherever I've gone, and with few exceptions, the clerks act as though the customer is an inconvenience. I can't count the number of times over the past few weeks that a cashier has been on a personal telephone call and never broke stride, never even looked at me; just points to the till, barks the amount, makes change and that's it: goes right on talking. I stood in the bank the other day while one of two tellers carried on a personal conversation and there were 3 people lined up waiting for service. It's a joke here, a real joke. I guess you have to be, or become very thick-skinned to live here."

"That's true of most of the country isn't it? I decided last night to take your advice about going to Europe, Hanna. I need a change. I need to wake up in the morning and expect to find crazy behavior the exception, rather than the norm."

"27 refugees, Cubans washed up not far from here last month. Did I tell you that?"

"No".

"Well, it was just down the beach, at the State Park. I thought to myself 'Well poor souls, they don't know what they're in for'. I imagine it will be better than what they had, or perhaps they are simply trading one hell for another."

A change is as good as a rest, my Granny always said. "Mad, have you ever asked Doris about her travels?"

"Oh please. Yes, yes. She claimed to have travelled all over the world with her soon to be ex-husband. Claimed that they were stationed in Germany with the military. Then I asked his rank. He was an NCO. Now I had a friend who lived there under those conditions and she, Sandy, told me that a regular rank and file Joe didn't earn enough to really do much over there. Sandy and Jim were not able to see much and the wife isn't able to work while there. I asked her about different places in England, France and so on, places I knew and that any traveller is familiar with. I asked her on two different occasions and both times she tried to change the subject. Those pale blue eyes flashed with anger and she looked frustrated."

"Well, her manner of speaking, everything about her belies her claims".

"That is not unusual here. Most of us are transplants. I suspect those who claim fantastic accomplishments are banking on the fact that no-one is going to go to the trouble to expose them. Insincere, purposeless, superficial lives. Yes we have an interesting collection of dreamers and drop outs."

CHAPTER 7

There is a race of men
That don't fit in
A race that can't sit still
So they break the hearts
Of kith and kin
And roam the world
At will

Robert Frost

The atmosphere was one of rootlessness, mistrust, alienation and self-deception. Everyone here looked and behaved pretty much the same; sort of a combination beach bum and lower middle class mentality. At a glance it was quite impossible to separate the tourist from the local. T-shirts, shorts, and sandals were the accepted dress code everywhere, though a second glance revealed a slight difference. the foreign tourists were casually dressed, yet neat, and carrying a lot less weight.

"The sun doesn't shine on the same Dog's ass every day, you know".

Old Ben had just celebrated his 82nd birthday with his fellow retirees at the community center next door. He said that he often used the above quote to "snap my grandchildren out of it when they get to whining".

"They lack inquisitiveness, curiosity. We had it; couldn't wait to grow up and travel around. This generation coming up just wants to be entertained; sit on their asses in ugly clothes and be entertained, preferably while holding on to a big mac and a 32 oz. bottle of coke. Dignity. Now what's that to them? Probably can't spell the word. You Know, some of the schools are trying to teach them table manners? What fork to use, all that stuff parents taught and would have been embarrassed if the kid didn't do right in public.

"We never were much good at geography in this country, but we've regressed. Right word? Yes, regressed. We got a new kind of peasant in this country. No King running it, we got corporations instead. Bill Gates - his fortune amounts to more than what the bottom forty percent got all put together. Medieval Europe all over again only worse. You could overthrow a monarch, can't overthrow a corporation.

"We got all this new technology now. should be good jobs available right? But our kids ain't ready, ain't educated, so now we got to import people from all over the world to fill the good jobs and our peasants are working the fast food line".

Emma strolled over to us. In her 90s, she was still trim. She walked across the street from her little house at the break of dawn each morning and jumped into the ocean. "Ben giving the world what for again? Says it's his age that accounts for his cantankerous old self, but I say he must have been even worse when he was younger. People usually mellow with age unless they have something awful wrong with 'em and Ben is too healthy. He'll likely outlive us all".

"What I'm sayin makes sense".

"So it does, but you need to tone it down some. He doesn't like to be corrected, but I always tell him that nasty doesn't like nice and that's why he gets ornery with me. He's an old union man. Makes him angry to see the young people let slip away all our generation worked to achieve without a fight. Don't blame him for that. Everything seems to be centered around the sensational now. Celebrities. Doesn't take much to become one. Just get into the kind of trouble that in the old days people would have been embarrassed to show their faces for, and you got yourself a book deal. Crazy stuff, Hanna."

I agreed and I felt sorry for these old people who couldn't quite enjoy themselves because they were concerned for their grandchildren and so unhappy with the way the country was headed.

"So, Emma, let me ask you" said Ben: "If you paid a visit to a neighbor's house and found it dirty and disorganized, a house full of people frightened to various degrees of one another to the point that they carried guns around by day, or slept with one beside them at night: one quarter of the kids in the house go to bed hungry, and every day a number of them get shot with their parents guns: One sixth of them don't have health insurance and most of the kids function below their grade level at school. So say one day you find yourself talking to one of the people who live in the house and he tells you that he lives in the greatest house on the block and he answers that it's the greatest house on the block because it has the greatest number of guns per person, per house and the most financial clout in the neighborhood. Now you tell me, Emma, what you would think of these neighbors? Oh and remember they don't know much at all about you because they haven't bothered to learn".

"Mad ought to be over here. She'd give us a Balzac quote or some quote" said Emma.

"How about: 'The peasant sees nothing beyond his own village'" I answered.

CHAPTER 8

I don't know what your destiny will be, but one thing I do know;
the only ones among you who will be truly happy
will be those who have sought and found how to serve.

Albert Schweitzer

I met a great many interesting people next door at the little community center and through them found the real Key Largo.

Tony

Tony, now in his 80s, grew up on Madison Avenue and 55th Street, in a Manhattan brownstone. He was one of seven children in an Italian family that had worked their way to the upper east side from the poor immigrant neighborhoods of the lower east side. His childhood in the brownstone in what is grandly known to the locals there as the silk stalking district was cut short by the death of his father at the age of 37 from bleeding ulcers. His father earned 90 a week and paid 90 a month rent on their home.

"Both parents did not have to work back then to provide for the family when the father of the house had a decent job and my father had worked his way up to bank manager. Nowadays a lot of professional couples both work just to make ends meet. We had neighbors then too. There are no neighbors anymore. Look around. Everybody locks themselves up, afraid of everybody else. No sense of community anymore.

"But then a large part of the problem is that people want it all now and right now. International travel, VCRs, CDs, big house, a wedding that costs thousands of dollars and one hundred dollar sneakers for the six year old. They eat dinner out more often than they eat at home and fast food is entertainment. That's why we are known round the world now as the nation of fat people and that includes the kids. Yep. Kids, parents, everybody stressed out and spent out. Then they go and spend some more to lose the fat, and get someone to teach them how to exercise. Then the stress about the debts mount and they have to mortgage the house to pay a shrink; family counseling you know, because by this time they can't stand each other.

"There's a woman brings her two kids here to play on the beach. She tells me that she spends the money she takes home on sitters and toys for the kids and eating out because after work she's too tired to cook. So I asked her why, when she is married to a professional man who earns good money, she doesn't stay home and look after them herself? And you know what she told me? "Hell" she said: "I don't want to stay home with those howling brats"".

Jude

At 65 years of age she divorced her husband of 15 years and retired to Key Largo. A pushy, bossy woman, Jude ordered rather than invited her neighbors to her quarterly barbecues. She wore her eyebrows bushy, her hair unkempt; her finger nails were cracked and dirty and her face incredibly wrinkled for one her age. I suspect the result of neglect was always bare of make-up. She bragged about the cost of every new article of clothing she purchased. "Well, a four hundred dollar dress and a two hundred dollar pair of shoes makes me feel more confident". She shared this bit of information with us one evening after dinner at her home. I admit to having begged Mad to accept the invitation to satisfy my curiosity about this odd creature, knowing full well that curiosity was Jude's only reason for extending us the invitation. So I felt we were even on that score. Now, over coffee in her living room, we were treated to the sight of our hostess flossing her teeth as she proceeded to expound on the social benefits of being well-dressed. I had passed by her house onc late afternoon as she, having just returned from a shopping trip to Miami, waded through her garden in her two hundred dollar shoes to pull a few vegetables for her dinner. She was a sight to behold whatever she was doing and Mad had commented: "She simply does not see herself" No. She imagined each of us saw that which she envisioned herself to be.

Jude carried what I came to refer to as her real life fiction to extremes however, for Jude had no compunctions about making up the lives of everyone around her to suit her idea of who and what they were. These were without exception always very unflattering scenarios and as inaccurate as her self-perception appeared to be. I offer as an example of Jude's proclivity for spreading canard, her opinion of one Miss Bell, the dedicated volunteer lady known and loved by everyone in the community.

Firstly, Miss Bell was not a miss at all, and had not been referred to as such since her first marriage at the age of 17. Now 53 she had buried her third husband just 4 years prior to our meeting. True, she was a conservative dresser and true, she did not frequent the bars in town, but she had been dating a retired psychology professor from Boston for the past 3 years, and unbeknownst to Jude led an active social life away from the prying eyes of the tiny Key Largo establishment. She and Art frequented the museums, best restaurants, and prestigious cultural events that the city of Miami had to offer and both were involved in various charity drives. Consequently, whenever Jetta heard some of the rumors Jude floated about her being an old maid without a life, she laughed so hard the tears ran down her cheeks, and grabbing her stomach once for effect, literally threw herself out of her chair.

"Oh yes: did you know that I stay, how does

she put it, behind closed doors? And that there are times that I don't talk to a soul for days on end? The other day she said: "Miss Bell, you haven't been out of your house for at least five days". Well, you know I let her think whatever she likes. Of course I'm up and out by six a.m. many mornings. Art picks me up and we drive off somewhere, staying away for days at a time. We return late and I have the house lights on timers and well, you know, I get the impression that Jude believes that if she hasn't heard or seen something, then it hasn't happened. She assumes so much. Everyone around here refers to me as Miss Bell, but that's just a southern way of addressing a woman. Initially someone thought that my given name was Bell and it stuck. She assumes I'm broke, as well as a spinster, too, because I don't flaunt money. She's always trying to get me to eat at some expensive restaurant with her and offers to pay my way. claims that I'm too shy to let her. It has never dawned on the poor soul, I guess, that I simply do not enjoy her company. Unbelievable woman. Says everything with such authority. She dumbfounds people, you know. Most just stare, and let her talk while they work out an escape plan.

"One afternoon, late, she called me and told me to meet her at such and such, a restaurant down the Keys- Marathon, I think it was; well anyway, I said "Jude, I've just started a good new book and I'm enjoying myself at home right now". which was true. "Well, you aren't doing anything important so I'll see you there at six" she said and hung up.

"I didn't show. Art would like to tell her off, but I sort of enjoy the game. Nasty of me. But I could never tolerate a bully. And I don't respect people who behave vindictively, so I sit back and wait until they shoot themselves in the foot, which is something one can always count on Jude's sort to do. She loves to brag; will describe in minute detail every detail of whatever trips she has taken over the years. She finishes by telling you where you SHOULD spend your next vacation. Kind of acts like she discovered the world. She might have spent her time better working to discover herself. Poor soul."

"Jude has those parties every three months, doesn't she?" I asked Jetta.

"Yes and no one ever reciprocates. Not one of us ever warmed to the idea of committing ourselves to forming a dinner club, but she persists. Lately fewer and fewer of the neighbors have been attending her get-togethers. One day I'll look out and see her sitting there all alone, surrounded by enough food to cater a banquet for old King Henry the Eighth. She just doesn't get it. Have you ever watched that British comedy on PBS - the one about the woman so obsessed by appearance, and status? Always hosting the candlelight dinners. And the family she is so ashamed of. Well, that's our Jude, though far less sophisticated than the character Hyacinth".

Well, that's insecurity for you; talk at people and order them around. She never learned to let things just take their course, as my granny used to say. Let friendship build, rather than force people into your company. She never learned, poor thing.

CHAPTER 9

"He who has health has hope,
And he who has hope has everything."

Arabian Proverb

Mrs. Beauchamp

I thought of Mrs. Beauchamp as "The old lady by the sea." She lived one block from Mad in a big old house on the beach. Alone, she collected bottles of distinct design and placed them round the inside of her garden wall. A nocturnal creature, she did not emerge from her home each day until the sun began to set. She puttered round her vast lawns and garden, then, when it grew too dark for her to see to work went back inside and to her parlor. Yes, Maimi Beauchamp was over 90 years old and the musty little room where her upright antique piano stood, as it had for the past 50 years, was still referred to by her as the parlor.

She switched on the lamp that occupied the middle of the piano, just right of the metronome. The antique brass base tarnished, its shade faded, and the dirty gold fringe all but deteriorated, was yet one of her most cherished possessions. It was a converted gas light given her by her mother the day she began to study piano. Mrs. Beauchamp played long into the night. Well preserved for her ninety plus years, she might have been mistaken for someone not much over seventy, in the right light. "I stay out of the sun" she told me.

It was said that she would do whatever she could for anyone and yet she cautioned: "I do not socialize but I am a good neighbor.

"Loneliness is one of mankind's greatest Fears, you know. Yet to me being alone is a kind of personal freedom. There is, of course, a marked difference between being alone and being lonely and often it is only a matter of perception. I've no close family within hundreds of miles to consider and I live as I please. I live in the immediate, but for the hours I play my piano each evening and reminisce. And I live alone here on the shore where my playing will not disturb anyone's sleep.

"I worked well into my sixties. Worked at the VA hospital in Miami. I began nursing after the war when I saw that I could not afford the time - time is a luxury - to pursue the musical career that my mother had wished for me. I dealt with the maimed, the helpless, and often the seemingly hopeless. At that time there was a sort of camaraderie among the staff and the patients. We had all been through so much during the war that we all just seemed to pull together instinctively. we were very optimistic about the future then. We all felt we belonged to the same club, so to speak. In spite of all the bustle and hustle and pressure, we had an inner peace. We felt we knew what we were about. It's the feeling I have living here alone in my grand old monster by the sea. They call me the hermit woman, those who have never ventured behind the garden walls to speak with me.

"But then they've no idea what I think of them, do they?" With a little laugh her face lit up, her smile grew wide and she was pretty. Then, with a wave, she turned and disappearing into her garden, was gone.

CHAPTER 10

"The test of first-rate intelligence is the ability to hold two opposed ideas in mind at the same time, and still retain the ability to function. One should, for example, be able to see that things are hopeless and yet be determined to make them better."

F. Scott Fitzgerald

Julie

Mrs. Beauchamp's granddaughter Julie had spent the months since graduation from Boston university with her grandmother. Julie stayed in the small guest quarters on the grounds and kept busy by compiling notes on her family's history and working part time at a local bar. Her goal for the next two years was to be invited to join the Peace Corps. She fulfilled the final requirement in the application process which were the physical check-up and tests at the VA hospital in Miami.

There she found not a safe haven, but a dissatisfied, surly group disrespectful of the people they were employed to serve. Because the services she required were all available in this one huge complex, Julie had chosen to have the work done here rather than the alternative of making appointments at various offices all over the area. She thought she would be saving time but this was not the case. In fact, what would have taken two to three weeks to complete ended up taking two and one half months and was spread over a period of three long days.

The doctor in charge of final consultation and signing the completed forms was a surly and arrogant creature. On two prior occasions his response to her greeting him good morning in passing him in the waiting area had been met with no more than a depreciatory smirk. when she did consult with him her few questions had been ignored and she had been forced to repeat them and wait patiently for an answer.

When she arrived at the women's center wing of the building she had been told that the VA "Takes poor people like you. They need the money. Not so many vets left. They're dying out. Oh, you're Peace Corps, Sorry. Thought you another vet, no money. I hate people coming here. Get tired of poor people, so stupid. Don't listen to me. Don't want health care professional. Want doctor, but we only consult doctor when we think there is problem. I six months training anyway doing this. Last woman here before you, she say where doctor? I tell her how it is, then she don't stay, she do. I tell her health professional take doctor's place, so they can pay less money. Oh well, she nothing but a prostitute anyway, probably, that's what come here lots. Nobodies". Some professional, thought Julie.

Though the experience was not one she would wish on anyone else, she appreciated the fact that it had opened her eyes to a world that relatively few others see. That of the disenfranchised, disrespected, and the ignorance of the local so-called health care professionals, those of whom none but the most ignorant would judge their patients on the basis of their opting to take advantage of the services they had earned the right to expect for serving their country.

Julie had been told that her last trip there was necessary. Rather than mail the results to her they insisted she make an appointment, ostensibly so that the surly doctor would have the opportunity to go over the results of her examinations and tests with her. the final day arrived and Julie was ushered into the doctor's examining room. There she was told to wait while he completed the forms. After being handed the completed forms and noting that absolutely nothing had been interpreted for her, nor was it about to be, she asked why two of the tests, RH factor, and TB had not been performed as requested. His answer? "We don't always do those" whatever that meant. They had taken all the extra blood necessary to perform all the tests. She decided that to argue with such people would be superfluous and taking what had been made available to her left doctor surly's office.

Julie now entered the restroom before leaving. she found one door left ajar though someone was occupying the cubicle, their collection of plastic bags and pathetic rags arranged round their feet. Julie glanced to her right and spotted another woman washing in the sink. Julie exited the restroom and as she made her way out the main door of the building, breathed a sigh of relief. Yet the outside main entrance was crowded with the homeless, crippled, some so badly-off, so filthy, that one could not tell at a glance whether one man was wearing socks, or no, those were his feet, unwashed and barely distinguishable from his worn shoes.

It was naturally a sunny, beautiful southern Florida day and as Julie walked to the metro entrance she wondered for perhaps the thousandth time, what this country was really all about and a new question developed. Did she really want to represent this?

CHAPTER 11

And when ye reap the harvest of your land,
thou shalt not wholly reap the corners of thy field,
neither shalt thou gather the gleanings of thy harvest.

And thou shalt not glean thy vineyard,
neither shalt thou gather every grape of thy vineyard;
thou shalt leave them for the poor and stranger.

The Book of Leviticus

Tony's granddaughter Angela was mid-forties, divorced, and in search of a new beginning.

"Life is like a puzzle you know. You think you have laid it all out before you. You set goals, make plans, you work hard at fitting it all together and then one day find that someone has come along and stolen a piece when you weren't looking. You can't complete your puzzle; your plan won't work the way it was designed to. And suddenly you find yourself being accused of having had no plan, no goals in the first place. What is it about people that will not allow them to admit that one cannot control everything and that consequently we are at times faced with a curve in the road, and forced to take a detour, make a new plan? Is it fear? I believe so. I believe that it takes courage to admit that we may not be able to have everything our way, always. Courage to accept the truth that in this life we will be confronted with problems not of our making.

"Granddad started me thinking along these lines. His old friend Pete had been missing for three years and suddenly his daughter called Grand last week and told him that her father had been found at a Salvation Army shelter in New Mexico. Well, you know we were just happy that he had been found and always have been angry about the stigma attached to people who find themselves in circumstances like that. So granddad walked over to the neighborhood bar for his usual night cap that night and his gossip session with the boys. He was so darned happy about finding Pete and told his buddies about it. Immediately they told him to keep his distance. "Let the guy's family handle it. Guy's probably a bum now. Drugs, all that stuff, you shouldn't get involved". Granddad was appalled, amazed as he always is when people assume the worst about another without the benefit of facts.

"Pete was an English professor, very well respected. Then about thirty years ago he was driving home from a faculty meeting and it was wet. It had been raining buckets for days. He was forced off the road by an out of control truck heading straight toward him, struck a telephone pole and the pole fell hitting the roof of his car rendering him unconscious. He did not regain consciousness for a month and when he did it was discovered that his short term memory had been affected.

He suffered with depression. He'd forget names, dates, had to make lists of all the little every day chores we undertake without even consciously paying attention, like the dirty clothes go in the hamper, the garbage is put out Tuesday, that sort of thing. Then he concluded that he was getting worse and didn't want to burden his married children, who were raising children of their own. Therefore in a last-ditch attempt at some bit of independence he decided, without consulting anyone, to drive his car to the Salvation Army and there he turned over his car, household possessions and accounts, in return for a place to stay and supervision. It was much better than a nursing home he said, in that he was allowed to make himself useful working at whatever chores needed tending, and he loved the Christmas season. Said he felt proud to be trusted to ring the bell for the collection kettle and trusted with the money collected. So here is a man who spent his life working, paying taxes, raising and educating kids being judged, as granddad says, by some ne'er-do-well in a bar. That is pervasive in our society, isn't it, the penchant for judging one guilty until proven innocent? "Easier that way" he says, "throw away people." Then he told me the story about his mother and how she coped during the depression.

"During the dirty thirties the homeless out of work men were often referred to as hobos. They travelled from one town to another hoping to find any kind of work, enough to keep body and soul together and allow them to reunite with their families. They'd knock on kitchen doors asking for work and accept a sandwich as payment, just something to eat. Granddad's mother always invited them in. She'd fix them something then sit and visit with them while they ate. Said she wanted them to feel the dignity of being a guest, rather than a beggar, as some referred to these people. Then as they were leaving she handed them a bag with an extra lunch to take on the road and thanked them for their visit.

"Incredible enough, and then you find out that at the time she was a very young woman, thirty something, and had her own family to care for, often staying up nights and through the night to finish some sewing she had taken in to make ends meet. Well, after a few months' time she found herself so swamped with "visitors" that she had to cut back on the sit down lunches and began handing out whatever she could afford to on any given day. Then one afternoon she told one of these men that she could not understand why she had been singled out, more so than her neighbors; asking her to follow him to the curb outside of her front door, he crouched down and pointed to an X that had been scratched there. I wonder if that is where the expression, 'so and so is a mark' came from? "Well the point is, lots of people were marks and most of the family and their friends felt compassion for the downtrodden as they were called then.

"So many stereotypes. Listen to what I overheard in the beauty salon the other day.

"I was sitting in the waiting area and on a Saturday you know how noisy it is, so to compensate everyone shouts to be heard. I was sitting behind the partition and tossing aside a magazine I had been looking at I closed my eyes. That's when I became aware of the conversation taking place closest to me. Rose was the name of the customer they were talking about, Sarah Rose. The older lady having her hair done was going on about how nice Sarah was. She apparently worked as a bar maid in a saloon that this whisky-voiced woman frequented. Well, whisky voice was speculating about the wedding dress that Sarah had chosen for her wedding that weekend and the church and so on, when the hair dresser interrupted to inform her that Sarah was Jewish. "Jewish? Oh and here I've been thinking how nice she is and I've been friendly toward her. Well, you never know do you?" "Nope" said the hair dresser, "you never can tell who you're dealing with nowadays. Have to just be careful I guess." I thought "no, sure can't tell", because if I hadn't overheard the conversation I'd have seen only a smiley-faced little blonde, chattering away as she applied hair color to the head of a matronly sixty something woman. No, I really would not have known what I was actually dealing with.

"That reminds me; Great Grand was Jewish and I think about all her good deeds when I read about the southern Baptists and their claims of owning the keys to heaven and their superior Christian family values, while they practice bigotry and racism."

"Yes, as far as I know Christ didn't discriminate."

"A friend of mine had a cousin who was married to a very successful businessman. Oil industry out west. They had two children and raised them in an upper middle-class neighborhood. The best schools, best clothes, and twenty-five dollar haircuts for the six year old girl; owned horses for their weekend recreation, the whole nine yards as they say. The marriage was a farce. Nothing more than daddy bringing home the bacon and mommy amusing herself while the kids were at school. They were four strangers living in that house. Terrible atmosphere. The kids fought, the parents didn't speak to each other only in the most sarcastic way – well, you get the picture. They finally divorced when the boy, the youngest of the two, enrolled in university.

"The children had always been A students, their father having encouraged them to love learning. The point of this story is the stereotyping so I'll get to it. The daughter ended up six months pregnant, unmarried, and unemployed at the age of twenty-four. Her reason for not completing her education was that it would have taken her too long. She said the money a vet made wouldn't have compensated her for all her efforts anyway.

Then the son quit university, lived in a condo his mother owned and did odd construction jobs around town. So my friend thought back to a time many years earlier when on a lovely spring day she had called the cousin and asked her if she had anything she could donate to the local charity. "I'll pick your things up and take them along with mine" she had told her. "Welfare people, down and outs, you don't know who's going to be using your things". Well my friend Annie, in one of her more spirited moods reminded the cousin of what she had said all those years earlier, after the cousin had finished telling her about her now grown children. "My children aren't in that category. They come from a good home".

"The bottom line here" said Annie "is that if you are raised well off and educated you have a right to be in an unfortunate position, because you're from "a better class" is how cousin put it. Then she went so far as to claim that her daughter was doing the country a service by staying home and 'nurturing' her child and the son was freeing up a job for someone else when he was unemployed and on the lamb".

"That cousin of Annie's, what is she saying? My children are creating job opportunities for others; I love it. It's not as though they were hanging out through necessity, but rather choice, sort of a charitable donation to the community."

CHAPTER 12

On fear
"You must do that thing, which you think you cannot do."

Eleanor Roosevelt

One Sunday Doris strolled out to the beach with a man Mad and I recalled seeing on one other occasion. We were introduced to him and then told that he was her boyfriend. Balding, of medium height and unexceptional build he appeared to ignore the presence of others and surveyed everything within view from behind an old fashioned pair of mirrored sunglasses. His days were spent cloistered within the confines of Doris's small apartment and only when he arrived home from work did he venture outside. His trips out were more often than not simply quick drives to the local fast food and he'd return in record time with bags of take-away for their dinner.

The few times we saw him out he appeared to walk with a practiced nonchalance, the studied unconcerned air of the self-conscious man unable to overcome his feelings of vulnerability and so Ken adopted what he no doubt believed to be the body language of one self-assured; a highball glass clutched in his hand offered security, at least temporarily.

Well, whoever he was, it appeared that he had decided to stay for a while. Doris informed Mad that he would be staying for a few weeks and from that time onward his mail would be redirected to her address. He began to settle in comfortably and Mad, who is a patient soul to a fault, became more annoyed than usual with this overbearing tenant, and her parasitic new boyfriend.

"Charlie always said that my worst character trait was keeping silent until I was absolutely bursting with anger. Then he'd have me rehearse what I wanted to say to my offender and I'd spend days practicing what the twins call my cool, in order to be effective when the confrontation took place".

Mt. Vesuvius he had dubbed her in the early days of their marriage. She had been eighteen, he thirty, and she jokes that he had practiced child-rearing before the boys came along, because of their age difference.

A week into Ken's stay his friend arrived. Tall, he must have been six foot three or four, and wore his hair pulled back in a ponytail three inches long. He had a thick untrimmed moustache, and his eyes, well who knows? Like his friend he wore the large mirrored sun glasses, reminiscent of the sixties B movie tough guy.

He was no more than twenty seven or eight, and was already carrying a beer belly round. Nothing distinguished him from hundreds of other transients in appearance; however his behavior was odd, perhaps more so than most. Whenever women and their children gathered at the beach next door he would venture out, and only then. At these times he spent long hours sitting in the heat in his friend's jeep, beer in hand, just watching. At other times, when the jeep was not parked in a convenient place, we stood at the window and observed him hiding behind the trees and bushes that grew along the wall, sometimes a camera in his free hand.

The voyeur and boyfriend left as silently as they had moved in. Mad asked Doris what the two men did for a living and Doris said that boyfriend was a teacher and that his friend was from New Orleans.

"Yes, but what does he do?"

"Oh he's rich" was the reply.

"Well, that's one heck of a job Description, Doris".

Doris had to laugh and then asked us if we wanted to join her at one of the bars later. We didn't, yet felt sorry for this woman whose life would once again be centered round the local watering holes.

Doris would stay until the house was sold and I, to amuse myself, would continue to roam the neighborhood in search of more stories.

CHAPTER 13

"At the very moment when we are struggling to sustain a sense of personal autonomy, we also get caught up in vital forces that are much larger than ourselves, so that while we may be the protagonists of our own lives, we are the extras or spear carriers in some larger drama."

Carl Jung

Jetta Belle

"Everything happens for a purpose, Hanna. The puzzle pieces of life fit together perfectly. It is called synchronicity, the connection between seemingly random events and thoughts".

This was the last time I would see Jetta. She had married her retired professor, Art, and was clearing up some last minute details before closing the door on her Key Largo home and this chapter of her life for good.

She had called Goodwill Industries to cart away her household furnishings and all but three suitcases that sat packed by the door she had given to charity. A donation to the animal shelter was ready to post, the envelope resting beside her purse. As a final gesture Jetta had wrapped a copy of Deepak Chopra's book, 'The Seven Spiritual Laws Of Success' in happy flowered tissue paper and after loading her luggage in Art's car, stepped over to Jude's mailbox and placed the gift inside.

"Forgiveness is the fragrance the violet sheds on the heel that has crushed it."

Mark Twain

Walking home after seeing Jetta on her way I thought about Mark Twain's quote. A sort of courage is needed to be able to forgive the way Jetta forgives, don't you think so, Mad? I always had and then I read somewhere that because forgiveness frees us up and lessens our own pain, that it could also be viewed as a kind of selfish act. Selfish in a positive way mind you, for it does more good than harm for all concerned. What is that saying of Raymond Ng's? Oh yes, 'The one who pursues revenge should dig two graves'. I guess that says it all.

Beware the hypocrites, however. Jetta is a strong, honest character but there are so many who preach one thing and practice another. That woman in the class I attended at the library is a good example. She wore a pin that said 'Jesus loves me' and every, or almost every sentence was interjected with references to the Lord.

There were three young Japanese women in the class. All had Masters degrees in English and they were taking the course so that they could volunteer to teach English as a second language and adult literacy. Well, this woman who claimed a very close association with Jesus spent the majority of her time staring over at the three Japanese women. It was frightening to watch because her expression was absolutely wicked, just hateful.

Then her friend, who claimed to be there as well for the purpose of doing good works for the community raised her hand. "Hey, do we get a tax break on this? I mean can we write our car expenses and gas off for income tax deduction?" Heads shot up and even the teacher, who must have seen her share by then was shocked.

"Hypocrisy. There are lots of stories to illustrate the hypocrisy that afflicts American society. Look to that article about the twelve year old boy in the wheelchair for another example. He suffers from muscular dystrophy and lives with his mother, a physical therapist, and his sister in a condo in Miami. Old people reside in the place and most of them are comfortable. They complain that he is two years too young to swim in the pool, even though the water is therapeutic for him. He has a hard time reaching the buzzer to get in the front door and the security guard does not assist him, claims that door man isn't in his job description. So the kid pulls pranks, buzzes other condos, rides his chair in places that are off-limits, kid things and do these bored oldies offer to do anything with him, for him? Goodness, no. What they do is spend lots of time and energy to work on getting the family out of the complex. And yet, Hanna, I'd bet the house that if a reporter came along and asked them about their beliefs regarding charity, family values, that to a person they would all claim to be God-fearing, God-loving folk. I get angry, so angry at all the lies, half-truths, and hypocrisy".

"Well, there's always Doris with her big smile and asking us to join her for drinks. Yet just the other day she was going on and on about you and the way you do not consume like most here. Guess she either thought I wouldn't tell you or doesn't care if I do. "Recycle crazy" Doris said. "Saves those containers you get when you buy something, like from the deli and uses them instead of buying storage things. Not that she buys much. She's not much of a consumer you know. Doesn't eat fast food, won't spend anything in a bar and tells me she'd rather pay a bit more for clothes so they'll last longer than buy much every season. Then she goes out of her way to donate her used things. Says it helps others and doesn't fill the garbage dumps up. She talks like that; very serious about the environment, all that. But I ask you, does that sound like fun? I'd rather consume it's the American way anyhow. Besides everybody does. We're here for a good time as far as I'm concerned. Let the grandkids worry about their environment or whatever, when they grow up. It's not my job. Know what I mean?"

"I looked at her books when I was up there. Lots of stuff about social issues. Oh and those old classics and all the serious writers. She says she likes to go to 'a quality' restaurant, but she says not too frequently or it isn't a treat. Then she likes to sit at her kitchen table and visit about travel and other cultures. I can't see that she has any fun thinking about other people, can you?"

Mad laughed and shook her head. “What, pray tell, does Doris do for fun? When she isn’t eating, drinking, or picking up strangers, what goes on in her mind? Now that interests me. I asked that question of a man I knew and he answered, “Nothing; I don’t think of anything. Well I think of what I’m going to do next, like where am I going to go? think about my investments, should I have a nap, normal stuff like that”. I wonder if he’s typical? Someone ought to take a poll; they take polls on everything else now.”

CHAPTER 14

"Man has lost his capacity to foresee and forestall.
He will end by destroying the earth".

Dr. Albert Schweitzer

Mad was curious about everything and perhaps too serious at times, yet far more content than her neighbors.

Mad and I had spent an evening a few weeks past discussing retirement. The former Chicago saloon owners had bought homes and retired six years ago and we were shocked to hear what one had to say.

"A lot of retirees talk about moving to Puerto Rico and the Bahamas, all those places, Central America and all that, but I won't even visit those places. I can't figure those guys out. Why would anyone want to move to one of those countries and live around poor people and all those blacks? It would be like moving to a ghetto."

"How do you know unless you travel there what it would be like?" asked Mad.

"Hell, I don't need to go to know that I don't want to live around a bunch of blacks. You got blacks, you got a ghetto".

I found it hard to believe that this man had said what he did and yet I had heard him with my own ears. Mad later told me that she believed his problem was that he was frightened of being a minority anywhere. Certainly little Belize, with its literacy rate of ninety-seven percent and its hard working friendly people can hardly be referred to as a ghetto.

And what of beautiful Nassau? I mentioned this but he changed the subject. I felt saddened to discover this man that we had considered a friend for so many years felt this way. Perhaps he had just recently let down his guard? Another old friend had just recently told us that he would move to Western Europe but that even after he learned the language he was afraid of being laughed at.

"Why" we asked "do you think you would be laughed at?"

"Well, I'd be speaking with an accent and you know we think people with accents sound stupid".

I told him that he was judging other nations by the plebeian attitudes of the United States, but I know that I had not convinced him that the world outside of our borders practiced a more tolerant and compassionate way of life. Even examples of my own experiences did nothing to change his mind.

Someone once wrote that testing an idea or a rule means looking for exceptions. Observation is the judge of what is so.

I met another retiree one morning who, in discussing the morning's news told me: "Well, we need to go ahead and starve those Cubans and Iranians, then they'll get rid of their leaders and they'll all be better off. We gotta back those sanctions."

"Indirect murder?" I asked.

"Well, we gotta do what's right."

"Fear motivates him and people like Him, Hanna" Mad had said. "He once told me that he was afraid to write a letter to the editor about something he felt strongly about."

"You never know these days" he said. "I can't say anything against the Government. Never know what could happen. Look at that Kenneth Starr. People get investigated. Even the President for foolin around. I like to say what I think, but it's dangerous, and lots of people I know feel the same way. They probably would be afraid to print what I had to say anyway, or don't care cause I'm just a regular person. Makes me angry Though; forty million spent investigating sex and our schools are fallin apart. And we're always hearing about family values, so where's the family values when over forty-five million people don't have health care and kids lose their parents because they couldn't get medical help? Hell, kids lose their lives".

CHAPTER 15

"Nothing is more powerful than an idea whose time has come."

Victor Hugo

"You know, Hanna, when circumstances change, and the change is not of one's doing, then one's outlook must change. Consciously and purposely living. How many of us simply go through life, go through the motions, out of habit or misplaced loyalty? More than we want to believe I'm sure.

"People vote the same party line regardless of the issues. Friday night is always spaghetti night and winter means travelling to Key Largo. Hey! Perhaps it's just lazy. Habit is easy, a creative life takes work, effort."

I knew a whole family, four kids and mum and dad when I was growing up, who had the attitude that life handed you what you were supposed to have. The crazy thing is that they were creative. You have to be creative to survive fairly well on very little. But they didn't know they were creative. They didn't see anything in themselves or anyone else other than what they could see physically.

After school we'd sit out on the porch steps in the old neighborhood like kids did then and talk. One afternoon after school I asked them what they were going to be when they grew up. Angie, the eldest, about fourteen at the time said: "'Going to be and want to be are two different things you know." Only fourteen and she was already negative and resigned to accepting whatever fate meted out to her. She also gave the impression that it was her mission in life to discourage others.

So I said: “Wait a minute. Goals. Remember goals? The future? We’re supposed to choose a trade or profession. Something we’re going to make a living at when we’re grown up”.

“You’re dreaming. What if you decide something and it doesn’t work out?”

So I said I’d switch to something else. “Only one way to find out and that’s try”.

“Ya”, the others chimed in. “All that work and you don’t make it”.

So I told them I was going to be a journalist. God it was awful; they all laughed and it seemed as though they might never stop.

“Who do you think you are?”

“Ya. Your parents aren’t PROFESSIONALS” they jeered.

So I told them that someone in the family had to be the first and that their attitude was that of eighteenth-Century England. But that even in those times the Lord of the Manor was in his position because some ancestor worked his way up in trade, or the military or something.

Well, then they started in with, “Oh, now she’s a fine lady. Going to marry a prince?”

And on and on it went.

Pathetic babble. Then the dream crusher, Angie, told me that I must think myself better than the rest, otherwise I’d be content to live the way they did.

“If you were meant to be somebody, you’d have been born to a different family, your Ladyship.”

"It's fate, and you shouldn't tempt fate, our ma says".

"Well, Angie, you draw really great, so why don't you see that as your fate and become a commercial artist, something like that?"

She never answered. They all just drifted away. One by one they walked into their house and I ran home to dinner. I never did have much to do with them after that. They'd look at me and laugh in the school yard, and never invited me to share the porch step after that.

I ran into Angie years later. It was a Sunday, and a beautiful spring day. She was with by now her four children in Central Park, living the life her mother, or fate as Angie believed, had meted out to her; harried, trying to keep track of all the kids, worn clothes, and a scowl. That's how I remember Angie.

"How did the rest turn out?"

"Just one, the youngest, Emily became an executive secretary somewhere in Manhattan. Nice apartment, clothes, according to Angie. But then she told me that they don't see her much. "Left the old neighborhood like you did. Too stuck up to bother." But Hanna, I'd bet the house that the silly stuck up business was a false claim. More than likely they had given her such a hard time that she had to stay away just out of self-preservation."

So habit was formed over the generations. Habit. All but Emily had the courage to break the old habit of shutting out new information.

CHAPTER 16

"If one advances confidently in the direction of his dreams, and endeavors to live the life which he has imagined, he will meet with a success unexpected in common hours."

Henry David Thoreau

Mad received an offer for the house just one day before we were alerted to the impending threat of hurricane George. My friend was now in the perfect position to advance in the direction of her dreams. Her long-held dream of wandering round Europe, writing, exploring and in general feeling unencumbered and free was soon to become a reality.

But first things first. We had to prepare the house for a possible beating from the approaching George.

It was late September, and at 5 a.m. on a Tuesday morning I had walked down the path to collect the morning paper. As I bent to pick the paper off the ground I was suddenly struck by the unusual quiet that seemed to envelope the area. The palm fronds that rustled in the sea breeze creating their musical tinkling sound as they brushed against one another hung motionless. The water that gently lapped at the shore at this time of morning lay still, an ocean of glass.

Eerie; beautiful, but eerie. The calm before the storm I remember thinking, and quickly turned the television channel to the weather after entering the house. The hurricane would hit the Florida Keys in approximately four days.

After breakfast Mad and I quickly packed our personal belongings in her van, then we started to hurricane-proof the house. There were shutters to fasten to windows and everything not stationary had to be placed in the garage under the house. We had stored jugs of water, and canned goods; by 5 p.m. we were ready and exhausted. We decided to leave the following morning at sunrise, around 7 a.m., two days before the official order to evacuate.

Wednesday

We placed our last-minute items and Mad's cat, Baby, in her van and after running round the house pulling cords on electrical appliances, locked the door and we were off.

We took highway 97 up the middle of the State and stopped in a little town named Clewiston. Population? Well not many. Concerned that there may be others looking for accommodation because of the storm, we foolishly took a couple of rooms in the first motel we stopped to enquire of. Fifty dollars a night was what the woman quoted, far too high for such a place, we said, but were told that though the lot was virtually empty the place was booked. Our rooms were identical. Both filthy, which assuaged Mad's guilt for having snuck her cat in.

We paid up front for two days and noted that it wasn't until the third day that the lot began to fill. Talking to one of the other guests we found that the price of a room had risen considerably higher during that time. Eighty-nine dollars was what one late-comer had paid and the couple in the end unit had been asked to pay an extra ten dollars a night to keep their little dog with them. Each morning the maid pounded on the door at between seven-thirty and eight a.m. Fortunately we were early risers and one or the other of us had gone out and rushed back with a take away breakfast from McDonalds by then and whoever was sitting Baby would holler they didn't need anything while the other asked for towels and handed out the trash can to be emptied. We took turns going for walks and shopping, the later limited to Wal-Mart, and K-Mart, These being the only department stores in the area. Mad had a horror of the cat escaping in fright should the maid open the door. The following Sunday we headed back to the Keys and after being allowed to sit in a line of traffic for one and one half hours that morning, were told by a state trooper to turn round and wait on the mainland.

"No-one is allowed in until 1 p.m." he said.

"so why not stop people at the junction 97 and US1?" I asked

"I don't make the rules, Ma'am."

"Who does?" I had asked in annoyance. He simply laughed and waved us to turn round. Well that was my one and only hurricane adventure.

Key Largo had fared very well. Yard waste was all any of us really had to labor over; nothing of any consequence was damaged. The lower and middle Keys were not as fortunate.

Trailers of all sizes and descriptions, as well as shanty houses, old apartment buildings, and house boats had been damaged beyond repair and in some cases, many cases, beyond recognition. Mother-in-law suites such as the studio Mad rented to Doris felt the force of George as well and left their tenants homeless.

Fifty percent of the Keys' inhabitants were service workers, minimum wage people just scrapping by, most without health, let alone household insurance.

Houseboat row, as it was called in Key West, was all but obliterated, much to the delight of the powers that be, who for years had fought to have the houseboats removed and "rid the area of these eyesores". That most of these people had nowhere else to go was of no consequence. Trailers were seen as eyesores as well and these two modes of living deemed trash. They would not be allowed to be replaced it was announced in the aftermath of the hurricane. Mother-in-law suites were not going to be allowed to be rebuilt as owners in many neighborhoods didn't like the idea of renters in their area. Affordable housing had been virtually non-existent before George, with people forced to pay outrageous sums for tiny rooms. Eight hundred dollars was not an unusual rent to pay for a tiny suite, utilities and phone not included.

And so it happened that the eyesores had finally been removed and with them, the people who could afford to live nowhere else and the services they provided.

These people left in droves and then the well-heeled began to complain about the lack of service, businesses understaffed, and so on and on, but then one can't have everything.

While all of this was happening my old friend was busy activating her dream. She planned to visit Canada and carry on to Europe from there. She had to visit a vet to obtain a health certificate for her cat in order to fly her across the international border. The initial conversation with the receptionist should have sent up a red flag.

There are mile markers standing roadside at every mile throughout the Keys and when asking directions one asks Bay side or Sea side? Unfortunately this receptionist was not sure which side of the island the clinic she was sitting in was on.

"Well are you on the same side as Publix or the opposite side? Oh, the other side of the highway. What side is that?"

"That's Bay side" Mad told her.

We took Baby over to the clinic and found a Forty-something receptionist with a little girl's voice and a blank expression. The price for the certificate had been quoted at forty dollars, yet when we arrived Mad was informed by the Vet, after he patted Baby and pronounced her very healthy indeed, that a sixteen dollar fee would have to be paid to yet another vet in a Government clinic in Miami.

This didn't sound kosher to us so we called US customs when we returned home. Once the agent stopped laughing he told us that the forty dollar certificate was sufficient. "It's for the benefit of the foreign country, you know, so that they are reassured there is nothing wrong with the animal they are letting in. sounds like somebody has a little extra business going on the side".

When the receptionist had filled the information in on the certificate she had asked where the cat was going and then when told Canada said: "Is that national or international?" Oh well. The whole thing had to be redone at any rate because she had classified Baby as a dog and entered the zip code of the foreign address where the phone number should have been placed. So you see nothing was working very smoothly here.

Doris now claimed to suffer from a variety of maladies; allergies, hypertension, a degenerative muscle disease: "Had it since I was little" and anxiety. The future owners of the house were uncertain as to whether they wanted to retain a tenant, but decided to see how well they were going to get along with her.

Doris arrived home from work with a pair of doves one Friday and told us that she was going to release them Sunday morning in honor of her boyfriend's recently deceased mother. Then she hurriedly entered her apartment and emerged an hour or so later. Dressed beautifully and expensively, she was all ready for a night on the town. Boyfriend arrived the following evening.

Hurricane George ushered a lot of people out of the Keys, including Mad and many, if not most, may now be a lot better off.

The month of October, and the last Mad would ever spend in Key Largo appeared to be one of the happiest periods in the twenty-five years I had known her. "Keep the best and leave the rest" she said as she went about packing up and that is exactly what she did. After bagging and boxing all but a few suitcases of her best things and the few items we needed to get by the last few days, she called Goodwill. They sent a large truck the morning of our last day there and we watched as they loaded everything up for transport to the mainland. She even gave them the old van.

The house was now wiped clean we took one last look round. Then locking the door, we descended the stairs and never looked back.

Ally, the realtor, kindly offered to drive us to the airport. "What do you two think of Cape Canaveral sending a seventy-seven year old former astronaut up into space?"

"Well Let's see" I said. "They are ostensibly testing the effects of weightlessness on the elderly. Are the seniors planning to relocate to some place exotic like a star ship or another planet?"

Though we all laughed we found the reality of what we considered a huge waste of money, money that could have been better spent caring for the elderly, an absurdity. Unconscionable, criminal, pathetic.

EPILOGUE

Mad is in France now, living there Full-time actually and very happily. She took Thoreau's' advice, went in the direction of her dreams and is living the life she had imagined.

She travelled round the first six months in Europe and then found a flat in Montmartre. It is close to the Sacré Coeur Cathedral and not far from the Moulin Rouge.

"It is such a romantic neighborhood, so historic, Hanna and it has always been one of my favorite places."

And yes, she remarried. Andre is in his early sixties, loves to travel, visit, dine out in the little French restaurants by candle light. Things Mad only fantasized about until now.

I've visited her a couple of times since she has settled in France. I've even had dates when on vacation there. European men don't toss aside the women when they near the forty, or even fifty age mark the way North American men do.

It has been two years since Mad and I flew out of Miami for the last time. It seems a much longer time; I reason that's because there is so much more to think about and enjoy. living in the present and moving forward tends to put the past just where it should be. In the case of Key Largo, it is but a netherworld not to be revisited.

In late October of 1998 hurricane Mitch wended its way through the Caribbean, causing a horrendous amount of damage. Over 11,000 lives were lost it was estimated, when on Wednesday November 4th a tornado struck Key Largo.

Emma and Jack wrote Mad telling her that all of Monroe County had been declared a disaster area by President Clinton and that Key Largo had suffered the most damage of all the Keys this time round. Once again those worst hit were those who could least afford the loss. Mad's former home lost its little screened-in porch and a few storm shutters; there was a huge loss of beautiful trees and plants but otherwise was not much worse off than after Hurricane George had paid his visit.

Pam across the street who had claimed to hate living in Key Largo now had something to bolster her argument for moving elsewhere. Or so it seemed until it became obvious that Bud, her husband of over forty years was actually in his glory. "He loves this" she told Emma one afternoon. "He loves all the yard work caused by the storm, finds it gives him even more work outside. Now he's running round to the neighbors when he runs out of his own work."

The Phillips, a man and his wife in their sixties had bought Mad's house and were now realizing Doris' full potential. She complained that the rain had wet her carpet because the old wooden storm shutters were warped and had let the wet in, declaring: "Next year it's going to be different. I'll have insurance." Though how that would have made a difference to her in that she did not own the carpets no one could quite understand. The telephone repair man arrived and Mrs. Phillips overheard Doris tell him that the line was old and snapped easily, complaining that it was because the owners were cheap and didn't replace anything. Everyone had a good laugh about that. She'd had boyfriend rush over to help her put the shutters up and when he asked her who had helped her before George struck, she told him that she had done all the work herself. Mad had sweat bullets helping her prepare that day, even assisting her in lifting furniture and placing cement blocks under everything to lift the naturally very expensive sofas and chairs should the rain cause any flooding.

The final straw for the Phillips was the barbecue Doris had for four male friends and during her house cleaning dragged the garbage bag down the drive, leaving the contents that had spilled through for the Phillips to clean up. And so Doris was given her walking papers.

The Sunday after Mitch struck saw the community center beach next door become a place of bedlam. Shrewish and likely overwrought mothers hollered at young children; a radio, turned up full volume, broadcasted a sports event for what seemed like hours and unsupervised children threw all the beach furniture into the water. The senior was still reliving his WW11 glory days by buzzing the neighborhood and the motor boats were back out travelling fast to nowhere. All in all paradise was lost as far as Mrs. Phillips was concerned.

The gentle, quiet speaking lady across the street told Mrs. Phillips that the supposed stray that Doris had claimed to have fed since a kitten was in fact hers and approximately 8 years old. "Just friendly, likes to visit the neighbors". She was horrified to learn that Mrs. Phillips had saved it from attempting to eat from a box of take-away chicken that Doris had set out for it one night.

Doris the menace was how Mrs. P. began to refer to her. "Who in hell feeds a cat chicken bones?" she said.

All in all I see the Keys as Plato's worst nightmare. "The triumph of the senses over the mind, of emotion over reason, of chaos over order, of the id over the superego. Dionysian abandon over apollonian harmony".

THE END

LETTERS FROM JULIE

CHAPTER 1

Sept. 15, 1998

Dear Hanna,

Grandmother Beauchamp says hello and asks that you pass on congratulations to Mad. Imagine, moving to Paris and marrying all within one year's time; we are very happy for her.

Your mission here was successful, while mine, I'm afraid was not. At least not yet. I'll tell you what has happened so far with the Peace Corps.

You'll recall all those trips I made to the horrible VA in Miami to complete the final phase of the application process? Well two weeks after my last visit there, (to the VA) I received a call from the Corps placement officer informing me that I had been assigned to leave for French Guyana this past April. He was irritated with me at first, telling me that my paperwork was to have been submitted at least by March, and here it is September. I explained that the recruiter had not provided me with the final forms until late April and that he had told me I would not be assigned until November.

"Well, we've just pulled out of four countries and now we have one hundred and sixty four people on our waiting list, so I guess you're number one sixty five," he said.

I was so angry, Hanna. How was I to know that even a Peace Corps recruiter was going to be just as incompetent as God knows how many others we are forced to deal with every day? There was no apology, of course, and I have had no further communication from them.

Grand told me to chalk it up to experience and carry on. Who knows, they may straighten things out and call me later on. In the meantime I'm going to start looking round for a job. I haven't yet succumbed to what they call (the Keys disease); in other words, I'm still motivated to find something to keep me busy.

Grand has been great. She told me to travel the Keys and work here and there. Generally enjoy myself, she is telling me until I decide what to do. I'll send you whatever interesting bits of info. I come across. Hope you'll be able to make use of some of it re: your book.

All for now

Sincerely,

Julie

CHAPTER 2

Oct. 1, 1998

Dear Hanna,

I've spent the past two weeks in Key West and returned home late last night. I can't say I enjoyed the place much, however it was interesting. One of those places you shouldn't miss seeing, and yet once is enough. It is very expensive, and the locals told me that the average worker leads a hand to mouth existence (if they're lucky). Affordable housing is a fantasy, with little efficiency apartments renting for eight hundred a month plus utilities. Wages, as you know are horribly low in the Keys, yet I was surprised to find they were no better even in Key West, the most expensive of all the islands. I read not long ago that it costs 8.5% more to live in Florida that in the rest of the nation as a whole, and that wages run 10% less in this State than in the rest of the nation. Phoney paradise, Hanna. But then you and Mad came to that conclusion some time back.

Anyway, I found that the workers looked a lot less happy than the travel brochures would have us believe. One told me that tips were their life's blood, so I reasoned service and attitude should have been a lot better if that were the case. But then another told me that the place is called The Conch Republic because of the independent "take us or leave us" attitude. Guess they can't have it both ways.

Many of the tourists appear to take advantage of the anti-social environment here. I was sitting in Sloppy Joes the other night when in walked a man and woman pushing a little dog in a baby stroller. They had the cold country pallor (snow white skin) prison pallor? Anyway, they were dressed up far more than the islander would be even to go out for dinner. She had obviously spent hours on her makeup (ready to go on stage); her hair looked prepared to withstand a wind of hurricane magnitude, and her nails were of the four in. highly glossed, acrylic variety. His thick white hair (top missing) was professionally coiffed, and he, very conscious of his new do, kept running his fingers through it, and tossing his head as he did so. They both seemed to be self-conscious and kept glancing round the room as though they expected, or rather desperately needed to be noticed. He was soft looking, his pale pock-marked face totally expressionless and she grinned in a phoney way at any small bit of attention that he deigned to pay her. The dog, in fact, was the primary focus of their attention and I noticed that hanging from the stroller handle was an airline baggage tag.

The rest of the bars customers looked like bike gang members and their women. The men and women were tattooed everywhere. Arms, legs, chests, backs, unbelievable. My God they looked filthy too. Baggy, dirty jeans, the waist bands belted under huge bellies, greasy hair, held back with faded kerchiefs, or tied back in a pony-tail, and most appeared to be late forties, or fifties plus.

What would Hemmingway have said? This wasn't the romantic, artsy atmosphere I had expected to find. Really it was more a purgatory for misfits and losers. Everyone bored, boring, and unwashed, and naturally, fat. I don't imagine it's easy waiting on these people for little more than survival wages. An editorial in one of the weekly Keys papers said that employee turnover in the Keys is two hundred to two hundred and fifty percent. No wonder. Beer budget wages and champagne prices are in effect everywhere.

Quite a few of the tourists I've spoken with agree that this is a unique place to visit, but they sure wouldn't want to live here. They agree with recent articles that decry the trashy strip mall, tee-shirt shop, fast food joint ugliness of the Keys and they are disenchanted with the cheap atmosphere. One British lady told me that she thought the Keys, particularly Key West, had a circus atmosphere. "Fun for a time, unique in its way, but who would want to live here? Perhaps it's not a conscious decision" she said: Then quoted Yogi Berra; "If you don't know where you're going in life, you're liable to end up somewhere else."

I'll end on this column note, and be off to bed. More soon.

Sincerely,

Julie

CHAPTER 3

Oct. 14, 1998

Dear Hanna,

I feel like Alice in Wonderland. I seem to be meeting the sort of strange creatures one expects one might in a strange upside down world. Grand recited the conversation that took place between Alice and the Cheshire Cat, when I complained to her last night.

"Would you tell me please which way I ought to go from here?" Alice asked.

"That depends a good deal on where you want to go." said the Cat.

"I don't much care where" said Alice.

"Then it doesn't matter which way you go" said the Cat.

"So long as I get somewhere" Alice added as in explanation.

"Oh, you're sure to do that" said the Cat.

I haven't told you about the mamma cat and her five kittens I found next door in an abandoned pool in the back of the vacant lot next door. This happened about two weeks ago and Grand told me a little story about the lady who owns the lot and once lived in the adjacent house.

Aileen was married to a local attorney. She had had the pool installed, reasoning that being a qualified swim instructor and having time on her hands she might contribute to the community by offering free lessons to the neighborhood children.

Apparently this didn't sit well with the neighbors. You know the type, Hanna, always preaching family values. Well they didn't want cars parked along their street and the sounds of children around for a few hours a day; they therefore took up a petition and put a stop to her good deed.

Aileen and her husband, disgusted, packed up and moved back to North Carolina. For quite a few years there has been some discussion about building a community pool; however the locals have been hesitant about sanctioning the project (don't want their taxes raised). Meanwhile they complain about the wayward kids. Dumb.

Back to my rescue effort. Months ago I noticed a rather small cat perched on our wall, though whenever I approached it would back away. I spied her on a couple of occasions eating the food that I put out for the tom that roams the neighborhood, though he has a home. Well I started putting food out on the wall for her and over time she allowed me to get closer and closer, until I was patting her.

Grand called the feline rescue league and Donna, the woman in charge, told her that if I could take the stray in she would arrange to take it. Three days later she gave us directions to a strip mall in one of the Keys twenty five minutes south of us and I met her there and handed over the cat. She apparently took it straight to a vet to be spade and after spaying this poor animal, they called me to come and take the cat back telling me that she had recently had kittens and to let her loose to find them. Sick people, Hanna. I asked them why on earth they didn't wait to spay her-wait until I'd found her kittens. Her she was sedated and feeling ill now. Well I get upset even writing about this after the fact. Anyway. The vet had said "Well she's here now". I take that to mean he wanted the business.

I brought her back home and once I saw she was able to move around without any trouble, I followed her to her little family. I left her with her kittens, with enough food and water to keep them overnight. Then before dawn broke the next morning I went over and with the assistance of a couple of neighbors' pet carriers managed to retrieve the whole family.

We put them out in Grand's screened-in porch and for eight days worked to tame the kittens which were six or seven weeks when I found them and eating on their own right alongside mamma. Some of them were quite wild because they had not had any human contact and we hoped that they would be adoptable once they left us. Donna had told me when I met her the first time that cats over six weeks were hard to adopt out in the Keys, but that she had a place she sent cats where they were kept regardless, never destroyed. Well we wanted to hand them over so that they would have a better chance of finding homes and the sooner the better for them. She takes all the cats that come in to her possession up to Broward county and told me that there are twice as many cats as people in the Keys, strays that is and strange as this sounds she said: "Well, it never gets cold here so they don't freeze and die off." I told her that in my opinion it was uncaring, irresponsible humans who were responsible for the suffering of these helpless animals and she gave me a look that could have killed. Odd. Who would have thought that the weather could be held responsible for the over-population of homeless creatures.

We left messages and finally Donna called telling me to drop my little cat family of once again at the unfeeling vets, adding in a curt, harsh voice "If you leave a pet carrier behind you don't get it back and I'd appreciate a donation if you don't mind. It costs a lot to look after these animals."

"Yes" I said. "I've spent over a week caring for them, three days rescuing them and this will be my third time transporting them. I've done my best, and of course I will leave a donation and please keep the pet carrier". She had told Grand when Grand called her the first time that she gets fifteen dollars each time she sends a blood sample from one of these rescued felines to a researcher in Broward County, and absolutely every feline donates a sample. This apparently offsets costs. The point is Hanna, I would not expect the woman to do what she does for nothing, yet why be so nasty when it was me contributing to her mission? I would do the same thing all over again for the innocents, Hanna. I just don't understand why some people are so damned nasty and for no reason, do you? Oh well, Grand told me to hope for the best where the poor creatures were concerned, knowing that I had done my best and push on. She does force me to let go of circumstances and people I cannot change, though she says it's as hard to do sometimes as pulling hens' teeth.

I'm off tomorrow a.m. to job hunt - I'll write you re: who and what I encounter in my search.

All for now.

Sincerely,

Julie

CHAPTER 4

Oct. 28, 1998

Dear Hanna,

Have you thought any more about paying us a visit round Christmas? It's not all so far off now. I drove Grand and her friend Mrs. Johns into Miami yesterday. Needed a break from the rigors of job hunting. We stopped in at the Wal-Mart in the Kendall area. What a hoot, Hanna. You'll have to see it. They don't trust their customers to walk from the electronics department to the check-out stand. Mrs. Johns decided to buy a new electric razor for her husband and what do you think? The clerk said it was store policy to walk the customer to the cashier for that sort of purchase. All the items in that department were locked away to boot and we had to find a clerk in order to look at anything, not that the clerk knew the merchandise anyway. Then Grand decided to call old Mrs. Preston to ask if she needed anything and we were directed to a pay phone outside. Lord, the phone was locked behind an iron cage; just enough room left to slide the quarter into the slot and stick your finger in to dial. No phone books of course, guess they've all been stolen, if they were ever placed there to begin with.

I got a call from the Peace Corps yesterday. Seems they are interested in my eligibility for assignment and asked that I obtain the last bit of information that the VA had been paid to collect but failed, this being my blood typing. I found a hospital in Homestead that will type my blood for the modest fee of eighteen dollars. Naturally I will need a note from a doctor before they can accept my money and perform the test. This is the fun part. I have called clinic after clinic. They want seventy dollars in order to furnish me with a note for the hospital lab, which will instruct the lab to take my blood and allow me to pay for the privilege of finding out whether I am Rh negative, p.oop positive or whatever the hell I am. One clinic told me that they charge forty five dollars and up and kept repeating this, said it depended on how long it would take. Still I didn't catch on. Then I called one last clinic and told the receptionist that I needed a doctor's note in order to get my blood typed. She kept telling me that I had to book an appointment for a physical and I kept repeating that I just wanted my blood typed. Finally I said, "You really don't know what I'm talking about do you?"

Her response was, "I don't care what you need. You have to have a physical if you want a note from the doctor".

Of course it may have helped my cause if she had been fluent in English, and also less hostile. God, Hanna, I am beginning to absolutely hate this place.

Old Dottie from across the street stopped her bicycle outside the mail box yesterday and decided to say hello. I'm collecting the mail and she found it important to cheer me up by sharing the fact that she had hit a bird on the way home from Miami the day before. I asked her if she had stopped to check how badly it was hurt and the ridiculous woman laughed. "Oh no I didn't, but it was a big tall bird so I figure it must have lived long enough anyhow."

I asked her then, "Did anyone else stop to help it?"

She said: "No. But it's not hurting now cause I'm sure the two cars behind me pretty well flattened it. It won't need no help. But my CAR, my CAR, you didn't ask me about that. I'm so lucky, I jumped out and checked as soon as I got home and there isn't a scratch on it."

Hanna, I grabbed the mail in one hand, slammed the box closed with the other and said "Well, It is very sad to hear a wild thing has been killed. No-one really cares that much, do they?" I turned and walked away. Mercifully I haven't seen her since. She's the woman who came over one evening and told us we had better join the community club. "The lights, the security night lights reflect onto your property you know." Never mind that we would be paying to use a beach when we have our own private beach just this side of our wall.

Word is leaking round that Grand is considering putting the house up for sale. Guess that's why the DOTTY ONE told Grand she had better replace her carpets, paint the beautiful dark wood paneling white, install modern windows to replace the jalousie, and lastly before departing our humble abode said "Julie, you need a tan."

She's jealous I'm sure of the house. Ocean front being as expensive as it is here and this big home sitting on a half-acre as well, makes it worth three times what she could ask for hers, even with our outdated carpets, ha!

As of last month a new law was introduced to the Keys. People are no longer permitted to rent their studio apartments, or whatever it was they rented out to tourists, for any less than twenty-eight days. Less than that and the owner is charged a fine of hundreds per day; they even said something about fining the renter. People were writing letters to the editor asking how they were going to find out who was renting to whom and for how long. I believe I have found the answer and so wrote a letter to the editor myself. I'll attach it to this. See what you think.

I'll sign off now. I'm going to go out before it gets dark and rake some seaweed, while I listen to the doves call goodnight to each other. That's one thing I will miss when I leave here.

All for now.

Sincerely,

Julie

Julie Beauchamp

11 Seaview Dr.

Key Largo, Florida 33037

To The Editor:

Regarding recent articles re: The ban on home owners renting to short term vacationers (less than 28 days duration). I have discovered the answer to the questions: How will this new law be enforced? Who will check to ensure the owners of these properties are complying with the law? How will these property checks be conducted?

For the answers to these questions, look no further than your neighbors.

At approximately 11AM on-January 19th. I answered a knock at my door and found a short elderly man accompanied by a woman who one may safely assume was his wife. I said hello, and the man quickly blurted out "Do you have a place to rent in your house?" Without stopping for breath – nor looking me in the eye - he nervously rubbed his chest, grinned, and continued quickly; "We have company coming who need a place to stay." I told him that I have a tenant and that she has been with the house for nearly two years. Ignoring my response he repeated; "Oh, we really need a place to put some people up for a little while."

I reiterated - "My tenant has lived here for nearly two years" and pointing toward her vehicle said: "That's her car sitting there."

"Oh, how long?"

"Two years" I replied. I then asked him where he lived, and he hesitatingly said: "Bonefish." He then said a quick thanks and hurried down my porch steps.

I find it extremely odd that someone who claims to live approximately three blocks away and whom I have never met in my life, would be knocking on my door looking for short-term accommodation at precisely the same time said accommodations have been deemed illegal. What do you think?

At best this is an insult to one's intelligence: At worst it is reminiscent of Nazi Germany, or the Soviet Union where the practice of spying on the affairs of one's neighbors was commonplace.

In conclusion: May I ask - Are there financial perks involved? Or have these pathetic little people simply decided to embark on this new activity out of boredom and stupidity?

Julie Beauchamp

CHAPTER 5

Nov. 12, 1998

Dear Hanna,

I'm still job hunting. I had picked up an employment application from the Humane Society a few weeks ago and returned there yesterday to hand it in and speak to the lady in charge. A short stocky woman with a closely-cropped head of white hair and the demeanor of a drill sergeant, she was obviously entirely dedicated to the animals in her care. As she ushered me through the tiny building (kept cleaner than a hospital) she described what my duties would be should I accept the job. The duties of the receptionist included everything from pitching in to care for the animals' physical needs to keeping books etc. Despite the small pay ($6.00 an hour) and only six hours a day five days a week, I was about to accept and gladly, as it would have given me the opportunity to spend time with the animals, when, out of the blue she said: "If you hate people you can't let on because they come in to make donations and then a lot of old people come in just to talk and pass the time".

Well, Hanna I'm friendly, and god knows, No-one likes to visit more than I do, so her comment made me wonder if she wasn't judging others by herself.

Then she went on to tell me some of the cruel things people do to animals, preparing me for what she said; "Comes through this door." I decided that if she had turned off to the human race I couldn't blame her in a way, but said I thought it best to focus on the kind people who make donations and are concerned for the poor little creatures.

Well, then she said; "I tell everyone that they had better not accept the job if they don't think they'll like me."

I decided that perhaps she doesn't dislike people, it's just that she's afraid they won't like her. What do you think?

She had looked at me when I'd first walked in and told me that I would not be able to wear the sort of clothes I was wearing at the time if I were going to work there because, as she put it; "If I need you to clean a cage you'll get shit all over your nice clothes." I guess you get the picture, Hanna. Then before the little tour she gave me she made a comment under her breath (not far enough under I'm afraid) about showing "Her ladyship round."

The day before this I had gone into a tee-shirt shop wearing khakis and yes, a tee-shirt, to apply for a cashier's position and met three middle-aged women. They were dressed for a night on the town, or perhaps the stage. Their eye makeup was so dark it looked as though they'd been in a fight and gotten the worst of it, and I hadn't seen the claw-like acrylic nails painted neat since a trip to Vegas. They stood at the front counter eating French fries and tuna salad sandwiches and gossiping.

I quickly completed the application form standing at the counter, and handed it to the one who appeared to be the star of the establishment. She looked me up and down and told me that I'd have to really dress up to work there (this tee-shirt shop) and that all the cosmetics were important. "We really, really, want to impress our customers that we are not just any tee-shop".

Well I am sure she has accomplished this end. Then she told me all about the history of the business how successful, how many shops they owned, were opening etc., very impressive. Lastly she said; "We don't pay more than six dollars an hour. We don't want people who need the money; we really, really, want people who love our clothes and love working with the tourists. Money isn't a priority." Well wages aren't, that's obvious, which of course places this little enterprise in the majority of those operating businesses in the Keys. Crazy. No. Greedy, and unconscionable is closer to the truth.

Nov. 20

I'll finish this and get it off to you today. I've accepted a little, and I mean little, in wages and hours, job. It is at a resort about twenty-five minutes' drive from home. It is part-time naturally; almost all the job here are. No benefits. Benefits don't kick in until a person has been employed for six months full-time here. That lets management off the hook as far as doing more than paying survival wages to a majority of their staff, and staff is something they are pathetically short of.

Apparently the company sent recruiters to Mackinaw Michigan to look for employees for our tourist season and few of the hundreds that were offered jobs showed up. Smart. I imagine they did their homework and came to the conclusion that living in paradise would not be much fun if one could not afford to eat. Out of their puny pay, barely more than minimum wage, the resort deducts $450.00 a month for staff accommodation. This consists of a small studio apartment, furnished with bed, dresser, tiny fridge, microwave, table and chair. This is one of the perks of working for the company, I am told. Speaking of food Hanna, what I have seen that is supposed to pass for the free employee lunch is truly an insult to any worker; anyone, no matter how far down the social ladder should be treated in so dehumanizing a manner. Three trips to the little room back of the main kitchen was enough for me.

The last time I happened to be walking through the door just as one of the kitchen staff walked up to the steam table and tossed two big bowls of what appeared to be kitchen leftovers on to it. It was gross, as though throwing food to hogs. The scraps were barely warm. What was supposed to pass for salad was wilted, and even the lettuce was rusted. All this mess of bacteria, as I came to regard it, was but one foot away from the trolley wherein dirty cutlery, cups, etc. are placed and the huge garbage container sits next to that. There must be a shortage of health inspectors down here.

The people who eat there are those who have no choice I am told. 99% are Haitians and Hispanics working for close to nothing and the poor could barely speak English so would have a hard time complaining and wouldn't dare anyway. Those of us who work in the shops either don't bother eating, or bring a sandwich and eat it out behind the resort kitchen.

I work twenty hours a week in the boutique and I'm alone except for the boutique manager darting in and out a few times a day. I am still not trained on the computerized cash register, though I've been there for one week. "Just keep a list of your mistakes darling." Everyone is darling. Six foot one wearing two inch heels most of the time. She is dark, very exotic looking and wears her hair waist length and her clothes painfully tight, the kind of jeans granny used to dare us to try to sit down in when we were in our early teens and before we knew better. Barefoot and neon painted toe nails peeking out of open toed shoes make quite a picture for the customers of the very expensive resort hotel boutique.

She keeps on the move all day dodging her husband and various and sundry boyfriends and running out to restaurants to keep lunch and dinner dates. She's the main topic of conversation round there, and seems to relish all the attention. It's as though she regards herself a celebrity of sorts, but then nowadays people are being celebrated for the darndest things, aren't they?

She says her husband's girlfriend and her boyfriend don't prevent her marriage from being (workable) as she puts it.

Christmas is a month away but we are playing Christmas music and she told me that she hates the season. I asked her when her children begin their holiday break. They are eleven and seven. "Oh I don't know; I guess they told me, but I wasn't paying any attention. I just hope my daughter won't tell her father that I was out all last night with my British boyfriend. She's a real daddy's girl. Can't keep a secret for me. Last night was the night he spends over at his girlfriend's anyway.

The Brit has been part of the equation for the last ten years and then there is a two year old. Somewhat invisible I think, as he is never mentioned except when the subject of day care costs arise, which has been often even in the short time I've been there.

Nov. 22

I'm awfully slow with this particular letter; I may get it off to you tomorrow however. I met the bold one's Mr. Brit yesterday. He's not Oxford believe me, but very crude, the equivalent of a Bronx public school dropout. He's convinced the poor ignorant soul, whose travel experience is nil, and whose world is the size of a pea that he is class and even owns a castle. The Castle Pub perhaps, but I don't quite see him riding to hounds with Charlie and the gang.

Just before closing he sauntered in wearing a towel round his swim trunks (I'm assuming he was wearing swim trunks, and ordered Vi to give him a message. I asked him if he vacationed here often and he said: "Every chance I get, luv. After last night I won't have to floss my teeth for days." So Hanna, I looked him right in the eye and said: "You know I've been to Manchester." He turned a bright shade of red, mumbled something about meeting Vi later, and hustled out of the shop. The little old lady who had been browsing the racks of overpriced goodies beat him to the door however. What a picture.

Nov. 23

Another day and more people with more problems. It seems to me that there are a lot of humans running around bored to death, in that if they didn't have a problem they feel a need to cause other people problems just for the hell of it. That is a sad fact of life here in paradise.

One customer in her mid-sixties told me that she had cancer, though it is in remission. She said that she and her husband were retired, and to make conversation I said I thought it must be nice to be able to retire and travel when and where one chose. "Oh, we can afford the resort and all that" she said but told me that the bad part of being retired was having people not know who you were. "They just see old people stumbling around, don't know what we've accomplished."

Granny said it sounds as though the Woman's spirit is as sick as her body, and perhaps the one led to the other.

Most of the guests are retirees, and don't appear to be nearly as happy as the advertisements would lead us to believe.

One lady and her husband came in so that she could try on swim suits, and she proceeded to model each and every one to get approval. They looked sixties, and she looked to be in better shape than he, though he had it all over her when it came to nasty. I felt sorry for her. She popped out of the dressing room in one suit after another, only to be demeaned by his depreciating laughter. "Keep looking. Hopefully you'll find something that doesn't emphasize your rolls".

While his wife was desperately trying to find a suit he'd approve of he decided to impress me by describing the neighborhood they lived in. "Costs one hundred thousand just to be considered eligible to buy there. That's money you have to put down and leave while they check you out, and then they let you know whether they're going to accept you into the community. We got our own air strip, country club, gourmet dining room, golf course, sailing, everything. All kinds of yachts parked there you know. We've got it all, even all school. It's gated. Lots of security. You can't just come in and shop at our center.

"A guest visits three times and in the market to buy isn't real welcome after that. You gotta get permission to invite guests in too. We like to keep it exclusive. Know what I mean? We don't want just anybody".

I told him that granny was acquainted with some of the residents in Ocean Reef. I didn't ask him whether the rumor that the tennis club had broken the exclusivity rule and invited some of their workmen to play in a tennis tournament was true. Apparently they had been losing badly.

Well he was a bit humbled. Or perhaps he was afraid that I would find out that he was not as big a player as he would have liked me to believe, because he suddenly confessed that his house was one of the smaller homes in this exclusive nineties commune. Shortly after this confession he approved a swim suit for the long-suffering wife, though still grumbling about her rolls. She by now was perspiring profusely, the water running down her face, her wig a bit askew, and near to tears.

Vi arrived to teach me how to run the computer monster exactly five minutes before I was to leave. Her heavy perfume and breath mints didn't hide the smell of alcohol. A woman walked in right behind her and continued a conversation they had begun god knows when.

What a mess. Four letter words were flying and she was going on about her unfaithful husband and the cheap dinner he'd bought her the night before. I decided that Vi had no time to work with me, told her so, and picking up my purse, left. As I opened the door to leave her silly friend said: "Oh sorry, ya'all. I'll be goin in a few days. Just got these problems ya know."

I have four days off now so I'm going to play tourist and visit some of the attractions in the Upper Keys, enjoy a dinner out and so on. All for now.

Sincerely,

Julie

P.S. We've big news.

Keeping it a surprise until you arrive for Christmas.

CHAPTER 6

Dec. 6, 1998

Dear Hanna,

Mum and dad flew in from London last Wednesday and I spent my free time showing them round Largo. It was a complete surprise, them visiting. I expected them to arrive closer to the holiday. Anyway, they can see I am none too happy here. Even my pay check was a joke. Twenty five percent deductions. According to a recent news article, Florida has what is called a regressive tax system, meaning the poor pay a higher percentage of their income in taxes than the wealthy. Then to add insult to injury, old Greenspan wants to eliminate the minimum wage, or he would if he could. Crazy. As things stand now it is impossible for many on the lower end of the economic scale to do more than barely survive. If I were not living with Grand I don't know what I'd do right now.

We went out to play tourist, and even that day as beautiful as it was perfect weather, was marred by nasty, unhappy people. We began the day at a resort that serves as a sort of marine sanctuary as well as hotel. While waiting for the boat to take us over to a neighboring island - there is a pioneer house there and various types of flora and fauna etc. - we stood on the end of the dock enjoying the pelicans. Beautiful birds, they were so tame the tourists got almost close enough to them to hand-feed them.

One of the pelicans was having a difficult time balancing on the thick wire it was perched upon, and mum and I followed the wire to the source of the bird's trouble. There at the entrance to the dock stood an idiot, mid-twenties. pony tail, of course, pink neon framed sunglasses, and dirty lime green shorts, shaking the wire for all he was worth Then, once he realized we were staring at him he suddenly let go the cable, and in a dead run headed our way. Once he got to our end he jumped up and down, ran and jumped repeatedly, frightening the birds away.

Mum said "What's your trouble?" and he answered, "I hate those birds." Then he just as quickly ran back to the boat reservation area. Real nutty, Hanna. I said "Oh, lovely people" just as he ran off, and hey, I got the strange looks from the crowd.

After our visit to the island, which was beautiful, and the tour guide a knowledgeable nice man, we drove over to the animal sanctuary. Unfortunately the resort offered dolphin and trained seal shows. Sad I always think. These beautiful animals made dependent upon people, and exploited for the sake of the dollar, but then so are most of the people here. This resort had more cats roaming round than Hemmingway's house in Key West. Unbelievable. At least they were fed and watered, poor creatures. They would come up and cry to get patted, yet there were signs warning the guests against patting the cats.

On our way home we stopped off at a strip mall so that mum and I could satisfy our bargain hunting urges. You know we love the dollar stores. Today's answer to the five and dime. You see all kinds of people in those stores from well-dressed to thrift shop queen. Well, I was standing at the wall of shelves cluttered with shampoos etc. and looking for the great bargain when a woman next to me said very loudly, "Sounds like a damn magpie", referring to a Spanish speaking woman a few feet away. "Can't even understand a word she's saying. Sounds like a damn magpie." She kept repeating this over and over, and I got the impression that the sound of the woman's voice was not the main source of anxiety of the thrift shop queen. A few doors down from the store we found a nice looking little restaurant and decided to eat lunch there before we left for home.

The waitress, a woman in her sixties glanced over at us as we entered and then continued talking to a man sitting at the counter. About ten minutes later she sauntered over to our table and said "Ya?" (American for may I take your order) dad decided. She took the orders and walked away. Twenty minutes later she brought the plates of food and left again. We had to ask for cutlery and call her back a third time to ask for our drinks. All this time she never said a word. Not to us at any rate. She was too busy telling another customer and his friend that if it's a half hour before closing she locks the door. "I don't give a damn. And they want nice, they can go somewhere else."

Someday, Hanna. At least I know now that it isn't just me who finds this country a negative depressing place to live now. Mum and dad told me that they wouldn't visit at all anymore if it were not for Grand and I.

"After all, if we want a break from chilly weather we can always go to the Caribbean, Bahamas, south of France and so many other places". Mum said. She figures that the pound's value against the dollar is the reason so many Brits are visiting, but that's her. She can't see the attraction for the place because of the poor service and rude people. No wonder seventy percent of Americans are suffering from acute loneliness according to the latest report by a research group.

Dec. 8, 1998

I just might get this in the mail today. I can now understand why you love writing. I've decided it is excellent therapy. I can vent without being argued with, interrupted, or walked away from, and I know that the reader can always toss it away and me none the wiser. Beautiful. Perhaps all therapists should direct their patients to hand in some written work before each session. And speaking of therapy dad says that I had better get on the ball and make a decision about where I am going to settle, at least for the next couple of years. Away from here he says or I'll be in therapy myself. I'm becoming much too morbid.

Dad told me that England, and perhaps the rest of the world, are having a good laugh re: the Minister Jerry Falwell's remarks about the kids show Teletubbies. Imagine getting paranoid about the color of a cartoon character? Lewis Timberlake writes in Born To Win that a Dr. Adrian once told an audience that God gives light to light. Mr. Timberlake took this to mean that the more you know, the more God lets you know. Conversely, the more you refuse to learn, the darker it gets for you intellectually. I'm afraid that some of the so-called leaders in American society are making us look to the rest of the world like a bunch of cave dwellers.

There are some things I will miss very much when I leave the Keys, not the least of which is the call of the Doves. It is wonderful to wake up to them calling good morning to one another, and then again at night as dark closes in they are particularly active again. I am always up before the sun, and love the silence of the early morning when it's just me and the squirrels and birds awake. The pleasure boats start motoring by before dawn on the weekends during the tourist season and fracture the sounds of nature. By eight on these mornings one has to listen hard for the rustle of palm fronds etc. It's a shame. There does not seem to be much respect for nature in this most beautiful of States. Mum read an article the other day in the Miami Herald about a group of Florida politicians dove hunting north of Tallahassee. How very sad. It would never have occurred to me that anyone would set out to kill even the doves. Perhaps I ought to send these bubbas a poem I came across recently.

Hunter's Letter

Remorse

By

Truman P. Reitmeyer, Philadelphia

A hunter shot at a flock of geese
That flew within his reach.

Two were stopped in their rapid flight
And fell on the sandy beach.

The male bird lay at the water's edge
And just before he died,

He faintly called to his wounded mate
And she dragged herself to his side.

She bent her head and crooned to him
In a way distressed and wild,
Caressing her one and only mate
As a mother would a child.

Then covering him with her broken wing
And gasping with failing breath,

She laid her head against his breast
A feeble honk-then death.

This story is true though crudely told
I was the man in the case.
I stood knee-deep in snow and cold
And the hot tears burned my face.

I buried the birds in the sand where they lay
Wrapped in my hunting coat,
And threw my gun and belt in the bay
When I crossed in the open boat.

Hunters will call me a right poor sport
And scoff at the thing I did.
But that day something broke in my heart,
And shoot again? God forbid!

I cried when I read this. Wish more people could take it to heart. I'll sign off now. We're all going out for dinner. All of us vegetarians. Are you coming down for the holiday?

All for now.

Sincerely, Julie

CHAPTER 7

Dec. 26, 1998

Dear Hanna,

It's boxing day back in Great Britain, Canada too, yet over here it's as though Christmas was not celebrated yesterday, and it must have been rather a Scrooge type affair for many. Mum and dad were amazed to see the garbage men collecting as usual. Those who wish to make an impression re: the unwashed masses tout family values; however, as mum says "Actions speak louder than words."

I'm still at the boutique, though not for much longer. At any rate, it is not the upscale establishment the outrageously high cost of rooms etc. would lead one to believe it is.

I suspect many of the American customers are nouveau riche, or on one of the cheap charter tours, because they are nothing if not rude. Really. They seem to enjoy in trashing the dressing rooms and then sauntering out without a thank you, kiss my ---, whatever. They're more the motel 6 variety than anything else. You know the type. Shorts and attire to board the plane, then drink too much and terrorize the other passengers.

Two women and their husbands came in this morning (clerks' nightmares). They had already checked out and claimed to be in a hurry as they were on their way to the airport. They grabbed and threw things on the counter like two bees in competition to see who could collect the most junk in the shortest period of time. And it is that, Hanna, overpriced junk. They charged round like the contestants in that goofy show – 'Supermarket Sweeps', or whatever it is called. When they did glance at a price I could hear one or the other comment that it had to be quality because it was expensive. Finally one tossed a last item in her pile and said: “Ring it up”. She literally threw the credit card in my direction, and then her friend followed suit.

Believe me I was working away as quickly as was humanly possible when one of the husbands said to his wife, “We don’t need all this stuff. Come on, we’ll be late”. Now wifey actually hollered at me, “Hey I said we were in a hurry, we want quick service and now!” Well, Hanna, the machine had rejected all four of the credit cards she had thrown at me, and I was afraid she’d start frothing at the mouth when she began to screech, “It’s your damned machine. Fix it. I’m not going to stand around waiting on some little clerk”. Well, I told her that I would like to complete the sale as quickly as she would, “So if you’ve no more credit cards to try, perhaps you’d like to pay cash.”

Just then the other witch began to toss cards my way, but horrors, these too were rejected. Now the husbands were livid; they were so angry with their wives. The men dragged some bills out of their pockets and tossed (yes all these people toss) them at me. The women meanwhile, demanded that I “get wrapping”. Then suddenly they grabbed bags and tissue paper out of my hands and stuffing their “junk” into large carry all bags bolted from the store, cursing me because of the credit card rejections.

The quiet and kindly Mexican cleaning lady had watched most of this performance from the relatively safe distance of approximately two yards and half-hidden behind a rack of floor-length beach dresses. “Sorry you treated so bad. I was in Canada last year. You know it’s better. Big difference. Polite, welcoming people. Not like here. Here they don’t care.”

Don’t care for man nor beast some of them. There is a small cat that lives at the hotel, and is cared for by the security chief. She’s fourteen years old, slow and frail, and spends most of her days in the shop under a table that is covered by a cloth that reaches the floor and affords her lots of privacy. Well just after lunch yesterday the young valet hopped into the shop and got down on his hands and knees beside the table. I asked him what he was doing, and the other valet who works the shift with him said: "Oh he likes to tease it".

"I just scare it". So I asked this nut how it was that a twenty something man justified getting his kicks frightening a poor old cat. I grabbed his arm and ordered him out as well. God, he is a mean looking bastard.

Slightly built, thin dirty blonde hair, rigid, taut body movements, ready to explode at any moment. And those small, pastel blue eyes are as cold as the pacific on a winter's day.

The local fishermen held their convention here this week. That was something to behold. However they did make the worst guests look somewhat better. They must have been so excited to be staying at this supposed upscale resort that they forgot to bathe and change clothes. Unshaven, and wearing ragged dirty clothes, filthy sneakers, their greasy dirty hair hanging beneath old ball caps, they spent a good part of the day standing round the courtyard leering at the female guests as they walked past. Very loud, colorful language echoed round the area all day, and the guests that did manage to brave their way past them and into the boutique complained that they would not even consider staying with us again.

Well I've spent my last day there. The only aspect of the job I will miss is the poor little cat. Other than that I feel a sense of great relief.

I'm going to post this and then spend the rest of the afternoon out back by the beach making a list of all the things need for the trip back to England. See you in a few weeks.

Sincerely,

Julie

EPILOGUE

CHAPTER 8

Julie's grandmother Beauchamp had been a nurse in England during the war years. She had met and married her American husband two years before VE day. The young couple moved to the United States when Julie's father was not much more than one year old. Julie's father returned to London, his birthplace, to complete graduate work in psychology, married a British girl shortly after graduation, and never left Britain. Julie, raised in London, moved to Boston to attend university and spend time getting to know her grandmother Beauchamp better. After graduating she therefore moved down to the Keys and lived with her grandmother for almost two years.

Julie told me that she had not expected her grandmother, now almost seventy-five years of age, to return to Britain after so long a time, and therefore no-one was no more surprised than Julie, when arriving home from work one afternoon Mrs. Beauchamp met her at the gate and made her announcement.

Old Mrs. Beauchamp is a quiet lady. She doesn't interfere and maintains she finds it best to "Keep one's own counsel." She had been contemplating the move for years, yet did not want to influence her granddaughter's decision in any way. "Julie, you see, had bought into the myth, as many foreign-born young people do, that America was a place of fun, freedom, and exceptional opportunities. Though sadly, experience has taught us that opportunity became opportunism quite some time ago. I feel it wise however, to allow the young to learn for themselves as much as possible".

"I believe we have become a nation of Job's comforters. In that I mean that the displaced and disenfranchised victims of the corporate welfare state are now being blamed for matters entirely beyond their control. Well, Hanna, I can't hide in the garden any longer and make believe that I am living in a paradise, just because I am able to admire a palm tree from the kitchen window. This is a fool's paradise now. A place where the wealthy take advantage of everyone and everything they possibly can, and the poor are increasingly to crime. Look at Miami and the state it's in. Fraud and white collar crimes of every description have become commonplace, almost expected, the norm. Pathetic really."

"You know that over a three day period this December, eighty three Cubans and twenty three Haitians waded ashore here. In Miami a group of refugees abandoned their old boat and walked into the lobby of an exclusive apartment condo and asked for assistance. I view the U.S. sanctions imposed upon Cuba as nothing more than an opportunity for this country to suck cheap labor out of that impoverished little country. They are starving there, so they scramble over to these shores and end up disposable commodities here. The old fool down the block verbalized what many are thinking when he said that he was happy to have the foreign peons, as he referred to them, over here. "They work cheap anyway, which is good for us," is exactly what he said."

"But how do you explain the fact that many of the Cuban residents here agree with the sanctions?"

"Easy. I recall a passage from Steinbeck's *The Winter Of Our Discontent*. He said that during the nineteenth century we did not see what we couldn't explain, and therefore a great part of the world was abandoned to children, insane people, fools, and mystics-who were more interested in what is than why it is."

"I know that Julie is confused, somewhat, and not sure of the next best course to take. Because of her dual citizenship she can join the Peace Corps, the toughest job you'll ever love they claim. she also wants to make her home in Britain. she wants to help people, give something back she says. I brought this old Chinese tale for her to read. Perhaps it will help her decide on her course for the coming two years. The Corps might give her time to take stock. Most people who join are either in a state of flux, or retired and wanting to feel useful."

This is the story of a woman grieving over a lost son, who went to a holy man to ask what prayers or magical incantations he had to offer to bring her son back to life. Instead of sending her away, or reasoning with her he asked that she fetch him a mustard seed from a home that had never known sorrow. "We will use it to drive the sorrow out of your life." The woman set out in search of the magical mustard seed and came first to a splendid mansion. She knocked at the door and said, "I am looking for a home that has never known sorrow. Is this such a place?" They told her that she had certainly come to the wrong place, and began to describe all the tragedies that had recently befallen them. The woman said to herself, "Who better to help these unfortunate people than I, who have had misfortunes of my own?"

She stayed to comfort them and then carried on in search of a home that had never known sorrow. But wherever she turned, in hovels and in palaces, she found one tale after another of sadness and misfortune. Ultimately, she became so involved in ministering to others that she forgot about her quest for the magical mustard seed, never realizing that it had in fact driven the sorrow out of her life.

Sometimes, Mrs. Beauchamp, the best cure for whatever is troubling one is to put one's attention on another.

"Her dream is to make a difference, and as Thoreau advised, "Go in the direction of your dreams, and live the life you've imagined." Mrs. B. just be happy that she imagines something worthwhile; so many don't. I have found a new direction at age fifty. Yes this time I will not simply be waving Bon Voyage at the airport gate and dreaming of Europe. I am going along. I've found a teaching job with an international school in Greece. If whole new vistas can open up for a fifty year old divorcee, then Julie at twenty eight should not be one bit discouraged for having not yet made her mark on the world yet".

Five days into the new year 1999, and we are saying goodbye to Key Largo for the last time.

Preparing for her long-awaited journey had breathed new life into grandmother Beauchamp. The impending move had acted as an adrenalin and she positively glowed. She seemed suddenly much younger than her seventy plus years, bustling round the big old house from pre-dawn till long after dark, never tiring, setting aside things for charity, sale, the garbage collector, and overseas. As it turned out, very little would leave the States with her. Sentimental keepsakes were packed into an old trunk and shipped ahead. As she had done fifty years earlier, she packed only three bags to carry with her to her final destination.

"Final destination. I'm living proof that we can never be sure what, if anything is to be final."

Grandmother Beauchamp. The petite elderly lady who lived at the beach, and whose trademark appearance was a large straw hat and flowered summer dress, was now transformed. "Dressed to kill, Herb would have said". She looked now every inch the Sophisticated senior, in her fashionable suit and all the right accessories. "All new for the trip you know. I wouldn't be caught dead strolling round Britain in one of my old Keys outfits."

Bon Voyage!

SISTERS AND OTHER STRANGERS

We opened the inn ten years ago today. Mrs. Lemieux, our next door neighbor, peeped in that first day and finding the prospect of having travellers coming and going very exciting, urged me to begin keeping a journal. She is over so often chatting up the guests that I don't think she'll find it necessary to read it. I am certain that Mrs. Lemieux knows as much as I about everyone who has passed through my home in the last decade. The little pub I have added was her idea as well. She thought it would give me more to do and she was right, of course and yes it has kept me from dwelling on the death of my husband Peter.

Peter had been in poor health for some years and it was he who suggested I open the little bed and breakfast I refer to as THE INN. "Something exclusively yours. Your own little enterprise. It will give you extra income and most importantly provide you with a steady stream of people, and lots of conversation."

Many of our guests are from North America, word of mouth providing the best advertisement. I often eat breakfast with my guests and find that the single people especially, enjoy a bit of company. They are often the first down in the morning and this is how I came to know so very much about some of the people who have passed my way.

Quite often as I am clearing the breakfast things away and busying myself about the house, I reflect upon some of their stories. As you will see, the brave faces they presented to the world seldom reflected their true feelings.

My house is fifty miles south of London by train and sits on a quiet street lined with cherry trees in the town of Tunbridge Wells. Built in 1780 the rooms are high ceilinged, the walls paneled with dark mahogany and bookshelves line the walls in the sitting room, filled with volumes as diverse as Thackery and Grisham. A fire crackles in every fireplace during the colder weather and my cat roams the halls welcoming our guests. The first of these was the lady from Florida.

MARY

Mary was thirty nine the winter she came to stay at the inn while looking for a place to live. Slightly built, she had a nervous energy and yet an introspective side to her that seemed to compliment her large, dark and fairly often sad eyes.

"My grandparents were from England" she told me during our first breakfast together. "I was ten years old when I became somewhat obsessed with the idea of living here myself. Circumstance and finance have prevented me from moving over until now however. So thirty years of fantasizing culminated in a few successful novels and finally enough financial backing to do as I please. I've been divorced for ten years now and my son is in university, so you see I'm in effect starting all over.

"You know, we see things more clearly when we decide to make a change, or is it the other way around? Perhaps we make a change because we see things more clearly. At any rate, the disparity between what I had and what I wanted had created a huge hole in my life. Back in the States I used to watch a particular chat show in the evening and one of these confirmed, (though by this time I hardly needed confirmation) that moving toward something else was in my best interest.

"This night the host had decided to answer questions of people chosen at random from the sidewalks of New York. The first question was put to Mr. Host by a well-dressed black man of about thirty years of age and a visitor from England. He asked the host why he thought Americans were hypocritical, materialistic, and superficial. Mr. Host had been railing against these self-same flaws in the American character for some time himself. Yet when the question was asked him he suddenly shouted; "Go back to London". Then he idiotically suggested that the young man could not have an objective opinion because he was from a foreign country. He concluded by jeering at England for its people being "so proper and polite". I decided that had I posed the question to Mr. Host I'd have been thinking by now "well I rest my case". The hair-trigger bigoted response revealed Mr. Host to epitomize that which he professed to despise.

"While waiting to board a plane for Europe I encountered a woman who reminded me of the hypocritical Mr. Host. We began talking and she told me that she lived in England. I told her of my desire to move here and she quickly said: "Europe for the Europeans". This took me by surprise and when I commented that I had spent some time in England and couldn't place her accent, she admitted having only lived here for the past twenty years and was in fact from Quincy Massachusetts. Now she quickly feigned concern over the possible loss of her U.S. passport should she become a British citizen. She represented much of what I disliked about the country I had been living in and I boarded my plane happily. 'I have been a stranger in a strange land' (Exodus 2:22) is the quote that came to mind as I fastened my seat belt".

Mary's little story caused me to reflect upon a few of my own travel experiences. The woman from Texas stood ahead of me in line waiting to board the plane. She turned to glance behind her and I noticed that her face make-up blended with the color of her big hair; bright orange from her jaw line to the top of her head, she effected an almost cartoon type character appearance. And this shade complimented her bright orange pantsuit, which was beaded with large amber and mauve bobbles, This fashion statement was accessorized by garish earrings, the fake jewels every color of the rainbow and so large they all but obliterated her ears. Heavy black false eyelashes and a handbag the size of a carry-on rounded out the look. My eyes moved downward and I discovered very long toe nails, orange of course, peeking out from open-toed spiked heeled sandals, so flimsy she teetered as she stood. Now as she began to move forward she quickly assumed the posture of an elderly woman; her body tilted forward at the waist and toes grasping the soles of her shoes she took a couple of steps before the line came to an abrupt halt. The young woman ahead of her made a comment and they began to talk. Tired and rumpled looking she was travelling with a child of about five years old. She told the orange woman ahead of me that her little girl was thirtieth generation Californian, and expressed great pride. That this claim, if it were true, would have placed her ancestors in the Golden State some six hundred years prior to their meeting, appeared to be lost on the orange woman who accepted the information as delightful news and was effusive with her compliments.

Once on board the plane I found myself seated next to one I thought of as 'manic man', a large man with a thick head of greying hair and well dressed in casual shirt and slacks. He looked neither right nor left, but alternated between chewing ice cubes and life savers for the duration of the trip. When offered refreshment by the flight attendant he peeked over the rims of his half glasses, and mumbled an answer. He never quit moving as he popped something into his mouth and attacked crossword puzzles one after the other with a voracity and nervous tension reminiscent of a class of college students, anxiously working their way through sets of true or false questions for a final exam. I hoped only that his puzzles would last as long as the flight, as a mother hopes to keep a child occupied with a coloring book and so prevent him from bouncing round a restaurant.

Across the aisle in the window seat an executive occupied himself with his laptop computer. He was a black man of about forty and next to him sat a Caucasian man of about the same age. Rather poorly dressed he turned his back toward the man in the window isle and amused himself by making disparaging remarks to his son of about nine years, while rolling his eyes and smirking. It appeared that no-one within his range of vision met with his approval and the man seated to his left was no exception as his body language spoke volumes.

I changed planes in New York and was soon on my way to London. A young American serviceman occupied the window seat to my right. He told me that he was from Arkansas and returning to England to complete his last assignment there. He marveled at the medical system in Britain with coverage for all and said that his main reason for joining the military had been the medical benefits for he now had a wife and child to consider. I expressed concern for the forty plus million Americans without health coverage and was shocked as he turned quickly toward me and viciously accused me of having a socialist attitude. "You want everybody to be the same" were his exact words. I shall never forget the contorted red and angry face. There was silence until the captain informed the passengers that we were flying over a part of Canada. The young man began to laugh derisively and said: "Oh wow, Canada". I asked if he had had a bad experience there and he responded: "No, never bin there, don't know nothin' bout it."

I imagine he considered himself patriotic. I wondered how many fools of his caliber represented the United States abroad.

Making my way through Gatwick Airport to board the train home I noted the change in atmosphere between the two countries. Tourists commented on the polite and efficient service they received from the airport staff and conductors stood on the platforms and visited with passengers waiting to make connections at the various stops along the rail line.

As I struggled with a large suitcase between trains a voice from behind me said: "Here, let me help you" and a lady of about forty wearing a beautiful sari stepped forward and together we carried my case to the car. Then as I attempted to board the next train a young man appeared out of nowhere, smiled, took my case from me, boarded the train with me and having settled me in my seat wished me a good trip and returned to the platform. Yes, people were much more relaxed here, certainly less impatient and hostile and consequently happier it appeared with themselves and others. And so you see my experiences allowed me to understand Mary.

One evening Mary and Mrs. Lemieux accompanied me to the neighborhood pub. I close my own early two nights a week and enjoy a bit of free time. We hadn't even had a chance to order our drinks when I was approached by a man and his wife looking for a room. The barman had told them about my little place. They were only too happy to sit with us and begin a conversation. They carried one small bag each and spent the first ten minutes of the evening extolling the virtues of travelling light. They made it clear to everyone within shouting distance that they had travelled as far as Italy on a prior occasion and were more than happy to offer advice to any who wished it.

He had been in the lumber business and she a retired elementary school teacher. Both were from the Canadian northwest and both were thoroughly obnoxious in their pushy behavior and yet pathetic in their need to be accepted as one of our group, which would have been easily forthcoming had they not appeared to be such braggarts. On the face of it they were a totally mismatched couple. However, once we became acquainted it became apparent that they could not have been more alike in their need for approval, and their penchant for trying to be the center of attention. Though neither had achieved particular public stature they put on quite a show of self-importance, perhaps predictably so. Their conversation was peppered with allusions to what they might have, or had almost achieved, if only. Each claimed great talent in their individual areas of alleged expertise. If only.

One morning at breakfast our lumberman announced to my unusually large group of assembled guests that he could have been the world's greatest singer and was in fact far better than any he had ever heard. This declaration was met with a stunned and embarrassed silence and a painful look of embarrassment from his wife. For her part she claimed to have risen in the teaching profession only as far as assistant school principal, but blamed short-sighted supervisors for her failure to excel past that point. It would have been appropriate for her to have said nothing of her life's disappointments; however as was the case with her husband, she appeared to be asking complete strangers to confirm her worth by accepting her claims at face value.

Now and then her husband would interject with the admonition; "You listen to her now". Her knowledge of Britain was delivered in a monotone, so rehearsed that one may have closed one's eyes and believed they were listening to her read from a text book on the subject. She went so far as to advise the other guests (in an authoritative voice) on points of interest, some of whom had lived here all of their lives. "She really knows her stuff" he said.

As one of my permanent guests, a retired professor later commented: "They have a neediness to be someone important. The wife's diatribes could best be described as pedantic and of course rehearsed and her husband sits so physically tense, and pre-occupied with what he is going to say at the first opportunity. Neither were the least bit interested in either each other or anyone else, of course."

His wife found his ability to force the focus of the groups attention upon himself disconcerting and in retaliation took it upon herself to tell him to be quiet, "While I retell this story accurately" she said. They had wanted to leave an impression and this much they did accomplish. The morning of their departure she pointed her index finger at everyone at the breakfast table and admonished all to be sure to visit them should any of us ever pass their way.

The pathetic couple, (for that is really how they appeared to us) clearly saw themselves as sophisticated world travellers. Although on closer inspection a two week guided tour and a two week trip on a budget that allowed for very few creature comforts belied that claim. The sub-standard accommodations they told us of, they rated as different because it was European, rather than cheap, demonstrated their novice approach to travel and a limited understanding of where they were.

Two months after this couple left, a lady and her friend arrived who told me that I had been recommended to them by the world travellers. One of the women, recently widowed, was tiny in stature and melancholic. Her husband had retired fifteen years prior to his death and refusing to travel he did no more than fish and watch old western movies. A professional couch potato is the way they described him. He ate too much and what with not getting any exercise destroyed his health.

Emily was her name and her friend told me about her. Anna said that Emily's husband had been a controlling man and true to that character trait he was very uncomfortable when not on his home turf. Emily never travelled without him but had attempted to content herself with magazines and stories of her friend's adventures. A lonely hard working woman, a nurse's aide, she had allowed Dean to convince her that she would be lost without him. She did not drive and toward the end of his life became anxious in crowds when alone. Although he appeared to be the strong silent hero to those who did not know him well, I believed that he was more dependent upon her than the other way round.

I stood talking with her in her kitchen one afternoon when suddenly he appeared in the door way and said abruptly; "Where's lunch? Don't we eat today because you have company?" She literally jumped toward the fridge and began to put a meal together. Under her breath and shaking a bit she said: "Oh, I feel so angry and frustrated and don't know what to do about it." I suggested she tell him off and tearfully she told me that she would pay later if she did. "I don't drive; he thinks it's best I don't because I get nervous. And what if I needed a ride to visit my friend on the farm? No I can't say anything."

"Breaks your heart, doesn't it? Later that evening as Emily and I sat at the dining room table talking quietly after dinner, she pointed into the living room where her family were all sitting glued to the television set and said sadly: "You see that? Well this is my life here. I sit here every night alone and they sit in there. And I wonder if there shouldn't be more to my life. I look at them and I think, well this is it, I may as well be invisible, and feel so lonely I want to cry. Unless of course one of them asks me to do something for them. Well as I listened I thought of the words to an old French song, something like (love is a child of liberty) and you know there was no liberty here."

"You can see her need to escape into magazines. Even dinner was a dehumanizing experience. He and the children in their late teens and early twenties would stand up and walk away after the meal was over. Never a thank you or excuse me, nothing. Dining out was the same thing. When he had finished eating he would stand, walk to the cashier, pay, and then continue out the door. It was unbelievable, really it was."

"I knew a man like that" I told Anna as I poured us a second cup of tea "I'll tell you about him and perhaps the story will instill some hope for you as regards your friend. He was the husband of an old school mate. Never left home until he was thirty-three years old. It's the same scenario. He held a position of control, although he was a college professor rather than a police officer. He sat around expecting to be waited upon when at home, and his hobby involved the sitting position as well. Poker was his choice when he decided to relax, which was often. Friday night, Saturday, and into the wee hours of Sunday morning. Then he slept all day Sunday in preparation for Monday morning, where, upon entering the college he was transformed into (as you so aptly put it, Anna) the strong silent type. No-one there knew of his temper tantrums, or the abuse his wife suffered and his colleagues regarded her as being somewhat beneath him. She was anxious, and unhappy looking and he often told her that he had made a mistake by marrying someone so far beneath him educationally. That is exactly how he said it.

"That he gambled much of his pay and it was left to her to deal with the creditors and make sure the children had food to eat, no-one was the wiser. Their four sons grew to be as selfish, violent, ill-mannered and yes, as charming socially as he. As you might imagine my friend was, after twenty years of marriage to this man quite beside herself and too frightened to move. Then one day a miracle happened. Laura's sister sent her a plane ticket for her birthday and told her she would meet her in Paris; they were taking a trip. For once in her life she found the strength to do for herself and to make a long story short, when she returned two months later she filed for divorce. She told me that she realized that it had been he who was weak and dependent. She had managed just fine and in foreign countries where she did not know the language. She met someone more successful than her former husband could ever hope to be and he treats her with respect. She has not looked back these ten plus years. So you see there is always hope and with a friend to encourage one things turn themselves round, or rather we turn ourselves round just that much sooner".

When I opened the inn I was amazed at the number of people who told me their stories. My friend Mrs. Lemieux says they know they may not pass this way again and it's sort of like meeting someone on a train. They talk together, happy to have someone to listen to them and secure in their knowledge that no-one in their inner circle will be any the wiser. It is a sort of therapy I guess and a comfort to me to know that I have been able to help a bit. Granted some of my guests refer people to me but they must not care about their stories being repeated or trust me very much. And then I don't say much other than to use a story as a positive example for someone in distress. No real names mentioned of course.

There was one lady who told me a story I thought worthy of a novel and I told her as much. She was here a year ago and has moved to Scotland. We keep in touch and with her permission I am including her story in my journal. I will call her Hanna, not her real name. She arrived here from New York and these are her words as near as I can remember.

Hanna

Goat's Landing is the name the town was known by, not it's real name, but the locals had dubbed it so in honor of the town character. He must have been over ninety, though no one was sure of his exact age. No-one was sure where he had come from either, just as they could not recall the town without him as a fixture there.

He did not confide in people. Indeed he barely mumbled hello if spoken to and was given the name Goat because of his long white hair and goatee; his personal hygiene left much to be desired as well, so it was as well that he did not encourage friendships. Nobody was really brave enough to come within a few feet of his person.

He lived in an old houseboat patched together with pieces of tin and discarded sheets of wood and it never left its berth at the far end of the dock in the village on the Gulf of Mexico. He spent his days riding an old bicycle around town collecting bottles, cans and his last stop was the processing plants. Here he gathered the discarded fish heads and tripe to feed to the town's stray cats.

Twice a day, morning and night, he set their meal out and the parade of cats could be seen making their way to the dock at the appointed time. They had become as much a fixture as the old man and somewhat of a tourist attraction.

I had moved there from New York City to work for a semi-retired financial analyst. I was his driver, laundress, cook, all round Girl Friday when he was there. I was his house sitter and travel companion when he decided to take a trip. I took the job so that I could devote my free time to writing. At the time it seemed a good idea you know. I had a house to myself without the burden of rent and all that sort of thing; however I paid dearly in other ways. I received a small stipend for my efforts and though the relationship was purely platonic the town's people assumed that I was his wife.

Having travelled throughout the south and read extensively regarding the culture there I believed I was prepared for the experience, a foolish assumption on my part. Goats Landing was an aberration. Its inhabitants proud of the fact that it was twenty five years at the very least behind its southern neighbors on every level.

The town straddled highway 98 and if you had blinked twice while driving through you would have missed it entirely. On either side of the highway sat weathered, abandoned buildings in danger of collapsing. Structures in this state of disrepair could be found throughout the town that branched out from the highway, and wound its way through dirt roads for the most part. Travel and single wide trailers, rusted and surrounded by piles of garbage shared the landscape with cracker houses that had not seen a coat of paint since they were built, if then. These places looked uninhabitable, though they were called home by most of the town's people.

There was not even a playground for the children who, for the most part entertained themselves by hanging round the IGA store on Saturday nights in particular, smoking, and waiting for older friends to purchase cheap beer.

I lived in a house at the beach accessed by a service road. I had no neighbors and often walked the thirty minute round trip to the post office to collect my mail each day. As often as not as I approached the main road there, seated under a tree, bicycles leaning against the old magnolia were the local drug dealers awaiting their customers. Dressed in filthy rags, their greasy long hair accessorized with a ball cap they watched and waited. Should a car slow to make the turn onto the main road they leapt from their haunches, hoping that it was a customer. They were a disgusting lot and although everyone was aware of the business they were in they were never bothered by the local police who seemed much too busy parked beside the local post office, their attention concentrated on catching a traveller passing through town. Chatting up the corner garage owners who appeared to have nothing more to do than sit outside the station on old crates watching the traffic roll past, was another favorite pastime.

Most of the locals found it odd that we did not fish and more odd still that one of my hobbies was reading; in fact some did not hide their amusement but laughed out loud at the prospect. But then the illiteracy rate there was 43%.

The postmaster was a round, bald, bespeckled man of about sixty years of age, and extremely hostile. Later on I would discover that these people appeared to be some ten-fifteen years older than their actual ages. Mr. Rebuff I'll call him, never could bring himself to do more than quote an amount to either the boss or I. Should either one of us ask him a question it was met with an irritated look and absolutely no reply.

Having been overcharged twice the boss came home one afternoon and complained to me. I called the Regional Head Office in Jacksonville and spoke with a supervisor. They asked for my name assuring me that it would be kept confidential; however they had to have it in order to register my complaint. After all Old Rebuff was an antagonistic fixture and had told the boss the first time he entered the post office that he hated the town and everyone in it. His sidekick, a woman with long dirty grey hair and dressed like a farm hand offered that she had lived in Goats Landing all of her life and did not like foreigners either. You may be aware that anyone not a southerner is considered a foreigner, even the boss who was American born and raised and retired military as well as wall street capitalist.

One week after I made my complaint Mr. Rebuff called to tell me that he had been advised of it and that he had an explanation for his behavior. Simply put: "I don know ya'll so it ain't my fault how I treat you people; cain't expect to be treated otherwise, you be'n a stranger and all."

Those basic character traits of integrity and responsibility were lacking, which put him in step with the very people he professed to hate. But then it is said that most people are more frightened of being an outcast than of death. Therefore I now considered him to be no more than a scared sheep. Pathetic way to live one's life is it not?

The town held a festival yearly to celebrate its identity as a fishing village and the boss decided that we should go and get to know the locals. We walked over to what might be laughingly called the downtown area and were immediately approached by a man and his wife who each carried a cardboard container containing shrimp in one side and cocktail sauce in the other. His wife shoved her container under my nose and demanded I try some. I picked one of the shrimp up and when I attempted to squeeze it from its shell discovered that it was raw and consequently tight in the shell. Now the fisherman grabbed it from me and with filthy hands and long fingernails encrusted with dirt struggled to work the meat loose, with no success naturally. His wife quickly snatched it from him and breaking the shell into half a dozen pieces handed me the, by this time battered and mangled morsel with the comment: "Well ya'll are from the north. Ah kin tell by the way ya'll talk. Ya don know how to eat ya'll." I commented that the shrimp was obviously raw, and they looked at me in disgust and walked away.

We carried on and finding a vendor selling used books I stopped. The seller, a stout little middle aged woman wearing a faded tee-shirt approached me instantly and said in a loud voice: "Ya'll better buy some to support the library". Yes, I said I hoped to find something. "Well they're all good; take 10" she said. Now as unbelievable as this sounds I found six books and when I held my money out to her she grabbed the bill from my hand and said, loudly of course, "Well ya'll better let me keep the change". I did let her keep the change too. I was kind of stunned by everything and only wanted to get away. We did quite a bit of walking that day and after leaving the stalls ended up outside a convenience store. A white pick-up was parked at the edge of the lot and in it sat an unshaven man with the standard long dirty hair and regulation ball cap. Beside him sat a stoic disheveled young woman staring straight ahead. As the hound in the bed of the truck barked its head off, the man devoured pieces of chicken one after another so quickly one might have assumed he hadn't eaten in a week, although his fat round face belied that assumption. I watched as he systematically worked his way through the box of fried chicken, tossing the bones out of his window as he worked his way through, then apparently satisfied he disposed of the container the same way he had disposed of the bones, and wiping his greasy mouth on the back of his hand slammed his foot on the gas pedal and drove off.

Well, I thought to myself, it is amazing the number of gross things one can see in only an hour in this place. But the day was not over. We stopped into the IGA supermarket, and searching one of the isles I overheard a conversation between an old man and the store manager. The older man asked if there was any dog food cheaper than what he saw on the shelves and when the answer was no, he said "Well, I guess ma dog will survive somehow". A young couple walked by and the older man stopped them to talk. The young man asked him if he were still cutting lawns and the answer was: "Ya sure, but I done cut two this week, so the old girl who lives three mile out will have to wait till next week". Now he proceeded to follow the couple down the aisle and round the store complaining of what he called his money problem.

"You have a sit down mower" the younger man said.

The old one replied; "Ya but I don wanna spend all that much time ont it."

Walking home I recalled a quote of Mark Twain's "I have been through some terrible things in my life some of which actually happened." And while he meant that most of what we fear does not come to pass, some of life's nastier day to day experiences had been felt all in one day. The boss didn't appear to find anything about these people particularly unusual. This may tell you something about the boss and I would find out more than I really cared to know before I left.

Our first night there we went to buy groceries and as I loaded the car he began talking to a man in the parking lot. The man stood there in his camouflage shirt, long greasy hair, ball cap, looking like most of the others I had seen, beside his pick-up truck, dog in the back and told Dale about the previous owners of the house we had just moved into. "Well ya'll, they always had a bunch of niggers around, lettin' 'em fish off a their dock an all." I was mortified, really I was. Yet the boss just laughed and said: "Well, he was a nice friendly guy anyway". He began playing poker with a group of locals soon after, very proud of his ability to make friends so quickly. Their use of that awful word and their ignorance and filth did not seem to bother him and he told me, laughing, that they ate pork chops smothered in gravy with their fingers the way one picks up a chicken leg. They dipped their bread in their chilli and joked about LETTING their wives go on a shopping spree at the Wal-Mart in the city as long as they did not complain about their gambling. As one said: "Beer, fishin' and gamblin'; that's all worth doin." The man that ran one of the poker games bragged about hiring poor blacks to work his peanut farm. "Ya don have to pay them niggers like ya would a white". Gross sub-human creatures these, but the boss said they were nice to him and apparently that was all that mattered to him.

I told him that it was a mistake to believe that niceness was synonymous with goodness. He laughed it off saying; "It isn't my business as long as they're nice to me".

Time passed and I wrote and kept to myself. Then one day a bank teller and the only friendly civilized person I had met asked me what I did with my time. I told her that I had come here to write and she said; "Oh I could never do that; I'm too logical." She was a nice lady however and told me once that she had been thinking, "people, when they get to our time of life should do something they want to do. There are no pockets in shrouds." She had lived day by day for the past twenty years she said. And she knew that because she was not from the town originally, though a southerner, still she would never be accepted as one of them. And she had married a local.

Most of the people here lived in abject Poverty and the lotto machine at the convenience store was never idle. One day it was so busy I left the store rather than wait; the machine was spitting out tickets so quickly and non-stop for so long I was surprised that it did not explode; ragtag people with neglected little bare-footed children in tow spending what ought to have gone for groceries on a dream. One woman who had been ahead of me at the market and had just used food stamps to purchase a few groceries had decided to leave her change here.

The parking lot of the market was always littered with paper, bottles and cans, the interior not much cleaner. Soda pop dried to the linoleum, broken eggs, their yolks left to dry on the dairy shelf, spoiled fruit tumbled to the floor and was walked through and boxes blocked the isles. A display crashed to the floor only seconds after I had pushed my cart past it. The young assistant manager laughed heartily, shrugged and with the toe of his dirty sneaker pushed some of the articles aside, making no attempt to clean up, much less apologize. An older cashier asked him if he was going to; "Tell her you're sorry". His reply was, "Who cares?". The cashiers usually stood with their backs facing away from approaching customers, but more often than not could be found grouped around one station gossiping. When a customer approached the gossip continued, the chatter broken by the question, paper or plastic? Grubby faded smocks partially covered worn tee-shirts and jeans. The hair was most often dirty, their faces masks that never responded to good morning or hello. The last time I went in the cashier refused to even quote the total, but pointed to the register instead. It was a common occurrence to pass through the store and pay without ever having exchanged a word. The only voice I heard was mine as I continued with my greetings.

Well, on this last visit I found myself standing at the counter looking at the three gallons of milk and two quarts of cream had just purchased until the clerk finally asked; "Do you want a bag?"

One morning I picked up the paper and was shocked to find an article about this horrible little town, front page item too. Apparently a couple who had moved to town about two years prior and had bought a deserted pub and refurbished it, were in big trouble. Their offense had been to hire two male strippers to perform the previous evening. However before the show was to commence one hundred of the locals (self-proclaimed god fearing Christians) had assembled for a meeting and invited the proprietors to be the guests of honor. The group's leader, a rotund woman of about sixty asked the pub owners, "How long you bin here?" Two years was the reply. Then with eyes narrowed to mere slits the Christian woman asked; "Ya'll wanna stay?" She told a reporter that the town was too wholesome and god-fearing for anyone to want to see the show, then demanded the local police prevent the men from performing for fear they would contaminate the audience. This now is as accurate an example of local logic as anyone will find. Though there was no local law prohibiting the entertainment and the pub was full of people waiting for the show to begin, the sheriff and his mugs sent the performers on their way.

The article ended with the group's leader quoted as saying that she considered this blemish on the face of humanity (a Mayberry). She claimed never to lock her door at night and left her car keys in the ignition and the car unlocked.

Our house had been broken into one month after we moved in and when Dale tracked a policeman down to report the crime the officer did not even take notes. Weeks later when Dale asked said officer if he had any new information the answer was; "Oh nothin to worry bout, we have some kids who do a little break an enter but we know who they are". End of story. Drug raids were carried out there and at election time the Bubba's focus was on crime prevention and cleaning up the town if elected as the next sheriff. Sort of belied the Mayberry angle did it not?

Only one person interviewed for the article had the courage to recognize the town for what it was. "Hypocrites; why don't they spend their time tackling the real problems of teen drug abuse, an epidemic in this town. Mayberry? No. All this makes me sick. They're just a bunch of hypocrites."

Yes, hypocrites and the smugly ignorant. This was a hiding place for those who worshiped conformity and found denial easier than facing real issues of importance. They are not unique however; the good Christian Baptists of a Havana Georgia church demonstrated their beliefs when they requested the exhumation of a young couple's mixed race baby from the church graveyard. After all, the poor little soul had been born half black.

Not long into my stay a woman who lived down the road called and asked me how I liked living there. I told her it was a fine place to write. Then she asked me how long I planned to stay and did I attend church. I said no and she said "Well everyone goes to church; it's all there is to do". As for how long I planned to stay I told her I'd let her know. As for church, well, I thought to myself I have the most beautiful church. I look out of my window and enjoy some of the most beautiful nature in the world. I say my own private prayers, a nice conversation with the one who created all of this and I'm satisfied. I don't need to rub shoulders with the bigots and the hypocrites to show my appreciation.

Dale decided one day that the time had arrived for him to admit he needed a hearing aid. The salesman visiting the neighboring town sent him to a clinic there to have his ears flushed. A seemingly simple procedure and they assured him that they had the equipment. Well, into the clinic he walked and was ushered into the examining room. His blood pressure and weight was taken, his heart listened to, and finally the ear flushing equipment was produced. Voila! A Q-Tip. Yes, this was the deep cleaning mechanism that would allow the extremely small hearing aid to be fitted. This doctor missed the class that admonished, (never put anything smaller than your elbow in your ear) and charged fifty five dollars for his expertise.

They must have been used to people not paying attention and placed everyone at the same level of pathetic ignorance. Unfortunately Dale did nothing to dispel their assumption. The medical system there is a money-making venture and Dale's insurance did not cover any of this, not that it was proper procedure. Have you ever known anyone to submit to a blood pressure, weight check etc. in order to have their ear cleaned with a Q-Tip?

Of course I did witness an instance where the doctor should have been listened to, but ignorance again intervened. A young woman stood outside a convenience store while the male she was with made a call on the pay phone. An elderly local walked up to her and asked her how her child (a girl of about two years old seated in a broken-down stroller) and caked with dirt was doing. "Oh, she's okay I guess. Doctor says her throat's infected and I should take her bottle away". Just then the child dropped the bottle to the ground, retrieved it and stuck the nipple back into her mouth. "Don't you pay no mind to them doctors. They don't know nothing" the old man said.

Finding health insurance was as irritating an experience as most other business transactions here. The first agent I called claimed there was a doctors network in the area and that I would have to choose a doctor from a preferred list; managed care they call it. He refused to make an office appointment for me to sign the papers and told me he would come by my house to collect my cheque etc. He never did materialize and when I called his office and left a message it was ignored. I called another agent, this time in the city.

"Oh yes" he told me. "Your insurance kicks in the moment you get your blood test, which I can arrange for inside of the next two weeks. We arrange for a technician to come to your home; now that's service right?" Well I drove to the city, paid the man with a check and never heard from him again. Months and numerous calls later I called the issuer and asked they cancel my application and return the money. They advised me that they did not send technicians round to take tests, did not even require physicals in some cases and it took sixty to ninety day before one was covered after signing with them.

They like to check your medical history, you know, to make certain that you are not in need of treatment before they will agree to cover you. A pre-existing condition prohibits you from obtaining insurance in most cases. Well finally I found another agent, paid and then was asked to fill out the forms. I had to spell Vancouver for the agent, that being my place of birth.

Then an argument ensued. Simply put, the woman had a problem understanding that one quarter paid yearly meant every three months; she insisted it meant every four months. She was absolutely certain that one quarter meant that she should divide three into a twelve month period. With the assistance of her supervisor the matter was finally settled. It was now time to close the transaction. "Goin out a the country anywheres in the next six months?"

"Belize".

"How'd ya'll spell that?"

I spelled the word and ask why it was necessary to ask.

"Well ya'll, if ya were goin to a dangerous place, then you won't be covered. Belize ain't in no war or anythin, is it?"

I think you get the picture.

As it turned out it was possible to purchase insurance without it being a managed care program, thereby choosing one's own doctor. There was no such thing as a policy that covered one for regular medical checkups and should one become involved in an accident one had better pray that it does not take the paramedics too long to decide which hospital to take you to. After all it has to be willing to accept your policy. The deductible ranges anywhere from five hundred dollars on up and coverage insures you for eighty to ninety percent of care. A person would not want to be hurt too badly; it is not uncommon for homes to be lost and bank accounts to be wiped out because of medical costs.

Our vehicle was no more secure than our persons. When I took the car in to have the air conditioning repaired the first two garages told me to trade the car in. "It's five years old anyway"' said one. I did find a man who replaced the water pump but as it turned out that was not the problem and it did not get repaired properly until I took a trip to New York.

Apart from the infamous American road rage to be concerned with I could never understand why the drivers in this part of the country had an aversion to using signal lights. Ignoring the fact that this is just common courtesy (and courtesy was easily and readily ignored here) the practice prevents accidents. Dale followed a pickup truck out of a parking lot one afternoon and in accordance with local practice the driver of the other car slammed on his brakes without signaling. Yes, brake then signal is the custom if they signal at all. Anyway, it was very minor and did not warrant a police call but the man insisted, and pointing to a faded grey tee-shirt with the word 'rescue' printed across the front said: "Look, I know what I'm sayin. It's what I do for a livin." We called and the man in the faded shirt sat in his truck and waited with his dog, his gun mounted in the rear window and now and again adjusted his requisite ball cap. Finally the police arrived and we exchanged information. Whatever he had done for a living was a memory according to the information because he was unemployed. His truck had Georgia plates and he was a Florida resident. Naturally Dale had to pay for the accident, though it was caused by the other man. Apparently there is a lot of that sort of thing going on there.

Dale never did recognize the behavior of the locals as but a microcosm of what was happening in the whole of American society. He did not seem to care at any rate about anything that did not affect him directly and materially. His homes were over-decorated to say the least and every picture framed had not one image of another human being with the exception of himself. Now the exception to this was the collages he had assembled and hung, of all places, in his bathrooms over the toilets. It looked like a sort of trophy collection. All were of past wives and girlfriends.

He used to tell me that only peons concern themselves with the disadvantaged and that his time was infinitely more valuable than that. I asked him if he believed his life to be of more value than others. "That's one way of putting it" he said. "Don't tell me about judging people by their characters rather than their pocketbooks. Obviously the person with the most money is more important in society than the rest. We're less expendable. The man with the money gets respect, he makes the rules."

I've always believed that those who did not respect themselves did not respect others. How very sad that his opinion of himself hinged only on what he owned.

I did not see much to indicate the people here respected themselves. Not only was this indicated by the extent to which they neglected themselves, but in the way they treated others and their environment. Roadside garbage was just part of the landscape. Liquor bottles, cans, even bags of household garbage were tossed alongside the roads and onto people's front yards. Old young and in between simply opened the vehicle window and let fly with whatever they wanted to get rid of. One beautiful day as I drove along the shore admiring the view and wondering why those who lived here did not appear to appreciate it enough to want to care for it, a van came speeding along in the opposite direction and just as it was about to pass me the driver opened his window and let fly with a large bag. It hit my car, slid underneath and split. This I saw through my rear view mirror and just as I directed my attention to the road ahead once more, a pick-up passed me and as soon as it pulled in ahead of me paper cups came flying out of each window. Some days were like that.

The irony was that, while the locals were hostile to foreigners moving in and (changing the place) they seemed bent on changing it permanently by destroying it through neglect. Individualistic to a fault was how I felt about the people here and consequently selfish.

Dale said ornery, but he liked ornery people. "My favorite of all my girlfriends and wives was the ornery one. She'd get a cat and then get rid of it because I paid more attention to it than to her. I got a kick out of that. I wasn't raised that way. Dad was a good neighbor; he was so good it made me sick. Mom was a church-going woman. She even made friends with refugees and helped them. Very proper. I've dated different kinds but never would marry one. Jews are after the money and Asians figure they're smarter than us. I like Mexicans though; as tenants they're great. They all pull together and always come up with the rent and they work cheap if you want anything done. They're so poor they feel lucky to get anything so you don't have to give them much".

I asked him which, of all the different church denominations his parents had introduced him to he identified most with. "It didn't make any difference. It's like anything else; you take what you want at the time and if you get tired of it you move on to something else".

On the subject of education he said quite often that it was of no use unless it would earn real money. "It's a waste of money to educate someone otherwise." Each time the stock market rose it appeared to me that it was the result of massive lay-offs. "Someone has to lose and it isn't going to be the smart ones. The stupids are where they're supposed to be". This reminded me of a Henry Ward Beecher quote: "God has intended the little to be little, and the great to be great."

"Tom Wolfe was right" I said: "You brokers really do see yourselves as captains of the universe."

"Well it isn't the do-gooders and the peons that keep things going."

"But it is" I said. "Without the volunteers and all the charities and churches, society would be in a worse mess than it is now".

You know that by the time this conversation had taken place I felt as though I was living on another planet. The end came shortly after the poor little cat he had given me to care for had a litter of six kittens.

As Hanna began to tell me the story of the kittens I saw that she looked particularly sad. She turned her face away for a second, sighed and she would tell me later it felt that a weight had been lifted from her in the telling.

Dale told me that I was welcome to keep one and placing the others I kept the smallest kitten. He looked exactly like his mother, pure black with a bit of white fur under his chin. Like his mum he was timid and until I had earned his trust backed away from me as he had everyone else. Dale found it offensive; he said that the poor little thing was afraid of him. Well Max was a bit slow to take to the kitty litter too and I had been afraid that he would be abandoned by someone with not enough patience and so I kept him thinking that I was rescuing him. I had taken the others to the city and given them to a pet store thinking that anyone who was willing to search out and pay for one would surely care for it.

Once little Max turned nine weeks old I left for one week to visit my son. Well, Dale picked me up at the airport and we were not out of the terminal before he blurted out: "Your Max is no longer a member of my household. All he wanted was his mamma. Wouldn't sit on my knee, or let me pat him and me feeding the thing too. I don't want it around. A pet, or anything else, is there for pleasure or to be of use and that thing was neither so I got rid of it."

He told me that he had given him to the pet store but weeks later when I asked him to drop something at the charity across from the store he said: "I don't know where that is".

He had once commented that he thought Max was better suited to be an outdoor cat and when I remembered this I felt horrible. One morning not long after this I took a roll of film to be developed to the store in the town where I now did my shopping. It was a forty-five minute drive from where I lived. When I returned to collect my pictures the young clerk said; "You know, it's really weird. I found a little kitten in my yard about a month ago that looked just like the one in your pictures. Exactly like it, white hair under the chin and everything". For an instant I felt happy thinking that the poor little thing had been rescued. My heart sank as she continued however. "Yes, I wanted to keep him but he was too sick and I have a baby at home, so the vet said he shouldn't be around the baby and we took him into the animal shelter. I called a week later but the woman at the shelter said, when I asked her if he had been adopted; "Do you really want to know?"

I confronted Dale when I went home and of course I was crying. How could anyone throw a helpless animal like that by the side of the road?

"Have you no empathy for anyone or anything?" I asked and he raised himself from his chair and walked across the room without a word toward the table on which sat a large Dictionary and when I asked what he was doing he told me that he was going to look up the word.

Poor little Max. He'd been a happy little thing. I could hear his purr from across the room when mamma washed his little face. He'd try to climb my pant leg and when I set him on my lap he purred himself to sleep. At night he climbed up and under the bedspread finally making it as far as the bend in my arm and sleep. He swung from the tea towel and the baskets of artificial plants Dale had hung around the house and well, he was so full of life.

We were invited to the home of Dale's poker playing pal for thanksgiving. It would be my last there. His wife was the family anchor, her husband not having worked as a fisherman for over two years. She managed one of the convenience stores in town and as often as not left the house for work just as her husband was returning home in the wee hours of the morning. "I was darned near the only woman in town who knew what a pair of shoes were when we got here ten years ago. I was absolutely the only woman wearing make-up or doing my hair. Ya, they'd look at me as though I had two heads. Took about three years before anybody had much to do with me."

Now a lifetime Goats Landing resident spoke up. "Well, ya'll don't git it. It's not like we ain't frienly. We jus don bother with no outsiders. We sure never, never, would have one of 'em inside our house. No way".

As she babbled away working to justify her Ignorance, the image of a lady I had struck up a conversation with in London a few years earlier came to mind. I had asked her for directions to the market square and after about ten minutes of visiting she asked me if I would like to visit her for tea. "I'm off to visit my sister for a few days" she told me, picking up her overnight bag. "But when I return perhaps you'll come round to visit".

The self-proclaimed friendly woman's voice broke into my thoughts with: "Well, I'll tell ya what's wrong with Goats Landing. It's the way it's startin ta grow. There's two new buildins goin up on the water front, and they're tearin down the old ones. Don't look the same".

Our hostess said: "Well, there's nothin for the young here. Nothin, nowhere ta work and jus nothin for 'em ta do, play, nothin. Nothin but git inta trouble. So maybe we need somethin ta put life inta the place. What's gonna happen otherwise? What, If no new people come in? It's dyin quick, what with the net ban an all, an there's nothin for us here let alone tourists. All they do is stop for gas if we're lucky".

The ban had made a certain type of net called a gill net illegal to use. Apparently it took everything in its wake and some species of fish had been overfished for years. Some men cheated however, by venturing out in the wee hours between midnight and day break fishing under cover of dark. So while the locals complained about the fishing industry drying up they continued to contribute to its demise. A man could go out and return with seventy pounds of fish. They were desperate to survive however and most could do nothing else to earn a living.

The handyman who had worked round the house a bit had asked to leave his little boat at our dock. He said he was afraid of "people messing with it." Then one morning I looked out and watched as two men dragged the little boat away from the dock. The tide was out so far that one could have walked to the island a mile away. Well the boat sat on the mud and the men got into the boat, drank a can of pop, and after throwing their cans over the side stood up and grabbing a long pole attempted to move the boat. It was the most ridiculous thing I had ever seen and proof that life was indeed stranger than fiction. The owner of the boat later told me that the men were his kin. "I told 'em they could borrow the boat and thought they could catch some fish for dinner. Thought I was doin 'em a favor. Sure thought they'd wait till the tide came back before they took the boat out. Caint figure 'em sometimes. When they're with me ah make 'em pick up their trash too. Ya, lots of kin like that".

Well, back to the dinner. The friendly lady now abruptly turned everyone's attention toward her huge diamond ring. "It's payment for not leavin him when he was sick. Everybody knows that" she laughed.

Her husband had been in the lumber business and had prospered because of the recent expansion in the area. So while they disparaged growth and outsiders, they sat bragging about their new-found wealth. There they sat, he in his old ball cap, a scowl on his unshaven face, she barefoot and dressed in a faded top and a pair of shorts. Her hair askew, her face naked of make-up she told the group: "Whenever I fixed up when I was young, everybody would say, so where you goin? Now I'd as like they see this." And she stood and waved her hand past the faces of those seated for all to admire the diamond that Elizabeth Taylor might have been proud to own. An older lady announced that she had given a pair of diamond earrings away to a young girl as a graduation present the previous spring.

Diamond Lil said "Oh, but that's stupid, but if it's kin it's okay. It was kin wasn't it?"

"No" the other said. "It was not kin but a friend's granddaughter. Gave 'em to her cause I've no place to wear 'em. You know there's no place to wear nice stuff here anyways and I'm gettin too old now; probably never will go anywheres now and it made the kid happy".

"Not kin? Well I still say it's stupid givin ta outsiders."

This caused the older woman to remark that she had done volunteer work for many years and that was giving to outsiders.

Having to have the last word, Diamond Lil ended the conversation by declaring: "Want ya ta work for nothing, some people; well that's stupid too. Why the hell yea ever do somethin like that?"

As we sat attempting to eat, people came and went. All the men wore the requisite ball cap even while they ate. All had long dirty hair and no one ever excused themselves as they left. Two little boys, miniatures of the adult males, ran back and forth past the table, in the front door and out the back. The men and women who had finished eating lit cigarettes irrespective of the fact that some had not finished their meal.

"Times sure have changed" said the boys' grandfather. "Kids nowdays don't sit at the table. They just carry their food around with em".

The children and their parents lived in the grandparents' home. The daughter worked as a store clerk and following in her mother's footsteps supported her husband. He had been sitting on the porch when we arrived and I noted might have been cloned from any of the other men in town. His legs outstretched in front of him and one hand rubbing his belly, he looked up as we approached and said only three words: "I already et."

As Dale and I finished our meal and I very happily contemplated my escape, the dinner conversation became a debate almost on who of them had had the most favored childhood. Those who had indoor toilets won the day, all heartily agreed.

"Ya, we don't know how lucky we are" one commented. "Not everybody around today has an indoor toilet".

Indeed that was true. I had read articles in the paper about people living in sheds and shacks with no plumbing and unable to have their electricity turned on. Much of the rural south looked like a third world country.

Beginning the day after Thanksgiving the charities began soliciting for donations and the stories of those needing help were heart-breaking, all the more so because this is such a wealthy country.

Old people had to choose between buying their medicine and buying food and there were instances of the ill and elderly freezing to death in winter.

Christmas was upon us, but there was very little festive feeling here. I was living alone most of the time in the beach house about a half mile from the center of the shabby, tiny, northern Florida town. The morning was overcast, and a heavy fog blanketed the Gulf, and so I set off on my walk later than usual.

I made my way along the old dirt road to the center of town and completed my usual rounds, checking the post box for mail, and the convenience store for the newspaper. It was a lonely time, my greetings of hello or good morning were met with the same stony silences as usual. I was an outsider here, a foreigner from the north, and may as well have been from another planet, I thought, as I made my way back to the house along the same desolate road.

Suddenly, in mid-stride I was stopped by something rubbing up against my right leg. I looked down and into the huge brown eyes of a basset hound pup that could not have been more than four months old. I reached down to give her a pat and realized that she was thin, so thin in fact, that her small bones were beginning to protrude from her dusty, mangy coat. I could have almost counted her ribs, but though she was slow and weak, she had such heart. She forced all of her energy into wagging her tail, staying close by my side all the way to the house.

Golden in color, big ears flopping, big sad eyes glistening whenever she looked up at me, the pats I gave her excited her beyond description and her tail wagged faster and faster in excitement.

I set the only animal food I had on hand down for her as soon as we reached the house and a big bowl of water and she inhaled everything I offered. She had quite a time deciding between the affection she so desperately craved and the food she so badly needed. It took at least an hour before she calmed down, finally lying at my feet, her head resting on my slipper, my hand stroking her head to reassure her.

What kind of people treated an animal this way? The rumors I had heard of men getting these hunting dogs for the season and then abandoning them had been substantiated in numerous newspaper reports, and editorials and the Humane Society was constantly pleading with people to show compassion for these helpless creatures.

I had seen dogs of every description running free here, all of them thin and obviously neglected. Should this beautiful pup be left to fend for herself, she too, if she survived, would soon breed more little ones to suffer along with her.

Well, suffer she had and with fleas that caused her to groan in anguish periodically. I had nowhere to keep her as I did not own this house and so I called a clinic in Tallahassee that claimed to keep animals for extended periods; one dog had lived there for a year before being adopted after being nursed back to health.

The following morning, having eaten all she cared to, she lay on the sun deck, nose tilted toward the sky, face turned toward the gentle sea breeze and looked at peace. I have never found the words to adequately express the feeling that welled inside me at that moment and spilled over, soaking my face with tears as I sat beside her, my hand on her head, knowing I would have to give her up and praying that someone would soon come along to love and protect her.

I drove her to the clinic and carried her in my arms to the reception desk. They asked me if I wanted to give her a name. "Noel" I said. Christmas was just two weeks away. Everyone there appeared to be as taken with her as I, and there were a few eyes glistening, as were mine. They told me that I was welcome to visit her as often as I wished, until she was adopted, and I carried her, following behind the attendant to the dog run in the back and waited until he had given her water. She seemed comfortable before I said my goodbye.

On the hour drive home I recalled something Lord Moran had written. Courage was a cold choice between two alternatives, he had said: And a fixed resolve not to quit. An act of renunciation that must be made not once, but many times by the power of the will.

Noel might have taught humankind a lesson. I know she gave me strength. A week and a half after arriving at the clinic, she was adopted by a couple who had met her only hours after I had left her, I was told, an older couple. It seemed too good to be true, but then it was Christmas, and her name was Noel.

I accompanied Dale on one last trip before I left. It was to Belize, a small country in Central America that had at one time been British Honduras. It had gained independence in 1981 and is now a member of the Commonwealth of Britain.

Now by the time I travelled to Belize I had, but for my trips out, spent two years living in an antagonistic society, a place where stone-faced people spoke in monosyllables when at all. We landed and as we entered the Small Belize airport I could feel the tension melt away. There was an easy graciousness about the people.

Their literacy rate was 90%, and they were adamant about protecting nature and their respect for all living things; this attitude was reflected in their kind and friendly natures. Indeed there is a growing number of expatriate American and Canadian people living there.

The day before we returned home I accompanied Dale on a walk round the neighborhood close to the hotel. Walking along the beach on the way back to the hotel he wanted to double back a block to take another look at a particular house. I agreed to wait a few minutes and sat down on the sea wall to enjoy the view of the harbor. The minutes passed and when I looked toward the direction he had walked I discovered that he was out of sight.

Past experience warned me that I could very well sit there long enough to bake beyond recognition in the hot sun and so I left and headed back to my room. He returned two hours later to the hotel.

He had treated the service people rudely of course throughout the trip. The sort of behavior that has given the American tourist a bad name throughout the world. One incident in particular stands out among all of the others. We were walking in downtown Belize and stopped at a stall to get a cold drink and something to eat. An East Indian gentleman and he was a gentleman, waited on us. He asked Dale if he would like another drink, and Dale said yes.

"Oh, I will pour it as soon as you finish that, sir."

"I want it now" Dale said.

"But sir, I can pour it in that same glass after you finish, not to waste".

"No, I want another cup."

So the polite and somewhat mystified man gave him a second plastic cup. Now as a final insult, when Dale paid the bill he told the man to keep the change, saying: "You keep it; it's not worth anything in American money anyway". The Belizians are poor in material wealth and Dale's hostile contemptuous attitude toward those less wealthy then himself paraded itself all over this little country.

I am positive that Dale never has asked himself how his behavior affects others. But then relating to others on a more meaningful level would have interfered with his ultimate aim, that of control and acquisition. His emphasis was on quick gratification. Yet while he collected things, he was never attached to them, for he said anything can be replaced. "The fun is in getting them". And so every material thing he acquired was stored and forgotten. It was the comfort of ownership he enjoyed. Everything and everyone was expendable. Yes, Belize was a society centered around people, while Dale's centered around things and it was easier to see who were the happier more fulfilled people.

His possessions eventually passed Dale. His every utterance related to things and money and naturally himself. To give away or discard anything: The mention of doing so would cause in him a great deal of anxiety and really the only time he showed any emotion was when I would suggest he donate something to a charity. He had even kept clothes that had hung in his closet for over twenty years. But then things were his obsession. Neurotic, he mirrored the society he had been raised in. Kindness was always a mask for exploitation, for his interests were purely selfish.

E. L. Doctorow made the point best when he quoted in The Book Of Daniel: "The art is not in giving your adversary nothing. But of giving him nothing while making him think that you are giving him something. For with nothing he has nothing to lose by going to war". That quote came to mind when, each time I would contribute to a charity, Dale would insist I get a receipt for income tax purposes and give it to him. Charity, I had thought was something someone offered for its own sake. I know of no other country that offers tax breaks as an incentive.

"People who have nothing are nothing." That was not a sentiment unique to Dale. However, it seemed to echo throughout the society. I always took it to mean that those who believed this must also believe that two thirds of the planet need not exist, for they were unable or in some cases unwilling to consume and hoard. Oh well, you see I began to think these kinds of thoughts more and more often and if not for the fact that I lived within a beautiful natural environment that provided solace, I could have gone a bit mad.

Woods surrounded the beach house and my closest neighbors were the squirrels, water fowl and gulls that perched by the dozen on the dock. The kitchen table sat in front of the window facing the ocean and this is where I spent my time writing. One morning while drinking my first coffee and scribbling notes, I was startled by the most horrible shriek. Dropping my pen I ran outside and followed the cries round to the beach side of the house. There I found a frightened water fowl caught in a large crab trap. I ran to the shed and all I could find were a pair of little clippers, of the sort we use to prune plants.

I worked for over half an hour feverishly snipping away at the wires, while the bird cried and I, with perspiration dripping down my face prayed, every so often turning to the creature to whisper it's alright, it's alright. Then realizing that I had finally broken through enough wire, forced an opening in the cage and stepping back said: "You're free." Unusually quiet now, it hesitated and then in an instant darted up and spreading silver wings flew out to sea. I cried tears of relief and felt a sense of joy at having been able to save this beautiful creature and I felt as though he had carried a part of me to freedom as well.

And so my friend Hanna is free. She writes now about happy times and lives just outside Edinburgh Scotland in a fair sized village. In spite of her unhappiness, friends had told her that she was crazy to leave her security for she knew not what. But then she told me she quoted Zorba the Greek to them: "A man needs a little madness or else he never dares cut the rope and be free."

The Ladies From Dover And Wales

They had met during world war two driving for the RAF. Friends for over fifty years, they could not have been more different. Mary of Dover was slightly built, well dressed and friendly. Her friend Jean was squarely built, with salt and pepper hair cut short, non-descript clothing, and a permanent scowl. Hostile and belligerent she mistook my friend Sarah for an American and proceeded to make unkind remarks about the large portions of food served in restaurants there. "Waffles smothered in all that butter and syrup and French fried potatoes, as you call your chips there first thing in the morning. Really".

Taken aback, Sarah said "Well, I have had many interesting experiences with food during my travels round the world. The diversity makes life interesting however, don't you think? Now kidney is what I was offered in northern England and livers, which we would not eat in America at breakfast. But it's just a difference in custom". Now Jean shot from the room without a word and much to the embarrassment of her friend.

Mary, eyebrows slightly raised said: "She must have had an unfortunate experience in America. It is too bad she had stereotyped everyone from across the pond. I've always thought so at any rate.

"One loses the opportunity to make new friends that way. This is the first I've seen her since she lost her husband. That's four years now. She always did hold a grudge, poor thing and usually traps herself into a corner. She tried to run her own bed and breakfast when she moved from Manchester to Wales. Really shouldn't have. She isn't a people person".

Sarah had returned to visit a ninety-six year old aunt, all that was left of her family. She had been an only child and her parents had not wanted her to marry and leave the country. Her husband had been posted in England during the war and she had met him one evening walking past her home in the town of Tunbridge. She had been working in London then and told many an interesting story of how she had managed to get home on the train each evening after her shift at a shop in spite of blackouts, delays and at times no small bit of confusion.

Well love won out and shortly after the war ended she left by boat to join her groom who had by then returned to Canada. "Oh, this to do about food reminds me of my first few hours on Canadian soil. We disembarked and the first thing they did was sit us down to lunch. Silly isn't it but what always comes to mind is a sandwich. Yes, a peanut butter sandwich. And they had put jelly in it and we war brides looked at each other and said: 'Oh they've put sweet in the peanut butter' but not one of us said a word about it.

"They were so helpful and were doing their best to make us welcome, you know. So much was different that way but then that's life isn't it?"

Two young sisters

They looked much younger than their actual ages, which they were not shy about admitting. Gloria the blonde was a lively, smiling, bubbly personality. Her sister Abby was dark and ill at ease in her new surroundings. Gloria, forty and self-effacing was well travelled and quite worldly; Abby was authoritative, preferred talking to listening, and we discovered gleaned much of her experience from books rather than experience.

She quoted the experts on whatever subject, verbatim, hoping to drive home a point she wanted to make. Yet it was obvious that she was detached from the subject emotionally and therefore she was rather unconvincing. Gloria was animated. Willing to listen and it was apparent that she had done her thinking independently after gathering all the facts she could in regard to whatever subject interested her. She advised me that a cousin by the name of Mrs. Swan would visit soon with a friend and tried to prepare me for the meeting, yet Mrs. Swan had to be encountered to be believed.

Mrs. Swan or Tara The Terrible

The complaints started as soon as Tara Swan and her friend Mrs. Hanks arrived. They were travelling Off-season to save money and ought to have expected dull, rainy weather and yet Tara Swan acted as though I had ordered up the dreary days especially for her. She spoke in a nasal, high pitched monotone and her grey eyes had no sparkle. Dead, cold, is the best way to describe the look unless she was in a particularly mean-spirited mood, at which time a small flicker of life would appear. She never went anywhere she said without "a good reason"; her reason for travelling to England was to keep her friend Janet Hanks company while Janet searched for her birth mother. Inward-looking and xenophobic, it was almost impossible to believe that she was related to the humanity conscious, and curious Gloria.

Tara Swan retired for the evening as rudely as she had arrived that morning. "Well I'm not interested in anything you two are talking about. Don't know anything about your history and don't care, so I'm going to bed. I mean this is a quaint looking town but God, why would I bother to know it?"

Janet, obviously shocked and embarrassed, took the opportunity of being left alone in my company to tell me a bit about Tara, I imagined as much to apologize for her friend's behavior, as to understand it herself; she began her story.

"We haven't spent much time together since high school, you know and that's some twenty five years ago. Oh a few days here and there every few years. She'd drop by for a short visit whenever she came to Vancouver to visit her grandmother. She was kind of eccentric even in high school but mum and I decided that it was her disturbing home life that was responsible for some of her attitude. She earned good grades by studying by rote, very mechanical, used to laugh and say that it was only important to remember the material long enough to get through the exam. So I guess you could say she never really participated, never learned and certainly never questioned.

"I remember one time her sister told her that she was lucky to have long dark lashes, as the boys considered them sexy. Well one morning I noticed her lashes were mere stubs and asked her what happened; she said that her reading glasses had worn them down. The real story didn't surface until years later. She began to wear her hair in a French roll, very severe all pulled back and pinned tight. She wore plain unattractive clothes and had only one date that I ever knew of, until college of course, and then she married the one man who asked her out.

"Insecure teenager my mam said, but during this trip I've come to realize that her problems with herself and the world have multiplied. The other kids used to tease her about growing up to be an old maid. She married and had two children you know and yet she does have some mannerisms that in the old days were referred to as spinsterish. She is very short with people and that adenoidal voice is irritating".

I had noticed that she walked stiffly. Her shoulders raised toward her ears, arms crossed tightly in front of her or straight by her sides and her steps were not much more than baby steps. She looked neither right nor left and fixed a tight smile on her thin compressed lips. A closed-in person I had thought at the time. Her voice literally became a high pitched squeal when she was excited about something and felt the need to sarcastically rebuke another's comment or opinion. Her hair was thin, a non-descript mousy brown worn in a short page boy, and according to Janet the style hadn't changed in twenty years. She wore little makeup and no jewelry, but her clothes were the most garish colors. Fire engine red, peacock blue and neon green appeared to be her favorites. It was winter and everything she brought with her was made of velour. All of her garments were boxy and uninteresting and the sort of thing one might find in the bargain basement of a department store.

She claimed she preferred wearing bright colors because they conveyed a cheery attitude, forgetting or perhaps never realizing that the sum is equal only to its parts.

"No", Janet told me; "She was not impressed with university and had only stayed one term. She disagreed with the professor's methods of teaching she said. She had been enrolled in the education program. When I asked why she had not transferred to another faculty, she told me that there was simply nothing that the university had to offer that interested her. That raised a red flag you know and less than one year after quitting school she married a young man who had just graduated the faculty of engineering.

"Her one interest she said was Shakespeare, and I suggested we visit his birth place at Stratford Upon Avon while we are here. I actually thought she'd have jumped at the chance and was taken aback when she screeched: "Why no; we came here for a reason, we didn't come here to sightsee". "So you see what I've been up against, don't you".

"But you'd kept in touch during the years and never knew this side of her".

"Exactly. Looking back I realize that the infrequent visits had always been about her unhappy marriage, her children, and a birthday card here, a Christmas card there and living thousands of miles apart, well.

"You know, her husband became quite successful. Before they married she agreed not to have children, however he was a good father in spite of Tara claiming two accidents. It is he they are close to now. He remarried and the woman is a cook; she was a cook for a living is what I mean. Everyone laughed, I'm told, when they heard the news. I learned this from a cousin of hers I ran into just two days before we left on this trip. Apparently Tara had spent her married life dragging Jon and the two children to fast food restaurants for dinner, or serving waffles for the evening meal. I can't understand how nor why he lived that way for years but I assume it was for the children.

"Years ago her sister told me that she was afraid of Tara and that no-one dare say anything to her to make her angry. I chalked it up to sisterly rivalry at the time; we were only kids. Having spent the better part of three weeks with her now I see that she can be very cutting. Doesn't spare one's feelings. She remarked when she arrived in Vancouver to live after her divorce, that we sure had a lot of Vietnamese moving in, Then went on to complain; "They all live in one house and save their money and buy restaurants and hire their own; well if that's the way they want to live".

"What way? "I had asked. "They work hard, look after themselves and contribute. What is the problem, Tara?" But then she assumed her poker face and Looked right through me. She had made disparaging remarks about other groups as well, including the population of East Indians in London. I'm mortified you know. I had not realized she was so very bigoted. She doesn't mind saying things within ear shot of others either. I told her that she risked hurting the feelings of people and she said: "Well that's their problem".

"It's backfired however and with her own children. Her husband took up with the new woman in his life only one month after the divorce and she bragged about telling her own children that she had never loved him anyway. Just married him because she was ready for a physical relationship. I can't imagine how she believed this would make her look superior in anyone's eyes, let alone her children's. She confided in me that she only slept with him when she felt desperate to do so. They never travelled anywhere unless she knew someone at their point of destination either. It's as though she sees pleasure for its own sake wrong somehow. I asked her yesterday if this were not the case and she said: "Well I am not going to spend money or time on anything just for the sake of fun. There has to be a reason for doing everything".

"I've wondered if having the children wasn't a way to justify having sex. As crazy as that sounds in this day and age; she was raised catholic. "I must justify everything I do, to myself you understand and I don't care what anyone else thinks". That included those she has referred to as "stupid marriage counselors."

"Tara lamented the few sticks of furniture she got in her divorce settlement, but this was before she moved to the city in which I live. I couldn't believe it when I went over to help her unpack. The pathetic possessions consisted of a silver tea service, antique furniture, Waterford crystal and so on. Oh, I'm upset, more so than I realized. She had a few people over the week before we left on this trip (which had been planned and paid for months ago) and anyway that was embarrassing as well. One of the ladies remarked on how good the Nanaimo bars were and asked Tara to pass the tray so that she could have another. Tara hopped up so quickly she nearly overturned her chair and squealed; "I didn't spend all morning making goodies so that everyone could eat them all up". Then she giggled in that silly way that's supposed to lighten the mood I guess and grabbing the tray rushed to the cupboard, put the contents into a container and then straight into the freezer.

"Well that day she said the craziest thing. She told everyone at the table that she had advised her daughter never to marry, to just fool around. "I don't even believe in love, silly emotion if it even exists." One of the women contradicted her and her face turned white and her eyes that steely cold, white rage I call it. It must have been what her sister had been referring to all those years ago. Well, then she gave that shriek of a laugh and told us that the subject was closed and that she wanted to talk about something else".

I mentioned to Janet that Tara had asked me where all the English were. "All I saw were East Indians in London" was what she had said. Having asked her where they stayed while there I discovered that she had stayed in an economy hotel and had never left the two block radius round her hotel and the silly

woman believed that she knew all about England. She had no natural curiosity about anything outside herself. "I'm not interested. You sound like Janet; she wanted me to run up to Stratford just because I memorize lines from Shakespeare's plays. I told her don't be stupid. I like being on stage that's all".

"Have you more projects lined up?" I asked

"No. They've told me in Vancouver that I should study Voice; well I'm not changing myself because they tell me to".

Indeed. I walked to the market later that afternoon wondering how anyone could behave so rudely and yet be unaware of it.

Janet later told me that Tara had advised her while on this trip that she never apologizes for anything. "I never say I'm sorry for anything, that's admitting you're wrong. Gives the other guy the upper hand. A stupid thing to do".

I help with the local charity when I Can and one morning just as they were coming down to breakfast I was completing a phone call related to calling friends and acquaintances about donating clothing and household items for our center. "I'll be out most the morning" I told them. "My turn to pick up donations".

"Oh, I have a cousin like that," Tara said. "Always asking people to donate. Gives things away. Crazy. I told her she was crazy. You never know who will get your things. If I can't sell something, I throw it out".

I was glad to get out of house that morning. Granted we don't have to and aren't expected to like everyone we meet, but this was the woman from hell. Why, only last night and sitting in my front room belittling me for planning a trip abroad next summer. "Running away from yourself? That's what I call it when people run around all over hell's half acre for no reason". I'm thinking she must be trying to project an image of a contented soul by never venturing far from home base. Is she thinking her life appears so full that nothing else can matter outside of herself? And of course the reverse is true.

What sort of thoughts did she think? What did she think about? What kind of life is generated in a bubble anyway? A life unlived.

Could be the title for a book. Such a stingy life too. Stingy about material things, emotion, people. Janet tells me that she never introduced her husband's friends to hers, nor any family member to a friend. Told Janet she didn't believe in introducing people of different social status. Never believed in compromise either. What had she said? Oh yes: "Never compromise. Win, win, otherwise you lose control." But what had she won?

Three weeks into their stay with me, Tara came down late in the evening and announced that she was leaving for home as soon as possible. We were clearing up in the pub and talking away. We'd drank goodness knows how many cups of tea and a quarter bottle of brandy while we were at it as well. Well, just as we had cleared the last of the things away Tara appeared in the doorway. "What could you possibly want to sit around talking about till all hours? You should clean up in the morning before you open. Of course, I can't see why you need a pub anyway. Silly. I'm thinking that I'm so bored here I'll go home earlier than planned. I hate spending money to stay in someone else's house when I'd be more comfortable at home anyway".

"That's blunt, anyway". I said that, couldn't help myself.

She giggled. "That's me, independent" she said and turned on her heel and left the room. Next morning Janet arranged for Tara's ticket to be changed at the local travel center and three days later Janet accompanied miss independent to the station to catch her train to London, Janet all the while assuring her that she would make it home just fine on her own. Unfortunate the sister being afraid of her; such a waste of time fearing the fearful. Of course it was easier for me to be Objective as I wasn't involved. She was obsessed by the idea of having security. Love, freedom, change of any kind must have threatened her, threatened her false sense of security.

Janet and I keep in touch. In her last letter she wrote that Tara had moved. "Rents a room and stores all her things in the basement of the house. Squirreled her money away and lives very nearly like a pauper though she doesn't have to". Janet ran into Tara's brother not long ago. He's an older brother by about two years. He was dubbed 'the banker'; not connected to the world of high finance in any legal sense, he made withdrawals with a hastily scribbled note and a toy gun.

He was thirteen when he and a friend decided to hitch a ride one summer. They agreed along the way that a little extra money would come in handy and the driver of the first car that stopped became their benefactor."

Jack claims that he doesn't remember who planned the attack, but that they both pounced on the old gentleman at the same time, beat him and stole his wallet. That was the start of his sordid career. Juvenile home for three and one half years and he said he learned a great deal there.

"I was stunned to hear it" Janet said and added; "I remember the conversation as though it were yesterday. Who wouldn't? It was the first and only time I've ever been told a story like it. Well here it is as near as I can remember:

"He has been a member of society for ten years now and told me he wished he'd have discovered life could be so good years ago.

"Age is what set me straight more than anything," he said.

"The last time he was incarcerated he was over forty, soon to be released, and looking around the lunch room one day contemplated futures of the older men. Some would never get out, others did not want to, as there was nothing for them out in the world anymore.

"How do you start over when you're in your sixties or seventies? I decided I'd never return" he said.

"Initially he had wanted to get hold of money to run from home with. Then as the years wore on it was money to start over and show everyone that as he put it, "I could be somebody."

"In and out, I've been in and out since I was thirteen. More in than out I guess. Rapes, all the stuff you see on television, these things happen. Then as you get older your reputation grows right along with you, grows with the rap sheet and suddenly you have a kind of status and you're somebody, at least on the inside. But then you begin to age and you realize that there aren't going to be any more chances for work, a wife, children. Life inside was like living the life of a gerbil. Like those rats Tara keeps in cages. They're the only kind of pet she's ever had you know, the kind you keep in cages. Guess she figures they can't run away from her. Anyway I began to feel like one of those rats. Running around on that little wheel. Wheel's supposed to amuse them, but it's the owners who are amused. I started to see the prison guards, officials that way. I didn't own myself, never had I guess. Back when we were kids the adults owned you. They could pretty well do as they pleased too, get drunk, beat you, starve you, leave you in dirty ragged clothes, the whole bit. So that's how it started. Just trying to escape. But I only traded one cage for another. It's over now, but it's the memories that can get to you if you let them. Our old dad towards the end got the snakes. Used to keep a shotgun under his bed and they tell me that whenever he fell asleep, whoever was around would sneak in and unload it so that if he came to and tried to shoot at the rats and things he saw crawling all over his body he wouldn't kill himself. I don't know that they did him any favors to tell you the truth. Mum had been long gone by then, married another drunk I hear.

I remember one of the times they left us alone to go out drinking. Somebody broke in. It wasn't the best neighborhood as you can imagine. Anyhow we four kids were in bed, all sleeping in two beds squeezed into the same room. We heard something, then kept our eyes shut pretending to be asleep. A light passed over our faces, must have been a flashlight. Nothing happened. There sure wasn't anything worth stealing. Anyway Tara told that story to her husband right in front of me and he complimented her on having been smart enough to tell us all to pretend to be asleep until the burglar left. Of course she did not tell him that we had been lying there petrified that it was our parents come home drunk. I didn't say anything. I knew that she'd faked a good home life in order to get him to marry her. Guess he never knew about the old man staggering up the street, a patch over one eye to correct the double vision. Tara always worried about me embarrassing her. My reputation you know. But that's as far as the caring went. It's like when we were kids and I used to get teased all the time because I was fat. She teased right along with the neighbor kids, and didn't want me to walk down the street with her. I cried sometimes. Told her it hurt my feelings.

"But you know something? (and this is kinda creepy) she said: "feelings? that's stupid."

Mrs. Lemieux told me a story just last week, a story worthy of a television movie in our opinion, but I'll let you be the judge. It was told her by a gentleman friend who visits from time to time. He is from a small farming community in western Canada.

Two Sisters

For the most part, the community had been settled by Americans. They began moving north in the early 1900s after being offered ownership of as much land as they were willing to homestead. They formed a tightly knit community, its inhabitants related by blood and marriage. As is true of small communities births, marriages, and deaths are one of the main topics of conversation among the older population. Most the seniors can be found hunched over cups of coffee at the local co-op cafeteria any day of the week but Sundays. Closed Sundays, the little coffee shops and diners along main street absorb the co-op regulars. It's a pretty street. Six blocks long, clean sidewalks, nicely kept shops, and well-dressed locals. Friendly and relaxed and in typical small town fashion aware when a newcomer has entered. all heads turn when someone from outside enters an establishment and you won't be left to sit alone for long before someone steps up to welcome you.

Yes, everyone knows everyone else, all the day to day happenings, and of course the town's history, its characters both living and dead. As is the case with every small town they do have their (characters) though it is agreed that none will ever compare to THE SISTERS, daughters of one of the town's first settlers.

Emma Jane and Edna Sue belonged to the Whitfield family. Their father had immigrated from the States from Kentucky with three of their younger siblings from a Kentucky hollow to take advantage of the Canadian Government's offer to homestead. At the time it was common for the Government to recruit south of the border as well as Europe, for people willing to settle the northern reaches of provinces famous for their cold winters and naturally because of the harsh environmental conditions an incentive was offered.

The Whitfields bragged of being related to the famous Hogg family of Texas, claiming the sisters Ima and Ura Hogg as distant cousins. They also claimed ancestry dating back to the Mayflower pilgrims, though it was in 1783 that their forefathers arrived from Scotland. And of course no Kentucky family was complete without the requisite Cherokee ancestor. Though not to be outdone the sisters insisted their Cherokee ancestor to be no less than a princess, first daughter of a tribal chief.

Safe to say that the sisters, having been raised with a fictional past saw nothing unusual in creating a fictional present as long as it was to their benefit. The altered reality of the family history was passed along to successive generations and those who would dismiss it as nothing more than tall stories (after having done their research) were said to be unsupportive of their own and rebuffed as family traitors.

The patriarch of the clan, a failed farmer and justice of the peace in his ole Kentucky hollow, elevated his stature to that of former judge when he reached his new home. An older brother of the sisters having completed the eighth grade commenced teaching in the one room hollow school house, but once he reached his new home became a former mathematics professor. The professor blamed the British for the American prohibition era, insisting that it had been a sinister plot cooked up among unscrupulous U.S. Government agents and the British Government calculated to increase the import of alcohol when what he called "the dry spell" was over. Therefore he claimed it his patriotic duty to make and sell moonshine before fleeing north to join his family. Reality was whatever the family decided it to be, and their motto being "the end justifies the means" they lived accordingly.

Legend has it that Emma the eldest daughter, blonde, green eyed and at five foot ten inches tall as slim as a reed, had at an, early age married a wealthy man. This then was the explanation given for her quickly acquired wealth. With his financial backing she had opened a haberdashers on Madison Avenue in New York City was the story she told. The bemused town folk appeared to accept her explanation at face value. I say bemused because none were quite so naive.

In fact, she had married a tug boat captain and while he was away for long periods the sisters were free to amuse themselves as they saw fit. They enjoyed a grand life while making the best of a lonely situation. Though they were likely the least lonely ladies in New York City and certainly two of the busiest. Dressed in the finest, most expensive fashions of the day they played hostess to many of the most prominent men in the Borough of Manhattan. That their wealth, lifestyle, six figure income and prominent connections were derived from the little shop challenged the imagination and yet their kin (none of whom ever visited New York City) applauded their resourcefulness, and their ability (to make friends) so effortlessly and quickly. Their virtues were never questioned and they were made much of when they paid their most infrequent visits to the north country.

Edna Sue had dark red hair and blue eyes that at times appeared to be almost transparent. Two inches shorter than Emma and fuller of figure, she occasionally took a back seat to Emma. Yet she had the best sense of humor of the two and with her devil may care manner had no trouble attracting admirers. Whatever their physical and personality differences they were a team and would remain so well into their nineties, at which time first Edna, and then Emma passed away within two years of one another.

Born in Kentucky in 1880 and 1881 respectively, Emma and Edna were as close as two sisters could possibly be. That they arrived at a time when their father had given up any hope of recovering the ill-gotten gains he had accumulated before the civil war meant that they had been born to poverty and desperation. Those less critical of them suggested this as the reason for their (ambition) as some delicately referred to their calling.

They were eighteen and nineteen years of age when their father, lamenting his inability to prosper without the use of slave labor decided to take advantage of the opportunity to move north. He loaded two wagons of his own with family members and provisions and together with half a dozen other like-minded families formed a wagon train and headed north. The sisters meanwhile headed east with whatever bits of finery they had managed to gather together and with their southern charms made their way alone.

That neither sang, danced, played a musical instrument, or had advanced past the sixth grade in their academic pursuits deterred them not in the least. They had not even the working experience of shop clerk or maid; therefore the kin marveled at their ingenuity.

Emma was not long in finding a husband - one Derek Thayer, tug boat captain. He, madly in love with the angel haired Emma wasted no time in settling her into a decent apartment and supplying her with the best furnishings and clothing he could afford before leaving for another work assignment. Thus Emma and Edna had their start and Emma now a married woman, a veil however thin of respectability.

The sisters prospered quickly and the following year moved to a considerably larger and much more lavishly decorated, though gaudy apartment. Their business now took them on trips to cities such as New Orleans and San Francisco and ocean voyages to Europe. Their companions were always gentlemen of the highest social standing.

Their lives progressed in this fashion for seven years and then an accident one foggy night changed their lives forever. It was late fall when Derek Thayer's tug suffered an explosion just thirty minutes before entering its berth at a New York City pier. Most of his crew were killed and Emma spent the following five days keeping a vigil by Derek's hospital bed.

His body was swathed in bandages, his face half blown away. On the morning of the sixth day it was over. He never regained consciousness.

Emma rushed back to her apartment, emerging only to attend Derek's funeral. Two weeks later having settled her financial affairs and giving all but one suitcase of her personal belongings away (having kept the least ostentatious of her possessions) she boarded a train for the wild west. Though at the time she swore that she was relinquishing all her material wealth ostensibly due to her sorrow (some said guilt) she nevertheless retained stocks and properties that would one day cause her to be recognized as one of the wealthiest people in the territory she ran to after Derek's death.

The small one bedroom wooden house she insisted upon moving into when she arrived in Bearclaw, where her father and the rest of her kin now lived (Edna excepted) caused shock waves to run throughout the community. The naive believed that she had entered a period of great repentance.

Almost one year later she married a farmer. Andre was barely literate, and though three years her junior he appeared to be much older. It was rumored that he had never been with a woman and most of the locals were convinced that he had never worn a clean item of clothing in his life, but simply recycled the least dirty of his raggedy things.

With his front teeth missing and a heavy head of black hair that one of his brothers would on occasion take a pair of kitchen shears to, Andre Leroux was a most unlikely husband for the still beautiful Emma. While there were those who reasoned that Emma had entered this most questionable of marriages because of a protracted period of grief, they soon came to realize what most everyone had known all along: The Leroux brothers were the wealthiest farmers for thousands of miles, collectively and independently.

Emma's spirits lifted considerably after this marriage, so much so, that she began to travel again, Most often to visit Edna. Edna was by now dividing her time up between Seattle, San Francisco and a few other port cities she enjoyed calling home now and again. She was now a nurse they said and in great demand in areas where construction and dock workers sometimes suffered serious injury. No-one ever challenged the explanations the sisters gave to account for their comings and goings. They simply enjoyed the stories as a sort of entertainment.

Emma's sense of style resurfaced as well, though her more sophisticated, or at least expensive wearing apparel was reserved for travel to and from Bearclaw. Ten years after the tug boat explosion Edna gave birth to a baby girl and assumed a new surname and widowhood as well. A most unfortunate construction accident had claimed the life of her husband she said.

No-one had been advised of the marriage or death until the birth of her-daughter. At the age of two little Charlotte had been given to Emma to raise. Edna, Emma told everyone, was busy performing her nursing duties and could not raise Charlotte alone. Nursing proved a lucrative profession for Edna, who eventually owned several apartment buildings in and around a number of coastal cities.

Edna became even more brash in her speech and tougher of manner. Both sisters were now notorious for their rude and abrupt language. It was said that most of those they came into daily contact with quaked in anticipation of their arrival. The local bank manager was not above being at Emma's beck and call and could be ordered to meet her anywhere and at any time of the day or night. On one such occasion in the middle of December, the temperature hovering around thirty degrees below zero Fahrenheit she called him from the hairdressers and told him to meet her at precisely the moment she expected to be ready to leave. The poor man was five minutes late and when he arrived found Emma seated outside the shop in her warm car. Angry at his tardiness and therefore refusing to budge from the relative comfort of her vehicle, left running while she had had her hair done she cracked her window just enough to allow him to slip the documents through.

He was forced to stand in the terrible cold until she dismissed him. She and Edna were in their sixties by this time and all pretense to civil behavior had long since ceased to be of concern to them. They were by now unquestionably very wealthy women and as their wealth had grown so too had their penchant for treating others as inferiors; prime testimony to the saying "money doesn't buy class."

During the summer months Edna visited the prairie town that Emma called home and Emma travelled south to visit Edna during the cold winter months, now with Charlotte's son in tow. He was a handsome child with black hair and huge brown eyes, well-built and admired for his looks. Unfortunately his temperament was another matter. He had no friends, and spoke to everyone in the manner of his grandmother and great aunt Emma. In fact no child was either inclined, or allowed to associate with him. His grandmother had spent his sixteenth summer as the uninvited guest of a niece and her family on a farm near Bearclaw. Her preferred mode of entertainment was to sit on the sun deck drinking bourbon and make a game of counting the number of flies she could swat with her unusually large fly swatter.

Deeply contemplative (between the last dead fly and the next sip of bourbon) she came to the conclusion that little Ronnie would be happier if he were to return to San Francisco with her. Two weeks before classes began they arrived south of the border and he was promptly spirited away to a private boarding school where, she had presumed, he may have a captive group in which to find some friends.

Over the ensuing ten years Ronnie proved himself worthy of the Whitfield heritage. Socially inept, he fell in with boys more interested in playing pool than academics shortly before graduating from high school. He narrowly edged his way into acceptance at the local university, finally spending no more than one semester there.

Three failed businesses financed by his grandmother and three failed marriages and two children later he celebrated his thirtieth birthday. His telephone calls to the sisters were made for no reason other than to solicit money.

Once Emma celebrated her eightieth birthday she decided that she was no longer fit to travel and therefore never again laid eyes on the young man she had raised. Edna died at the age of ninety and her estate was bequeathed to Charlotte and Ronnie. Emma had sent Charlotte away abruptly at the age of fifteen and Charlotte was never seen in Bearclaw after that. Emma had done the same with a niece some thirty years earlier. At the time the niece was but thirteen years old. The child was the daughter of the older brother, the ne'er do well you will recall who claimed himself a professor and who abandoned his children after his wife left him to whomever would take them. The young niece was placed by Emma in an orphanage in the city and left there with only the clothes on her back. Emma had accused her of being a cry baby and thoroughly unmanageable after she had attempted to run away in the wee hours of a morning. Once abandoned to the orphanage she was never heard of again.

Charlotte had lived an isolated existence with Emma and Andre on the farm. She had a few girlfriends and had never been allowed to spend time in the company of boys. Therefore it came as a shock when just three years after Charlotte's sudden departure, Emma returned from a visit to San Francisco with two and one half year old Ronnie. From this time onward Emma never spoke to Andre other than to give orders. And two days after her return with Ronnie Andre signed his entire estate over to Emma.

One wonders if Emma suffered even a slight twitch of conscience over her abandonment of the young niece when the scenario was replayed with Charlotte. If so, she certainly never showed any sign of remorse.

Now in their mid-eighties Emma and Andre were too old and infirm to maintain their home on the farm, and turning the labor over to nephews she and Andre moved into the shabby little house in town. It now mirrored the age and neglect of its occupants.

They subsisted on the provisions offered them by a kindly women's group from one of the town's churches. Emma was not about to pay for someone to do her grocery shopping and certainly none in town felt inclined to go out of their way to do favors for perhaps the most disrespected couple in the area. Having eschewed any services that required payment and never having been church goers Emma and Andre marveled at the charity offered them. Emma declared sardonically that the women were: "Just a silly group of frightened fools hoping to secure a place in a mythical heaven by racking up points with the mythical man upstairs." Edna had once said that she didn't believe in charity and the sisters had always been suspicious of those who would be kind for kindness sake.

Andre and Emma might be found any day of the week in the front room of the dilapidated little house, planted squarely in front of their small black and white television set, their only visitors the bank manager, attorney, doctor, and the church women.

Eventually Emma decided that it was time for them to enter the nursing home and she made arrangements for she and Andre to share the same room. No doubt because of his increasing senility she may have wanted to be present to keep a lock on his tongue. So now they sat. Each in a bed, Emma had her trunk placed at the foot of hers, locked. It held documents that only the bank manager and attorney were privy to on those occasions when they were summoned. The key was kept securely round her neck on an old shoe lace she had decided was good enough to do the job. And Andre had his toe; yes, his toe. Some fifty years earlier he had lost it in a farm accident and unable to have it reattached had pickled - well preserved it somehow and placed it lovingly in a little jewelry box. He had found it great fun to whip the little box out of his pocket and pop the lid to frighten unsuspecting children and now the nursing home attendants were the recipients of his humor.

Andre was the first to die and Emma followed within the year. It shocked no-one that the only people to attend her funeral were a few of the church ladies, the banker, the attorney, a long absent yet greedy nephew and his wife and Charlotte and Ronnie. Mother and son had arrived the morning of the funeral, spent three days in town meeting with the attorney and bank manager and left, the sole beneficiaries of Emma's estate. Charlotte left somewhat the worse for wear, having closed the hotel pub each night.

Though Ronnie and Charlotte were reportedly left sums of money in the millions of dollars, no one expected the money to benefit them for very long. Each-were impoverished in a spiritual sense and had spared no expense thus far trying to buy happiness. From rags to riches to rags goes an old American prophecy.

The Broom Man

The first week of April a couple from America arrived, for what they told me would be a five day stay. She was a German woman, he an American and apparently quite well off, if we are to believe his bragging about stock holdings and successful business dealings. He spent at least fifteen to twenty minutes on the telephone at least once and sometimes twice a day talking to his stock broker long distance and yet he was stingy enough to ask for a reduction on the price of their room because they did not eat the full English breakfast each morning. You see how very interesting, if not at times irritating, my little enterprise can be occasionally.

I call this man the (broom man) because that is what he sold and claimed to have achieved wealth in the broom business. He had no children and the woman with him was not his wife, but a live-in girlfriend of a dozen years. He had no relatives at all and complained that his brokers and attorneys were constantly hounding him about making a will. Understandable, one would think as he was now in his eighty-fifth year. At any rate each of these people vied for Executorship of said will. Apparently one stood to gain a princely sum as administrator of such a large estate. Broom man's paramount concern was the problem of what to do with his fortune, having been forced to admit that he could not take any of it with him.

I was tempted to tell him that there are no pockets in shrouds. His girlfriend favored the suggestion of one broker, which was to leave a sizeable portion of his estate to a university. Not for scholarship funding or anything of that sort, but rather for the construction of a building with his name on it. I had been drawn into the conversation and even asked my opinion which surprised me because I did not know these people and as the days passed decided that I would rather not. They were the most dedicated drinkers I had ever had stay and made my pub their home away from home every night from opening to closing. Well this particular evening as I had been asked my opinion and they insisted I have one, I suggested he leave something to children's charities, homeless people, that sort of thing. After all, the percentage of children that go to bed hungry in the wealthiest country in the world is over 25%, so there was obviously a need there.

His friend, I'll call Gerda, said with some Disdain: "I hate people. I'd sooner he leave it to animals. Who cares about other people's kids? And besides who knows who will be using the money? Where we live I operate a booth at a swap meet on weekends and I always keep my eye on the Mexican kids. I watch them extra close; everyone knows their parents teach them to steal. So I think, why help kids who are going to grow up to be criminals anyway?"

A German war bride, she had entered the United States with her American serviceman husband shortly after world war two had ended. He had been a gambler and died just as their only child, a daughter, graduated high school. The broom man at this point loudly and laughingly told one and all that he had inherited Gerda. She and her husband had been renting a house from broom man at the time of the husband's death. Oddly Gerda laughed along with him and showed not the least bit of embarrassment.

Broom man bragged that he had made his start in business by hiring illegal Mexican aliens to make his brooms, therefore paying less than minimum wage for his labor costs. Eventually he farmed the work out south of the border, cutting his expenses again considerably. "Times have changed. Young people don't have the opportunities I had back then. Now the good Samaritans and bleeding hearts are ranting about the exploitation of immigrants. A person has to be careful, so a lot of us just moved the damned business out of the country".

They did not stay but four days. This was as well because some of my customers were not dropping in for their usual night caps; those who came were disgusted with the couple and spent very little time and even Mrs. Lemieux said: "Jan, I'll ask you to fill me in later. They're just too much."

The final evening of their stay Broom man, upon ordering his eighth drink of the evening, lifted his glass and informed everyone present that his house was the house of love. Poor old Mrs. Briggs, ninety two and still spry, fairly flew out the door at this point, and did not return for a week. "I know it's the house of love" he boomed. "Just look at our dogs, right Gerda? Hell, animals are sensitive; they know about people. I don't know how they'll take it when I die, they may even have to be destroyed. Yeah Gerda and the dogs, now that's love, right Gerda? Don't need nobody else." I couldn't help but believe that it was just as well.

Mrs. Lemieux, after listening to the story of the broom man said: "Jan, do you remember that Alexis de Tocqueville wrote: "Nothing is so petty, so insipid, so-anti-poetic, as life in the United States."

The Uncles

Shortly after broom man and his mistress departed a young couple arrived from Canada. They were on their way to visit his mum up in Edinburgh. The second evening of their stay a group arrived at the pub after attending a funeral. "You know the last time I saw any of my relatives on my dad's side of the family was at a funeral" Bill said. "It is also the last funeral I've had to attend. Funny how I'm reminded of those people from so long ago and so far away; I have not thought of them in years. You're friends with mum so might find the story interesting. She told me you are keeping a journal.

"Anyway, mum told me when I was in my late teens and asked about that side of the family why she had felt that she must protect me from them. Consequently, we had little to do with them. They were four uncles of my father's, all insurance salesmen. They met three times a year at my grandmother's home, Thanksgiving, Christmas, and First of July.

"They were small in stature, expensively dressed and hopelessly alcoholic. Eccentric, well into their sixties they were wearing bowler hats, and having spats made to order. Now no-one would even know what a pair of spats were, those fancy little coverings men used to wear over their shoes to dress them up. Mum said they went out of fashion with the muskrat coat as far as she could tell; she'd only seen them worn in old movies on the late show. Well, she met them in the late sixties, so you get the picture.

"Fancy vests and watch fobs were part of their wardrobe as well. On these special occasions the four would gather in their sister's living room and challenge one another as to who could hold the most liquor. Poke 'er back was the common command as the one who finished the drink first stood, his empty glass raised and ready for the next round. To sip your drink, rather than guzzle it, meant that you were not a real man as far as they were concerned. Their wives followed their husbands by about two hours, having been detained at their jobs as shop clerks until closing time. These women were the true bread winners of the family. They paid the bills, raised the children and kept the small rented homes and apartments cleaned. They were tidy little women and nicely dressed, although their clothing was not nearly of the quality their husbands demanded for themselves.

"An hour or so after the wives arrived, the conversation would predictably turn to how difficult the insurance business was and the hard luck the men were having. Though after thirty years with no success only the brothers were shocked at their poor sales ability. The little they did earn found its way to the clothing stores and the liquor stores. All four however, claimed and adamantly so; "Clothes make the man. Look successful and you'll be successful" they shouted in unison and draining what was left in the glasses cheered each other and poured another drink.

"They were certain that what they called their "natty appearance" would eventually turn things around. Their children, all girls, had fled long before mum met them and had all made horrible multiple marriages. Each had married a succession of abusive, self-centered, alcoholic men.

"Once in their sixties they began passing away with not more than a year of two between funerals. None even reached the age of sixty-five. All were cremated. The service hastily arranged and the dandy eulogized by a minister who had no knowledge of the deceased other than what he had been told by the widow. Understandably this had been rather limited in scope. After all, they felt that they had worked so hard to save face all those years and had "no intention of airing our dirty laundry in public at this late date. So we'll keep it quick and simple. If more were said everyone would know that it was lies anyway" said one. "You know if we make them sound too good people may think them worse than they were, though I don't see how that's possible" said another.

"After the service a large party was held at the home of whichever daughter was married at the time. It actually was a party. It certainly was not a solemn gathering of bereaved. Pathetically, it was the deceased's end that was being celebrated, rather than his life. Mum said it was almost ghoulish. The daughters got drunk rather quickly and then all the cousins together felt free to compare horror stories of abuse.

"They only saw me a couple of times. We were visiting my grandfather or aunt and they would turn up hoping to sell my parents insurance. Paribas mum said. They did the same with every family member and shirt tail relative, no matter how remote. She says their most profitable years must have been during those times when the next generation was setting up house. They had an antagonistic attitude toward children, referred to them as little tads, as in tadpoles and a frequent comment of theirs was: "You listen to your elders and your bettors".

"You bettors?" Mum once said and quickly picked me up and left the room. Weak people need someone to lord it over she always says and who is weaker than children, animals, and at the time many of the women.

"Their wives had long since given up and with drink in hand toasted themselves with; "Well, if you can't lick 'em join 'em." All but one of the wives who, if unable to find an excuse to avoid a family gathering would nurse one drink and leave early. She was the only one of all these parents who managed to raise a child well, a son. She had kept him apart from the family. Helen was her name and her husband was the first to die. After that she became a model for older women's clothes and travelled, created for herself a good life really. Mum says that if she had a fault it's that she didn't break away sooner."

Adam and Joan

They seemed a happy couple, or at least content with each other. Both widowed, Adam and Joan had "found each other " as Joan put it in the late autumn two years ago. "It was an art exhibit we attended separately and then we recognized each other a few weeks later at a book reading. Oh, I had so many outside interests then. All sorts of volunteer and cultural events to attend to and a diverse group of friends".

She was petite, not more than five feet tall if that and quiet spoken. He was a big man and it was obvious that in his youth he had been quite good looking. Joan asked about the area, the history of the town and well, was simply curious about everything, and everyone. Adam on the other hand preferred the sound of his own voice to any other. He gave the impression that what he did not already know was not worth knowing. He was relaxed and happy as long as he was doing the talking and was the protagonist in every one of his very long and drawn out stories. And all were meant to be very flattering to himself.

He told us that he had worked all over the United States all of his working life. A jack of all trades and to hear him tell it, a master of all as well. According to him, one course in a particular trade or profession had enabled him to master the subject. "I told one of my sons that you may as well say I have seven degrees." He began ticking off the subject from electrician to environmentalist and concluded by saying that a course in a subject was really all one needed to become an expert, if one was smart enough.

Ann and Joe, that's Mrs. Lemieux and her Husband, were visiting one evening and noticed as I had that whenever one of us attempted to enter the conversation, Adam fixed them with a cold stare and very obviously waited until they had finished speaking, never acknowledging what they had to say, but simply carrying on from where he had left off. Joe said that he reminded him of a record where someone had lifted the needle for a few seconds and then let it drop back into place. Joan was careful not to say much and on those infrequent occasions when she did Adam dismissed her opinions as no more than cute, as a self-centered adult might condescend to a small child.

Joan had never travelled until she met Adam. They were from New York and she had never been outside of her tri-state area, she told Ann and Joe. To their credit Joan and Adam were very youthful seventy somethings physically, however it was clear the relationship was patterned on the male, female roles of a bygone era.

I Asked: "What made you decide that you wanted to leave everything for long periods of time and so suddenly too, to travel?"

"Oh I was blackmailed into it " she said sweetly, glancing over at Adam and then looking quickly away. It was apparent that his interests were now their interests.

"Investment meetings are one of the ways I like to spend an afternoon every month or so. The last one was great. Remember, Joan a couple of the gals had big rings on almost every finger? They're making money".

"Yes" Joan said: "One of the women sat beside me and at one point waved her hand in front of me and said: "Well I know what I'm doing, don't I". So that I would notice all the big rings".

"How very tacky" Ann blurted out, for she is not one to keep quiet.

To this Adam responded, "Oh no, not tacky, no way. They were great big expensive rings". And at this point Joan looked away once more.

Our discussion of charity work reminded Adam who had just entered the pub and was ready to take over the conversation for the evening of one of the things he liked to do. "Goodwill; It's a charity outfit you know. Well I like going on the second Thursday of every month for the 25% discounts". This after spending the better part of every evening bragging about his properties and investments was a bit much and it created an uncomfortable silence as no one knew quite how to respond.

Joan related a bit of what her marriage had been like one afternoon while walking to the market with Ann.

"Every time he invested in the stock market I knew to write it off as money spent and forget about it. Caused me less stress that way. He was always concocting some scheme to make money. Even bee-keeping toward the end." Later on Joan told me that she admired Ann and what she perceived as her "gift"

"Yes, I believe she has the gift of seeing past the mask a lot of people wear; their facade. It's a gift, isn't it, to be able to see the truth before it's too late".

Good Friends

I've a plaque that hangs on my kitchen wall and it says: 'A Friend Is Someone Who Walks In When Everyone Else Walks Out'.

How true that is, don't you think?

Well Ann and Joe are two such people. They are in their fifties, not much older than I. A perfect match, they both have a great sense of humor and are great listeners, two attributes which not only make them wonderful friends and neighbors to have, but make for a happy marriage as well.

They pop in and out of here any time and every day. I like that: it's like family, as are my regular guests and pub customers. Everyone needs to have people they care for and who cares for them in their lives and I am well aware of the fact that too many people today are not so fortunate. Well, just reading through my journal is clarification of this sad truth.

Ann and Joe met in France at one of those little outdoor cafes on a beautiful spring day, just like a couple might in one of those old romantic movies. She was alone holding a book and "pretending to read". Joe introduced himself and asked if he might join her, all the other tables being full.

They had been married for five years before Joe admitted that he purposely had been arriving too late to find a table, thereby hoping to find a lady alone and all the other places occupied. His American ingenuity, he joked.

Well, they hit it off right away and knowing Ann that had to have been the case because she is not the sort to have spent time with him otherwise. "Never have been one to settle, you know." She had read years earlier a bit of advice: Better to be alone than to wish you were. Some of my guests may have benefited from this bit of wisdom.

Peter and I met Ann and Joe when we arrived here looking for a place that would be suitable to set up as a bed and breakfast. But I'm getting ahead of myself now; perhaps I ought to tell you why I moved back to England and how I met Peter.

I was born in London England in 1952 to an American father and British mother. They met in London during the war, married, and he returned here after his discharge at war's end. I was one year old when they decided to move to New York City and having been born seven years after their marriage I am their only child.

Throughout my childhood I travelled across the Atlantic during school vacations visiting my grandparents here and making friends over the years, so that I've always felt this was my home as well. Actually I feel at home anywhere rather than just one spot on the globe. This is very good luck, for I would not want to feel restricted or afraid as do the people of Goat's Landing.

There are those who have told me that there is no such thing as luck, and yet I think to myself whenever I hear this; Isn't being born to loving, responsible parents luck? After all we've nothing to say about where or to whom we will be born. We can't control everything outside of ourselves no matter how hard we work or how well-intentioned we are, so that a loving background and an education goes a long way in helping one overcome the rough spots as we travel through this life.

I established myself as a teacher after graduation because that is what I wanted to do and I believe the students knew that I was interested in helping them. I had met not a few teachers in the States who were teaching because it meant job security and benefits. In many places one didn't even need an education degree.

I enjoyed writing and sold a few short stories and articles. I never shared my personal problems with job, life in general and therefore people perceived me as problem free. When someone like me does need a shoulder then no-one seems to want to listen. I guess they were just too used to me being the listener. They tended to say things like, "you? You never have problems; you can't have, you're our rock".

One morning during the Christmas season of 1978 I looked at myself in the mirror and decided that it was time for a change. The schools, indeed the country was becoming more violent and I was involved with a man neurotic in his self-absorption. He was a psychologist who one day told me that he had finally freed himself of the burden of emotional attachments. "It impedes optimal functioning".

Hanna's story of the Broker reminded me so much of this man I had known that I found it especially easy to empathize with her.

Like the broom man and the Broker his sense of identity was now tied to his possessions and he ceased to exist outside of what he owned. How different are the Lemieux' who are secure within themselves and refuse to allow society to dictate their worth.

Life, I had read should be an expanding spiral and mine had become a closed circle: It was time to make changes, for the minute one settles for less than they deserve, one gets even less than one settled for. The reality of my situation was far more anxiety producing, than change.

I walked the streets of Manhattan most of that morning. Down Madison Avenue window shopping, over to Macy's on Thirty-Second, then over to Broadway and a stop at my favorite vendors Mr. Martini, for a Kosher dog heaped with sauerkraut and a little conversation. The smiling face and kind word of this aged vendor cheered me as it always had and carried me out of the fog I had been walking in all morning.

I headed toward Central Park now, knowing that I would find activity there. It was the Christmas season and it would be an especially cheerful place. The past few weeks had seen a frenzy of decorating; indeed all of New York was beautiful, dressed in millions of lights. The store windows beckoned and entertained prospective customers and people rushed around madly shopping for friends and loved ones.

I found myself at Warman Rink watching the children skate, many with parents in tow celebrating the season and couples walked hand in hand, or arms round each other, smiling, transfixed and absorbed with each other's company as though there were no others. And I was alone. As I began walking back to my apartment a light snow began to fall and snowflakes mingled with my tears.

I did not return to teach after the holiday, but packed my things and sub-let my apartment. I flew to the Bahamas. I was definitely going to, rather than running from, as one unhappy colleague had suggested. There are those who cannot tolerate change, even in others. I believe it makes them feel insecure.

It was good to distance myself from all that had been familiar; cleared the cobwebs. It was a dream come true to be able to walk and think without any outside interference, demands, or restrictions. Then one afternoon I bought a local newspaper and out of curiosity read through the classified adds. This is how I found Peter. I spotted a help wanted ad for a nanny and called and made an appointment.

Two days later I arrived at his winter home in Nassau and interviewed for the position. The children, a girl of nine years and a boy of eleven simply needed a chaperone when their father needed quiet time. He was a London businessman who had lost his wife one year earlier. Well, just as in all good romance novels, the younger woman hired to help with the children eventually became the wife and step-mum. We returned to London together and had a child of our own, now grown. And so my life's journey had brought me back to my beginnings, and happily so.

I told Ann that I think people should complain about injustice, as I did by leaving a bad situation, or at least using their voices rather than sitting around hoping for things to get better and all the while they just slide along getting worse. "Never happen; most people are sheep and afraid to be labeled complainers, or different because of their points of view. They go along because it's easier not to rock the proverbial boat. Don't have the stuff our ancestors had. Organizing unions, fighting for fair treatment of the poor, children, helpless animals, a national health care system. All concessions were won in addressing these issues because people had the gumption to complain".

"So complainants don't bother me. It's the yes men; yes, they're the ones I don't have a lot of respect for".

Well, I've come to the end of this journal.

I will begin another while in France this spring. It should be an interesting month, more new people, more stories. Yes, as long as there are people and someone interested in watching and listening there will be stories.

MY TWO GRANNIES

I was ten years old the summer Pops died. He was my grandpa on mum's side. Until the day of his funeral I thought I knew everyone in the family pretty well.

It was after the funeral however, with my two grannies sitting, talking under the big willow trees in our back yard that I learned there was a lot more to Helena than her clothes, travel and book signings and much more to Lottie than her cooking, baking, and rushing round after everyone.

On the surface they appeared to be very different people. Dad's mum Helena was a big city granny, who everyone said always looked prepared for a photo shoot. Lottie, mum's mum was the prairie granny. As likely as not she could meet you at the door wearing an old faded t-shirt, jeans and those loafers that let her big toe poke through the top. Helena didn't meet you at the door and announce that she had made your favorite for dinner. Helena arrived by plane and told you all about the house in Nassau on the beach. There was no toe peeking out from an old loafer, just perfectly manicured nails looking up at you from an expensive pair of sandals. The slacks and top were perfectly coordinated and as for dinner, I always got to choose the restaurant.

The day of the funeral was warm, at least for mid-June on the prairie. At around three in the afternoon I decided to climb to my tree house. Sometimes it feels good just to sit up high and listen to the birds sing and it was especially good today, because the house was full of sad people trying to cheer each other up.

I had gotten comfortable on my sleeping bag, my lunch all set up and I admit I was looking forward to eavesdropping on whatever conversations floated my way, when along came my two grannies and sat down on a couple of lawn chairs almost directly beneath me.

They arranged a little table with a plate of those tiny finger sandwiches adults like to eat on such occasions, a bottle of white wine, and an ash tray. They behaved the way they always did when they got together; except this time the talk was less about the present than about the past, and what they had wanted, and what they had gotten, or never got, or were afraid to ask for, or wish they hadn't asked for, and well, it sounded as though mum, dad, and me were the best part of everything when it came right down to it. This was real nice, especially since they didn't even know that I was listening.

I had read some of granny Helena's stories, or tried to, but granny Lottie hadn't written any stories. I guessed that she had been too busy looking after everyone to travel and write and so I didn't know as much about her, although we had spent more time together.

Granny Helena had had her share of troubles, but on the surface they seemed exciting, even fun at times. Granny Lottie, on the other hand, had kept her troubles to herself, at least until today.

Helena was fifty-two years old now and Lottie fifty-nine. Helena had recently remarried. Charles Graham, her new husband was a retired financier. Lottie had buried her husband today, retired fireman, Ray Murphy.

Lottie and Ray had been born the same month of the same year, she on the fifth of May and he on the fifteenth. They always celebrated on the fifteenth and Lottie spent that day of the year as she always had; cooking, cleaning and baking their birthday cake. On Helena's birthday she had enjoyed the museums of Florence, Italy; dining in a fine restaurant and helping her husband plan their trip to Monaco. While one woman was being feted like a Queen, the other was working like a Queen bee.

Lottie didn't mind delaying her birthday celebration. Lottie didn't mind doing all the work. Lottie didn't mind putting everyone else before her. Lottie never minded. Lottie was lying, at least to herself, Helena often thought. Underappreciated, overworked and lonely Lottie.

Helena never voiced these opinions. Lottie's daughter and Helena's son had married thirteen years earlier and Helena enjoyed her visits and liked to believe she never interfered.

Now as the two women sat talking in the deepening twilight, the minutes ticked by as the discussion of the day's events progressed to an examination of past events.

Lottie: This is my favorite time of day, peaceful. Everything is done and everyone is satisfied, hopefully.

Helena: My favorite time of day has always been early morning. Fresh, new; I love watching the sun rise over the ocean, and listening to the birds chirping as I wonder what surprises the new day will bring. To me this is the most exciting time of day.

Lottie: Exciting? I never thought much about excitement. Perhaps that's why I have never really experienced any. When I think about it, life is the same old, same old, except when there is a special occasion; like Christmas, birthdays, Easter, and then it's work. What is Lottie going to make, bring, do for us? I sound boring, and bitter don't I?

Helena: No. Just taken for granted, predictable and tired of monotony.

Lottie: That's kind, but I know.

Helena: Know what?

Lottie: Your life is so much more exciting, interesting, and unusual than mine.

Helena: And at times it has been extremely lonely, so much so that on a few occasions I hoped not to wake up in the morning. Sometimes it has been frightening. I joke about being financially challenged, yet looking back I sometimes wonder how I came through it all sane, let alone successful. Those times I found myself buying canned goods and whatever else at the dollar store and thanking God that I had the six-fifty an hour job. Now that was frightening. I was glad to make the rent on that one room apartment that was my side of the funny little duplex in Reno, Nevada. Horrible experience Reno. I would pray, oh God, how I have made mistakes in my life to come to this. But then I realized that I had to travel down that particular road to come to the place that I was meant to be and believing in a kind and loving God kept me afloat. Me with my up and down life would at times wonder what you thought of me, Lottie.

Lottie: I just thought that at least you had dreams and that you grabbed the fear and made it work for you.

Helena: It worked for me. I don't preach, Lottie. You know I don't even attend church much, but I sure do pray, and really, at my darkest hour I do believe that God came through for me. Of course we have to help ourselves as well. We can't just sit and wait for a miracle. I always have believed however, that when God saw me trying so hard he did kick in with some help. Sometimes I got more than I asked for. I was always afraid to ask for much. A carry over from Childhood, you know. I had parents who saw their children as a drain on them, a problem to be endured and I believe that I was even afraid that the Almighty would see me that way as well. Crazy thoughts, Lottie. Crazy thoughts are what happen to abused kids and later in life, crazy lives as well.

Lottie: So you are saying pray.

Helena: Sure. Thank God for the good times. Keep hoping. Just believe that things happen for a reason. When we are doing the best we know how, then whatever happens, happens because it is supposed to be that way.

Lottie: How can this be for the best?

Helena: I asked that when no matter what I did to make things right, everything failed. Look at me now however; I am so much better off in every way than I could have ever imagined.

Lottie: I have felt lonely. So lonely I have wanted to cry, even with the family all around.

Helena: When we don't feel listened to, or understood and perhaps we feel taken for granted, it is natural to feel lonely.

Lottie: That's it. I have dreams too; sometimes I have looked at your life and thought it was a dream. You've lived your life no matter what anyone thought, or said of the risks you took. I have never been able to do that. Convention, others' opinions have played such a huge part in my life. I feel cheated. I even feel cheated by death now. I never could get Ray to do anything out of the ordinary. He wouldn't take even one trip to England with me and of course I felt both frightened and guilty about going alone. I always caved in. I always thought that, well, we at least will have each other for companionship in later life. Now I don't even have that much. Not only that, I don't even have any memories of us doing anything together but the same damned old things. When I think of it, it was all maintenance. The grocery, dinner at the crummy local diner.

Helena: and sometimes I envied your ordinary stuff.

Lottie: sometimes.

Helena: Alright I have to laugh. Yes it was only sometimes. And yet I wanted some of the routine. No; perhaps what I wanted was ordinary, but in an extraordinary way. I finally found it. I paid the price. Life on the edge financially, loneliness, abuse, all the mean circumstances.

Lottie: How did you keep going?

Helena: I believed. I believed that I would eventually overcome all the hardships. I prayed and I never lost faith.

Lottie: Even in the worst of times?

Helena: Especially then. Rebuild life. I have rebuilt often. It beats bitterness, living in the past, all the self-defeating behaviors. A prime example was the old man that worked at the poison factory.

Lottie: Your last Reno job where they made plastics?

Helena: Right. I was sent there by a temporary agency. One of the temps, a man of about sixty likened it to slavery. Modern day slavery he called it. It was just that. Seven dollars an hour, and no health benefits. The owner, an old German never looked at a temp and if one said good morning he ignored it. None of the supervisors acknowledged the existence of a temp either. I mentioned this to one of the permanent staff and was informed that no-one would recognize a staff member until they had decided that they might ask them to become permanent. Everyone had been hired that way. So I said; "So that is when you become a human being, when they decide to hire you permanently?" He said "yes" and I walked away wondering why anyone would want to be a permanent part of that poisoned environment and gradually I found my answer. The noise from the machines was deafening and the fumes from the chemicals - formaldehyde, poly resin, acrylic and god knows what else, caused everyone's eyes to burn, caused tiredness, headaches and the fine dust could have done the lungs no good. The dust was so prevalent that we were told never to leave a box of plastics that we were working on exposed. When we left our work station for a break we had to be sure that the precious product was covered with plastic to protect it. The staff were in no way protected however. A large poster hung in the staff room, the filthy staff room, and it detailed the various dangers of exposure to these chemicals, and the proper protective gear one was supposed to wear, masks etc. yet when I asked I simply got a look and was ignored. Paper dust masks were all I ever saw and they were few. There were radios at some of the work stations, left I was told by a supervisor by staff who had quit. I had thought they were placed there by management to break the monotony, silly me. I spent eight weeks there and it was during my very last day that sprinklers were installed in the staff room, though the plant had been in operation for over eight years. The floor was cement and standing in one spot working was painful on the legs and the old man was due for a third operation to have his veins stripped. He had survived five heart attacks, had kidney problems, liver, and God knew what else. The point is however, that his attitude had kept him stuck in this awful kind of work. He said he wasn't close to his two grown daughters, or their children and did not care whether his ex-wife was alive or dead. She apparently was from a wealthy family of old money. All he talked about was money in terms of other people's money of course. He had lost everything forty years prior and never got past that. Never forgive, never forget he said was his motto and it sure had not done him anything but harm. I ought to have suggested that he write things out as a sort of therapy, but he was too far gone for that I am certain. One day I did say "It's Friday, be happy, look forward to the weekend". But his response was that all he'd probably do was loose money gambling anyway. Then I said, "Say a prayer and thank God you are not worse off". He never spoke to me after that. The old owner's grandson had worked in the factory for five years and had risen to assistant manager. He was always helpful, friendly and smiling, then he began missing work a day here, a day there, three days straight, and suddenly word went round that he had just been fired by his grandfather, or rather, grandpa had had grandma, who worked in the office do the deed for him. He hadn't looked well, and though I don't know for certain I suspect the chemicals could have done him no good over such a long period. In fact I called OSHA and was told that everyone reacted differently and as little as two weeks could cause bladder, liver, heart, lung problems. Frightening. I didn't take long to find out that most of the staff were registered felons and if not that, then there was the woman on the run from California who had taken her son out of State against a court order. Another was a single woman raising a thirteen year old daughter and living in a cheap motel, then the thirty something who had three teens at home, and whose husband never seemed to be able to find a job to suit him. They had all moved in with granny nine years earlier and it didn't look as though they would be leaving any time soon. Thirty something walked with the aid of a crutch and kept to herself at breaks; reading thrift store paperbacks, she said, were her greatest escape from life. When you signed on with the temporary agency you signed a contract that stated you could not leave them and accept employment permanently with the company that you had been assigned until you had completed ninety days working through the agency. If the company wanted to hire you permanently before that time period was complete they had to buy your contract out. Interestingly, the only contracts that the poison factory bought out were those of the felons. The rest were advised at the end of shift on Friday whether to return for the coming week. Six weeks was all one of the felons spent as a temp before the factory paid for the agency to release him. The others spent from two to three months, yet were advised well in advance that they were (going to go permanent) as they referred to it.

Lottie: Unbelievable. Were they any better workers than the rest?

Helena: Not that I, or even they could see. In fact one was arrested for not registering a change of address and God knows what else, as he was kept incarcerated for one week and all the old German owner did was tell him that he was missed when he finally returned to work. Only one of the three had what I call a man's haircut. The other two had waist length hair that they pulled into a pony tail while working. All were so covered with tattoos that I secretly dubbed them the green hornets. Arms, backs of hands, even their necks were tattooed all round. They looked like what you would expect gang bangers, bikers to look like and had the filthy language and personalities to match. Their talk was nothing short of infantile. No interests other than drinking beer all weekend and nothing to brag about but how much time they had served and how many times they had been arrested. The old owner's grandson kept his musical equipment at the two long hairs place, a trailer in a part of the outlying area known for the fact that it was felon heaven. One long hair told me one day that the place was changing; it used to be at least ninety percent cons and it was down to about sixty-five percent. Well once I discovered that grandson was a buddy of some of the worst society had to offer, I began to see the light. The preferential hiring, time off for bad behavior, all of it seemed to point to a family of owners who were less than stellar pillars of the community. Then I find that they had moved the business to Reno from Auburn California because of trouble with environmental restrictions. Birds of a feather flock together my granny always said. Vultures all. And the con with the man cut a dangerous psycho. He had been picked up as well for failing to register and I kept checking the paper and sure enough the arrest was detailed just as he described it. At any rate I happened to mention one day to thirty something (you have to talk a bit and be friendly enough to get along) that I had a crazy neighbor that the landlord was finally evicting. Man cut had heard me talking in the staff room and came over to my station later that day to offer his services. "Where do you live?" he asked and I lied naturally. Then he said "How about I come over and intimidate your neighbor for you?"

Lottie: Good God, what did you do?

Helena: I calmly smiled and said "No thanks, it's taken care of". Then that Friday he walked up behind me at the time clock at end of shift and said "How about a beer?" I told him no thanks, very pleasantly, and added that I had lots to do after work. Following Monday, I am at my station and he walked over, slammed his hands palms down on the counter and said "You live alone, right? All alone. Have a nice weekend?" So I pleasantly said "Yes, was yours nice?" He stood back, shocked I believe that he could not intimidate me and repeated "You live alone anyway". and I said "Well, the Landlord is right next door which is nice". Nutty as a fruit cake. On another occasion not long after this he was sent to take over my station so that I could take my break. When he returned he told me that he listened to the same station as I listened while he worked on his art. I asked what sort of art he worked at, and he replied "Flowers, Picass, DRAGONS". The huge emphasis on the last and the anger might have sent most women running for cover. Yet recall that I had worked probation in New York and along with my psychology degree felt more confident than many, yet very, very concerned by now. I wanted to run myself, but decided to finish the month rather than allow the cons to think I was intimidated, as I believed that would get them excited enough to try to find out where I lived and don't forget by this time I did not trust the owners any more than I did the cons. The owner's son worked there as well, and though he was with the Sheriff's department, a deputy they said, that was no reason to trust him. At least not in that so typically high town. He wore a gold necklace around his neck and a diamond earring in his left ear and together with the curly below the ears hair, he looked nothing like the cops I was used to working with and he certainly was not undercover material.

Lottie: You see, that's what I mean. I could never have withstood that.

Helena: It took its toll, Lottie. I developed a major bladder infection and it frightened the hell out of me. Stress? Not being able to empty my bladder at the moment I needed to as I had been advised by a doctor twenty years earlier? The chemicals? That last thought was the worst. I finally quit. Never showed up for my Friday shift. Called the agency the night before and left a message. The medication was too strong for me to be able to work at any rate. I had worked there for eight weeks. I even returned to my station early many times after breaks using the excuse that because I did not wear a watch I would rather be early than late, but all the while simply happy to cut my time around the felons short. Well the girl who had sent me to the job feigned all the concern and compassion in the world when I told her of my medical problem, then asked me when I would be able to return and turned cold when I informed her not at all, but asked if she had anywhere else to send me. She said no quickly but that she would let me know. I remained pleasant to the end, thinking that all I wanted to do was retrieve my last two pay checks and get out of town. In fact I even added how disappointed I was to have to leave such a wonderful family-owned business.

Lottie: Unbelievable.

Helena: So was the price of the visit to the walk-in Medi-Quik clinic. One hundred and sixty dollars. This covered a urine sample, blood pressure check, looked in one ear, listened to my heart, asked a few questions, felt my belly and gave me three horse pills. They did not inform me of side effects etc. and when I returned two days later to find out what the results of the urine test were they said call back Monday. The one day results had stretched to five. I asked for a prescription in case I had a return of blood and she gave me what I asked for saying that they were no more than two dollars a pill. The pharmacy said differently - ten dollars a pill, forty something for four. The lady at the pharmacy told me that I had been given the strongest meds, short of an IV and that if it were her body and pocket book she would hold off to see if they were needed. I took her advice. She added that the clinic in question is known to overprescribe.

Lottie: Well all of it is unreal to me. It is like something from another planet. A B movie of the week. Or...

Helena: A book, Lottie.

Lottie: God, yes. What am I thinking? Yes that is where all your stories came from, real life. What a life. The people, men who rented next door, however. How many? Five? The last you said you would tell me about and how the poor old landlord came round to being a good man.

Helena: Yes, there's that story and the Vault. Notice how all the Reno stories are alike in their examples of abusive behavior.

Unwarranted, unbelievable abusive behavior, visited by the miserables upon one another. And oh, my little Mormon friend. Did I tell you her cancer had returned? That is part of the story of the vault and Keno at The Silver Star Casino. The older lady we had worked with at the outlet store appeared at the Keno counter one night and told me that our little friend had had a very bad prognosis. My little Mormon friend at the outlet store had told me that Reno was dangerous, particularly to a single woman such as myself. She had said that even though she had a happy marriage, she hated the town and even a contented home life could not make up for all that was wrong there. I thought about her when I was working at the poison factory. She would have been appalled to see me there. Get out, get out while you still have a future to look forward to living. I know that she must have had many regrets when her cancer returned. They stayed she told me, because of the financial security his job provided and now look what putting off living the life you desire had led to. So Lottie, I am thinking these thoughts and I turn on the television this particular night and the movie is one about the Jewish ghetto in Poland during the second world war. One prisoner of the ghetto said to the other "Fight back and if you can't fight back, run and if you can't run, hide. It is your duty to survive." I was feeling that way myself in Reno and the poison factory was the proverbial straw that broke the camel's back. I had told consciously work to combat the stress at work and the idiot that had moved in next door had only compounded the stress I was under. Idiot is the way the policeman had referred to him and it fit perfectly.

Andy lived in the other side of the little duplex for exactly four months and for the entire duration did nothing but irritate. The landlord downstairs and the old Irish man in the back of that side, as well as the young student in one room were all beside themselves, as was I for lack of sleep. Andy had rented the front room, had access to the kitchen and bathroom and paid only sixty dollars a week, but you would have thought he owned the place. He ran water at all hours of the night and paced back and forth across the floor in hard soled shoes. He constantly rearranged furniture and hollered, rather than talked on his cell phone. All these crazy behaviors got him attention from both the landlord and I, but he needed more because he soon began running the vacuum cleaner after midnight and then took to drilling. He claimed to head a much in demand western band, but as time wore on and his behavior became more and more outrageous, he appeared to work less and less often until he was not seen leaving for work at all the last two months. I noticed his clothes getting dirtier and dirtier, until the last week of his stay he was seen coming and going in the same pair of old black shorts that stopped just above the knee. It looked to me as though he had cut the legs off of a pair of cheap cotton pants. The landlord could not figure out the cause of the black stain in the bottom of the bath tub until I told him that Andy had decided to not bother wearing shoes any longer.

I would sit typing in the window and look up to see him heading toward his car barefoot. It was always the same scenario, slam the door, slam the gate, and dial his cell phone while opening the car door. He'd speed off and be back in ten minutes, then again, and this could go on for hours. Oh, and no shirt, and a pair of sun glasses completed the picture.

Lottie: Were you not scared?

Helena: No. I was disgusted. I reasoned that he most certainly was doing drugs and the condition he left the place in confirmed my suspicions. You had to see it, Lottie. He was outside working on his car one afternoon when I went out to check the mail and he told me that all the noise was because he was doing so much work to make the place perfect. "You should see the kitchen floor" he said. "I have at least eight coats on it and it is beautiful". He also told me that he had moved the landlord's furniture out to make way for his good furnishings, because he claimed he could not live with junk.

The reality we found was far different than that which had lived in Andy's imagination; four weeks behind on his rent the Landlord finally was able to convince a judge to evict him. The sheriff returned from court with the Landlord and told him that he could not break the door in, but would stand there with him while he did so. He had to break in because Andy had changed the locks once he was asked to leave.

I returned from the poison factory to find poor old Ollie standing in the middle of one of the worst scenes imaginable. There was nothing but an old filthy mattress lying in one corner of the sleeping room. The floor, carpet, and appliances could not have been filthier. He had even left food to rot in the oven. I found out that the drilling was nothing more than lines and lines of screws drilled round the walls about one foot from the ceiling and he had installed police locks on all the windows and doors. Well, as I stood talking to Ollie he drove up and demanded the rest of his things - a box of torn books, actually they were stacked in plastic milk crates, a bike, and he picked up a piece of bicycle tire tread from beside the porch and one of those padded blankets they use for padding things on moving trucks. This he threw over his shoulder and as he turned to walk to his car he told us that we would be sorry. He was returning to break all the windows and kick in all the doors in the house. Pathetic.

The police came and told us that they could not do anything until something happened and that we had to witness the event. I gave the cop Andy's license plate numbers, yes he had two old sport cars, one full of junk parked across the street. The cop, to his credit stayed and talked with us for a half hour and then sympathetically told Ollie that he would keep an eye on the duplex for a while. We never did see the drug addict again and the next day I noticed that the other old car was gone.

Lottie: It's the stuff of a B movie. Really, Helena. And this was the neighborhood that was supposed to be old, established and one of the safest in Reno?

Helena: Yes. Complete with the students raising hell across the street and the twenty something in the duplex next door inviting students who passed by to drink beer with him, filling whole garbage cans with bottles and even barbecuing on the front lawn one evening. He loudly bragged about all the drugs he did and even pulled his car on to his neighbors' lawn one day and began washing it, all the while his four letter word rap music blasting from his stereo. Unbelievable people, Lottie. The felons at work claim that it's all freedom of speech and people should do whatever they like. Well, that's the neighborhood. Looking back it is hard to believe that I was able to work on five hours disturbed sleep many a night and yet remain as sane and healthy as I did.

Lottie: Now tell me about the vault. It's going to start getting chilly out here at night on the old prairie.

Helena: Oh the vault, Lottie. The very last of my gruesome hotel experiences. This hotel I was told catered mostly to the locals and as I needed a job and quickly, I took the position as vault cashier. I convinced myself that it would be interesting to see just what a strictly locals hotel would be like. It was hell and the letters written back and forth between myself and the personnel director are illustrative of the kinds of people who work in the casino business.

There is the old saying 'thou protesteth too loudly' and the job orientation was indicative of that. It was really nothing more than an hour's long emphasis on the loyalty, honesty and wonderful work atmosphere we were about to enter and management's pride in its staff not having joined a union. That in itself should tip anyone off to the fact that they are entering a master slave environment.

I was required to lift twenty-two pound bags of money, coin and casino tokens, as the gambling chips are called. Well I had been told that much, but no one had informed me that I would also be window cashier to the bartenders and all other hotel staff requiring floats, restaurants, cages, you name it-- anyone cashing in or out and of course inevitably they were the run of the mill, rude and impatient type slaves. I would be in the middle of making up a cart for the cage, or change booth and someone would appear at the window demanding service or vice versa.

Only I was responsible for balancing and filling the orders from every corner of the hotel. Filling orders and keeping shelves stocked with hundreds of bags of coin and chips required not only speed, but strength and there was the paperwork involved. It was the work of two people I was doing for my seven dollars an hour, no benefits and a free meal it took five minutes to walk to and I was required to tip the cafeteria staff for putting it on the plate. Sure wonderful to see people so happy with these circumstances that they don't want to join a union.

I lasted one week in that job and was offered a transfer to the Keno department where, I was to discover they could not keep new hires and my letter to management emphasizes the reasons for that.

What a horror the Keno job was. Yet I give myself credit for fighting to keep it. The diner customers, fat slobs barely able to waddle in and many unable to fit behind the table in a booth, snapping their fingers for attention and talking with the food half chewed in their mouths, grease dripping down their fat double chins, angry when they lost their fifty cent Keno bet. Then there were the crude, demeaning, demanding drunks at the bars who treated the female employees as though we were retired hookers lucky to be running round making bets in the hope of receiving a half dollar, or if we were fortunate a whole dollar tip.

Heather Whittaker
Phone-323-4470

5-11-02

Dear Mr. Holder,

I am attaching a copy of a letter I have written to Mr. Skaggs. Your staff are advised that you can be relied upon to address those problems that are brought to your attention. I am therefore sending this along to you for your consideration.

Sincerely,

Heather C. Whittaker

Heather Whittaker
Phone-323-4470

5-11-02

Dear Mr. Skaggs,

At approximately eleven-thirty a.m., yesterday I left a message on Rick's office answering machine. This, as you will recall, had been your instruction. After four p.m. that same day he finally returned my call by leaving me a message that said "I thought you'd be in at four to work anyway, and had a meeting from two to three-thirty, but any time you care to come in we can visit."

On page 19 of the Silver Club's employee handbook it states that one of the instances where an employee may file a grievance directly with Human Resources first, rather than meeting with their department head would (2) If a safety hazard existed that threatened the health/safety of an employee or a customer. (3) If the grievance directly involves the dept. head, and the employee can reasonably demonstrate that the dept. head may not be able to deal with the situation effectively.

The fact that Rick took me to task for reporting the heavy smoking taking place within arm's reach of an oxygen tank, I believe demonstrates that he is not up to the task. in fact there was no good reason to blatantly make it common knowledge that I had been the person to cause this practice to cease.

(Pg 5) An impartial investigation will be undertaken immediately. The company not only prohibits harassment but also prohibits any retaliation against any employee who, in good faith, has registered a complaint. Interesting. I was the person to sign forms taking full responsibility for tickets supposedly gone missing and that Mary appeared to be free of any responsibility for the chaos that ensued that Friday night, after she had gone unaccompanied to the restaurant to allegedly set things straight. I was rudely sent home that Friday only half way through my shift-then told to come to work Saturday and when I arrived Saturday told that the schedule had been changed. That is a day and a half of work lost. Now on Thursday evening I was approached by Mikel in the restaurant and informed that if I had a problem with staff I should talk to staff and that I should not go around talking about people. Mikel also told me and very aggressively, that I had no right to go talking to Human Resources. I explained to her that the problem was of no concern to staff and that it had been a problem that concerned a customer, security being called, and tickets. Mikel refused to accept my explanation, and the next thing I see is her at the Keno desk talking with Mary, then shortly thereafter I walked by the bar outside the restaurant and stopped beside her to collect from a customer and noted that she was filling out a complaint form. From there I find her handing a folded paper to Lil. Mary denied knowing anything and I therefore walked over, retrieved the paper and handed it to the by this time, red faced Mary.

I told Mary that what was transpiring was making me angry and she quickly informed me that she would send me home right then if I was angry and that she was not going to have anyone fighting. I had not indicated in any way that I would lower myself by fighting. Ridiculous behavior is it not? Mikel, a grown woman, telling me that I had caused a lot of trouble for the staff, and all because these women can no longer smoke on the job and only feet from an oxygen tank.

It was after this instance with Mikel, that a ticket Mary sold me and the only one I had to deliver as the restaurant was very slow, was claimed to have gone missing. Now I returned to Mary and told her that a customer claimed his ticket missing, and that it was ridiculous because it was the only one I had been holding and her response was that she couldn't say what had happened to it between me taking it and arriving at the restaurant. Lauren suggested to Mary that she accompany me back to the restaurant, but Mary refused, telling me that I should tell the customer that he would have to pay for another. In fact there were two tickets totaling $3.50. Now the customer walked back to Keno with me and he and Mary disappeared for a short time and upon their return had in their hands two tickets smeared with grease. Obviously these had been tossed away and retrieved as Mary's need arose.

The restaurant had been virtually empty all evening and I had made a point of confirming with each and every customer that the ticket I was delivering was without question theirs. When I pointed this out to Mary she returned to the restaurant and came back to Keno with the news that I had confused the tickets and gave the first gentleman's tickets to the only other two men in the restaurant.

I was sent for my third break of the evening at approximately 11:10 that evening and at 11:30 Mary arrived in the break room to ask me if I wanted an early out. This was as well a good excuse for her to take a cigarette break. At any rate I laughed and said I could not imagine how I could make such a mistake, therefore she relaxed and told me that she had been in the business since she was twenty-one years old and that customers could be dishonest, but that I just did not know how to handle these things. She continued on to say that she might have to offer free dinners etc. to keep the night's customer happy. I have no doubt that the man will be happy to accept a comp. for assisting Mary.

I told Mary that I found it amazing that I could have worked for eleven years for a stockbroker and yet could not deliver two Keno tickets and she turned beet red and responded that I must clock out within the next four minutes. I did just that.

Now let us be clear Mr. Skaggs. Before being employed by Mr. Gould in Las Vegas I worked for the Department of Probation in New York City-Manhattan borough; I was very good at what I did. I have interviewed thousands of shall we say, people on the fringe of society. I know when I am being lied to, lied about and in general jerked around. I also have a B.A. in psychology and I am seldom wrong in my assessment of a situation. You have a sorry situation here. You have staff giving out free drink tickets to boyfriends and on their days off spending their free time drinking at the hotel, obviously free of charge.

I am an honest woman, who wanted to do a Day's work and go home; however I have been subjected to slander and the blatant intentional affliction of emotional and consequently monetary distress. I have lost wages and been forced to spend my time working to set this, my worst employment experience to rights.

Rick did nothing but make excuses for the staff smoking by telling me that he bent the rules to give them a break when they're busy. He is no doubt very angry at being exposed. You appear to have the fox guarding the hen house and the inmates running the asylum. Mary, it appears has convinced the other staff members that I am their enemy. Perhaps if I had not been present when a customer (Ron) laughingly accused Mary of having a buzz on and she laughingly went along, she may not have seen fit to instigate the problems we are now forced to deal with.

Your hotel is not standing by its commitment to its code of conduct, or it's grievance procedures. At the same time libel is an offense and one I am not prepared to tolerate. At the very least a letter of apology I believe is in order. Under the circumstances it is a modest request, and may save all of us time and money.

Heather C. Whittaker

The upstairs bar and it was approximately twenty steps to run up and down, catered to the couples for the most part, that is when the wife was not off working, then it was the husband or boyfriend sitting there complaining about not winning, money problems, and kids they could not seem to manage. Irresponsible whackos and the next generation following right behind them by the sounds of it.

The letter in response to mine from personnel rewriting all that had taken place was and is priceless in its bazaar attempt to alter reality. But then that's the casino business, or any business that employs those barely hanging by a finger nail on the fringes of society.

Look at the sixty year old man at the factory. He claimed to have held more executive positions than an army, but his filthy language and demeanor shouted prison and often he would forget he had told other stories and in an effort to import his vast knowledge on every subject whenever one of the other ex-cons mentioned something about probation rules etc. he was right there filling them in on conditions in Oregon. One afternoon I entered the staff room and he was hard at it, telling the con who had just been released from his week in the local jail that judges came down hard when it had anything to do with kids, especially women judges. "That's why I don't go nowhere and never get stuck in a crowd; I'm afraid they'll pick me up."

I will never forget hearing that said.

We hear that people deserve second chances, yet listening to the trash brag about their exploits makes one wonder just how many second chances one deserves and to do what?

Lottie: It sounds like you were fed up with everything.

Helena: And so disappointed. I suppose I had simply watched too many Frank Capra movies as a kid. I was searching for the

America of my ideals and like Columbus I found something else entirely.

Lottie: You did enjoy some great times however.

Helena: I did and I would not change a thing. We have to take the good with the bad. Churchill summed it up best I believe. "Life is a whole and good and ill must be accepted together. The journey has been enjoyable and well worth making-once." - Sir Winston Churchill

Lottie: You are just sorry that society has fallen so far, so fast.

Helena: Exactly. And where do you go but down when you don't respect yourself? You don't respect others either. And life becomes more chaotic with each passing year.

Lottie: I have read your stories. All of those jobs and all of the abuse. I, on the other hand kept my nose to the proverbial grindstone thinking about the pension that would follow. I could not have endured your experiences, but you are now on top of the world.

Helena: There is a price for everything and I guess knowing whether or not we are prepared to pay the price dictates a lot of our behaviors. Remember, risk is the price we pay for opportunity. Just looking for work required a great deal of stamina in Reno, in particular. Time after time I would fill out an Application; a worker would take it to the boss and the boss, a female, would emerge from the back office a moment later, look at me and tell me the job had been filled. One day I decided to do a little research and started calling the businesses a few hours after applying whenever this happened. I would ask if they were still looking for help and without fail every time I called I was told yes and to go in and apply. Sound crazy?

Lottie: Yes.

Helena: Well, on every occasion the boss had been the typical Reno woman. Unkempt, faded clothes, overweight. You get the picture. The bottom line was that anyone with self-esteem was paying the price for those who, for whatever reason had long since given up. Though male, the manager of Albertson's supermarket was another sorry case. I applied there because it was close to my little place and when he looked at my resume he commented that I had had interesting jobs and had travelled and enjoyed myself before - as I had told him - semi-retiring to Reno. I went for the mandatory urine test as I had many times prior to this and had never had a problem, yet this time they told me that I did not have enough impurities in my urine to test it for drugs. The very next time I went for such a test I told this story to the lab tech and she laughed and told me that she had never heard of anything so ridiculous. After that I shopped there a few more times and I was as pleasant as ever, but he was rude and hostile toward me. The best defense of the ignorant is always offence. Miserable people are always more than happy to spread their misery round. I fervently prayed for courage and stamina and I believe that my prayers were answered. I decided that my stories may help others weather life's hardships. Telling myself that things will get better in God's time helped me through. Prayer and patience, Lottie. I didn't give up on God and he didn't give up on me.

Lottie: What was the worst part of all you had to contend with?

Helena: The realization that my friends were fair weather friends I had never asked, but given and yet when a phone call or note would have been so welcome, one by one I ceased to hear from people as my situation worsened. Near the end of my Reno experience, not a soul called or wrote, with the exception of my young friend dating back to my teaching experience in South Korea. I turned it round however and decided that it was for the best. It would free me to do for those who were deserving, once I made it through the hard times. There are those who may think that having lived the good life in comparison to what I was living -well, the memories should have caused me to be depressed. I turned that around as well and decided that I had been lucky to have had what I did, at least materially and that the worst would end eventually. At least I had lived many experiences and enjoyed much that most people only fantasize about. You know the poison factory was simply the last in a long series of job experiences that confirmed the existence of Dickensian working conditions in America. Bitter, abused and neglected people, fearful of complaining. The Government locks people up now and holds them without pressing charge, allowing them an attorney, or even contact with family members, wonderfully democratic. The worker who told me she thought we had lost our guts in America seemed to be on to something. It is easier to wave a flag, hustle off to buy a big mac than fight for what is just, easier and less risky. The old Irishman who had rented a room next door called Reno a sewer and told me that he was staying long enough to sell his van and move to Cuba. He wanted to spend the remainder of his life in a nice warm climate. He was concerned that if he ever wanted to return to visit he would be fined eight thousand dollars for having set foot in Cuba. He had moved to the States in nineteen forty-nine and had become an American citizen, yet even that gesture had not meant anything as far as the treatment he had received was concerned. Belittled and referred to as a foreigner all of his life, at seventy-six he had finally had enough.

Lottie: Somehow I don't feel quite as sorry for myself as I did. I have regrets, things I wanted to do and did not do for myself, but I still have time.

Helena: You have time and be happy and grateful that Ray did not suffer.

Lottie: He had regrets. He wanted to have been more, accomplished more, realized more success. He did always play it safe though. I guess you can't have it both ways. What was it you wrote? Yes. Risk is the price we pay for opportunity. He never took risks. Maybe that embarrassed him. I've wondered about that at times, but he never suffered in ways you have described. What will I do now? I am alone in my little home.

Helena: You can retire which is something you have wanted to do for years. I recall you telling me that the reason you kept working was so that the two of you would not become irritated with each other, together all day with nothing to do. Be thankful for the good parts of life you have enjoyed. An example is the working conditions I have described and that you have never had to suffer. Allow yourself to do something just for you; visit me in Nassau. It is alright to enjoy what you have earned. For years I feared success; Crazily enough I saw the plights of those around me and thought that I should feel guilty for being better off. Now I realize that in order to help others, I had to help myself first.

So there they were plotting a new beginning for granny Lottie. Most of what I heard was about granny Helena, but later on I realized that the hard luck stories she had told that day helped granny Lottie to feel less sorry for herself, less depressed the adults say. She started to feel more gratitude for what she had and less cheated out of what she didn't have, may not have.

One nice thing about living on the prairie is that the twilight lingers and the darkness kind of creeps in slowly. My grannies' voices, and the descending darkness sent me to sleep and I awoke to the sounds of them calling my name.

They said it had just gotten dark, so I know I didn't miss much. I had missed the last part about the new plans for us to travel to Nassau to granny Helena's, but they filled me in while they were tucking me into bed that night.

When I said my prayers before sleep, I said thanks for granny Helena taking all those risks, and thank you for Lottie always having been there. I guess sometimes a kid just gets lucky and gets the best of both kinds of people.

THE CHAPEL

CHAPTER 1 - DEAR JACK

July 1, 01

Dear Jack,

Well I have finally found a job outside of the casinos while I patiently await the replies from agents to my query letters. It, the chapel, is a family owned affair. Junior, the grandson of the woman who established the business in 1955 is the boss, according to his father. I've been there only one week and already I have misgivings. The staff, all part time dislike Junior intensely. He apparently has accused them on occasion of stealing such ridiculous things as rice; we make up little packages - one tablespoon, in a bit of plastic tied with a colored bow as a favor for the customers, naturally the favor costs twenty-five cents a pop. At any rate the forty-six year old Junior appears to have overstepped his bounds on more than one occasion where staff are concerned. I do not want to get involved in any friction and have gone to work and kept quiet. However Junior is most irritating and I believe I will need allies.

I am the only full-timer there. I open at 9 a.m. and am relieved at either 4 p.m. or 5 p.m. by an eighty-four year old retired school teacher Sunday through Thursdays. She has worked part-time at the Chapel for sixteen years now and dislikes Junior as much as anyone. When I started I loved the idea of working independently in the old refurbished house. It is at least one hundred years old. I cleaned the fridge and sorted supplies etc. Rachel, (the elderly lady) had warned me against doing too much, or to use her words, "No more than absolutely necessary." she said that he would not appreciate anything and would only find something to complain about-regardless. In fact he gets angry when he can't find anything to pick at us about. None of the ministers can stand to be around him. The ministers who perform the civil ceremonies drive from chapel to chapel when needed. We have their cell phone numbers and when someone arrives to get married we call whoever is on duty and they pop in ten minutes later to perform the ceremony.

Earlene is the only minister willing to sit at Junior's chapel full-time on a Saturday. Earlene's story is one of desperation and she will do whatever she believes she must to survive. Naturally, this being Nevada one may as well write 'victim' across their forehead as let anyone know that they are in desperate circumstances; as the vultures will then smell blood and not hesitate to move in to take advantage.

Earlene spends three days a week cleaning the homes of a minister, his daughter, and their church and this covers the rent and utilities on a small house on the minister's compound. She says that the living room is so small you can stand in the middle of the room and stretching your arms out touch the opposite walls at the same time.

It sounds almost like a cult to me. It is out of town just off the highway on the way to Carson City. The compound has six homes all occupied by various and sundry relatives and Earlene. Those who work for the old minister work an average of sixty hours a week. When factored in at about five fifty an hour Earlene barely earns minimum wage.

Earlene is an attractive fifty-six year old woman who has a husband in prison - another minister no less. He is incarcerated for child molestation and she claims he is innocent and I believe that she really believes what she tells me. She tolerates a good deal of abuse and prays for his release soon, though he was sentenced to forty years.

The two twenty-one year old ladies who work at the Chapel on Saturdays and the odd week night each have two tiny children at home. They have to put up with Junior as well in order to assist their husbands with the household income.

It is rather difficult to describe junior; personality disorder, sociopathy comes to mind. He has absolutely no empathy for man nor beast, is arrogant, rude and basically oblivious to any societal norms. He never apologizes for anything and if he does make a mistake is quick to find someone else to blame. Always ready to pounce, he is red in the face and on the verge of an angry outburst. His alternate expression is absolutely blank.

His young nieces and nephews refer to him as uncle monster and no-one has much to do with him. His father is personable and pops in on occasion - Monday mornings usually to go through the previous week's business receipts. I am told that his father is Junior's only family contact on a regular basis.

The girl I replaced at the Chapel made off with twelve hundred dollars. Junior has renters who drop into the Chapel to pay their monthly rent and apparently she pocketed some of the rents.

Well, Jack, I am tired now. Write me soon regarding your plans for the European trip. It sounds wonderful.

All for now.

As Ever,

Aileen

CHAPTER 2 - NICKELS AND DIMES

July 21, 01

Dear Jack,

Well I am still at it, working the Chapel. When I hired on Jr. told me that although the pay was only six-fifty an hour I would get ten percent commission on whatever I sold. Well, besides cleaning, making bouquets, etc. I sold the bouquets, rice etc. pretty well, and expected approximately one hundred dollars at month's end tacked on to my pay but ah, Junior informed me the other day that my commission will not start until I have been there a full month. Typical of Reno to screw the foreigner - that would be anyone living here less than a decade I suspect, and screwed by the sociopath to boot.

To add insult to injury he - because I had been short ten cents here and twenty five there at the end of the day now and then - told me that he hated to think he was buying my cigarettes. So the young ones own the rice and I the small change. I guess he doesn't think I look like much of a cook.

Of course all this mean behavior causes negative reactions in the staff. Last Sunday was the second Sunday I have walked into a mess left by the young mammas. I presume they intend to work as little as possible and that of course affects me in the long run.

I wonder what I'll find tomorrow morning? Will the old lady have written that she left one hundred dollars for me in float money and then leave ninety-eight fifty in the leather purse? Will all the garbage cans be full and rice strewn throughout the building for me to spend hours vacuuming up?

It is a crying shame. Literally a crying shame that a person can show up early for work each day, do more than expected, treat everyone respectfully and end up the recipient of trashy behavior. No pun intended.

Thursday is my last work day of the work week and on the way home I stopped into the grocery store for a few items. A woman standing behind me in line was holding a greeting card and in the course of our short conversation she looked me right in the eye and said. "Let go and let God. Everything will be fine; don't even think about work or the nasty boss after you walk out that door. Just enjoy your home." The thing is, Jack, I had not said a word to her about myself. I thanked her though and told her that I was feeling down and that she must have been sent to cheer me. I wonder if we don't attract what we need at certain times in life?

Denise, one of the young ones at the Chapel needed two hundred dollars so that her Mexican husband could apply for his U.S. citizenship. Earlene told Denise that she would pray that the money would come and one day later Denise's father called and offered the money as a gift.

Do you think I should ask Earlene to say a prayer regarding my finding a literary agent post haste? I would like to get out of this nasty town with something to show for the time spent here.

I have made the best of the little studio, choosing to see it as a little cottage, and pretending not to care that I have only a two burner hot plate to cook on, an ancient fridge that I have to defrost every two weeks and now a toilet that has a broken handle. I reach down the tank and pull up on the plunger in order to get it to flush. I feel so close to leaving that I do not want to ask the old Irishman to fix it. I don't expect him to refund my deposit anyway not after the way he balked at having the one phone jack in the place made functional. Hollering the day after I moved in that I did not need a phone, that lots of people don't have phones and then commenting that it was a good thing that he had a deposit after I informed him that it was the law that a Landlord supply at least one working jack.

I did tell you about being charged an extra twenty-five dollars rent because of my cat Baby, although these carpets are filthy and ragged, and pieced together. The furniture is scarred, goodwill stuff, and washing the bathroom walls did not make that much difference to the appearance of the place as it is in need of a paint job. I stuck a brick that I found at the corner of the house in the window to hold it open and put a bit of tape over the hole in the screen to keep the bugs out.

I can't have been any thriftier. I shop at Ross Dress For Less, which is a good idea for anyone looking for quality goods at lower prices; it's just that I really have no choice at present. My days off, well, I spend one hour at the laundry mat, that's if I am too tired to go over after work on my Friday. I look forward to the people magazine that comes out every Friday and I don't purchase it every Friday anymore either, not since the price has gone up so ridiculously in the past year. It has become an extravagance. I've no television as I decided that I'm best to keep writing and trying to find an agent and reading to stay sane than to be spending extra for cable. I admit however, that when I see the odd nice movie, or biography advertised in the paper I wish I had the little box sitting on my table.

Hope this does not sound like pity me stuff. I don't feel that way really; just stating the facts. Looking positively at this situation I like to think, hell I do believe that success will taste that much sweeter because I have gone through so much to get where I am going.

I have learned that attitude is everything from all of these experiences. After all, without a positive attitude could one have remained sane and healthy? Imagine moving from Malibu to Hicksville and not getting depressed?

Having you to talk with is great therapy of course. I can't imagine anyone else having the patience to follow my saga and keep encouraging me the way you do. Actually, I find encouragement in dealing with some of the Chapel customers as well. There was the wedding I call the blind man's wedding. The groom, a blind man, very charismatic, beautiful kind personality and sophisticated. His bride my age, and as lovely a person as he, told me that it was her forth and his sixth wedding. I saw it as two good souls finally finding each other, although many people would, I realize see this many attempts at happiness as negative. I give them credit for not giving up; theirs was a lovely wedding, well-dressed people, at least the Sunday best clothes had been dragged out of the closet by every last one. Most of the customers turn up in jeans, even shorts and old t-shirts. I suppose nothing seems very special to these people, not even their wedding day. Some couples you never forget, like the man who had to turn himself in to a prison in California, and his bride, front teeth missing, yet worrying if her hair looked good enough for the Polaroid I had been handed to take to record this event for posterity. She wearing ragged cutoff jeans, and he in a faded t-shirt that had written on the front 'No Fear'.

The East Indian weddings tend to be beautiful events, taken seriously by all the guests. The clothes are the best they can afford, the people are polite, though unruly in that they will sneak in food and drink to the Chapel - apparently part of the marriage custom and they leave garbage all over the place, but then they pay extra for the clean-up with no complaints.

Sunday tomorrow and I open the Chapel and close at five. It's Reverend Thomas tomorrow. He officiates at weddings only on Sundays. The rest of the week he services slot machines at one of the casinos on the State line. Poor man. No one likes him because he talks non-stop and appears to think he knows more than he does. He is a saint compared to the boss however, and hates Reno and wants desperately to move back home to upstate New York.

Arnie is the minister I like, after poor Earlene. Arnie wears colorful shades, turns up as quick as an apparition when called upon and sees the boss as no more than the village idiot.

Junior, being paranoid has warned all of us to look out for the ministers. He claims they steal when your back is turned. Film, toilet paper, you name it, according to Junior nothing is safe, not even us. He claims they all want to talk us into working for them.

It is the pits to hate the thought of going to work in the morning. Hopefully it will not be for much longer here though.

I suspect that my typing has piqued the curiosity of the Landlord, or the tenant in the room next door, whom I refer to as one-eyed Jack, him having only one eye. The window being open, I chance to notice a figure flit by out of the corner of my eye. Oh yes, they bob and weave past the window on such nights, hoping to get an idea of what I am doing and then the garbage will be gone through before pick up on Wednesday.

Weird place, Jack, where the ice cream truck drives up and down the block at between thirty and forty miles an hour and the police informed me at approximately one o'clock in the morning on Friday, that they had warned the so-called students in the animal house across the street that they were going to start ID checks if they got any more calls regarding disturbances. This after my calling an average of two and three times a month for the last ten months. As you know I have had to call three times in one night on occasion.

It's a good thing that Friday was a day off as all hell broke loose over forty idiots at that house according to the cops. I looked out and they reminded me of a bunch of lemmings, literally, dozens of young men, peaked caps on backward, long shorts and white t's, mumbling, shouting obscenities, moving from one foot to the other in the middle of the road.

Cars would honk to try and pass and the creatures would holler and curse them, then one of the fools parked his car in the drive next door to me and set the alarm system off, leaned on the trunk of my car and just waited. I threw my bath robe on and asked him what the hell he was doing and he hollered "here's the bitch, gee I apologize". So I told him to save the apology for the police as they were on their way. He backed his car off and ran screaming that the police were coming and by god all the lights at the house went out and you could hear a pin drop in less than a minute. Just goes to show you how chicken shit bullies really are, which is why they bully in the first place. Like the boss, I figure he'd be pushing a shopping cart if it were not for his family and I suspect he is well aware of the fact.

Well I had better close for now Jack. I will read some positive bit of work like Deepak Chopra or some Oprahism to ease me to sleep. That little routine has worked for me all these many nights here.

I hope to have good, no, great news for you soon. In the meantime God Bless, take care.

As ever,

Aileen

CHAPTER 3 - DEAR ME

And what do I make of all of this? I refuse to allow myself to get down in the mouth by feeling sorry for myself, but it is not easy to keep up the good fight some days, no, not at all easy. I arrive at the Chapel at eight-thirty in the morning, though I am paid from nine; I like to have everything ready for the start of the day.

This morning the boss arrived early as he does on Monday mornings to go through the tin box and add up the week's sales. It was eleven o'clock and here he came papers in hand. He has something to go over with me he says. Fine. I am thirty dollars short in cash for one day last week he tells me. How? Oh but you are twenty nine twenty five over the following day so that makes up for it. I know he is lying. I don't trust him as far as I can throw him and consequently I count every penny at least three times before I deposit the day's balance in the tin box each night.

A few weeks ago he told me that I was fifty five cents short one day and twenty two the following. He added he didn't like to think he was buying anyone's cigarettes. So I told him to take the shortfall out of my pay. Now it is escalating. We don't take it out of your pay he says, we just go along until we get mad. As far as I am concerned he is as mad as a hatter anyway. Text book psycho.

There is of course the old woman to contend with as well. Eighty-four, though at first meeting she might be all of seventy. Left an extra twenty dollars in the float, but entered that she had left only one hundred on her sheet the night before. I had not made a sale yet that morning when the boss arrived and showed him what she had done. He defends her; she is old, yet another day he will tell me that she would never make a mistake, she is always totally accurate when it comes to money. I must never criticize the old woman I learn as it leads to vindictive actions later on his part. Ah, now he returns a few hours later. My printing is not neat enough. Another day, everything is in perfect order, clean etc., ah, he has found a spot on the glass door.

I am sitting at the desk listening to yet more criticism and tell him that all I want to do is work my best and go home at the end of the day. He turns a bright red as he often does and his expression turns mean, as nasty as humanly, or rather inhumanly possible. Whenever he walks into the reception area customers react. Bodies stiffen, eyes grow wide, he gives off an angry, hostile feeling, vibes some people call it. Then there was the woman in the wheelchair who arrived in a van to attend a concert next door. Her daughter asked if it would be alright to leave the van parked in the lot, the lot being empty late in the day. "No you can't" he almost shouts, bringing the woman and her daughter close-to tears.

Even the ministers are close to using the word 'hate' in relation to Jr. Earlene is talking to me at the reception desk one afternoon when he walks in. She very nearly visibly shudders and makes an excuse to leave. The following day she stops to talk after performing a wedding. After the newlyweds leave she tells me that it is not safe here. It is not safe if you do not have a lot of money. There are a lot of crazy things can happen to innocent people. Her face looks serious. Then a few days later Patty the photographer from next door tells me that on a Saturday morning she and the three part-timers were sitting in the Chapel kitchen discussing how well they liked me, and Jr. informed them that he was thinking of firing me. I wasn't catching on he said. To what? they had asked. The job was hardly rocket science and I was a very good Worker, good with the customers too. His face turned red, again the mean look. Perhaps, I said to Patty his problem was that I had indeed caught on to him. That, and the fact that everyone disliked the last full-timer, and he had liked her and was upset when she had quit. She had apparently been very nasty with everyone. I expect he liked having one of his own kind around.

I am alone here. I hate the thought of leaving my little place, as shabby as it is before the weather cools off, and/or I find a literary agent to commit. I am unable to sleep through the night now however. Psychopaths frighten me, Cleckley - Mask Of Sanity - said it was a healthy fear and one that ought to be paid attention to.

No compassion, no empathy, no soul. They are not human. I see the rage in this man. The mean looks, the disparaging comments about virtually everyone. Patty is about to end her agreement to shoot at the Chapel. To hell with the bit of extra business she tells me; her hair feels like it is going to stand on end when he enters the room, he gives her the creeps. Get out of here she tells me, it is not worth it.

She rents the whole bottom floor of the Two-storey brick apartment building next door. Self-made in only three years, she has built up a little photography business that supports her well and she is moving forward. When she moved in she tells me he told her she'd never make it. Nice welcome.

He is so malicious he did not want her to succeed, even though a studio next to a Chapel would mean a good business collaboration. But then if it were not for his family he would very likely be on the street and no doubt is aware of the fact.

It is the opportunity to create the pretty bouquets and the customers that keep me going. Customers like the group from Walnut Creek. Four middle-aged women waiting for the bride and groom and the rest of the guests to arrive. One, the most outgoing spotted the young couple and their friend arrive. The man and two young women were jean-clad, clean but obviously poor and they had driven from the bay area and were going to have to drive right back after the ceremony as money was tight. Yet they wanted desperately to marry.

They were polite, nervous as well and as I say, travelling on a shoe string. The little group of four led by the outgoing one took up a collection and offered it to the young couple and their friend as they walked back to the reception area from the small Chapel after their ceremony.

"It's for you to go for a celebration dinner now" the leader told them "And may I take your picture and send it to you? I'll take your address and send them on next week".

Their own party was arriving now, groom in tux, bride in beautiful white dress. The little group were teary-eyed and so appreciative as they left. the good Samaritans saw their emotional reaction as proof that they were not treated well often, not accustomed to kindness the leader said. "I am so happy we did that" she said. "It makes our day, doesn't it?"

How different from Jr. I think. Jr. Who, when the young part-timer Dee was pregnant and standing on swollen feet was handed two opera tickets by an appreciative customer had them grabbed from her hands by Jr. who informed her that his grandmother would appreciate them.

Ah well and now it is my day off; I can linger a bit longer over my coffee listen to the birds sing and at night the crickets talk. My cat purrs and each day I check the mail hoping to find a letter from the literary agent that is going to represent me. In the morning the birds sing, my cat purrs and another hopeful day begins. And the crickets talk me to sleep, my cat purrs and I say my evening prayer.

Epilogue

Sweetpeas Flowers And Such. My own little wedding boutique. How wonderful it would be; a peaceful little place all my own, close to the ocean. My own little safe haven named for my sweet little granddaughter Sweetpea, for that is the nickname I gave her even before she was born. Victoria. Yes the queen city. The Florida of Canada.

Better than Florida though. Kind, clean, polite, pretty. Yes, a peaceful little place by the sea.

And it is another day off and I am cleaning my little place and sitting at the laundry mat thinking of Jr. and my lonely yet hopeful life, and Sweetpea and I decide to put the cart before the proverbial horse be brave and quit the job and drive north, home and somehow, someway, the agent will materialize and my life will all come together. And the birds sing, Baby purrs and I've come a long, long way from the dark days of Malibu and I'm going home.

THE CHILDREN OF THE ORCHARD

CHAPTER ONE

Nestled in the desert dry river valley, dwarfed by the snowcapped Rocky Mountain peaks that loomed in the distance, stood the orchards of Baptist County.

Cherry trees predominate now, since the apple industry has all but disappeared due to foreign competition. The valley, once lush and green as far as the eye could see thanks entirely to irrigation, is now being reclaimed by the desert, the land bought up by developers speculating in low cost housing. The less affluent retirees from the surrounding area are choosing to live in the valley because of its Nevada-type summer weather and milder, at least by Northwest standards, winters.

The town center stands down river, straddling both banks of the mighty Columbia River. It is at the south end of town that the Mexican laborers live, as well as the working poor whites. Their homes, most often no more than one bedroom shanties, these people comprise most of the town's population. Their labors in turn generate most of the town's wealth.

At the peak of one of the eastern hills overlooking this valley stands the Underman house. Fortress-like, glistening white in the oppressive summer's heat, it appears to stand guard over its twenty acres of orchards that stretch down toward the river and North and South as far as the eye can see.

Ladders dot the landscape from five o'clock in the morning until it is too unbearably hot for the Mexican workers to continue picking.

The workers are paid $3.85 an hour for every lug of cherries picked. A lug is a thirty pound box. A lug was a thirty pound box in 1985 and $3.85 was the wage paid then as well. It is now the summer of the year 2000.

CHAPTER TWO

"We have to keep the prices down for the consumer. The chemical sprays cost more than they did when we started out, so we have to cut costs somewhere or it cuts into our profits. We have our own to think about. Besides, if they don't like it they can always go back to Mexico. They're not educated, so what can they expect? It's better than what they have south of the border, so they keep coming back and they shouldn't complain"

The man, small framed and no taller than five foot three flitted from one project round the yard to the next, head held back, eyes cast down on everything and everyone; he reminded me more of a nervous peacock than a human being.

He referred to himself as an entrepreneur. An entrepreneur who had in fact inherited a small fortune, thereby enabling him to invest in local businesses and finally the fruit orchards. It has been said however, that no man has the best of it all of the time and this was now the Undermans' reality. All but one of four restaurants had now gone out of business. Their eldest son, a high school drop-out, and father of eight by two wives, the second common law, would soon close the doors on the fourth.

Everyone in the valley was hurting. Revenues were not nearly what they had been even one year earlier, so in order to boost sales the wonderkind had decided that opening the mom and pop cafe twenty-four hours a day and spending money on radio and print advertising was the answer to his dilemma.

"I'm going after an untapped resource" Jerry arrogantly told his father one afternoon. "You notice we don't get any Mexicans coming in? So I've paid for the commercial on the Spanish-speaking radio station, and the outside Bar B-Q celebration in honor of my thirty-fourth birthday, with hot dogs, hamburgers, and sodas going for twenty-five cents a pop should bring us to their attention, right?"

"Oh yes" Mr. Underman said. "Everyone's attention. And from now on we will have the poorest people in the community coming in for meals that cost between five and ten dollars a plate, when all they can afford is a ninety cent taco on a good day."

The peacock was angry and yet strangely, shrunk before his ridiculous son. Indeed, these parents appeared to be subservient to all four children.

Jerry was the eldest. He was tall, sharp featured and his expression always angry. His body taut, small eyes glaring just like dad, he, quite appropriately had no friends, his children avoided contact as much as possible and it was said one pet pooch after another ran away from home.

Children, it is said, learn by example and perhaps Jerry had taken his training all too seriously. I say this because of the treatment I had observed the Undermans' dog subjected to. A big sad eyed St. Bernard, Boris was left to linger day in and day out with never a kind word or a pat. His coat molting in the summer's heat was left unbrushed, the hair matted and falling off in chunks, filthy, and tangled with bits of yard waste.

Boris' eyes teared up and the dirt and dust clung to his wet face. His nose was caked with at least a quarter inch of dirt, one nostril half closed, and most painful of all the nails on his hind paws were left to grow into his flesh. Fortunately, Sam, the youngest son and one who visited with his wife as infrequently as possible arrived for a weekend and Karly, a veterinarian's assistant trimmed poor Boris's nails. I brushed him as often as possible and washed his face and other than this bit of affection he received no attention at all. Every evening after his own dinner Mr. Underman took two minutes to dump some food into Boris bowl and often I found the water bowl nearly empty and was told that it did not matter as Boris could drink from the puddles in the orchard. Indeed water contaminated by the chemicals that had been used to spray the fruit trees.

Soon after I arrived I commented that Boris seemed lonely and the response that I received from Mrs. Underman was "Well we just got him to use as a guard dog. He's not really a pet."

Rags the cat did not appear to fare much better. His bowl left empty of water, he often ran up to the master bedroom to drink from the toilet. His long Angora hair was never brushed and he would eventually require an operation to remove the mass of hair balls that had accumulated in his stomach. "I've too much to do to worry about hair ball medicine" Mr. Underman informed me one day in his heavy Dutch accent.

"I have all the weeding to do at the Church. Church meetings to attend. Yes the Church keeps us busy. We are good Christians you know. Not that we do good works to get to heaven. Good works don't matter when it comes to getting to heaven. Believing in Jesus is the only thing that matters. Nothing else makes a bit of difference."

"Absolutely nothing you do or don't do matters. You will never be good enough anyway. So as long as you believe in Jesus, no matter what else you do, you're saved." It was then that I asked him whether he thought the child, animal abuser, murderer, had a better chance of going to heaven than the kind, compassionate Jew, Buddhist, Muslim, as long as the offender believed in Jesus.

"All those not Christians are going to burn in the fires of hell; I don't care what they do good on earth."

Southern Baptists is what the Undermans were and it appeared interpreted the bible literally if not very conveniently; I say conveniently because of their cruelty toward their animals, as well as their rude, arrogant, intolerant and often cruel attitude toward those outside of their extremely close circle. A circle so small it consisted of only those of their immediate family and members of their church.

Even the church members with whom they worshiped every Sunday were not invited to enter their home. Gradually I developed the belief that behind the thick stone walls of this fortress lurked not only an us against them attitude, but something much more destructive.

Weeks of observation would eventually reveal the truth of the Underman household to me. For the initial few weeks of my stay the truth would lie buried in the pages of area newspapers, some five years old. News items forgotten by the outsider as just one more example of a lost and hypocritical society, yet buried in the consciousness of the embarrassed locals.

CHAPTER THREE

I became a houseguest through the intervention of a lifelong friend of mine, and a close relative of Mrs. Underman. My host was reluctant at best, yet Mrs. Underman had succeeded in convincing him that I should stay for at least a short while as a favor to her cousin and wanting to appear the magnanimous Christian he then sanctioned my visit.

Oddly, I had been looking for a safe haven while going through a nasty separation and divorce. The irony was not lost on Mrs. Underman.

When he was not present Mrs. Underman, starved for company was tempted to talk of things that would have caused Mr. Underman to stroke. Not that she dared say much, but a comment here and there about him or one of the children and her eyes tearing spontaneously and frequently caused me to take more notice of the family dynamics. "It's odd; Jerry is so nice when he's sick really, his whole personality changes. I always think that it's too bad he isn't sick more often."

Misha, the third child, was the same according to her mother. "Very insecure, both of them and I don't know why". She said this with tears in her eyes. "You'll see, she's here every day. Every afternoon she comes over. I don't know what she'll do if something happens to us. She's angry like Jerry too. I worry about that too. He thinks he owns the restaurant. He lets his kids think he owns it. We need to make a proper will or there will be a horrible fight when we're gone. We own the business and he just manages it. It will be split four ways, everything will. He refuses to believe it though."

"Well, I'm just preparing you. They aren't friendly. They're worried that we'll spend some of their inheritance on someone else. They don't have friends anyway. Their personalities are like their dad's. Sam is different. Everyone loves Sam. He and Karly don't come around much However; when they come to town they go to her parents and visit friends. Sometimes they come to town and never drop by. He doesn't care about the money. He's kind, and always had friends and I know he'll do alright for himself no matter what happens. He's too independent for his dad, I know that".

Those first few weeks Mr. U. Seemed not to mind my presence; in fact, he would pat my back and make a point of visiting – well, at least acknowledging my presence when he strode through the door. It was not until he asked me what my University major had been and upon discovering that it was psychology, he became cold, and belligerent. And of course there was the incident of the prospective employer asking me to go and live in his house. Mr. U's response had been to blame the victim, by asking me what I had done to cause the elderly German rest home owner to do such a thing. I would come to learn that Mr. Underman's personality leant itself to the blame the victim attitude and unfortunately I would discover that there were more than a few victims.

After what I began to call the silly old man incident, Mr. Underman's personality changed for the worse. His good mornings were cold and I was not invited to eat breakfast with them before leaving the house to look for work. Now at dinner time he did not take his place at the table; instead he put his feet up in the living room and waited for Mrs. Underman to bring him his plate as was their custom. He was after all the ruler and consequently his wife waited upon him, even to the point where should he be standing in the kitchen when the food was ready to dish up he would walk to the living room to wait for his wife to bring everything to him. Over time I began to view her as the embodiment of a Stepford wife.

We might be seated at the dining room table, she and I talking and when he entered the house just the barely perceptible wag of his index finger would cause her to hop quickly up from her chair and silently follow him into another room. She then never returned. She trained quickly to this new behavior and after only two such admonishments would, upon hearing him approach either quickly get up and rush to the kitchen, or if busy with some project nod to me to leave the room and emerge after a few moments with a big smile and a hello.

After a short time she too began to take her meals alongside him in the living room and I, claiming to be a kitchen table type of person stayed put and ate alone.

The television was turned on in the morning at one end of the house and the stereo in the middle of the house, it sat in the huge family room that separated the main living areas from the bedroom and bathroom leading to the pool area at the far end of this cavernous cold monster. Both were turned on high volume and the noise never abated until they retired at night, close to midnight. It was one big noise factory and though huge in area, a prison to its inhabitants nevertheless.

Misha visited as often as her mother had warned and always in frustration and anger at something her husband had done or not done, or just life in general. A miserable creature, she had developed shunning to a science. With a cursory hello to me, but not on every occasion mind you, she entered, sat down and proceeded to complain. On one visit she walked into the kitchen, made a pot of coffee and returned with a mug for her and her mother, then sat down and swiveled her chair toward her mother and began to talk to her.

She wore her hair waist length and as it was thin, she had it permed into kinky locks that she seemed obsessed with as she was forever flopping it this way and that. Long red nails adorned her fingers and here and there one spotted a little rhinestone embedded in a nail, much like the stone that had bordered the black satin shoes that had mysteriously disappeared from my closet shortly after I had arrived. You see, Misha appeared to love visiting the house so much that she could be found there when no one was home.

On one occasion I returned in the late afternoon and as I made my way to my room in the back of the house I heard a door slam. As I put my hand on the door knob to the bedroom to open it I turned and spotted Misha sitting at the sewing machine across the hall. I said hello and she responded without turning to look at me. When her mum arrived home she asked me if Misha had been there and I told her yes, apparently to do some sewing. "Oh, she doesn't sew. What would she want with the sewing room?" There was a confused look on her face, and then a sad recognition. And I out a two hundred dollar pair of shoes. I had met Jerry only once until the evening of his birthday dinner. He arrived with his 23 year old wife and all eight children, proceeded to drink rye whisky as though it were water and insulted his eldest daughter, a beautiful fifteen year old by telling her that he had always thought of cheerleaders as no more that prostitutes. She had told me on an earlier occasion that she couldn't wait to leave home and attend university. "The internet is my only social life and I only get to use that when I visit my mum on weekends. We aren't allowed to have friends."

Indeed in the two months I stayed at that house there was never a phone call or a visit from anyone save a family member or someone from their church calling regarding a church event.

One evening Mrs. Underman told me that she did not intend to golf the following morning and yet as I was preparing to leave on the morning in question there she sat at the kitchen table, hurriedly working on her hair and make-up. "I wasn't going to go but I found out that my friend will be there and I don't want to miss this chance to see her." This was indeed a prison and my intuition told me that the invisible bars were intended more to hold secrets in than keep people out.

One evening the Undermans were invited to dinner at the home of a foreign missionary who would be leaving the country soon.

They readied themselves and drank one huge glass of wine each. They were as nervous as if they had been invited to speak at a gala affair. They kept repeating that "Oh well, we won't be long, two hours at most." Nervously looking toward each other as though for reassurance that all would be fine. When I suggested that they may have such a good time that they won't want to rush home they looked at me astonished.

Mary and her husband and two small boys came the following weekend for a visit. This then was the child that Mr. Underman had become so excited while describing her to me that Mrs. Underman had become uncomfortable.

It was after this breakfast conversation that I had taken particular notice of the huge framed portrait that hung over Mr. Underman's desk. It was of Mary and occupied what was to him the most important place in the house, his space exclusively.

It was almost embarrassing to hear him carry on about this favored child. His excitement and tone of voice took on the flavor of a man in love, rather than a man praising a daughter. Mary and her little family arrived with two dogs. Their dogs were fed once a day which meant that Boris' food was confiscated for the remainder of their stay so as not to interfere with their animals' eating practices. Her parents smoked cigarettes and were ordered outside while they were visiting. Amazingly, the mouse as I had secretly nicknamed Mary took over the house and with her father's blessing. In a very stern voice - unfriendly would be an understatement - I was ordered to remove all vestiges of my existence from the bathroom that I had been using. I complied and shined the room up especially for the impending visit. It was checked and double-checked by daddy in preparation for her arrival, the clean hand towel that I had placed beside the sink for the visitors removed by him just before their arrival. Once there Mary ruled and her mother became invisible to her father with the exception of her usefulness regarding meal preparation and of course caring for the children.

Jerry's children arrived on Sunday morning to join them for breakfast and the ensuing diatribe compliments of Mr. Underman took place.

"Well what are you kids going to be when you grow up?" No answer. "Well you had better think about it otherwise you'll be bums like the bums you see on the street. The homeless. They're all lazy. Don't want to work. Just live off other people. See, that's what happens when you don't have a real job, when you don't study something that makes sense."

There were two coffee cups sitting beside his plate and an empty chair next to him; this was the only seat left open and obviously I was to occupy it. "See, there are two cups here and one is for me and one is for the bum."

As I dished food on to my plate I happened to glance quickly in his wife's direction and her shiny eyes looked into mine. Even the little children were dumbfounded and strangely silent. Smiling, I placed my plate and a fresh cup of coffee in my place, took my seat and commented that he must be hooked on caffeine even more so than I for he had not one but was drinking two at a time now. There was a collective sense of relief that went round the table - the best way to describe it would be, well to make it analogous with that of a giant balloon too full of air and ready to burst when suddenly someone comes along and releases the excess oxygen. Statues, frozen in anticipation, miraculously coming to life. Mr. Underman I thought, you flatter me; why, you have attributed fantastic powers of perception upon me. Truth be told, his behavior, his belligerence toward me who had done no more than major in a subject he attributed wondrous power to had caused me to pay more notice to him and his family's situation than one in my position normally would have. I unfortunately at the time was embroiled in a nasty domestic battle and wearing myself to a frazzle looking for work and my own apartment.

This then was the man who made a point of saying grace before each meal and at least half a dozen times a day, actually saying;

"I'm a good Christian." I thought at the time, I will soon be away from this house, but what of these little children and what he is teaching them?

The sainted Mary would, in time, show herself for what she was as well. I had been raised to believe that it was simply good manners to help out about the house when staying with anyone and therefore one morning I proceeded to unload the dishwasher and as I was placing the cutlery in the drawer Mary passing through the kitchen, glanced my way and when I looked up to say good morning she sneered and made a disparaging sound. I dismissed it as an apparition I neither understood, nor wanted to spend time working to understand. But when the following morning after breakfast I offered to tidy up saying, "I don't mind doing that; you're so busy with your kids" and she responded nastily and without looking toward me; "Well I don't mind either. Okay? Okay?" Oh my, yes there was really something wrong here.

As was the case with her father the mouse referred to the bible and Jesus and Christianity an inordinate number of times over very short periods. Mrs. Underman and I stood talking in the kitchen one afternoon when suddenly Mary appeared - husband in tow and stopped to tell her mother that - she held the bible up - "We're going out to read the bible." There was no response from us, so she repeated it again, turned and marched out of the kitchen.

CHAPTER FOUR

You could smell fear in this house, feel it, almost taste it. I spent most of my time searching for a job, walking, brushing Boris, reading, writing and in short made myself very scarce. I sensed the antagonism and though I was cheerful, appreciative, and polite the antagonism grew worse. I found an attorney in the yellow pages of the phone book and when I told them his name, I noted the fear than played across the faces of Mr. and Mrs. Underman.

"What is it?" I asked. "Do you know something negative about him? Perhaps I shouldn't use him? What is it?"

"Oh it's just that he worked for us a while ago. Can't remember what it was about. Some class action suit".

"Was he no good?" I asked.

"Oh yes, he won for us."

"Well, he said oh you're at the Undermans as soon as I finished giving him your phone number. That's unusual isn't it? He recognized the phone number. Must have some memory. You're sure he's okay?"

"Oh sure" Mrs. Underman said. It was just that she was worried that he would expect them to pay. "Don't tell him you are friends with us, not related in any way. Just say we're doing a favor for a friend having you here".

"Well" I said "That after all is the exact truth. I met with him and he told me that he would take my case on a contingency basis".

Months passed, two to be exact. He never returned my phone calls then one day a letter arrived in the mail from him informing me that he was dropping my case. A bill was also mailed to me, a bill for services never sanctioned by me. I had neither signed anything nor sanctioned anything. What was happening here? What were these people all about?

I stood in the kitchen reading the correspondence from the shyster and upon finishing - I had read it aloud to them- Mr. Underman laughed. The control freak, the little man with the big chip on his shoulder, insecure, arrogant, the good Christian laughed. The control freak was fearful as is the case with all control freaks. This one had a strong propensity to blame the victim; this one had dysfunctional angry, insecure children; this one hid from the world, this one had some awful things to hide from the world.

No wonder Mrs. Underman hid candy in cupboards, cakes behind plates, smoked three packs of cigarettes a day, drank rye whisky from 4 till 8, and kept the noise of TV and stereo on all day to drown out her thoughts.

I would subsequently discover that the attorney had never sent the letter he had alleged to have sent to my ex-husband and another attorney had informed me that it was illegal for this first to have accepted a case on a contingency basis when there was no claim of child support involved.

That evening I sat at the dining room table looking through the paper for apartments to rent. We were alone, Mrs. Underman and I.

"Well it's a nice little town, quiet, seems like nothing really bad ever happens here. Peaceful."

Mrs. Underman's response was; "Oh there was trouble about five years ago. You remember, all the papers were full of the case about the child abuse allegations involving the children at the bible studies, child care and so on. Well that was this town".

"What happened?"

"Oh someone was just jealous or angry about something and started a rumor. But a class action suit was filed and everything eventually died down. People have short memories. They had a good lawyer, no-one was ever able to prove anything against the people accused."

"And the lawyer? " and her eyes tear up, as has become her habit and she's sorry about my bad luck.

Mr. Underman was back by the pool tonight preparing it for his grandchildren's visit the next day. I had never been invited to swim in the pool. Mrs. Underman never went in either. Just once I saw her standing by the edge staring at him; he was in the water with the kids. He only ever swam with the kids, never alone, never when any of his grown children had joined in. He did not care for any of the children being alone in the same room with me, would interrupt if one of them came over to me to say anything. His body was always taut, his eyes cold, angry.

Conversation had always been impossible with this man, even before his fears of exposure got the better of him. One could not enter into a discussion with him; the eyes would glass over, he may look away and tap his fingers on the table top or simply glare until the other had quit speaking. Shamelessly, he would resume his monologue and more often than not it was a long spiel designed to impress the other with his superior knowledge on a subject he obviously knew nothing about, thus having the opposite of the intended desired effect. His sense of humor consisted entirely of poking fun at his wife.

His demand for undivided attention reached the point of ridiculousness, an example being a long explanation of where and exactly why he had decided to pull weeds in whatever particular patch of garden on whatever day at whatever time ad-nauseam. He became so frustrated when not the automatic center of his small universe that he would quickly clam up and if the table tapping, angry glaring-eyed intimidation tactic on occasion did not work, his last resort was to stand-as erect as a tiny toy soldier, slam hands palms down on the table and march off.

Karly's mum called one morning and left a message on the answering machine - nice lady, just thought it would be nice for them to get together as they hadn't seen each other since their children's wedding 6 months earlier. Mrs. Underman told Mr. Underman as we sat drinking our final cup of coffee after breakfast.

"Did you call her back?" he demanded in his most intimidating and what I came to call his S.S. voice.

"No" she replied. He relaxed instantly. "Well they are alright, but they are simple people" he said with a shrug. "There is no need to become involved". No indeed I thought, and lucky for the in-laws.

I had to give Misha credit for possessing some bit of honesty, no matter how crass. One day she said to me; "You need to watch out for me. I can get in a mood, so don't ever cross me even unintentionally." I could not but smile; after all I had developed this opinion of her weeks earlier.

One evening about a week into my stay Sam and Karly arrived and the Undermans asked them and me to join them in watching a video highly recommended by the Church. It was a little film depicting the book of Genesis. The Undermans were very animated in their praise of the picture. Violent, the volume tuned as loudly as the television would allow, the moaning, shouting, hells fires and damnation burned away. As the minutes ticked by, then so did Karly's and my patience, until both of us finally excused ourselves, and left the room. As we made our way to our respective bedrooms we heard the shouts, applause and laughter of the good Christian couple as evidently those who were not believers in the Messiah were being depicted thrown to the fires of hell.

It was mid-week into the last week of my stay at the fortress when Misha came round with her two children. The girl was twelve years old and began a discussion regarding plans for an upcoming birthday for one of Mary's children. I sat, my back to the television reading the paper. Mrs. Underman sat at the end of the table, the television off to her right, she just able to peek at it over my head. And so began the party plans.

Laura was asking about the party plans, time it was to start etc. when suddenly she said "Why are you nodding at Hedy?"

"Oh I was just looking at the TV"

"No you weren't; you were looking at - pointing your head at Hedy. Hey, now you're kicking me. Hey, Grand, why are you acting weird?"

Well I got lucky the next day; I took the classified ads and stopping at a pay phone outside a Walmart called on an ad for a cheap room. Drove straight there and handed the nice retired couple three hundred dollars for a month of peace in the small studio, a converted shed really, yet with all of the amenities that sat in the corner of their perfectly groomed back yard. I will always wonder just how they were going to deal with me staying there, yet not invited to participate in their grandchild's fifth birthday party. But thankfully I would never have to find out. I drove back to the house and told Mrs Underman that I had found a place and could move in right away, to which she responded "Oh, tomorrow morning is soon enough".

I packed and washed my bedding and returned it to the bed while they were all at Church that morning. I was just finishing up as Mary's husband began dishing up a big smorgasbord of biscuits and chili and any number of wonderful things. Mrs Underman invited me to take a biscuit and come out to have a last coffee with her. No-one else said a word to me really; I was invisible to them or at least that was their goal - to make me invisible and as soon as possible.

"Ah well" I told her as we sat on the wall nibbling our biscuits. "It will be good for me to have some private time - a little place of my own before I leave for England" for I had found employment finally and fortunately far away. Sam had offered to adopt my cat but Mr Underman had put the kibosh on that. Yes, Sam 28, married, and living 200 miles away was apparently not capable of deciding whether or not he should have a cat.

"I'll need to find a home for Baby too."

Now Mrs. Underman looked down at her hands and said "I don't know how you do it."

"What? Do what?"

"Be independent. Go off alone. You're better than me. You're better, that's all. I couldn't do it."

He came out just then, and decided to water some flowers not three yards from where we were sitting. She said something to him about the grandkids, once twice, three times she repeated herself. he never responded. I asked if his hearing could be that bad. No of course not she said, "He's just ignoring me as usual." Like all those evenings I'd heard her calling him to dinner; he well within earshot and marching in 15 minutes, 30 minutes later and informing her That of course he'd heard her but was involved in thinking about something more important. The arrogant little turd I thought to myself.

I said my goodbyes and drove to my little safe haven. Unpacking my car I discovered a bag with a few things that Mrs. Underman knew I liked to eat, as well as two cold beers. She had given me a hug when I was leaving and telling me about the beer said: "I figured you could use them, especially today".

The first night in my little place was pure heaven. I lay down on my hide-a-bed, my cat curled round my foot and scenes from the preceding two months passed before me like scenes from a B-movie;

little snippets of conversations, impressions, feelings generated by people I had never before known and would not come into contact with again.

Iris, Mr. Underman's sister. All gold jewelry, bleached blond teased hair, bragging as did Jerry about how she had fired yet another worker from her restaurant. She ridiculed one of her waitresses who, though the girl had a psychology degree was waitressing. Fixing me with a hard, cold stare, she belligerently told me that such degrees were obviously useless, to which I replied; "Not at all. I always credit my training with helping me deal with the most disagreeable people."

Mrs. Underman asked me to help her in the kitchen a few minutes later and told me that we should have left the room as soon as the sister had arrived. "I am only allowed to stay just to say hello when any of his family come over, unless they invite me to stay and visit. They like to talk by themselves with no outsiders." The wife an outsider; a servant it appeared in every sense of the word.

"And did you move to America alone?" I had asked Mr. Underman one day.

"No. My parents moved us all over here after the war was over. We arrived in forty-six" His head tilted back arrogantly; he continued that his family were never poor immigrants. "We came with money. My father did well during the war. He was an engineer. We came out of it very well financially. Of course it was not pleasant. I saw people shot not two-feet away from me."

I am standing in the kitchen talking with Mrs. Underman as she prepares dinner and I commented that the surname of Underman does not sound particularly Dutch.

"No. Well, they dropped an 'n' from the surname. Two 'n's' at the end would sound Jewish. The Nazis asked his dad to work for them because he was an engineer, but he turned them down."

I am thinking, turned down a job with the Nazi regime and not only live to talk about it, but come out of the war prosperous? This woman must think I have just fallen off the back of a turnip truck.

What I actually say however, is; "Two 'n's' would not have been healthy in Nazi occupied Holland would it?"

"No" she said "And you never know who people are nowadays; they change their names." And I recall her telling me that I am better than her because I am independent. And the tears in her eyes. And one afternoon she commented that she thought my writing was a good thing and that she hoped I got published. And that perhaps what I was writing could help someone someday and she had not asked what I had been writing. Perhaps she did not need, or hoped she did not need to ask.

He made a point of saying that he had to be off to the post office to mail a letter to his friend in Germany. "Ah, best friends since boyhood, same clubs, activities." He knew that I was on to him, dared me to comment. For his wife's sake I said nothing. Like his children, he was angry.

Mrs. Underman and I and Misha and her twelve year old daughter are in the dining room seated at the table talking. Twelve year old Laura is seated at the end of the table closest to the throughway to the living room. Mr. Underman walking through stopped, tipped Laura's head back and kissed her full on the mouth. Mrs. Underman froze, her eyes watering and Misha stiffening, looking frightened and Laura said: "Oh Grandpa, yuk. You know I hate that." And wiped her mouth, displeased, but not taken a back, surprised. He laughed, glanced round the table in his manner, eyes down cast, head back, an arrogant belligerent expression on his face and left, he said for the Church to do some work there, laughing his way out of the door.

And I remember that afternoon I heard people in the pool and walked to the kitchen to ask Mrs. Underman if she were going to swim that day as well. She looked startled and together we walked to the back of the house and the huge indoor pool enclosed as was the house behind the same brick fortress-like wall. We stood at the edge of the water, she stone-faced looked no, starred straight at him without moving, and it seemed to me without breathing.

Her hands were on her hips. She just stood, stood like a rock. He finally said something about the grandchildren begging to swim right then, all of them under seven. I found it odd that no-one was ever invited into the pool but the grandchildren and that grandpa was the only adult to ever spend time with them there. Misha's little six year old son had a black eye and when I asked him how he got it he said: "I don't know. I know my daddy didn't do it." And he was called into the other room just then. None of these ten grandchildren were allowed to have a friend to their home or to visit a friend's home. Eventually none were allowed in the same room with me and whenever one walked over to me to say anything they were interrupted by one of the adults. Perhaps they had been told that their lives were normal and the parents and indeed grandpa was afraid of them talking. I suspect this to be the case. This was not a family. This was a cult, its leader a twisted, controlling monster.

He loved war movies, despite claiming to have suffered so during the war. He hated and belittled romantic films, kept his family isolated, all but the youngest who refused to go along to some extent. He was however financially supported by daddy. His wife worked, while he remained at home year after year, ostensibly waiting to hear if he had been accepted to a university of his choice.

Misha had been offered a job working with computers and daddy told her to turn it down. He would pay her to not work, rather than have her work and embarrass him by earning only twelve dollars an hour. My belief is that he wanted his children to have as little contact as possible with the outside world, or anyone who may get close enough to them to open their eyes. None of them had any close friends, the sort one can confide in.

I am sitting out on my little porch in the sun talking with my Landlord one afternoon and a truck is slowing up in the lane.

I recognize Jerry, squinting at my car, then speeding away. Checking to see if I am still in town? I call Mrs. Underman to say hello and the monster answers curtly; "She is busy cleaning the house. What do you want?"

I tell him I just wanted to say hello and ask if any mail had arrived there for me, perhaps squeaked through the change of address order I had put in at the post office.

"No mail" he says, and then angrily, "Oh, one envelope from an agent" and then his voice rising; "What that is about?" Broken English and heavy accent kicks in whenever he is disturbed. "If there is mail I will put it at the back door, stuck in the molding beside the door and you can get it without bothering to knock." Frightened little man. Very little man I think, in every sense of the word.

I feel less safe now. Jerry snooping, angry faced. Daddy paranoid. I must plan to leave sooner than I might have.

I am feeling guilty about Boris. I want to have him rescued. Indeed I want to have all those poor little innocent children rescued, but how? The Nazi monster is friendly with the lawyer, that much is certain and now I fear for what could happen to me.

I cry. I cry for the poor dog, the poor little children and even the pathetic parents, so brainwashed, frightened, or greedy, as to allow a second generation to suffer. Or were they really their father's children as Mrs. Underman had intimated? Angry, arrogant, selfishly believing they were beyond reproach?

I never found a home for Baby and have her still. I did not stay more than four weeks in my little studio in Baptist County. I drove away, feeling guilt, fear and anger and sorrow myself. I am free of the place and the people. I am free of their prison and it is two years behind me now. But what of the children, the children of the orchard?

AT A DISCOUNT

CHAPTER 1 - THE LINE

Six dollars and thirty cents an hour, clock out and in for your half hour lunch break, seven and one half hours of paid work time a day, gross pay forty seven dollars and twenty five cents per day.

The health benefits will not be offered until the employee has worked for four months and deductions will be ninety dollars per month or forty five dollars per pay check. Welcome to the world of the working poor.

The associates as they are called are a motley crew, yet all have one thing in common; all are poor. Not the sort of poor that my grandmother would refer to as financially challenged, temporarily short on cash for whatever reason, but the kind of poor she defined as being spiritually broken, having surrendered, lost motivation, determination, or perhaps never possessed anything bur poor character and attitude anyway. So then, according to my granny's definition these people were indeed poor and frighteningly never had been, nor would they ever be anything other than dispossessed. In fact it appeared that the harder they worked, the more they were taken advantage of and the more they lost. Up until about six months ago the company provided a nice cake whenever an employee had a birthday to celebrate and if the staff were willing to alter their hours to accommodate a shipment, or sale a pizza would be delivered for lunch. No more however; you can't keep the shareholders happy now unless you squeeze as much as possible in profits out of the business; dear Mr. Scrooge knew that much.

But then one did receive a ten percent discount on merchandise from the first day of employment and every so often the company offered associate discount days, wonderful days where the pathetically overworked and underpaid were given the opportunity to spend what they could not afford and receive a thirty to fifty percent discount over and above their ten percent, on the flawed, poorly made, or rejected catalogue merchandise at Discount Heaven.

Bigotry, ignorance, (one and the same) a disinterest in anything other than a quick fix via junk food, gambling, booze, or cheap clothes defined most of these poor souls lives. You could not claim to be human and not feel compassion for these people and yet their meanness, a meanness borne of hopelessness, threatened to discourage even the most patient of us.

This was the contemporary version of the Dickensian factory. A warehouse, filthy, rodent infested, asbestos insulation hanging from the ceiling and prevented from falling on the heads of the workers by wire strung from one beam to the next.

There were six stations situated on either side of the assembly line. A line consisting of a crude un-motorized contraption two foot wide and inset with steel rollers on which cardboard boxes were pushed along by the worker. The boxes contained everything from shoes to nuts, to be processed (tagged) and placed on the racks, or cages that sat to the right of each station.

Pull racks were maneuvered by the processor to any spot available, until they were cleared to be taken to the floor (department store area).

All new hires were trained on the cash registers at the entrance to the store. Therefore anyone could be called upon to fill in when the store was busy. Of eight check-out stands there were never more than two manned at any given time. When there were no floor clerks to fill in, as often was the case, a voice would call over a speaker asking for any available help to come forward. The customers would then find themselves being checked out by a jean clad, dead eyed, shabby soul just out from the processing room warehouse, dusty hands and all, bagging and making change. And anxious to scurry back to their little station where they were free to carry on with their crude jokes, jibes back and forth, complaints regarding children, sex lives, money, all interspersed with the foul language and profanities seldom, if ever, heard in a civilized work place. Yet even the head cashier, nicely dressed, groomed, and claiming to own a home in a better than average new neighborhood with her husband of some forty odd years, displayed her rough and true character when, the morning of September eleventh she stated matter of factly; "We shouldn't let any of those people into our country, even for vacations. Any of those dark people from those countries, and include the Jews in that." Tall, stern, and as mean as you might ever have the misfortune to meet.

CHAPTER 2 - THE CHARACTERS

Two of the women in processing were simply Housewives, women who had spent their years since high school graduation raising families and were new to the workforce. With no work experience outside of the home and liking the hours of eight to four, Monday through Friday they found themselves in an environment that they claimed they were too ashamed to admit to their families exactly how little they earned, or the true condition of the place. Most of the women however, were hard scrabble. They had worked other warehouses and judging from some of their remarks had not gotten along and quit.

Teeth were missing and or yellowed, broken, hair let go, no make-up, broken nails, old dirty sneakers and shabby faded tops and jeans; this was the crew. Not all, but most had lost their self-respect many years ago and consequently cared little or nothing for anyone, even themselves.

One such person was Selma. From Kentucky originally, she had moved to Reno some twenty years earlier. She stood on the line one day reminiscing of how she had begun life here in a cheap motel that had no hot water and no sheets on the bed, no towels. Now twenty years later she was living in a broken down rented trailer, with her two illegitimate children, a boyfriend and about to be evicted.

"The toilet's leakin' anyways; might even fall through the floor. An when I tried to open the window it fell outside onta the groun." Her fifteen year old daughter was pregnant and had dyed her hair purple: "That's the style." The eleven year old son visits his father a few blocks from the broken down trailer. "His daddy lives in that motel where that little girl was murdered by her step-daddy. I was sure we was gonna see my son on TV cause they was all over that place, all the reporters, and TV people."

The little guy works at a service station evenings and weekends, cleaning up, doing whatever he can to earn a bit of extra money. Gave his mother one hundred dollars one day. He had saved it over a period of months and told her that he wanted to go with his soccer team to San Francisco in the spring, a trip that would cost one hundred dollars. Laughing she told the line group that he had given her the money asking that she give it back in the spring; she took the money. It was a sort of, I help you now mom, you help me later. I hope he will not be disappointed.

Selma would not have been more than thirty five years old, if that, judging by the dates estimated in relation to her daily monologues of children, men, and money; however she appeared much older. Her complexion is sallow, hair lank and lifeless, eyes a blank stare, emotionless; but for the flicker of sadness periodically crossing her face, she might have been an abused rag doll.

Selma had the bad teeth of the permanently impoverished and neglected; she never smiled and I suspected she was ashamed. However Selma had the most infectious laugh I have ever heard in my life. Unfortunately Selma seemed only to laugh while working the line and bantering back and forth with Teresa. Teresa is a twenty-three year old Mexican girl. Teresa arrived here when she was only three years old; she is the sixth of a family of eight children. The twin brothers were born a few months after her parents arrived in Reno. Teresa was a baby when her parents left Mexico and did not recognize them when she arrived with her five siblings. She had apparently clung to her older sister and cried that the sister was her mother. One story she was told of her life in Mexico was of ants crawling up her baby bottle and into her throat. Teresa never talked much however about anything other than money. She was forever begging Selma to go out with her after work, or to a fast food for lunch. I could not understand why she did not have friends her age, until she talked one day of owing everyone she knew; apparently she had no idea how much she owed whom and this came to include those who worked at the store and warehouse.

She was living with her second live-in boyfriend and even owed him money. She had clothes piled on shelves at her little station, six pair of jeans, sweaters, slippers and planned to buy them pay day. "Wanting something is the same as needing something, Isn't it?"

She visited the food bank the other day. "I had to. I can't afford to buy food." Teresa clears about eight hundred a month and shares expenses with John. "I can't let him know I care for him too much or he'll probably kick me out."

Selma: "But he's good to you, girl".

Teresa: "Yeah I know. He loans me money".

Selma: "My boyfriend earns five hundred a week, girl and he don't do nothin'. That's why I got this shit job, so's I can feed my kids, girl. I toll him I'm gonna beat the black outta his ass, he don't do sometin. He was outta work for a month or so, mind, but still, girl, quit complainin, you young, girl; go do sompin for your own self, but get while you can too". (laugh)

I glance across the line at Kerry, the quiet Mormon woman, proper housewife. We make eye contact and shake our heads, just a bit. We do not want to be noticed. We do not wish to invite any verbal abuse.

Selma: "Think you're better than us?"

Teresa: "Yeah, well fuck them".

Selma: "They speak real nice. No money complainin. You notice?"

Teresa: “Yeah, well we’re just as good as them, and we can kick their asses. Those out on the floor too. big deal. Head cashier. Nice house. So what? Anyone can get a house if they have money”.

Selma: “She got a husband, girl”.

Selma, with the black dialect was white. Our supervisor was away on vacation the week this incident took place. These two partners in negativity let go all of their pent-up hostilities and finally the manager was called. I have no idea who called him; I had been too stunned to do more than stand there kicking myself for having fallen into such a horrible place. Mr. T. did nothing but stand and listen as the two pathetic creatures hollered all their complaints; he shrugged, turned and walked out. Nothing more was ever mentioned of the incident by anyone. Incredible.

Norma had worked the floor for fifteen years, left for four years when her husband died and returned to work part-time in the processing division. Norma was a seventy something woman of character. She was friendly, kind, and polite, however she was not shy about speaking up. She told Teresa not to talk to her if she could not control her language and then went on to tell her that her mother washed her mouth out with soap when she talked like that. “Nothing wrong with that either; society is going to hell now.”

Selma: “I’m goin to the health department. I’m goin to Mr. Russ. Polyvinyl chloride. I worked with this stuff in another place and they gave us gloves, an a mask to wear. These jackets say China too. China? Oh no!. I feel my hans burnin. I’m gonna sue. Why we handlin these here jackets without gloves when they say polyvinyl chloride anyway? AN these are kids jackets too. Poor little kids”.

Turning to Teresa Selma said: “We all gonna die, girl. You know that? We all gonna die. Yeah I’m goin to Mr. Russ an gettin a note to see the company doctor and then the health department. I’m gonna put an end to this shit, girl”.

Teresa: "An end to our jobs".

Selma: Laughing. "No, we gonna clean up, girl. Don't you see? We gonna sue. We gonna clean up. We gonna break this place, girl".

Off Selma went. Lost five hours work and ended up with a pair of plastic gloves and a small jar of cream for her hands.

Jeri, one of the line workers had decided that she was better suited to fulfill the duties of supervisor than crew member and to that end walked round inspecting others work, critiquing everyone on the efficiency of their performance (yes Jeri was a surly soul) and in general was simply a nuisance to be tolerated.

Jeri was at least six foot tall, over two hundred pounds, wore filthy tee-shirts, and had her short, straight greasy black hair shaved in a one inch square diameter over each ear. She spoke of having two daughters, though that fact was the only indication that this person was of the female gender and if she spoke of men at all it was despairingly.

She arrived at the warehouse one hour early every morning, yet did not clock in until the appointed time. When the rest of the crew arrived for work there we found Jeri pacing round, hands in pockets and hovering close to the time clock as punch in time grew nearer. "Just to make sure that no one punches in too early."

Jeri's buddy appeared to be Trudy the troll. At barely five feet tall, with waist length grey hair, not a scratch of make-up, face a blank, she walked with her arms dangling down the sides of her body as though they were semi-attached. Starring straight ahead, eyes unfocused, she never responded to a good morning, good night, or good day. Shoulders hunched forward, back rounded as a turtle's, she shuffled through life in her dirty worn sneakers in a daze. Only when talking with Jeri did she come alive and sound as though she was a member of the human race. Subjects such as prisons, drugs, alcoholism, or manic depression were of particular interest to her and she appeared to be quite knowledgeable in those areas.

Beatrice, a short, round, granny type seventy something, stood at her station directly behind me. Sat behind me would be more accurate, as she was the only employee furnished with a chair. It was a high backed padded stool and at least no-one complained about her preferential treatment. she was after all, elderly and in poor health. She went through the day with the blank stare of most of the others, though if I smiled and said hello she came alive and smiled. She never hesitated to point out quietly and kindly to me any possible error I was headed for; she simply loved being in her own little world. Bea worked a thirty hour week, the final eight hours worked on a Saturday, alone. "No radio, no silly talk, bad language, noise, just peace and quiet and that's how I like it". Bea said this to me one afternoon with a shy smile when I asked her how she liked working alone.

Behind Bea stood Selma and then there was Nancy. Sixty five years old and sporting the mushroom cut made popular in the seventies, she stood the live long day correcting, criticizing, and counseling the other line workers. She had an insulting comment to make about every piece of merchandise that came into her hands and 'weren't' and 'gonna' were integral to this alleged former teacher's speech.

The local school district was so desperate for teachers they had sent flyers through the mail in an effort to recruit and yet this woman who made some sort of reference every day to her education degree, arthritic fingers, and penury, stood on the line.

"If it weren't for Mike I'd be living in a box on these wages." Mike was her live-in boyfriend. Mike worked as a cabinet maker and shared what she referred to as her tin can. "My trailer is so small, one step and you're across the room".

Four years earlier, her husband of twenty years and ten years her junior had thrown her clothes into the yard and locked her out of their California home. She claimed to have received half of everything, property, stocks, etc. etc. and yet she was broke. A bitter woman talking as though it had all happened yesterday. "The judge thought I was a bitch because I thought he should award me alimony. I fully expected alimony because after all I am ten years older than him and should have been supported in my old age." Her manner of speech was affected and she took great pains to enunciate each word very carefully; even 'ain't', 'weren't' and 'gonna' received special attention. She claimed to listen only to classical music, yet when I asked her which were her favorite pieces she told me that she never discussed it with anyone as most people's ignorance of that type of music made any discussion a waste of her time.

So these were the women, not one of whom were capable of carrying on a conversation, save for the Mormon lady, and elderly Norma.

Kerry: "We have lived here for fifteen years. It required patience, and four years of trying before even one of our neighbors would acknowledge us when we said good morning. We wish we had never moved here. My husband was transferred here however, so we accepted the transfer because he needed the work. It has been a horrible struggle raising our children here. We only have three years to go and we are out of here. A few years ago we thought we had gotten lucky and were getting a transfer to California and believe me when it did not come through we all cried. Even the children, sixteen and seventeen can't wait to move and this is really the only place they have called home. No. You will find no quality people here".

CHAPTER 3 - THE MEN

Fred was a slight. wiry man with an accent that suggested he had learned his English at a British prep school; English obviously was his second language. He was difficult to place, yet reminded me a great deal of one of my cousin's husbands, a polite, positive, and optimistic man from Macau.

Fred did not use the foul language, street talk, of the other men that he worked with; these men were laborers, unloading the trucks, unpacking the cartons and cleaning up round the warehouse. Not a pleasant job and yet Fred arrived each morning cheerful, always saying things like "You never know what the new day will bring. It's great; I love the start of a new day." I found out later that poor Fred made a habit of driving over the state line on his days off to buy lotto tickets in California. Kerry, Norma and I found Fred's optimistic outlook encouraging, no matter the reason for it, though the others appeared to be irritated by his refusal to complain. Misery of course does love company.

The rest of the men were indistinguishable, all using the same epithets, disparaging women, loving violent movies and of course all had the requisite fat belly hanging over the low slung belt.

Benny was the sorriest of the lot, the hanger man. He had spent the past eighteen years at this warehouse, most of which had been spent on the men's side until about three years ago. He now sorted hangers and had become very territorial about his little place in the big ugly warehouse.

Each of our stations was equipped with racks for holding hangers of every description. One afternoon I returned to my station to find a row of my hangers gone. Benny, realizing I was back to work, quickly appeared beside me and told me that the hangers he had taken were the hangers used for heavy clothes and that he was not letting me take any until I needed them. I laughed, excused myself and replaced the hangers.

Benny had a problem with Ziggy, the young Mexican worker and enjoyed making fun of Ziggy, imitating him mockingly when he heard him speaking Spanish. Benny liked to creep round the cartons and spy on Kerry as she worked, and once grabbed Nat and tried to hug her. Benny was a sixty something with an IQ of about ninety and Benny was not just slow, he was potentially dangerous.

Nat talked incessantly about never having enough time for her church. Nat claimed that her husband made wonderful money and that she never had to work. Nat had been experiencing horrible back pain and had to make an appointment with her doctor, therefore Nat came in one hour early that day to make up for the hour's pay she would lose later on.

CHAPTER 4 - QUITTING TIME

The supervisor, Lil, was married to an alcoholic and all three sons had succumbed as well. Her great fear was that her grandchildren would end the same way. Lil drove a pick-up and spent her free time alone in the desert looking for rocks. Lil claimed that the reason the people here were so mean and negative was simply that they were poor. Sorry, Lil, somehow I doubt that if a million dollars were thrown into the laps of these people tomorrow they would miraculously become any more civilized that what they were right now. In fact truth be told, I suspect that nine or ten of them would be just as broke next year this time as they are right now.

It is a sad day when one cannot even feel comfortable sitting down to eat one's pathetic little sandwich that one has prepared for that half hour when one is allowed to clock in and out to eat the pathetic little sandwich, on one's own time of course. Yet this sadly was the case. The last straw. The final chapter in the saga of what I would come to consider Hanna's year in hell.

Lunch breaks were varied and when it came time for my break I found myself with two choices; either sit with the men, or with the three stooges. These three were Val, Dixie and Anita.

Anita was always going on about her busy schedule involving her two teenage children and their sports activities. Anita ate a tomato concoction for breakfast, break, lunch and when you got within one foot of her while she was speaking, you were knocked over by the stench of alcohol seeping from her lungs.

Dixie talked as though she knew everything about child rearing and yet one afternoon she was irate over the fact that truants were now being picked up at an alarming rate. "It don't do no good anyways. If the stupid teachers would just make school more fun, then maybe the kids wouldn't be runnin off".

Val's children were twenty-one and twenty-five. "Oh, they been gone on their own now for a few years. But anyways, as you say, you'd think the cops would be goin after real crooks, stead a kids. I know how you feel, Anita. Mine were always bein picked up, an sometimes Jake would tell me to not bother pickin him up from juvie some weekends, cause he'd laugh that he'd just be back in on Monday anyways. Hell It became the family joke".

During the lunch break Anita, on this day was anxiously awaiting a call from her son. He was to call her on her cell phone to arrange to meet her at Juvenile Hall for an interview.

I considered myself fortunate to have been assigned the twelve o'clock lunch break, as otherwise I would have had to endure Jeri. When she wanted to make a point she would bang the table with her fists like a bar room brawling man for emphasis. And as Teresa had said; "You don't want to try to squeeze by her in close quarters, cause she likes to bang you with her boobs whenever she gets the chance."

Unkindly, one day in irritation I thought to myself; the manners of goats and the IQ's of gnats. I was sorry for thinking that way and decided that it was as good an indication as any that I should give notice. In my ten weeks at Discount Heaven, six had quit and three had been fired for absenteeism.

One afternoon Mrs. Wald came into the warehouse and announced that whenever on cash everyone had better remember to ask every customer that came through the check out if they wanted to apply for a store credit card. "Forget once it's a warning; twice, you're written up and three times you're out the door". She said "These are orders from headquarters from Dallas Texas." She had one heck of a delivery. No wonder she had been dubbed "The Warden" by the prisoners of poverty.

I am standing tagging shirts. Mrs. Wald is leaving the room. People are shaking their heads, heads down. What had the business section quoted this morning? Oh yes, profits up 7% twenty five million over the financial analysts estimates for this year. Push those credit cards or you're out the door, you poor pathetic peon. Straight out of Dickens, and ironically, Christmas was only weeks away.

staff meeting the following morning. Nora is given three prizes for exceptional customer service skills. Nora, who never returns a greeting, never answers a question, sour Nora who never acknowledges the assistance we give her at the till. She must have been saving all her energy for the customers.

Skinny, blond Debbie has to take a few hours off this afternoon to appear in court to seek a restraining order against her daughter's father. He will be released from prison soon. How does she manage on her six thirty an hour with a four year old daughter to support? Her boyfriend babysits while she worked. One year ago she had a car accident and though she and her daughter were not injured, her car was a write-off according to her. And she never received a cent although it was the other drivers fault. Why? She could not afford to carry insurance.

Cigarettes. She is always begging a cigarette. "Do you want one of these?" She asked one day then added. "I am always bumming and can never pay anyone back."

Dora quit during my second week of Employment; she too had a husband soon to be released from prison. However they and their two year old daughter were moving back to California.

Teresa finally got fired. She had said that she would as soon be fired than quit. No one understood this because she had not been employed more than two months and therefore was not entitled to collect unemployment.

Mr. B fired her for telling Mrs. Wald off. She had bragged to everyone that when Mrs. Wald asked her what she was doing just standing around she had answered; "Nothing. At six dollars and thirty cents an hour what do you want anyway?"

Selma quit the following week. Two peas in a pod. I theorized that one could not function without the other as back up.

CHAPTER 5 - CHRISTMAS

It is getting colder now. I am also unemployed and yet I do not feel frightened. At least for the following two weeks I feel liberated while searching for something else to do to earn my living.

I accepted another warehouse job from a temporary agency. The woman had told me that it was simple scanning items. "No lifting." The warehouse is freezing. The young girl could not have been more than twenty, who the agency had sent along as well had driven one and one half hours from Quincy California to work. The agency had told her as well, "Just wear a tee-shirt and jeans. Poor young soul did not know any better and shook like a leaf all day.

We worked together lifting heavy boxed Christmas trees, having to lift and turn them in order to scan the bar codes. Seven dollars an hour and of course no benefits. We were supposed to move quickly as well. Unbelievably, they wanted us to scan one every three minutes. A computer took care of the count. Slave labor was all it was. Half hour lunch and we had to clock in and out for that. We had to lock our purses in our trunks as there were no accommodations made for them.

The second day we were split up, each given our own computer and belt to work from. The young one was told to scan from boxes placed on her belt by one of the men if they were too heavy for her to lift. I was given the job of lifting the trees to scan all by myself. The second day was my last. I, at one hundred pounds could not lift half my weight and more all day every few minutes.

When I told the temporary agency worker what had transpired she said simply; "Well you won't be lifting trees every day."

Apparently the supervisor had had one woman downsized to a janitor position and another fired even though they were short-handed. Why? Well she, indeed all the supervisors get bonuses for producing with the least amount of outlay for wages. Alana was working through her last day our first day there and she told us that she was leaving before she dropped dead. "The faster and harder you work, the more they push till you want to cry. Nothing is worth this torture."

I pull up to my little duplex and Buddy is at the gate, tail wagging. It sounds so simple doesn't it? Get a job, work hard, and take a paycheck home. However there is nothing simple where abuse is concerned, abuse in its many forms, verbal, shunning, physical, and I have lived it all in Reno.

I have become astute at spotting it before I get involved now, which is bad in that I am not working yet after two weeks of looking for employment.

I very nearly hired on at the care Home, eight dollars an hour working in the Alzheimer's ward. After I accepted the position they gave me a stack of papers to fill out at home. I was signing everything away. My right to privacy - they wanted to be able to check my credit rating - no compensation for at work injury – clock out for lunch ten minutes late and you are docked a half hour anyway - clock in ten minutes late and you are docked an hour on your shift. No problem with me being late; I am always early. Next paper and I am reading that there is absolutely no excused absences, not for sickness, accident, none whatsoever and I read this stipulation reiterated goodness knows how many times over, said how many ways all down the paper. Then the last page informs me that if I have to leave their employ for whatever reason before the ninety days are up, or if I am fired for being absent the company will deduct one hundred and forty one dollars and some cents compensation for the examination and tests that I am required to take. All worded in an extremely hostile tone. None of the usual we are happy to welcome you on board sort of thing.

Just take no prisoners, peons. I asked the director to discuss some of the issues with me and she quickly grabbed the papers from my hands and told me to go home and think about it. "Let me know tomorrow if you want to work here or not."

No wonder their ad runs almost every week and the woman I was replacing, I was told had run off crying and quit. Lovely people. God protect the poor souls living there.

Well the Landlord has agreed not to put the plastic over my windows this winter. Thank goodness. Nothing like looking through grubby plastic four months out of a year. Not that I believe I will stay much longer. I am wearing out, not physically but financially and I am as lonely as I can Imagine it is possible to be at times.

The man with the one good eye knocked on my door this afternoon. He offered me his microwave and a skillet free. He is leaving, says he has found a better deal. I feel sorry now for complaining about his loud television; He was always nice. On the other hand I had to have my sleep in order to survive the pressures on these jobs. Unnecessary pressures, created by unhappy, unkind people ninety nine percent of the time.

I read in the paper this morning that the editor of the Battle Mountain Nevada paper was fired just the other day for allowing an uncomplimentary article to be published about the little hick town. Apparently it even got published in the Washington Post. So much for freedom of speech. But then nasty people do not appreciate having their cover blown. Most bullies do not. My experiences in Reno have confirmed that fact very well.

EPILOGUE

A NEW YEAR

I applied for another job after Christmas. The advertisement said; $300.00 hire on bonus, $8.00 an hour guaranteed, day shifts. I return on the appointed day for the interview and orientation. We are told of the importance of dressing well for the job of telemarketing to the existing customers of the various companies we are calling for. It is the 27th of December and we are told that because the company cannot begin training us until January 2nd we cannot be paid the hire on bonus. The reason for this? We are beginning our training after the last day of the month. We are given folders of company information and the health insurance plan is touted as being one of the very best this human resource worker has ever seen. And she will see us on the 2nd and we are lucky to be coming on board.

On New Year's Eve I receive a call from what I would eventually come to regard as the INHUMAN resource worker. She tells me that she has been directed to call all the new hires and inform them of a start delay. We will not be able to start work until the 16th of the month.

I spend the two weeks looking for other work, turn down two lower paying jobs just days before the 16th arrives. I am up early, dressed well, shiny, optimistic, despite my intuitive warning regarding this company. I drive over to the office and recalling a phone call I had made just two days prior regarding the job and confirmation of the start date, I park and walk to the office door.

Inside a darkened office the silence is deafening. The office is empty but for an over-fed young man in what appears to be his early twenties. He is sitting at an empty desk and when I tell him that I am supposed to start this morning he says simply; "Office closed yesterday". Poker faced, the stupid blank stare looking through me, he repeats, "Office closed". I tell him that I had called to confirm the job only two days prior. "Lovely people" I say. Not too dishonest, but then this is Reno. "Sorry about that" he says almost laughingly. I turn to walk out just as a young woman is walking in the door. "Office closed" he repeats and she glances at me and says, "At least they could have told us the truth and saved us the trip here". She is almost in tears. Yes lovely people here.

It really is time to leave Reno. I wanted to survive the winter, save a bit, wait for warmer weather to make my trip. It is prophetic the way everything is winding down here, however.

Even the local rag has cut me off. Yes. They sent me a bill for three months delivery. I only owed six weeks. The following day the paper never arrived. I called and told them that someone had added an extra three weeks to the already inflated bill sent me. Added an extra twenty one dollars to the total in pen. I had never heard of a paper cutting a customer off before they had had an opportunity to pay an over-inflated bill. The girl I spoke to then offered to resume delivery if I wanted to opt for the convenience of automatic payment. all I had to do was give her my credit card number. I thought not.

Oh well, it was a good omen, another sign telling me to quit procrastinating. The few women at Discount Heaven who had treated me as a human being had told me to leave while I could. "This town will break you," one had said. "Get out before you go broke," another had told me and the kind Mormon lady said: "I would leave tomorrow if I could."

I am making plans to leave now. Always hopeful, I keep checking the mail for that letter regarding my book. I have a few things to take care of like the fact that a credit card offered me should have arrived two weeks ago and having never arrived I informed the company, which had to cancel the original and issue a new card.

I found it peculiar that the woman asked me where I was born when in the process of confirming my identity. No-one had asked that before. Perhaps we have reached a new level of paranoia in the country.

Well it hardly matters. I am leaving now.

UP THE DANUBE
or
THE EXPERIENCES OF A LADY IN BLACK
THE CHARACTERS

Ninety four tourists (46 British, 3 Canadians from Montreal, 43 Germans, and 1 American, 1 Lady in black)
20 crew members

THE SETTING

The Danube River, a broken down river cabin cruiser and the countries of Hungary, Austria, and Germany.

The plane touched down in Budapest at 8:05 a.m. Budapest time. It was a Friday morning and the two had been travelling since 7:00 a.m. the previous morning, Miami time. She had been driving and half way to the Miami airport had hit something and the left front tire had gone flat just before the toll booth; but then she had to slow for the tow anyway.

Well never mind. The boss, angered, told her that after fixing the flat he would drive the rest of the way. She was obviously incompetent he said, otherwise she would have surely missed what neither had seen. And so began (The trip).

The shuttle bus dropped them at the IBIS HOTEL at 10 a.m. and after a one hour nap, shower and change of clothes, the two headed down stairs. The Lady stopped at the reception desk to enquire of the clerk directions to the nearest restaurant where they might have a bit of breakfast. (It had been a dozen hours since their last meal) unless one factors in the small package of pretzels and coffee on board Delta just before landing.

"Ah yes madam, restaurants every couple of blocks in Budapest. Eating is most important here."

But no, it was not to be. The Boss declared that he had no intention of wasting time and that they would start off walking. "I want to see the Parliament buildings, and two other sights and you can find something there."

Years ago the Lady had seen a movie. Perhaps you too have seen it: 'The Out Of Towners'. Ah well, her shoes were not broken, she had at least been allowed a coffee at the hotel and Budapest looked like a rather safe city. And so they began to walk. Surely the light summer breeze would finish drying her hair. One is not always allowed time for such things. They walked and over the course of one hour arrived at the Parliament buildings (very lovely) and she spied a restaurant. She approached excitedly, her smile disappearing as she grabbed hold of the large bronze door handle and caught sight of herself in the glass door.

The hair; thick, curly and cut to just below the ear, had done as she expected it would. Damp yet in some areas, her hair, windblown, the curl curlier as always in the humidity, gave one the impression that she had just survived an electrical shock. Ah but she carried hair spray and a comb in her bag and would dart into the restroom before all of the patrons in the upscale Bistro had noticed her.

Coffee and an egg sandwich would be fine (anything would have been fine at that point) and would she mind sharing with the boss to save valuable walking time? Why no, not after he had promised that if half a pica of bread spread with the egg mixture was not enough she might have more.

"Sorry Madame, no more egg." Said by a waiter who after one look at the travellers, had not been keen on their patronage; (the boss had been wearing shorts).

A long day this. Though the walk across the bridge from Buda to Pest had been beautiful, one weakens on little food. "Always thinking of your stomach" the Boss told this 100 pound bundle of energy at one point. But she had insisted upon stopping to purchase the small bag of chips and a mineral water. Then a half minute run and she had caught up with him. Victory!

The evening passed pleasantly. The boss and the Lady dined AL-FRESCO, a delightful little Greek restaurant, just an eight block walk from the hotel. Owned by, or in part, by a thirty something from Los Angeles, who told the couple that his parents visited him in Europe and that he hadn't returned home for years. The lady was beginning to understand why.

Saturday 8:00 a.m., horrible sleep, as is to be expected the first day when one is recovering, or trying to recover, from jet-lag. Off they were on the tour however. Coffee and a light breakfast in the breakfast room of the hotel, before the mini-van arrived to collect them.

Franz Josef and Elizabeth the 1st Of Austria's castle was the most beautiful of any the lady had yet seen. The grandeur, the pleasure of walking there had kept the Lady intrigued and awake throughout the tour and had sustained her until the van had cleared the palace gates. Then head bobbing she slept until she was abruptly awakened and told that they would not be dropped off at the hotel but downtown and had only to walk 12 blocks back to the IBIS.

Grudgingly he agreed to take a cab, then after hollering at the driver that the fare was too high (which it was) continued on angrily, too loud to notice that the driver had dropped the fare in half. He paid the original fare and stormed away.

She had only 3 hours to kill and yet with the luggage in the luggage room and having checked out of her room by the appointed time, many hours before actually, the 3 hours may as well have been

3 days. More coffee and yet the caffeine was now failing to work its magic. A little over an hour in the comfortable lounge chair, head bobbing up and down, she awakened to the sounds of gentle laughter of the few bar patrons, who politely glanced away when she opened her eyes and gazed round the room. Now she made her way a few blocks down the street, found a Bistro, ate a tuna sandwich and yes, one more coffee. One half hour and the bus would collect them and drive them to the river cruiser.

The Boss returns. No bus arrives. Another cab and finally they are welcomed aboard the Wilhelm Tell, the Boss curiously stopping to ask (and in all seriousness) if this was the same Wilhelm Tell who had shot the apple off a guy's head back in England). And so began the voyage!

CHAPTER 2

Their first evening on board the passengers were introduced to the crew, and issued their (permanent) seating assignments in the dining area.

Dinner: Saturday 6:30 p.m.

The Boss and the Lady find they will take their meals with a French Canadian couple from Montreal Canada and their sixteen year old daughter. This was a pleasure for the Lady, because of the fact that she had been born with dual citizenship and had spent most of her life in Canada. They introduced themselves and then the Boss, having decided to initiate a conversation asked: "So when are you separating from Canada?"

Lady and the Montrealers stared open-mouthed, in shock, then suddenly all four broke out in raucous laughter. The Lady, by way of explanation, told the family that the Boss was an American and this disclosure appeared to satisfy the Belores. Now with patience and an obvious touch of sympathy, Pierre attempted to educate (in broken English) the Boss, as to the complexities of Quebec politics, adding that not all Quebecers were interested in creating a sovereign nation.

The meal progressed pleasantly, with Lady and the Montrealers exchanging stories of life in the great white north. East versus west, that sort of thing. All rose after the last drop of after dinner coffee had been drunk and as Lady turned to follow the Boss up the staircase, she overheard Helene pleading with the waiter for a change in eating companions. By no means could he change the table assignments this frustrated soul was informed. Lady then backed down two steps and told Helene that she was in for a unique experience, to which Helene replied, "Like family" and laughing, both women said goodnight.

Breakfast: Sunday 8:00 a.m.

Lady and the boss arrived at table first. Just as coffee was being served the Belores and their daughter arrived. Though no older than his early fifties, she perhaps mid-forties, he was a rather staid individual. His wife and daughter would tease later that this was the nature of an engineer. "Meticulous with detail, he fails to see the big pictures."

Pierre, tall, about six foot three had the habit of bending his arms at the elbow and rubbing the palms of his hands together, in the fashion of the child anticipating an exciting event. He held his head slightly back and this gave the impression that he was looking down slightly at the rest of us (which of course he was).

Pierre spoke every word distinctly and would emphasize what he considered the fine points of his discussion by placing the thumb and middle finger of his right hand together and jabbing the air in front of him ever so slightly. When building to an exciting crescendo, the large dark brown eyes behind the black rimmed glasses opened so wide that one became aware of nothing else but two huge marbles, rolling round in a cream colored casing.

While initially, one might get the impression that this man considered himself to be an expert on every topic; the Lady came to the conclusion that he was simply talking incessantly to practice every English word he had only recently learned. One had to admire his concentration. It came to light over the course of many one-sided conversations that Pierre, while he may have wanted to appear worldly, had in fact travelled little and only in the controlled environment of a cruise ship. "Ah when on a cruise one has not to worry about getting lost and wasting valuable travel time. Oh and finding lodging that may be too expensive and missing trains and all of that, you see. One knows where they sleep every night and the tour guide plans and executes the sight-seeing."

He spent the final three days of the voyage worrying about catching the train from Regensburg to Munich, where, their flight would leave to spirit them home. He had the reservationist on the boat make a train reservation, had it confirmed the next day, and so on each day, until he decided they must depart for the train three hours early. Poor man. As any traveller knew and had informed him, the trains left every forty-five minutes and one purchased one's ticket and hopped aboard. First come, first served.

Alex, the sophisticated daughter, articulate in both English and French (she had run home from school three years earlier and informed her mother that she would attend an English school) was tutoring her mother in English and to their credit, over the two weeks Mama learned quite quickly. A friendly, well mannered, well groomed lady with a healthy sense of humor, Helene, as it turned out helped make the journey bearable for the Lady.

"Is e always like this?" Helene, head in hands exclaimed one afternoon at lunch, when once again the Boss hopped up to run to the other side of the dining area, as he did during each meal (countless times) for fear of missing something. Back and forth from one side of the room to the other, looking out the windows.

"I don't know ow you stand it."

However Lady knew that no amount of pleading would change the behavior of the Boss, for consideration for others had never been an issue for him. Even the irritated stares of the other diners, as he made his way between their tables, failed to have an effect and gradually Lady came to realize that many of the passengers had decided that he was in her care and began to blame her for not being able to control him. Of course truth be told, he was simply selfish to the nth degree, and far from requiring care, though the same could not be claimed for many after they had experienced the Boss.

Ah, the pleasant British from places such as Bath, London, Herefordshire, and Edinburgh, to name but a few. The Lady passed many pleasant hours in their company, while the boss spent his time running from side to side of the ship, or planted firmly in the center of the deck above, fearful of missing a sight along the river. And how fortunate these ladies were, their husbands attentive, and not far from them.

Lady took note, as she had a few years earlier while on a trip to England, that the British chattered and laughed and generally enjoyed themselves, while the humorless Germans, dour, and rather sour looking, responded very little, if at all to a friendly greeting and appeared to take everything very seriously, whether eating sausage, drinking beer, or playing cards.

The two Japanese women, quiet and conspicuously inconspicuous, spent their days staring out the windows of the lounge at the passing scenery (though they did not run from side to side) and drinking prodigious amounts of orange juice, while watching the rest of the inhabitants (one needed a break from the scenery on occasion) of what might be euphemistically referred to as a floating seniors center ingest copious amounts of coffee, tea and alcohol. There was not much to distinguish the appearance of the British passengers from that of the Germans, save for the fact that the Brits were, as they say, a bit more spiffy and were not as inclined as the Germans to wear socks in their sandals. The Lady found the Japanese women glancing at the socks in the sandals and wondered if Japanese men were inclined toward this unique fashion statement.

This being a small river cruiser there was little in the way of activity, but for two afternoons during the two weeks of incarceration. On one occasion the tall, good looking, though rather sad but pleasant dining captain offered two hours of demonstration in napkin folding, in which the guests were encouraged to participate and on another occasion the rolly polly happy chef offered strudel-making exercises (the later served as desert that very evening).

Shortly before the cruise ended (and what an ending it was) the Boss felt obliged to inform his table, "We will be released at nine a.m. on Saturday."

The following morning, the Boss, the Lady and a bus load of passengers, were taken on a tour of yet another beautiful little village on the Danube and the excursion included a visit to yet another Cathedral. All went well that day, but it was not to last. The passengers had been told that the boat would be leaving port as soon as the tour ended and all right thinking people, (those well aware that the world did not spin on its axis solely for their benefit and that captains did not hold ships for wayward souls) boarded the vessel. Lady placed her foot on the gangplank and Boss told her he was going to take a walk around the immediate area. "Oh but we are pulling out right away" said she. To which he replied: "God damn it, I'll walk when I want to. They won't take off without me." So with a sigh, but held head high (as she was not responsible for his behavior) Lady made her way to the lounge, found a chair facing the window and as she bent over her coffee cup she heard a sudden loud burst of laughter from behind. Her head popped up and to her horror she saw the Boss, running as fast as nature would allow as the boat slowly backed away from the shore. The gangplank rose gently and out of reach of the erstwhile Boss.

With the assistance of one of the deck hands, a stocky German girl who obviously did not suffer fools lightly (she cussed at the Boss in German as he made the jump from shore to ship) he made it back on board. Straight into the lounge he strode, as arrogant as a peacock and informed Lady that it was no big deal.

"I could have swum to the boat if I'd had to."

"But are you sure they would have thrown you a rope?" she asked.

He spun round then and walking back to the cabin was again read the riot act, this time by the captain's first mate, she a young woman of about twenty eight, sporting long curly hair and about five foot ten and of athletic build, who until this incident had treated Lady differentially, but who now treated Lady with a somewhat friendly manner. Was she sorry for her, or simply no longer jealous of the young woman who accompanied the wealthy older man? Surely no-one could envy Lady by this time.

"Like a little child," Helene said that night at dinner. Boss was well out of earshot so to speak, on the other side of the room checking the scenery.

Well tomorrow was another day and beautiful Vienna with its church spires, squares and shops and palace, should have offered some respite from the so far unhappy experience in which Lady found herself trapped. But it was not to be.

The motley crew set off once again by bus for the center of the city and a grand tour of the palace there. Upon leaving the palace Boss told Lady that he was going to spend their shore time there climbing the hill outside the gardens, in order to reach a monument at the top. Lady left him and finding a little sidewalk cafe enjoyed a cappuccino, then proceeded to walk round the city alone. Peering in shop windows and watching the pedestrians, she slowly made her way back to the Cathedral and spent some time patting the horses stationed there, harnessed as they were in the heat to their carriages, lonely in their burdens, much like the Lady herself.

On the bus back to the ship Boss inquired of Lady in a loud voice: "If you moved to England would you try to talk like them?" Obviously angry with her for leaving him to do his own climbing.

Lady replied: "I believe I would just be myself."

CHAPTER 3

The fifth evening aboard ship Boss had insisted that Lady change places at the dining table with him. This particular table was at the end of the room and one side of the table had the view to outside partially obscured by a wall. Now two nights before they were to disembark, the little group sat waiting for their dinners to be served.

"Would you pull the curtain back just a bit?" Helene asked.

"Yes" said Lady "We little people would like to see as much as we can as well." Laughter burst forth, even from Boss, who, to Lady's surprise turned a bit red in the face.

The crash happened the following afternoon. It was five minutes to twelve as Lady remembers it. She was walking through the foyer on her way to the stairs down to the dining room and as she turned to look over her shoulder to see if Boss was going to accompany her, it happened. The boat, having lurched all morning, speeding and slowing down since leaving port at 3 a.m., was, as many had commented, going much too fast to enter the approaching lock. In a flash Lady was on the floor. The boat had smashed full speed into the concrete wall. Her left shoulder felt as though it had been driven in to the carpet, the iron mockup of a ship painted bright red that had been standing against the wall flew up and bounced off her leg, just as the woman from Edinburgh fell hard, slamming to the floor on her back before she too bounced off of Lady.

The woman's husband rushed to her, and looking toward Lady told her to lie still. "She has hit her head" Lady told him, to which he replied: "You have to think of yourself." Lady struggled to sit and looking toward the lounge saw the woman from London, her face dripping blood. The Boss appeared, and looking down at Lady said: "Well, you're probably alright. Here I'll set you in this chair". And pulling her up under the arms he dumped her in a nearby arm chair and said: "Well there's nothing I can do, so sit there until help arrives" then childishly he added excitedly, "I'm going to go and see the damage done to the boat."

"Astonishing behavior," commented one Brit. "Astonishing, boorish, and he has behaved this way the entire cruise. He has no consideration for a living soul and not even any compassion for his companion. Astonishing really." Added his wife.

"Well, he is the stereotypical ugly American isn't he? If I were you, my dear, I would definitely be moving back to Vancouver, England, or wherever you like, but my God, do something different."

"Yes he won't be made ambassador to a foreign country will he? I've tried to keep my dignity because I am not responsible for his behavior, yet I realize everyone has to have been made aware of the way he has behaved."

Four were taken to the local hospital for x-rays. The fourth, an elderly gentleman, managed to escape with a bandage over a cut under his eye. Lady escaped with bruises, an extremely sore painful shoulder and a rude awakening. Well, she thought as the cab drove her back to the boat, perhaps some people do need a good shaking.

She entered the reception area and a half dozen British women approached, asking how she was and in horror telling her that Boss had gotten on the bus transporting the German speakers to the hotel. "He said he was bored hanging around the boat and wanted to walk in Regensburg rather than waste any more time. I've never seen anyone like him; at least I don't recall it, thank goodness." All was a blur, even the face of the woman who spoke these words wasn't quite clear at the moment. Well at least there were those who expressed concern.

The bus arrived to take the English speakers in to town and at the entrance to the hotel someone pointed telling Lady that he had arrived. "Well no cast, you're fine. Want to go for a walk?"

"Peraps" said Helene. "We will go to my room first and I will fix a sling for the arm. This should av been done I think."

The police who had interviewed Lady had been less than honest. The form they asked her to sign would allow her compensation should the liner be found to have been at fault. "A mechanical failure?" she had asked. "Oh yes." Then she found the tiny English print that stated she was prepared to testify that the captain's negligence had caused the accident. In pain she had not thoroughly read the document before signing.

"Oh well the captain is probably at fault. He's a Swede." And the other officer laughed at his remark. These two have not yet recovered from the second world war mused Lady, and she handed the document to the officer.

As the man had said she would have to look after herself. Flying back to the states she would pass the time by planning her move.

The sling was now in place and the Belores suggested dinner and drinks. Over dinner Pierre related his experience of the crash as being "verrrrry wet, yes? I am standing at the wash basin, no? And rinsing a few leetle things, me, when suddenly the water she comes all down from my ed to my feet. Terrible, no?"

Later that evening Lady agreed to a walk. Some fresh air and to stretch her legs would be good. And she enjoyed the pleasant little neighborhood, in the pleasant German town. But as ever was the case, nothing was ever enough for Boss. When she decided that she must return to sit and relax, he, in spite of her pain and injuries, accused her of not wanting to do anything but talk, drink coffee and smoke cigarettes.

Ah the train trip the next day was as abusive as had been any other day during the trip. Lady was happy to find a seat close to the entrance to the train, but this was not good enough. Carrying her own two rather heavy carry-on bags, she followed him two cars further (he had to have a window that did not block the view). Two nights and one more day thought Lady.

They stayed in the City Centre Hotel at the Munich train station and the walk round the city was enjoyable. Boss was even considerate, allowing Lady to stop for a coffee and food when the need arose. He had complained of feeling tired.

"Ah, the Dutch waiter had been so kind when she returned to the boat. Fixing me the plate of cheese, bread and grapes. And the glass of wine. A treat from him. No charge." And as she rose to leave he had rushed over and with a concerned expression on his face asked what had happened to her husband. She told him. "Such a shame on him. Yes very bad. I am sorry." He'd said, his voice kind.

And the ship's officer. Helping out, was how they had explained the presence of another captain. His own ship had been stranded in Belgrade because of the war. Lady walked past the reception desk to say good-bye. "Why?" he asked: "Why does he behave so?"

"Because he does not care" she said.

"Good luck" he told her.

That second day on board and the toilets backed up into the shower stalls of the first nineteen cabins. A harbinger of things to come she had thought at the time. Repaired before nightfall. A bottle of champagne left in the cabin as an apology. Boss had put it in his bag.

The Lady in black. Well she had purchased a lot of black, greys, white, and creams. Good thing she'd thought. She'd at least felt stylish. Stylish. Her grandmother, a fashion designer had used the term so often. A bit classy? The expensive shops in Munich and Vienna had the same sorts of clothes displayed in their windows. She was feeling very European, very confident. No one could have known how she'd cut corners to save for the few items she'd purchased for the trip. It was to have been such a lovely trip. The black suit she'd worn to her father's funeral the month before hung in her closet at home. Black. The insecure American mood was black. He was anxious on foreign soil, which was why he had to feel in control of something, someone. "You have to take care of yourself " the man had told her.

Ah but it is over now. "It was time for my fortune to turn rounds" She told me when we met.

It was late September then. September in Paris. I noticed her sitting alone at the little umbrella table outside Madame Maries. Her little cat now and again peeked out of the carrier she had placed on the chair beside her.

Her fortune had changed for the better just two weeks after her return to the states. The book she had been working on for over three years was finally recognized as having merit. This had afforded her the means to free herself from her tormentor. Even her little cat was in jeopardy of losing his claws. A threat the Boss had made because he said: "She's not a loving cat to me. If she were I wouldn't care so much that she might scratch my furniture."

Of course her good fortune is mine. We would not have met had she not moved to Paris and I should still be single, never having known The Lady In Black, and her little chat noir.

BLIND EXIT 90265

CHAPTER 1 - THE DARK

"I have felt the wind,
of the wings of madness."

Baudelaire

It was the eve of my fiftieth birthday and I am standing alone on the deck of my Malibu beach house, clutching a ten dollar flea market sweater around me, as I watch the fog envelope Catalina Island and weep, praying to God to give me the courage to jump. It is high tide. The waves will carry me out to sea. No one will have to bother with my corpse. That's good; even better, it will not cost a cent. No, my demise will not cost anyone either time or money, no dressing for the funeral service, the phoney eulogy, what would they have to say? Gee she was great, the trips, the money, when she had it to give. Died broke you know. Never could manage money. Wasted all those years trying to get published. Shouldn't have kept giving. Stupid.

Should I leave a note? Yes, I'll go in and write something for them to find. Can't simply disappear; too inconsiderate. Foolish me. I begin writing. Baby hops up on my lap. Poor Baby. What did he say?

"She's useless, totally dependent, worthless, she's your cat alright." I look down and pat her on the head and she turns her eyes to mine and mews and what am I doing? Helpless cat. Am I as helpless as this poor creature? Do I jump into the polluted waters of Malibu beach, and prove the narcissistic, self-centered, controlling man correct? Destroy my perfectly healthy body, my future, leave the cat to be destroyed. Yes, these are the thoughts that ran through my befuddled mind that dreary spring night.

Was it the love of a cat, my baby granddaughter, or the respect for life, even my own pathetic life that saved me from ruin that year? I don't know, to be honest with you. All I know is that I am still here and the best of it is I am happy about it. Happy despite the fact that getting here was nothing short of a little journey through hell.

CHAPTER 2 - ESCAPE

"We should show life
neither as it is nor as it ought to be,
but as we see it in our dreams."

Anton Chekhov 1806-1904

This was not how I saw life in my dreams. this was more nightmare on PCH (Pacific Coast Highway to the uninitiated). There were only about four hours of the twenty four each and every day, that the surf did not smash, bang, boom, under said Malibu dream home and at night it pounded so hard that I feared the pilings might give way. The traffic roared by the bedroom window on the opposite side of the house, the four lane freeway from hell I called it. The new tenant upstairs, a transplanted Brit who claimed to produce rock videos, bought wane by the six pack, and appeared to work only on weekends. Beginning Friday night the crew would arrive and the same thumping tune would be played over and over again, whilst the high heels crossed the floor hour after hour and the furniture could be head sliding back and forth across the floor at odd intervals. I leave it to you to guess the nature of the art form being filmed. Sunday late and the crew are packing up their camera equipment.

Now Monday morning and the artists begin to straggle off. Miss heels is looking rather the worse for wear and the three or four men in the group appear to be exhausted. I on the other hand, accomplished nothing at all. I walk the beach, I take a drive down to the grocery at Topanga Canyon, venturing out when I sense a lull in the traffic. I am careful to fold the rear view mirror against the window when I leave the vehicle parked to go into the house; we've already lost two to being side swiped by traffic. Oh yes and when arriving home I learned early on to exit through the passenger side door of the vehicle, so that I and my few bags of food would not be spirited away along with the rear view mirror.

The houses on either side were built so close to ours that I could have reached out to touch someone, should I have been so inclined. But I found it enough to allow the aroma from their nightly barbeque to waft through the windows without complaint and pray for a reversal in the direction the wind was blowing.

There was nowhere to run, nowhere to hide. I felt trapped. Hell I was trapped. Emotionally, mentally, physically and financially, or so I thought until that sorry night, the eve of my birthday and there I stood on deck, surrounded by pigeon poo, the birds nestled in for the night cooing contentedly, as I contemplated my permanent move.

Ah well, so I was still alive, but that did not mean I had given up on finding a change. The noise, the traffic the dog poop on the beach, the nouveau riche, noses up in the air; were they snooty, or just trying to ignore the poop? The poor Mexican women waiting at bus stops along the highway. Let's see, they had cleaned the homes of the wealthy all day, cared for the children, for likely little more than minimum wage and were now waiting for the bus that would carry them back to their hovel in East L.A. And this was paradise.

I drove the silly sports car with the envelope windows that I could barely see out of down to the shopping center and the bank, the crowd gathered round, cameras pulled out, car blocked, couldn't move, people waving, smiling, me crawling along. Find a parking spot quickly, smile, open door, take deep breath, all the while, they're snapping away.

"Who is she?"

"I don't know?" Snap, snap.

"She might be somebody, keep snapping." And I'd thought I was nuts.

I make it into the bank. Close account.

"How are you today?" The manager asked, big smile.

"Been better" I answer.

"Don't blame you" he says.

My birthday; happy birthday to me.

Drive to travel agency. Pay cash for ticket. "Our clientele rarely pay cash" says the unkempt girl in the too tight shirt who informs me that she is an actress. Wonderful, I tell her so, and wish her all the luck, all the best, just let me out of here.

Back home. Booked two weeks ahead to get the cheaper fare. I obviously was not an actress. Just a poor writer. My clothes fit and I was well groomed. But then I was not making a personal statement. No tacky chic. Nothing like the director's wife who walked her little dog that wore the rhinestone collar on the beach and never acknowledged a smile, or a good morning. Just a scowl, until the day big guy was walking with me and introduced himself and told her he had just bought up the beach. Ah, now we were suddenly human, or close, I was not yet dressed in tacky chic. I was thereafter permitted to smile and say hello to her little dog, however.

The plane ticket is hidden in my closet. I feel a bit of power now, a bit of control. Yet I am frightened, anxious, exhilarated, nervous. Full of self-doubt one moment, and confidence, and optimism the next. Fearing the unknown, I am impatient, I am a mess.

A woman is like a tea bag.
You never know how strong she is
until she gets into hot water.

Eleanor Roosevelt
former First Lady and social reformer

He's gone again. I am usually alone. Now I am plunked down in the land of LA, dear me. I decide to clean my closets. I set out one box to take to the charity, another for cleaning rags. I clean house within an inch of my life. Always makes me feel more in control when I am organized. A place for everything, everything in its place. Feel I've accomplished something today. One day at a time, first things first, even if it's only the closet.

I've seen the homeless here. Pushing their carts up and down the PCH. There must be a charity drop somewhere. I read that the good people at city council out of the bigness of their hearts did provide a bus for shelter during the winter months.

I drive over to Venice. Lots of charity shops there. I drop the box. Over to the drug store to pick up a few last minute items for the trip. Exit the store. Hand the tattered, tired woman leaning against the building beside her cart a few dollars. "God bless you" she says. God bless us all I think.

I leave on a morning flight tomorrow. I'm packed. I'm scared. I don't want to end up like the woman at the drug store. Can't think like that. Got to be strong. I open the paper and decide to read a bit and try to relax before I try to sleep. What does it say? Third wealthiest economy in the world, California, a very wealthy state. Big deals, big wheels. Read further. LA county has one of the poorest school districts in the nation. Teacher begs for wash machine and clothes dryer, so that the children can bring their second set of clothes to school to be cleaned, that is if they are fortunate enough to own a second set of clothes. Some children don't attend school because they are too ashamed of the rags they are forced to wear.

And I glance out the window and watch the ribbon of traffic lights travelling along the highway, the waves lapping the shore and I remember the kids at the beach the other day. Half a dozen kids, not more than twelve, thirteen, laughing, having fun, great clothes, all running toward the chauffeured Limo waiting to take them home.

There is something very wrong here. I am powerless, powerless to help much more than donate old clothes, give a dollar here and there. Powerless to close my eyes to all the suffering I see about me. How is it that others don't notice? He tells me I'm a peon for being concerned for all the disadvantaged. He thought I had more class than that he tells me. Hopeless, useless, powerless, frightened. I must get out of here.

I go to bed. My grandmother always said that to close your eyes, say a prayer and drift off to sleep worked wonders for how you'd feel in the morning. "No sense in sitting up worrying; a good rest and you'll have enough courage to face the next day."

The following morning I am at LAX bright and early. I'm Fine; baggage checked, and cat safe in her carry-on slung over my right shoulder. Quite a way to begin the next year of my life.

I've thousands of miles to travel. I sit and I wait, and Robert Frost's poem comes to mind. "The woods are lovely, dark and deep but I've miles to go before I sleep, For I have promises to keep". Something close to that anyway. Yes, promises to keep. Must promise to be true to myself. And now we are boarding the plane. And I'm strong and brave and all those good things and if I can just keep up all this positive self-talk I'll make it.

CHAPTER 3 - BETRAYAL

I am no longer wealthy by association. I am no longer cared for financially, supported, able to give, trips, money, invitations to visit whatever beach house, in whatever area. I am no longer welcome. I'm stupid. I'm naive. A poor planner. A whiner. Cry baby. Have no right to expect help; everyone has their own lives and problems to deal with.

"You know what? I'm going to buy you a pot."

"A pot?" I responded, confused.

"Yes, a pot. Cause you don't have a pot to piss in, nor a window to throw it out of. No window to throw it out of, oh I won't waste the money on a pot." And she laughed. How sad. The relatives, the so called friends.

"Well good luck" they said. "Keep in touch. Let me know how it's going. Hope you don't end up homeless".

"What about here?" I asked. "Jobs, apartments?"

"You'll be fine," they said. "Just find a cheap weekly till you get on your feet somewhere."

I had purchased a used car. It had low gas mileage, was in good condition, nice looking, nothing to be ashamed of. I drove, drove, drove, from town to town, city to city and "Stay a few days till you decide where you want to go" they said. "Get rid of that cat" they said. "I don't know of anything you can afford to rent" they said. "You don't eat much, so food won't be a problem, not like for a normal person" they said. And they were too busy to talk long when I called. And letters were never answered. And God bless me, I said.

Stripped of the social and material trappings society has come to worship, am I now a useless, worthless, helpless creature? Am I as worthless, useless, and helpless as he had warned and now particularly so?

Suddenly everyone was very busy. Suddenly they all had problems to deal with, whereas prior to my arrival, they had all claimed to be leading wonderfully idyllic lives. Busy, burdened, or fearful? The fear of misfortune rubbing off, as easily as had good fortune? Embarrassment at being associated with a little woman unable to find work, an affordable place to live and so eccentric as to refuse to destroy her cat.

Now as I drove past open fields and road signs asking me to return and others beckoning me to stop, stay a while, it occurred to me that Baby and I were a pretty good team. Both of us were considered useless, helpless, and very definitely expendable. I related to her reliance upon me, her need. Yes, I could empathize. And my empathy for the gentle creature ignited a fire in me, the fire I needed to fight for my own survival, to nurture myself as well as I did this little four legged animal.

With my new found freedom I had packed my car the night before my departure and had slept the sleep of a child at peace and the following morning as my hosts departed for church, I had hit the open road.

CHAPTER 4 - THE OPEN ROAD

As I drove I recalled a book I had been assigned to read in my second year of university. Zen AND THE ART OF MOTORCYCLE MAINTENANCE. Well was I not in rather the same circumstance as far as searching was concerned? Perhaps the search to reclaim the self can be the most challenging that we will ever undertake.

A false sense of security is what I had been relying upon to see me through the years I now realized. False sense of man, family, friends. My fears of loneliness, rejection, friendlessness, impoverishment, abandonment, derision and decay had put my buried self on hold for a very long time.

Pat Conroy the author of THE PRINCE OF TIDES has said that he doesn't think one learns much from winning; it just feels good. But he said "Loss you think about, because loss makes you change the way you do things". Yes it was far past time I changed the way I did things. Well, these are the kinds of things I thought about on the open road.

Change can be difficult and so I had adapted to the regularity of a rather irregular life. Perhaps it is easier, at least for a time to adapt, rather than face the unknown.

I feared failure. What if I did not get it right this time? What if I am disappointed in my new life? Will I displease others? And then success, what if I am successful in putting victimhood behind me? What will others then demand of me?

Dennis O'Grady - yes, that was the author - TAKING THE FEAR OUT OF CHANGE. Yes that was it. That was the book. Oh yes, I had done my homework. Master fear and move on. Disrupt your routine. I had read it all. Psyched myself up so often and then finally and it took almost a fatal act on my part, but finally I had put into motion that which I had believed to be the right thing to do for my survival. All that reading finally paid off. I was not only alive, but with each passing day on the road I became stronger, less fearful, and more determined to prove to myself that I could succeed.

Leaving my relationship meant changing every aspect of my life. Not a small adjustment. Now why had I expected people who had been living lives of such routine that they knew exactly what they would be eating for dinner one week to the day from this, to understand the emotion, regret, fear, and apprehension that I was experiencing? Why did I expect people who answered "I can't imagine being in your position" answered angrily and fearfully my question, "You can imagine how I feel can't you?" And I said well that is empathy and they looked fearful and said they did not want to feel any of that, thank you. And I am driving and I am thinking, chicken shits, and I'm feeling much, much stronger now.

Well now I know for certain where I don't want to be and indeed whom I don't any longer want to associate with. Now as I drive I feel stronger, less burdened, less apt to concern myself with the opinions of people who, truth be told, are but shells themselves. There is a me here and I must get in touch with her. I must put her first, look after her, be kind and understanding of her, put her life back together.

Up until now it had always been about someone else. I needed to be needed. My needs coming after everyone else's wants. Now I needed to focus. I needed the solitude that would bring clarity and insight to what had been a tumultuous life. I needed this total independence. I needed the open road.

CHAPTER 5 - REFLECTION

"It has long since come to my attention that people of accomplishment
rarely stayed back and let things happen to them.
They went out and happened to things".

Elinor Smith - aviator and writer

Why don't you quit this silly writing? Why can't you just be content? Get a little job in a store. You're always doing charity work. Go volunteer somewhere. Be normal like the rest of us. Normal. Yes normal. Quit daydreaming about being someone you're not. Who do you think you are anyway?

Who? Who? Who? Why? Why? Why?

Why couldn't I be like them is what they were asking. I must have thought myself better than they, to believe I deserved more. Why didn't I just submerge myself to an even greater extent. Give up travel, writing, be content with what Thoreau called A life of quiet desperation. Give up hopes, dreams, why not simply die inside and make everyone feel much more comfortable? Why did I have to be me? That's what they were saying.

And I pass another road sign thanking me for visiting Washington, The Evergreen State.

And as the evening approached I checked into the Motel 6, settled Baby, ate my 7-11 hot dog, drank my Styrofoam cup of tea, showered, and asking God for the courage to continue on, fell asleep.

Shabby towns, pretty cities, from Wenatchee to Olympia, Portland, the days pass and as the days pass peacefully along the road to

God only knows what destination, so do the fear and panic that had had me in their grip. Concerns? I had a few, yes, money depleting, where to settle? Yet I had made it farther than I would have dared imagine only months earlier.

The adrenalin of adventure kicked in. I began to enjoy the exploration, the sights, the independence, discovery. I was going to be alright. Somehow I would even succeed, eventually. I was me, unapologetically me, and free. I had made it to the other side. I had crossed the river of fear, the mountains of regret. I'd found emotional equilibrium, balance and the next challenge was to find a home.

And as Robert Frost had written - The woods are lovely dark and deep, but I had miles to go before I was to sleep.

CHAPTER 6 - THE LANDING

"Life is mostly froth and bubble,
two things stand in stone.
Kindness in another's trouble,
Courage in our own."

Anonymous

I had spent money on the nursing assistant's course in Washington. I was going to care for the elderly in the homes. Yes, I was going to be paid seven dollars an hour, no benefits for six months and on and on. I drove and stopped in the towns along route 395. Now I was headed south once more. Pretty towns and the signs advertised friendly people. Friendly in relation to the size of one's pocket book. Not mentioned. Must not have had room on the sign to fit it all in.

I stop at a Wal-Mart to buy some much needed necessities, like 89¢ shampoo, and cat food for 88¢ as advertised. I carry on. I stop at the Family Dollar on a driving break. I observe the poor and unhappy looking people, in the friendly, happy towns, and in my mind's eye I compare them to the rich unhappy people sitting stone faced on little chairs outside the gourmet coffee shops in places like Malibu. All the lonely people, all the unconnected people. Rich, poor, Fila or Faded Glory didn't seem to matter much.

Perhaps they've nothing to believe in anymore. The Faded Glory crown have either quit trying or were afraid to dream a dream in the first place. The Fila elite have achieved a great deal and yet find that it wasn't everything they had hoped it would be and have shut down.

It's a lonely feeling knowing that you are the only one who believes in you and yet I decided it was alright. After all I thought, I am the one in charge here and so it follows I've 100% backing. It doesn't get any better than that does it?

Positive self-talk the psychology books call it, perhaps makes all the difference when working to move from Faded Glory to Fila, and enjoying the ride.

And where to land. Quickly get a job, an affordable place. And a friend, the only one left not afraid of my situation suggests Reno Nevada. He has a cousin there. It could at least provide a place to stop, and begin again.

And I'm driving down 395 south and it's late and I stop in a little mom and pop motel for the night in some small Oregon town. The light rain feels good on my face as I struggle with the bags into the tiny unit at the back of the building. Moist, warm, and I recall Key Largo and I stop. I can't stay here, can't afford it. Now sleep I tell myself and look forward to the new adventure tomorrow. And tomorrow the adventure begins.

CHAPTER 7 - THE BEGINNING

I won't stay in Reno but a year if that, I know it. But I will make the best of it and get back on my feet. I'm hesitant about leaving the cozy Oregon motel unit. I want to be somewhere closer to the sea than Reno. But I forge ahead, and soon I am on the road to Reno. It is beautiful country, the drive through Susanville California and on through the Sierra and I know it is going to be a challenge, but thank goodness I am finally up to it.

Highway 395, off at Oddie Blvd. and on to Wells Ave., and there is the Motel 6 I had called ahead and arranged for a room by the week, a bit cheaper than daily and somewhere to stay until I found an apartment.

I call my connections. First Abe. Has lived here three years. Calls himself a travel writer. Doesn't publish, but because of one article published some ten years earlier for a now defunct travel magazine, his name is somehow in a system that allows him use of a card, that in turn allows him to scam cheap hotel rates, free bus passes and a few morsels of food whenever he feels the need of a holiday. A holiday from what?

My mother, she's in a home. Twenty five hundred a month you understand, and when I try to show her apartments she doesn't like any of them.

"Where do you work?"

"Well I have disability".

"What sort of disability?"

"Eyes. They close every four months unless I get my medication. That's why I came to Reno. The benefits. They didn't understand me in Seattle, threatened to cut me off. A great social worker helped me set up here. Nice apartment, everything. You got to know the system, you understand". Laughs. And on he talks about his mother and how she is spending her money in the home and his last great trip and all the freebees.

"Well, I was given your name by Joanne and she thought you would be able to assist me in apartment hunting, show me the ropes here so to speak".

"Oh, Joanne. Rich. Do you understand her house is worth at least two hundred thousand? Inherited it. I told her to move here so that I could look after her in her old age though she travels and works you never know, never know. She's older than me, by ten years but we had a relationship you understand. She must be sixty-five now. Looks great though. We broke up that night we were in a grocery store in Seattle and she was ready to leave and I was on the phone. I told her of course I was on the phone I'm a New Yorker, we talk on the phone. She walked right by me and out the door. Of course I know lots of rich older women; they won't introduce me to their friends though. All they want is sex. How is your settlement going? Of course you have to get some money out of this, right? Got to run. Call me when you get a place. I'll take you to dinner, maybe I know of a job. You want a job?"

"Of course I want a job. I have to live, pay bills".

"Okay, okay, I see. Well I gotta go. I got to organize all these travel brochures, unpack. So be well, be well, call me later".

a nut, I say to myself. Yet I am curious. what does this kook look like? For the following couple of days I am busy apartment hunting, job hunting and each night before sleep I read a few pages of Deepak Chopra's Seven Spiritual Laws Of success. The book is so worn by now it looks like an old woman's worn bible.

Now I call my next contact. Seventy-three year old man. Cousin of my friend Jack and so surely he will be a normal human being. I talk with him; Very friendly man, helpful, insists upon picking me up to apartment hunt. The car leaves a great deal to be desired and I am being generous. I enter the passenger side and he tells me the glove compartment will not close, but it won't hurt anything to just let it rest on my knees. It is a tiny compact hatchback so tiny my five foot one hundred pound frame would be uncomfortable sitting behind the wheel, but there he sits, the six foot three man with the requisite paunch behind the wheel and we pull away from the motel.

There is a nasty smell emanating from the back of the so-called vehicle and two dogs in need of a bath repose on a filthy mat. "Never leave the dogs. Two hours max is all I keep them out in the car however, or they get restless".

We arrive at the apartment complex and a woman in her seventies wearing a grey pony- tail, sweats, and Nikes shows me a suite that is not for rent. The suite I would be renting isn't ready. Carpets not cleaned. No curtains yet. She talks non-stop about the history of the building and how it was a haven for the rich and famous seeking quickie divorces in the thirties and forties. All the units came complete with silverware, the good stuff too, and crystal and I would like to see the one unit I would be renting. And I have to ask three times and have decided that this old woman with the pony-tail and the gift for gab is not to be trusted.

Cousin sees things differently however and telling me he has been a Landlord for years claims to believe this old hag is but a rough-hewn desert rat, and really none other than the salt of the earth.

Salt of the earth now wants twenty five dollars. "A fee dear. Everyone does it. It's to check your credit rating and of course you get it back when you move in".

I don't like it but cousin insists that there's no problem and these two twits smile happily as I hand over my twenty five dollars, imagining correctly that it has taken wing and will not be making a return flight.

Cousin returns me to the motel and hands me the classified section of the local paper as I crawl out of the puddle jumper. That night at the motel I weigh all I've seen so far in the matter of apartments. They all want double security deposits because of my cat and all inform me that the cat deposit which equals mine is non-refundable - a gift one woman called it and this on top of the fifty to one hundred extra per month rent for the cat. When I tell them that spade female cats do not spray, I am met with blank, or most often angry stares.

I sit now at the little table by the motel window searching the ads for studio apartments. Hopefully furnished. I see one and only one. I believe I've looked at everything else in the city by this time. I call and an elderly man with an Irish brogue answers. He wants three fifty-five. A cat, well I don't want pets but for three eighty you can have it. He asks my age and tells me that he has had it with the students, the drinking, the loud music. The neighborhood is within walking distance of the university, and after moving in I soon find out about the torment he is referring to when the street livens up and the houses begin to rock on the weekends in particular.

I call cousin next morning and tell him I found a place.

"Good thing I gave you that paper" he says in all seriousness when he arrives to drive me over to meet Paddy. Good thing you encouraged me to throw twenty five dollars away I think.

It is a nice little place, though the carpet is filthy and the first I'd seen laid out in patches. The furniture is of the Salvation Army style and there is a brown film over everything suggesting an empty abode for quite some months. I take it. I can clean it and at least it is a little duplex with a little front yard, white picket fence, trellis and all. I won't have people walking over my head, banging around below, someone snoring on either side I think.

Back to the motel and before I leave the puddle jumper cousin tells me to be sure and tell Jack how he helped me find my little place. "I want to get back with the family" says he, "and let's face it, who knows where you'd be if I hadn't given you the classified section". Right you are.

"Now I'll pick you up tomorrow and help you take your things in, well, lead you over there and then I have yard work to do and after that I'll take you to dinner. No, day after tomorrow I'll do the yard work, then I'll pick you up and take you to dinner to celebrate you finding a new place".

"Sounds fine and the weather is lovely, I'd be happy to do some yard work". This was true. I had been driving and spent so much time in motels that yard work sounded like a treat.

A beautiful Saturday morning, autumn and the leaves just beginning to turn, not a breeze, sun shining, all is right with my little world at least for today at any rate. I have wondered for so many months that my little place has begun to feel like a small palace. My safe haven. My own address. My cat happy, content not to be on the move. In fact when I open the door she bolts underneath the bed, frightened that she'll be spending another day driving and so I arrive at the house of Jacks cousin.

The house unfortunately smells like the car and is every bit as clean. Dark and dingy it reeks of unwashed clothing, dog, and garbage cans bursting and begging to be emptied. I sit on a wee corner of the living room couch, it covered with a blanket the likes of which has not been washed since it was bought. Shelves, walls, tables, are piled high with such clutter you don't know for sure what exactly you are looking at. The kitchen cupboard doors hang open, full shelves, though no dishes, those are piled on the counters caked with old food. Tables, window sills, everything is nothing but dirt and clutter. One has to walk through the bedroom to get to the bathroom and it would not be advised unless one was terribly desperate. The bed is a single wide bowed in the center like a hammock and covered with an old blanket of the type on the couch. The bathroom another storehouse for clutter and one would not want to linger there either.

Ah well. After a coffee drunk from a cup that looked rather suspect, yet I calmed myself with the thought that the class of wine I would order at dinner later would kill any germs that may have invaded myself, we are out in the back yard, cousin showing me round. As it turns out he owns not only his little house, a duplex, him occupying the one side, but the three others round the duplex. all of them paid for and rented out. Apparently he owns a fifth house in Alaska. He spends six months a year there and enjoys the check all Alaska residents do each year, royalties from the oil revenues. Then he is determined to keep a mortgage on it as it is useful for some sort of tax write off. all this and he lives like a welfare recipient in the worst of circumstances. Just as I am contemplating his odd living conditions he tells me that as far as he is concerned Jack has some really weird friends.

"Oh" I say and ask who exactly.

"Well there was the time I was living in San Francisco and Jack and a girlfriend and another friend of his knocked on my door just as the police were coming up the stairs to interview me about the prostitute who had just made off with a roll of money".

"And what did they do that made you think them weird?"

"Well, they made a big deal of it. Like they were horrified and the girlfriend wouldn't even stay for a coffee".

OH.

It's a fine little restaurant. Looks like an old houseboat outside and in, which is why this old merchant marine no doubt frequents the place. After we order our drinks and decide on the meal to come, the conversation drifts back to where it had left off in the yard that afternoon. He had offered me a look at his memoirs, three thick books nicely put together and labeled say 1935-1956 etc. and all the photographs inside of women, and all of them Asian and Philippino prostitutes.

Now at the restaurant he begins to reminisce about the good old days. the adventure on the high seas, the prostitutes, regulars, one in every port, and all very happy to see him on his stops. He then tells me he cannot be just friends with a woman he is attracted to. Case in point. He asked a woman he had known for a time if she would marry him as he wanted to see what it would be like to get married but the woman suggested they just be, or remain friends and he told her that he cannot be friends with a woman he is physically attracted to.

Dinner over, he drives me back to my little cottage and just as I turn to say thank you while at the same time opening the door to Iet myself out, he grabbed his crotch. I said a quick good night and thanks again and he kept staring straight ahead motionless and not so much as a good night. He did however call me next day to remind me to tell Jack how much a help he'd been.

Abe now calls and invites me to dinner. It is a buffet he tells me. It is at a bank. Apparently three or four times a year the bank offers a lovely bunch of food and wine and displays paintings for the pleasure of their customers, no matter the size of their bank balance. This is good because Abe later reveals that he deposited only one hundred dollars, this after finding out about the free food and drink once a year.

Abe is very proud of not knowing how to drive, this according to Abe is the sign of a true New Yorker. Abe of course moved out west twenty six years earlier, but does not drive, does not take walks either because according to Abe there are no interesting window shopping expeditions to go on, no streets crowded with people, no hustle and bustle, so why bother.

It follows that for Abe to partake of the free food and drink he will need a car to get him to the bank and as I am most curious to take a look at this odd duck I accept his most generous invitation. I drive to his apartment complex, park, pick my way through the courtyard and walk up two flights of stairs in forty degree weather and knock on Abe's door. I wait, knock again, and finally the door opens a crack to reveal a face as white as a sheet and the face says simply, "Abe".

I respond "I'm Aileen" and again he says "Abe. I'll be down in a minute. Is your car downstairs?"

"Yes, Abe"

"I'll be down in a minute". this I thought was going to be one interesting dinner.

I walked around to keep warm, and fifteen minutes later Abe emerged. Abe, I found was well over six feet tall, soft looking, hair well past his ears, dyed black, though with a bit of grey strategically left showing at the temples in order to, I supposed, effect that natural look. In the light of the bank I noticed he had not the small creases round the eyes of even a thirty something, though he claimed his age as fifty five. His skin was a prison pallor white and his lips looked as though they had undergone collagen treatments. His eyelids had obviously had a bit of fine tuning and when he spoke he posed and pouted the collagen lips.

He was not shy about filling two bread and butter plates at a time with h'orderves and questioning the bar server about the age and quality of the free wine. In short Abe would have been a total embarrassment had I not decided to chalk the occasion up to experience, relieved in knowing that I would never see any of these people again.

Abe talked of nothing but Abe. Abe sought to impress by claiming to know many very wealthy people and his adventures in reading seemed to consist of nothing more than a who's who of who owns what where and how much everyone from Oprah to Trump was worth. Abe was nuts. Abe looked like a tall version of Michael

Jackson with even the fragile nose about to disappear. Any money he had siphoned from wealthy and no doubt desperate women had obviously gone into the surgeon's pocket.

Abe hated his mother, claiming she had had him committed to a home for mentally ill teens when he was seventeen. Abe claimed to have dated movie stars and models and ran with the club 52 Crown while living in Manhattan. Abe protected everyone's privacy though by not naming names, though I had not asked and was obviously not the least bit interested in his celebrity fantasy. What I was interested in was finding employment, something unfortunately terribly foreign to Abe. After all, Abe's eyes closed every four months if he did not get his medication. I hesitated to point out that blind people held jobs. Abe was different.

"You have to understand that I am a travel writer. Never mind about being published, that's unimportant. You have to understand that that is my identity. It is logical than that because I don't see myself any other way; I obviously can't do anything else. I mean it is hard for me. I can't find a woman who has her own money and is willing to clean and do laundry and share the expenses at least".

"And what would you be doing, Abe?"

"Well, I am told I am talented in the bedroom and she could have her own room. I don't like to share a bedroom. Well, they're all so selfish".

Yes, Abe was nuts.

CHAPTER 8 - SURVIVAL

"Treat everyone with politeness,
even those who are rude to you
not because they are nice,
but because you are."

Anonymous

Jobs. The little city had lots and lots of jobs to be filled. The majority of course were casino jobs. Low pay, in most cases little more than minimum wage, no benefits for six months and if one worked downtown parking would be a problem. The spaces, half empty anyway, were reserved for guests, therefore if you needed parking you were charged a fee. A real good deal was the reduced rate of only thirty five dollars a month deducted from the $6.50 an hour pay check. I was fortunate however to land my first casino job in the vault of the family owned and operated Eldorado Hotel Casino. I could walk the two long blocks from the bowling center parking garage to the hotel and not have to pay a fee as until the bowlers descended on the town in February the garage was virtually deserted. After that it would cost sixty dollars a month for the privilege of earning $8.50 an hour. As you will see, I lasted only two months in the Dickensian environment before becoming very ill and being forced to quit however.

The vault

Who were these people willing to work in the bowels of the hotel? What was it like to stand for five hours at a time counting hundreds of thousands of dollars, under the watchful eye of the casino surveillance cameras? What was it like to have nothing more to look forward to in the course of an eight hour shift than the free lunch in the staff cafeteria? Could the working conditions have been worse? Perhaps, but then I imagine the family dared only to try and get away with so much even in Reno Nevada.

The vault sat directly under the indoor parking garage of the hotel. Windowless, of course, there was no ventilation save for the vent that could be opened to allow the exhaust tainted air into the two dirty rooms, separated by a glass partition, that confined the docile labor force. Docile as far as management was concerned, yet like rats in a cage perceiving no personal power, they turned on each other for relief and as one of the damned put it for fun. Unruly kindergarten children, they cursed each other and the company, brought in bags of junk food each day, snacked constantly until lunch and then turning their frustration and anger inward overate and returning from lunch complained of discomfort, and overweight. Headaches followed and then a return to the ultimate outlet, foul language and belittling remarks and attacks upon each other.

They were living embodiments of people committed to living lives of not so quiet desperation.

My first morning I was told that I must leave my purse in one of the lockers outside of the room; a locker without a lock and I was informed that I was not to bring even my eye glass case into the room, for security purposes they said. Meanwhile they trucked in grocery bags of junk, from potato chips and dip to huge bags of cookies, and homemade goodies of all description, in filthy stained containers.

This was the room where the carts carrying the cans, the containers extracted from the slot machines were accepted. There were two long tables in the dingy, dirty room, with the stained water marked ceiling, and the worn cement floor, five people ringed these tables, taking turns pulling the thirty pound a piece cans from the carts, removing the money, sorting by machine and counting by denomination. Your hands became black as ink in no time and the sight of the dirty hands stuffing the mouths with garbage will I am sure remain with me. A half hour or even less would pass and the vent would be opened and the fan turned on to cool the grossly overweight, which was all but yours truly.

The cold air blew down my neck and chills ran through me. I comforted myself with the fact that this was simply a stop gap sort of job until I found another and I stood quietly working and allowed thought, pleasant, of another time and place comfort me.

I place the five dollar bill stack on the machine and they are talking trash, gibberish almost and I am driving the coastal highway in Florida and the butterflies envelope the car and the ocean waves pound the surf.

She says "Yea, so where would I go?"

"Where you goin?" Laugh; they all laugh.

Empty. Yes. Each can emptied has to be turned toward the camera; the person who has removed the cash says empty, another acknowledges and on it goes, hour after hour and the bills are banded in elastic bands and the chips counted and on, and on, and she says "It's his heart, all the cholesterol; anyway that's what the Dr. Said".

They don't wear make-up and they even cut their own hair. Their nails are unkempt, and any polish chipped. And I stand working and listening.

So, Janet to Dee: "Put on your old jeans with the holes and I'll take you to the woman's house; you know the one, every X-mas she hands out boxes of food, no questions asked and in the elevator down after the break I told Doug we gotta get another VCR, just have one in the bedroom, gotta have another for the living room. Remember about the clothes; you won't believe how much you'll save. Pays for the VCR".

"Hey" Janet said one day "You don't talk much" and shaking with barely contained anger, "You think your smarter, better than us".

"Yea" says Dee. "Just wait till menopause and all that style, beauty shop hair falls out like mine. I had better than you once".

And maybe the letter will be in the box when I arrive home, the letter from the literary agent and it's back to work and only three hours to go now.

Dee: "And when ma dies it's New Orleans for me. This may be her last X-mas so cheer up, why don't I?".

Doris: "And we took out a second mortgage on the house, no bigger than this room and paid the bills, and he puts $800.00 a month on credit cards at Wal-Mart; Fishing junk".

"Jerri, her right eye needs to be drained, two thousand dollars the Dr. told her. Better to let it drain on its own anyway he told her. High blood pressure, diabetes, husband dying of cancer. They say she was pretty good looking once, short, but she had been a stripper, husband never worked much, had to feed the three kids didn't she? Now she is sixty pounds overweight, looks after the granddaughter while her daughter works two nights a week. That is the daughter who was beaten by her husband then had him arrested".

Well each story is much like another. Violence and ignorance, filthy environments, hopelessness, helplessness, and anger lurking just beneath the surface.

I survived for two months almost to the day and then one morning, the cold air blowing, the fat women complaining of being hot and suffering high blood pressure and I coming down with the worst cold I can ever remember having I left three hours into the shift. I never returned. I called saying I was too ill to work the following day and then the supervisor called personnel and told them I had not called or shown up for two days. They were happy to tell me that anyway when I complained to the personal director of the verbal abuse and being told to put on my winter coat to work if I didn't like the cold. Guess this is a great example of what it meant to be frozen out.

Things happen for the best more often than not, at least for me, and so I spent two weeks the first three days of which were spent in bed, drinking the chicken soup that I always kept on hand in case of emergencies, my cat curled up close for comfort. I lay in bed thinking that I was fortunate to have a bit of a buffer thanks to my thrifty ways. I could pay the rent and keep going and be alright as long as I found a job within weeks; I would be able to maintain a bank balance of about two thousand.

The Dollar store, a wonderful place. Two for a dollar cans of vegetables, and a loaf of bread, the expensive heavy wheat only a dollar and lots of chicken soup two for a dollar and wasn't I fortunate to live only five minutes away.

Sniffling, wads of Kleenex stuffed into my purse, I get in the car and make my way to the Dollar store. To cheer myself up I splurge on a candle once a week. A scented candle, tuna two cans for a dollar for Baby and me and then the market and milk and the paper to check the classifieds. And I survive, and in two weeks to the day I am well enough to drive to the Hilton, a name synonymous with class and I apply and am given a job and thank God I'll have a pay check in two weeks and my savings will remain intact. Now I am a cashier in the buffet and now I have a brand new tormentor, but this time I go straight to personnel after only one week of suffering rather than two months and I am transferred to the new bingo dept. and a whole new abusive situation begins.

All of these months I am sending out query letters to literary agents, a fact which I believe kept me sane was my belief that one fine day a letter would arrive telling me I had found someone interested in my work. During these months of loneliness, penny pinching drudgery and abuse, Abe is still very much alive, out there on the other end of the phone, or the message; Coll, Abe, on the answering machine awaiting my return from the money pit.

"I have hope" I tell him once. "My writing will pull me through, I know I will make it, it just takes time that's all. And he said "let me ask you something. Do you have a computer?""

"A computer? No, I have an electric typewriter. Why?"

"Why?" he laughed "Because you are fooling yourself if you think that you can sell a book that is not typed on a computer. They'll see that letter and well, that will be the end of it. I'm a travel writer, I know. You can't work nowadays without a computer; the type doesn't look right; no way so forget about it".

He talks fast in New Yorkese and he is narcissistic enough to believe he knows everything about everything, and callous enough to hash the one hope of a lonely, hardworking and yet optimistic woman. I began to let the machine pick up calls even when I was home, but one evening, expecting my son to call, picked up and found Abe on the end of the line.

I was surprised somewhat because having called one night when I was so desperately sick he had said: "Don't talk, if you're sick, that's okay, don't talk. I just called to tell you that I finally bought insurance for my mother's funeral, casket and everything. A real deal, a real deal. You must understand only a New Yorker can find a real deal". Abe liked to say most things of great import at least twice. "And I got a haircut, a haircut; you wouldn't believe what I look like, but my mother, my mother, I went to visit her and she said you look like a hippy with your hair down past your ears, so don't visit me like that anymore. So you see I had to get it cut. It's like a crew cut. I'm afraid to go out, afraid to go out". Abe did not speak much in sentences either, it all ran together at a fast manic pace, as if to imply that whatever he was saying was terrifically important.

The next day he left a message saying his mother had suffered a cardiac arrest and fool that I am I picked up and he went on to say: "She didn't die, she didn't die, can you believe it? She didn't die. Even that did not kill her and she is spending twenty five hundred a month in that place. What is your place like?"

"Oh I must go now, Abe, just on my way out".

"Where - a date? Rich guy I hope. Hey you have to introduce me to some people when you land on your feet with the right people. You know what I mean?"

"Have to go, Abe".

It's spring now, and my favorite time of year. I feel good. I feel strong. I am making headway what with a bit of extra money to put away in the savings and I have even established credit with a new VISA card. My cupboard is full, my cat happy, the windows open, the Landlord having obligingly removed the plastic once the warmer weather arrived and despite the friction at work and clouds on that horizon, I feel that in general all is right in my little world.

"You must pick up, you must, if you are home pick up; this is a real emergency". The sunlight shinning through my window so beautifully, and my writing going so well and everything nice on this day off. Do I need Abe's emergency?

"You have a doctor now, don't you? You must have a doctor. You've been at the hotel a while and I need the name of a doctor".

"What are you talking about, Abe? I've been there two months and it takes six to establish medical".

"Oh, how would I know?"

"Why would you need my doctor, Abe?"

Frantically hollering that his doctor has cut him off his drugs, the drugs he needs to keep his eyes from closing every four months. He babbles on about me surely having a doctor, a name, anything, any connection. Then I asked what the name of the miracle drug is that keeps his eves from closing every four months.

"Valium. Valium. You probably never heard of it. It's a very special drug. Of course you're healthy, you don't know my suffering, you're healthy".

"Abe, Valium is a tranquilizer. Everyone this side of Mars has heard of Valium, the drug of choice for nervous hyper people. So this is the special drug taken for an eye problem? Your doctor must have cut you off because you were overdosing on it. I'm not a fool, Abe. No-one is really dumb enough to buy what you are trying to put over, even your doctor".

"What's the big deal? I need Valium. I need another doctor, you understand what I'm telling you?"

"Too bad, Abe. I don't know any doctors here and none anywhere who supplies Valium on command".

"I gotta go, I gotta go. This is terrible, terrible".

"Call the social worker who got you all the free goodies, Abe, the rent, Valium, everything. Tell her you need Therapy, Abe. I am serious Abe".

"Yea, yea, thanks. Therapy, that's what my mother said this morning when I told her I got cut off. Now you're just like my mother. She put me away at seventeen. All I need is Valium. Gotta go, be well. You're sure you don't know a doctor? You know people, you know people who have a doctor?"

"No, Abe".

I never heard again from Abe.

CHAPTER 9 - THE PLAYERS

Bingo, the new drug of choice. Lonely retired people, singles with few social skills, poor people for the most part looking for companionship, even if it is limited to exchanging a few words with the worker selling the cards, or the person sitting next complaining about never and almost never getting a win.

Cashed the welfare, or disability check, beginning of month is always busy, the end slow, a few buy only a six dollar pack telling you that the check hasn't arrived yet. Most don't say anything about the check, just buy light, look depressed and will be so until the check is cashed and the come in spending at least fifty for a session of ten games and running out during the break between sessions to load up on a bag of fries, hamburgers, tacos, whatever, to eat while waiting for the action to begin.

Goodwill clothes, battered shoes, unkempt and often dirty hair, the smell of poverty surrounding them, they come day in day out, seven days a week.

Perhaps two percent are just there for an hour of fun, tourists, a few well dressed women waiting for their husbands to meet them, just playing a little bingo for something to do to pass a little time, or as a few said somewhere to sit other than the slot machine stool when they get tired.

Then there are the hostile ninety-eight percent. Hard core gamblers with not enough, money to risk losing. Shabby, overweight from a diet of cheap junk food. Reformed alcoholics, drug addicts, replacing their addictions to drugs with gambling. Bingo the game associated with church fund raisers and county fairs is now big business.

They're angry. You sold them losing packs. None of the numbers you called did them any good. Then one of the young, overweight and angry employees decides that I don't fit the mold of a bingo collector. I don't gamble. She goes from table to table talking up the old customers she knows from the Sands and convinces them to write a letter to personnel complaining that I don't call well. All the while she and another young mom, her husband in prison in California for goodness knows what are divvying up the tips every week. One week I should have six days tips and get three. I have personnel look into the goings on in the back room out of sight with the box full of money. Meanwhile the manager is never there and by the time I quit in the midst of the verbal abuse from the customers, he is escorted off of the property by security. Barred from ever setting foot on Hilton property again due to the fact that he had stolen a goodly sum of money.

I'm asked out on a date by one of the casino games bosses. I meet him at the restaurant for dinner. He asks me if I attended university.

"Yes".

"What was your major?"

"Psychology".

"Oh" he says, turning red faced. "I'd better be careful".

"No need, I think. You are too insecure for me to date".

My last night at the Hilton the computer blacks out while I am calling, the customers start to throw a fit. I keep calm, telling them that it is the computer. the young one who claims to have a body full of tattoos (hubby in prison, two year old being cared for by her boyfriend while she is at work) runs up to the wagon all upset, pushing buttons, moving from one screen to another. She corrects the problem then she orders me off the wagon and takes over. I walk to the desk where the supervisor tells me that she is not going to have another riot in here and that I'd better smarten up or she will have me fired. At the end of the evening I clean the soda fountain. Not good enough for the tattooed one, I did not get in the drain cracks well enough. It will have to be reported.

I call in next day I won't be in. Day after they call begging me not to quit. One day later I tell personnel I have had enough. They put me down for rehire. They are sorry.

Once again I am looking for a job.

CHAPTER 10 - A ROOM IN RENO

Casino man called again. I met him at a restaurant, second dinner. Well why not? I thought. it might be interesting to see what he was about. Childish and I perceived a nasty temper when suddenly, just before the entree arrived he burst out; "Oh you'll probably leave town anytime; independent traveller." ASAP I decided.

Then the childish leaning across and rubbing my back saying "So how you doin?"

"Fine" I leaned away. Does not get the hint and again the attempt at the back rub. The stuff of sixteen year olds out on a second date. Fifty, he had told me. Then the conversation about being in the military and the prostitutes wanting him to take them back to the U.S. Now a military base and the live sex show on stage and he'd sure like to see more of me. Dinner is over thank God and he walks me to my car. As I open the door he grabs me, face red and looking angry.

"Thank you for dinner, lovely evening, very interesting, must go. Thanks again". And I pull away thinking that two dinners does not buy a trip to paradise and sure as hell not with this creep.

Happiness is coming home to my little room, Baby in the window waiting for me when I pull up and I lock the door and sigh a sigh of great relief.

Of course nothing is perfect; discovered that my Landlord could not resist going through my garbage after I had set it out in the can. I made sure after that not to put anything in the bag that contained the least bit of personal information, a good idea at any rate.

The Landlord's watering days are Wednesday and Saturday. He makes sure he uses his quota of time and turns the sprinklers on, three, full blast at 8 a.m. sharp on these days. Smart idea to shower before eight, as otherwise I am left with a trickle of water to dance under.

Mr. Irish is seventy-two and though his manner is older, he is lively, constantly working round the house and making improvements to the yard. He rides an old European bicycle probably brought over from Ireland I thought and once Buddy arrives he takes a few months break in the way of garbage snooping. Buddy is a beautiful golden Irish Setter, rescued from the pound by some friends of Mr. Irish who have decided to move back to the Emerald Isle and leave Buddy behind. I give Mr. Irish credit for taking him and each time he sees me he tells me how he rescued him from yet another horrible fate, that of being returned to the pound. The Irish couple had given buddy to a family with two girls ages ten and eleven, but apparently their father was afraid for the children to take the dog-for walks alone for fear they would be abducted.

Mr. Irish, I discover has lost his sense of smell which is why, when the ailing old alcoholic man next door died only hours after taking a taxi to the hospital one fine spring evening and Mr. Irish unplugged his fridge quickly, no doubt to save on the electric expenses, the meat began to spoil and I began to think it was the old man until I was advised otherwise. This caused me to rush to the dollar store and purchase at least half a dozen candles, scented naturally, close the heat vents, which mercifully I did not need anyway and thank God that it was spring and that I could open the windows.

The winter had not been the most comfortable, what with me not being able to adjust the heat, as Mr. Irish was in control of the thermostat. I decided that to his credit he did an admirable job of keeping me from freezing to death and thought he must have a soft spot in his old Irish heart for this little woman, until I overheard him talking to the neighbor one fine day. He, standing not far from my open window told the neighbor that he was sure I had lots of money, and was glad to have me renting the place.

He was not alone in his thoughts however, as that was the general consensus wherever I had worked. I finally came to the conclusion that perhaps because I wore makeup, didn't cut my own hair and pressed my clothes that I had established a reputation as someone of means.

CHAPTER 11 - SOLITUDE

Oh sure there were times when I felt very lonely. You know it is at those times when you read, or hear something that you want to share. You want to be able to turn to someone, or call someone up and share. Well, all my calling was long distance and I couldn't afford much of that and as for turning to someone, well, Baby doesn't talk much.

I began to gain clarity, insight and enjoy my independence, though it may have been somewhat restricted through lack of funds. I would have loved to attend a concert, a movie, a dinner in a good restaurant. I had my library card however, my writing, and all the memories, and visions of the great things to come to keep me occupied, not to mention all the daily chores, and errands of living.

The Nugget Casino would be the last Reno hotel that I would work in. And once again I applied and was given a job calling bingo. I had heard rumors here and there, most from old timers that the hotel was not a good place to work. Apart from having to find out for myself however and needing tips, not having learned how to tend bar or serve drinks, I paid the requisite forty dollar fee to the Sparks police department thereby obtaining a police card, and signed on.

For those of you who may still be living with the presumption that Nevada is part of the freedom loving U.S. of A. let me remind you that in order to work in this State in all but a few occupations, you are required to visit a police station, be finger printed, have your picture taken and be charged the princely sum of either fifty dollars, (Reno) or forty (Sparks) in order to earn your seven dollars an hour.

I didn't mind the job. In fact I liked the fast pace and variety. I would sell before a game, then call, clean tables, make coffee and the time passed quickly. The people were another matter however, though over the course of a few short weeks they began to relax, and many began visiting with me a bit.

As was ever the case in Reno the staff, once they found that higher education had meant more to me than high school began to adopt a new attitude. Again, one of the young women had a husband in prison in California and another was fighting to have her daughter returned to her amidst allegations that her boyfriend has abused the child. Then there was the supervisor on my shift, Marnie. Sixty something, she had left her husband fifteen years earlier and had apparently given up on men.

Marnie told me that she had left her husband because he gambled.

"You don't gamble" I said.

"Just nickel slots. I like the twenty four hour town".

Marnie had become friends with the young manager now barred from the Hilton when he had worked at the Nugget.

"I can't believe all the awful things people are saying about him" she said one day over lunch in the staff cafeteria. "We used to take my grandsons to the-bowling alley and we'd go for drinks after work". Poor woman. Lonely woman and as it turned out frustrated and vicious woman.

Every afternoon Marnie would join me for lunch and one day sitting across from me she suddenly said she wondered if I had not intimidated Leo. Me? The idea was absurd. However, I responded that I can't imagine how that would be unless it was my psychology degree, as he had reacted negatively to that bit of information on my resume. However being in a hurry, remember he did not spend much time at the office (at least during working hours).

He hired me anyway and after all, I had been sent to him by the personnel office. Well after that lunch Marnie never joined me again and now rather than speak, she began to bark orders, whether in front of customers or not.

She walked over and told me she was taking over my till as I was serving customers. She grabbed the shoulder of my shirt on another occasion and said: "You get up on that wagon. You're going to be late starting the session". If she looked at me at all it was with daggers and more often than not I was merely invisible, except on those occasions when she was ordering me round like Fido. Then one evening an elderly man began harassing me by hollering "wake up, wake up", as I was calling. Suddenly Marina was sent up to replace me and I thought no more of it until I heard that Marnie had told the manager that I had run from the wagon one night, completely abandoning my job.

Well Marina needed to get along with Marnie the supervisor; after all she needed the job in order to pay the attorney to work to have her child returned to her and the prison widow was supporting two children on her own. And so it went, once shunned by a few in a group the others follow like sheep and all but two gave me the time of day.

The manager when approached by me was kind enough to listen and asked me to (hang in there) until he could straighten things out. But then he, perhaps faced with a problem he would rather not deal with turned on me as well.

It was Sunday. Bingo Blowout. A ballroom filled with literally thousands of people paying eighty five dollars for the privilege of buying two packs of bingo cards and the opportunity to buy ever more as the day wore on in the hope of winning the big bucks, thousands per game.

I was given a plastic container full of two dollar tickets (Bonanzas). These are played at the end of the fifth session and an apron with a two hundred dollar float and assigned to the smoking section of the hall. In between arriving for work and starting, I had asked the Manager where to put my purse and he said: "Stick it under the stage. what's the matter? Are there diamonds in it? You worry about everything too much".

By the close of the Bonanza game I had sold six hundred and seventy five dollars' worth of tickets. It was my scheduled work day of eight hours and I had worked only six and a half, when a woman was directed to tell me to: "Go cash out, you're the first to leave".

I cashed out and asked about my hours only to be told you are only paid for hours worked. So I left for home, swollen legs, burning eyes, and sore throat from all the hours spent enveloped in the dense cloud of smoke.

The following day I arrived at work wishing I were anywhere else, but John Asquagas Nugget. I am on the floor, verifying bingos as they are called. In the two months that I had worked there I had asked repeatedly to be taught how to operate the little bingo machines some of the customers favored and was always told that I would be taught later. Well a poor man lost his bingo and suddenly I was the fool, and Marnie and Rose are standing to one side of the customer and me whispering and I could not stand another minute. I surprised myself, after all I had been through I would have thought that I could have at least finished the day. But no. I got my purse and left near to tears.

I felt better now walking to my car in the sunshine and why beat myself up? I had lived through it all. Sickness, loneliness, hurt, financial ruin, and I was not beaten. You see I believe that you are not beaten until you lie down and allow yourself to be abused without protest and that was never going to happen.

CHAPTER 12 - SUNDAY

Who were these people really? Looks like you have never had a care in the world. You're so confident and well kept. Like you never had a worry. Like you never in your life really had to work. Don't look like you need the money. What you doin? That was the well-dressed black lady from Seattle. Over the course of a few weeks we would visit a bit between sessions. Some evenings her husband would join her, but not often. "I shop and play bingo" she said. "I like to come to the Hilton and talk and look around".

Of course she was the one without a care or worry and I was the one who had to be there. It was a compliment I thought, being told that I, in effect, did not look desperate.

The tattooed one with her white eye liner, and artificial nails two inches long, told me that she missed the gang back in San Francisco. "I'm glad my brother still lives in the neighborhood, so I have a place to stay, and a little fun when I drive over to visit my husband every two weeks".

I'm five minutes from my little place now and I wonder at the path, the journey I have travelled. I am in a staff cafeteria with a former gang member reminiscing about her good old days in the neighborhood, picking away at the scraps trucked over from the various hotel restaurants. Leftovers. Listening.

"My mother died of aids just two days before my son was born. She was really beautiful. You couldn't even count the boyfriends she had, there were so many. She was only forty two when she died". I asked about the tattoo on her wrist and what it means. "It's Japanese. It means trust no one".

Baby is peeking out the window. As soon as she hears my car pull up she hops up on the sill, then dashes to the door to greet me. She needs her pats, and I need her to need my affection. We're safe, it's alright, I tell her. We're going to make it. I hear the sound of my own reassuring voice and I feel better.

I head for the shower and can't help remembering. Thoughts pop into my head for seemingly no good reason right now. The castles of Europe. We agreed we both hated cold weather, feared loneliness, poverty. Just bits of conversation here and there. He never wanted to discuss much; that would have meant getting too close, too intimate. Keep it light. Just that once we were walking around Dodge City, Kansas he was telling me about his grandfather, childhood in Kansas. I listened, happily, began to see this as an opportunity to share some of my own past. "I don't care about your life before and I don't want to listen to your boring childhood".

I turn the shower handle toward the cold, and the blast of chill water washes the tears away and I towel off and perhaps a nice cup of tea, as granny would have said, is what I need.

CHAPTER 13 - PEACE

Everyone ought to have the right to a little peace and quiet after a day's labor, or any day for that matter in one's own little place. The university students across the street in the house on the corner however, did not seem to agree. Any time seemed to be the right time for a party and my sad Sunday was to be no exception.

I had spent nine months calling the police almost every weekend. The house overflowed with hollering, fighting (at times the so-called party carried out into the street) and a mob would gather in front of my small abode ready to do battle. The truck stereos (a dog inevitably balanced precariously in the bed of the speeding truck) blasted away brakes squeal and the so-called students had to shout over the din to be heard. One twit, perhaps not invited to the celebrations would occasionally pull up, stop and sit honking his horn until an irate neighbor man began to scream bloody murder for the idiot to cease. There were mornings when I had had to leave for work in the vault with only four hours of sleep to see me through the day. Oh my delight at finding a swing shift job to lessen the stress. The police would arrive, all may be quiet for but half an hour, then begin again and back the police would come, though not as quickly on my second call.

The girls stood and shrieked, the boys, particularly articulately challenged seemed to speak in four letter words, every other word was 'fuck'. These were the hope for the future were they? The night the girl with waist length blond hair threw herself spastically round the porch, the scene back lit by the light from the open door, hollering to the two young men who were running round in their under shorts, get it up, get it up, was a personal favorite.

I never did understand why the police never did more than tell them to be quiet until I chanced to meet the Landlord there one afternoon, he, replacing a lawn sprinkler that one of his tenants had run over. He told me that the university police as far as he knew were told to take it easy with the kids. But the Reno police? "Oh well, who knew? I suppose they are healthy income". Then he told me that the house that was going up down the side street was going to be a two storey and watch who moved in.

"More students?"

"Definitely. You have to understand this is a university neighborhood". I expect that meant that it was synonymous with noise and abuse. He gave me his card and told me to call him the next time his tenants acted up. I thanked him and prayed to God I would be far and away very soon and the neighborhood as far as I was concerned was on its own.

It is a beautiful sunny day and car doors open, I am enjoying the breeze and the birds' song, as I squirt Windex (from a huge bottle purchased at the dollar store) onto my windshield and polish away with my dollar store paper towel. A fine day it is, when out of the other side of the duplex walks a man, sixtyish I am guessing, bald, and approaches to introduce himself. Ah, needed someone to tell his troubles to. On he went about losing everything to the casinos. His vehicle, everything. Terrible place to work the Atlantis he said. Told me he worked as a cashier there and watched people win money and after work he would cash his pay check and play the slots.

"You didn't see anyone lose?"

"I concentrated on the winners, wanted to be positive". He was serious.

I said "Tell me, would you walk out into the street and hand your money to a stranger?" thinking this a good analogy to throwing it away at a casino.

"Well" he said "I gave a man in a wheelchair a few bucks the other day".

"I'm not talking charity" I said, and explained.

"Oh" he said. "I am going to church now and God will help me".

"Oh" I said. "That's good, but you'll have to accept responsibility for your losses as well, so that you don't go back to doing the same old thing. Besides, do you think the casinos built all those monstrosities because of the fact that people were winning in them?"

He said "So you don't gamble?"

"No" I said. "Lost a quarter once a few days after moving to Vegas years ago and that ended my gambling career".

"Thought maybe you gambled, cause I see you aren't here that long by your plates. Washington. Do you drink?"

"I enjoy the odd glass of wine" I told him.

"Oh, okay" he said delightedly. "Maybe you'd like to go to church sometime, or breakfast".

I was finished with the car by now and wished him well, closing the door behind me.

He had told me that he came by his room next door by way of the bus stop a few steps away. Apparently Mr. Irish had been riding by slowly with Buddy and had stopped to pass the time of day, a lovely practice still held by the Europeans and the gambler had asked him if he knew of a place he might stay.

"There I stood with my one suitcase wondering what to do next" he said.

Yes, and I thought whatever it is you won't be doing it with me.

I had worked so hard, made so many sacrifices, that though I was sorry for the man, I also felt such irritation at yet another story of someone throwing everything away in the hope of quick, easy riches.

For the most part I enjoyed a peaceful existence at home, most especially on my days off, when I could write, read and take care of my few errands. Yet always in the back of my mind was the knowledge that I had not yet found a home and would have to leave here someday soon.

One morning at the Laundromat I met a young woman who, over the course of the wash and dry cycles told me that she had never felt happy in Reno.

"The People" she said "may act like they are your friend, but they turn on you and you don't know why. Backstabbers. I asked how long she had lived here.

"Thirteen years" she said. "Got pregnant, married, pregnant". Her husband worked two full time jobs in the hotels to support his little family. She drove up to my neighborhood to wash her clothes because it was quiet and safe up here she said. She lived in a neighborhood with gangs and noise and wanted to leave and go back to upstate New York but her husband wouldn't go.

"He came here to Reno sixteen years ago" she said "and it's all he knows of America. He was from Mexico. He was doing his best. He didn't want to Change". She drove her children out of her neighborhood to schools in better neighborhoods. She used another's address in order to do this and her main focus in life was keeping them safe. Just as I was leaving she told me that she did not think there was a hell in the afterlife; hell was right here, right now. She was living her hell.

CHAPTER 14 - SOON

My young friend, fellow teacher from my Korean adventure, called the other night. A second son was how I described him in my story about South Korea. I talked with Jack early one morning a few days ago, another sunny Sunday. He is thinking of going off to Europe in a month or so and in two months I hope to be leaving Reno. I have to work for a short while yet here, two months, no longer. I will take the bar tending job. Tips. Interesting people. I made it this far and now I am praying, waiting, praying some more, looking for the agents letter that says we have a book that is going to sell.

I have lived so many places, lived so many lives within this one existence. Where shall I go next? Will I look for a summer place? There are so many places on earth that offer summer almost year round. What of spring? Perhaps one can carry spring in the heart year round. Optimism, renewal, joy. Every day is new I told my son when he was very small. Every day you wake up ask yourself what experiences am I going to have today?

"I can scarcely wait till tomorrow
When a new life begins for me,
as it does each day, as it
does each day."

Stanley Kunitz

American Poet Laureate

NOT THE END

THE EULOGY

INTRODUCTION

May 2, 1999

Dear Hedy,

Thank you for writing. Getting a letter from a new found niece was quite a surprise. I'm happy to send along some of the family history. I don't know any more than what I was a witness to, as my mum never spoke of the Witcombs after leaving Mossbank.

My younger brother Norm didn't even know that your grandfather Jim was his dad until we sat down a couple of years ago and I finally told him the whole story. After years of searching I had finally located your dad and fortunately by this time he had retired where the whole saga began: In Mossbank.

As you know, your dad and I have had quite a few telephone conversations and letters have been exchanged, yet I haven't managed to get up there for a visit. I hope to make the trip soon however.

I'm enclosing this sometimes funny, sometimes sad, but never dull, bit of Witcomb life as I knew it. I look forward to meeting you when I visit your dad.

All the best,

Alex

Not long before Christmas of nineteen-Thirty-seven my mum got a job with a man who had four kids. We had been living in an old Scottish lady's place on 98th St. on welfare. This new job was on

104th Ave. just across the Street from the railroad freight sheds. The man's name was Jim Witcomb and this was the first time that there were other kids around. Five of us in all from the start of January. I started school with them after the holidays. This man had a team of horses and he was trying to make a living hauling freight with a big wagon. A few days before Christmas Jim's runaway wife had shown up with some presents for her four kids; her boyfriend was with her, his name was Don Stamp.

As I said, times were tough and one night everything was loaded into and tied to the big wagon; there was no room for us kids so we walked. We walked pretty well all night until we came to a new log house that was not completely finished. We moved in anyway, as I guess it was cheaper to move than to pay rent. I guess it was out in the Piney Grove area. I always wondered what the teacher thought on Monday morning when a whole new family walked in on her. We were only there for a little over a couple of months. Then we moved back to a little house not far from the Caulder yards. This time we started at the Norton school. Out back of the property it was all bush, but there was a fence all along there and there were large herds of cattle from time to time.

After school closed for the holidays the Witcomb kids all disappeared. I was told that they had gone up to Wildwood and Mossbank (which was where they'd all been born). That just left three of us at home. My mother said I was to call him uncle Jim.

All this time he was hauling wood from the Northeast Sawmill. The mill would cut the wood into stove wood lengths, then haul these out into the field and dump it in piles, then those piles were sold to a lot of guys like Jim. They were all trying to make a living finding customers for this fire wood. Quite often Jim would take me along to help and we would stop at a store where he would buy a package of tobacco for himself and a bottle of pop for me. After some time at this the Government opened up some more land for homesteading west of Mossbank, so Jim took off about the same time mum went to the hospital. I stayed the night at the neighbors, then I was taken to the Scottish lady on 98th St. After a few days mum came out of the hospital and now I had some competition. I had a new baby brother.

Jim was working on the homestead. Before he had left he'd given mum a list of all the customers who owed him money for the fire wood. I remember walking for what seemed like miles, pushing the baby buggy trying to get one or two dollars here and there.

While we were at Mrs. Campbell's (the Scottish lady) a charitable group called the Sunshine Club paid us a visit. They took us down to a thrift store where we got some clothing more suitable for the weather that was coming. Mum got a job at a place helping an elderly couple. The lady was so crippled up that she had to be lifted in and out of her bed on her chair. We were there maybe six weeks when the old man had finished his harvesting and I had to start back to school.

We got a couple of housekeeping rooms. I don't remember what Ave. but looking outside from the window at the end of the hall I could see the parliament buildings. I still went to school outside the city limits even though it was an awfully long walk. I was afraid they would make me change schools and I had seen enough different schools.

It was around March that I had to go to the hospital and have my tonsils and adenoids removed, then a few weeks later we were on our way to the coast. We stayed out there for two years and then headed back to Mossbank. Uncle Jim met us at the train station in the city. He had a team of horses and a sleigh and by the time we got to the homestead it was quite dark. It wasn't until daylight that we saw what was facing us. There were only enough trees cut around the house to make it possible to build the house. It had been built with poplar logs, and the roof and floors were covered with shiplap.

There was a trap door leading to the upstairs and a trap door leading down into the cellar. No way to let any light down there;

as a matter of fact there was only one small window in the downstairs part of the house, on the north end and one small window upstairs in the south end. The door was on the west side, where you only had to go about thirty feet and you were in the bush. Jim had a wooden cook stove as well as a big heater, almost like a barrel lying on its side, only it was big enough to put a four foot log into. You could sit beside it and roast the one side, but the other side of you would be freezing. There was the odd spot in the cabin where the chinking had come out and you could see the outside between the logs. By the time school time rolled around the Witcomb kids showed up and there were four of us then trudging the four and a half miles to School.

There were just two rows of desks and along one wall was a row for the colored kids. The white kids sat on the other side of the room. At the end of the day we walked the four and a half miles home, got on the end of an axe or saw and made sure there was enough wood cut for the next day.

Since there was no well, it was a matter of getting snow. You had to make sure that you didn't get some of those brown pellets that the rabbits left around. And since there was no out-house everyone tried to select a special place in the great outdoors. There were paths going in all directions.

We had about a dozen chickens and they were put in solitary confinement down in the cellar. There was a pile of hay stacked up in the yard with a pole fence around it. The few cows that we had were fed from that. We also had about five or six little pigs one time and at about one month old they tried to burrow in the hay. Unfortunately the pole fence was nothing more than a minor irritant to the cows, so they went over it and wiped out the little pigs.

Mum's bedroom was downstairs. The rest of us slept upstairs, which really was the warmest place in the house, providing the fire didn't go out, which happened often. It was also quite often that you'd wake up with snow drifting down on you from the cracks in the roof. The first six months we were there we were kept busy catching rabbits and fool hens. This turned out to be our main source of meat. We had no gun so we set snares for the rabbits, or at night you could go out by the pole fence around the hay stack, with an arm load of fire wood, or anything else that was frozen and knock over quite a few in an evening.

On into spring: Your uncle Harry and I sold so many dollars' worth of seeds for the Gold Medal Seed Co, that they gave us a single shot twenty-two. We got a box of shells and that was divided up twenty-five for Harry and twenty-five for me. We could go hunting big time now. Even hunting squirrels.

We'd hunt muskrat and skunks too and Jum Hickey in Mossbank would buy them from us. Our land itself was a series of swamp lands. Looking back on it I realize that Jim was working his heart out on some land that was never going to be a viable piece of farm land. There were a couple of meadows where we took some hay off there but as you moved across them with a mower, or a wagon, you could see the ground all around you just sinking like a bowl of Jell-O. Wherever the wagon wheels went you could see water in the ruts. He had done an awful amount of ditching trying to drain the water off and one of the ditches was about two hundred yards long and eight to ten feet deep. It's no wonder that the land is now a protected wild life area.

Toward the last he had trouble seeing because of cataracts. When your dad left I was given to understand that he had just gone to the neighboring town of Wildwood. It wasn't until sixty years later we met up again and he told me that he realized that there was no future there for him and he just walked away from everything.

We used to stop in at the Belvederes on the way to and from school. They had the little post office and we would walk to school with their kids.

I remember once when we took the small saddle horse (Marie) and hooked her to a small sleigh. We had to stop to open a gate to her place and she ran up on her heels and you should have seen the lunch pails flying. The kids hopped off and there we were picking up frozen biscuits out of the snow. She was the typical strawberry roan and that was the only time we tried that mode of transportation.

Your dad left. Then Jim's sister Cora got married. She had a real log cabin built and Harry went to help over there. One less mouth to feed. Now there was just three of us going back and forth to school. I have left a few things out since I'm not used to writing much, so I go back a bit.

I told you about the house. Well we had one chair. That was mum's, only it had no back. There was a bench between the table and the wall, then there were nail kegs and a big stump that made an ideal seat.

Jim would go and buy wheat, then take it to a mill in Wildwood to have it ground into flour, shorts, bran and bring it home to be used for our porridge in the morning. It was your aunt Willa's job in the evening to go through that and pick the weed seeds out of it. Then it was put on the back of the stove to soak and cook for breakfast in the morning. Sometimes the fire didn't last as long as it should have, then it became a matter of just warming it up, Sometimes to melting a bit of ice that had formed on it overnight. A good many times the milk was so scarce, it came down to just so many teaspoons full for each one.

That was cutting it pretty fine. Then there were times when the coal oil for the lamp ran out. What we had to do then was put a fair sized button in the center of a piece of cloth and tying a little bit of string around it, let it soak up some grease in a tin lid: Lighting it up, it didn't show much light, but at least you could make out where the middle of the table was and everyone knew where mouths were.

Spring time would come and with it the mosquitoes. There was no place to milk the cows but the old corral where the hay had been.

You'd get them into a corner so you could milk them, but first you had to make a smudge with the smoke to make it a little more bearable. I have forgotten how many chickens survived down in the cellar. But it got to be a job to build a fire in an old wash tub, then covering it with green grass and cow manure and putting that down the cellar and giving the house a real good smoking before going to bed. Sometimes it had to be done again about two in the morning. Is it any wonder after reading this, that your dad just up and walked away? After school let up in the summer of nineteen thirty-five Willa and Jim Jr. left. Young Jim would end up getting killed over in Italy during the war as you know and no one ever heard from or about Willa again.

I'd just turned fifteen about the middle of June and all that was left home now was mum and Jim, my little brother Norm, and me. Jim had planted a lot of potatoes in one end of the driest meadow. Not having the proper machinery, it was a poor job of ploughing. About the third or fourth of July, Mum and Jim and Norm took off for town leaving me to take the hoe to the potato patch. I started working around one end where it looked like the sod was going to outgrow the spuds and though it didn't look very impressive, trying to hoe that sod was a real tough job. The next day Jim jumped on me about not doing anything. I was holding a shovel and I don't know if he thought I was going to use it on him or not, but he grabbed it out of my hands and I was ordered off the place. It was just about noon, but there was no mention of after lunch, but leave right now. Mum gave me the five dollars a friend had sent her and she'd been saving. Then she came up with another one dollar and seventy five cents.

I made my way to an aunt's thousands of miles away, a story too long to tell here. Anyway Hedy, this answers some of your questions about your dads life and how I came to be a part and yet not a part of the Witcomb family.

I understand that life on the homestead came to an end sometime in nineteen-thirty--six. Jim just up and walked away one day and mum took Norm back to the coast. She married and had another son, Edward. Edward became a dentist, as is his son now. Edward's daughter is studying for her Master's degree in civil engineering over in England.

The way everybody is spread out reminds me of what happens when you throw a stone into the water and watch the ripples spread farther and farther, over the pond. Or perhaps drifting across the prairie, like a bunch of tumble weeds coming to rest who knows where?

This has taken longer than I thought to write. I guess I'd better wrap it up for now. I'm invited by some of my cousins to take a long driving vacation around the country and then end the journey with a cruise up to Alaska. Sounds like a busy time, but it's a once in a lifetime opportunity, so I have accepted their kind offer.

Who knows what the next year will bring?

I'll sign off now, and hope to see your dad and everyone up that way soon.

Love Adam

Who knew what the next year would bring? Not I. And even as we walked the corridors of the nursing home, his left hand in his left pants pocket, my arm through his he periodically looks to me and smiles and squeezes his left arm to his side, as if to say I'm glad you're close by. Even then, as we walk and I look at our reflections in the windows, he, about my height, but bent over slightly and our faces almost mirror images of each other, even then when I knew he was tired and wanted to leave, not even then did I dream that I would soon be writing his Eulogy.

Richard John Witcomb entered into eternal rest peacefully, late in the evening of Sunday May 30th.

He had come full circle, ending his days in the area where they had begun eighty-one years and eleven months earlier - the place he had always referred to as "My home."

He respected his heritage, never forgetting his roots, his people and where he came from, no matter how far afield he travelled.

He was born to poverty, in a tiny cabin not far from where his earthly remains will be interred in the shadow of the church built by his grandfather Cummings and just down the road from the one room school he had attended and where Mr. Harris, the kind respected teacher encouraged him to sing.

Dad dared to dream big dreams and was willing to work hard to achieve his goals, many of which he realized.

"You have to be an optimist, never give up and smile and you'll feel better" He had so often said. " You have to smile and greet people, then they're happy too and it all goes round, like the seasons. You plant a seed in the spring and before you know it a gorgeous flower blooms and that's the way the world works; you know that don't you?"

I believe that every soul gathered here today has a memory of dad bounding toward them, his hand raised in greeting, a smile on his face, just for them.

Dad revered the universe, and I've vivid memories of him on clear starlit nights pointing to the heavens as he named stars and explained the milky way.

Marveling at the sight he'd say; "The wonder of all this" and when he had a garden, arms waving excitedly as he pointed to the new growth, he'd inevitably end the tour by saying, "You have to respect all of this, you know that, don't you? You have to respect all of it because it's all a miracle. Creation, life, it's all a miracle."

Dad loved his world, his children, grandchildren, music, people and above all, never lost sight of the wonder of just being alive.

Yes, to the last he was looking for miracles. As he walked from one window to the next at the home he searched and then finally spotting a few buds on a little tree standing close to the glass, he tapped my hand, pointed and smiled, saying quietly; "Yes, oh yes."

Spring was his favorite time of year. "A time of new beginnings, the first bloom of the roses" He said. And so with this spring of nineteen-ninety-nine, Richard John Witcomb has found not an ending, but a new beginning, in God's heavenly garden: A peaceful, joyous place, where for him the roses will bloom throughout eternity.

CHAPTER 1

"The Man who dies rich dies disgraced"

Andrew Carnegie

Roses, I had asked my son to order roses. "His favorite flowers were roses." That had been the first thing I had said when he had called and told me. "Rose Garden. That's the name of the chapel grandpa chose, mum."

It was just past midnight New York time, Memorial day. Fitting, fitting that there should be a chapel named Rose Garden in this tiny northern town; one short main street. Fate. How well we realized we knew someone, once they are gone. And how much more we appreciate them, once it's too late.

This small carved wooden box placed in the center of a blanket of roses beneath the pulpit. My heart aches. The tears sting my eyes. I force myself to look there. I say a prayer. I hear Lenny's voice. "I ordered the carved wood. Grandpa would like that. A lumberman. He loved good wood, remember? Nice carved things." I remember.

I am alone. Oh there are people. People. Someone enters the room every minute, every two? They take a seat a few pews back. Close. I see a figure out of the corner of my eye. I feel their presence. I am comforted by this, yet I am alone. I am alone with my memories.

He has come full circle now, ending life where it began for him. Mossbank. A funny name for a town I had always thought. Mossbank, where my father's life began eighty-two years ago next month. Ending exactly one month short of his eighty-second birthday. And I remember. I wait now for the service to begin and I remember.

My father and mother were born one year apart, on opposite sides of the continent. He was born into a dirt poor southern family from eastern Kentucky. She, to descendants of Ellis Island immigrants. Her ancestry was ethnically diverse and her forefathers on her mother's side of the family, had been educated professional people. A fact my mother was never to let my father forget during their few years together.

Dad's ancestors had been poor farmers from England, who had found their way to the United States in 1783, by way of tramp steamer and not as dad would tell us, on the Mayflower. After the civil war between the States the family had been impoverished and would remain so for generations.

Grandma Eva bore four children in quick succession, in the one room shack, on the few swampy acres of land, in what had by then been christened Mossbank. Barefoot and penniless, she walked away when her eldest, my father, was only ten years of age. The last time she was seen in the town was on a hot summer's afternoon, walking barefoot in ankle deep dust, her face wet with her tears.

I have but one picture of her. She stands surrounded by her children, a sad expression on her face, eyes downcast. The children clutching at her skirts are ragged and unsmiling.

The year after grandma left for the city and remarried, grandpa took a lady in that he referred to as his housekeeper. She had one son my father's age, and together they would produce one more. This relationship did not last longer than four or five years however. Grandpa, having been diagnosed with cataracts and unable to provide, simply packed up and left one day. The housekeeper took her two boys and left.

Months earlier my father and one of his brothers had run off and a younger brother and sister were sent to live with an aunt. The aunt would send little Willa to an orphanage within the year. Willa would never be heard from again.

Mum was a city girl. Her dad was an Irish Catholic barkeeper and alcoholic and her mother a French, Austrian dressmaker, who, having fallen in love with the big handsome Irishman joined his church. This being a requirement if she hoped to marry him, as was the promise to raise their children Catholic. Far from being abused and/or neglected, my mother and her brother were, if anything, over indulged (as my grandmother has once put it).

They were provided with the best of everything and despite grandpa's drunken bouts, knew that they were loved. With fine clothes, music lessons and private schools, indeed they were the center of their parents universe.

Now these two people from such diverse backgrounds met while in their late twenties. She totally self- absorbed and grandiose, he lonely and insecure. They outwardly at least presented a quite different picture to the world. They both sang beautifully and she by then a concert pianist, accompanied their voices on the piano. Together they would have three children of their own.

At the time of my birth my parents were living in the second storey suite of my maternal grandparents old Victorian. I was five months old the first time dad left and not quite two years old the second time; my sister had arrived by then.

"You threw up every morning and insisted upon drinking out of your father's coffee cup and you rained tears."

"When you were two" my grandmother continued, " I took you to the park and my you ran and ran, your little arms outstretched, hollering that you wanted to be a bird. Even then, my poor darling, you wanted to fly away."

Throughout our very early years my father came and went. Four months, five months and when he returned he would have stories to tell of places he'd worked and things he'd seen.

We moved out of Grand's as we called her, just before my brother was born and into our first rental home. The house was across from Grand's and that was a comfort for I had never lived anywhere but under her roof.

When dad was away my Grand kept the clothes washed and food in the house. Often she would have to prepare a meal and stay over until we had eaten. She told stories, the kind of stories children love to hear and when dad returned he took over. His stories were not as funny however; in fact most of his stories were sad. I don't imagine he realized how the image of our dad suffering for lack of food and walking to school in bitter cold, affected us. And often I suspected he told such stories so that we might feel we had less to complain about.

People are entering the chapel in smaller numbers now. The service will begin soon. I glance again toward the small wooden box nestled in the blanket of roses.

"Rags to riches to rags." Someone had written a long time ago that this was the American experience. Who wrote that? I don't remember now. It doesn't matter now.

All those years of effort and struggle, of fighting the demon depressions that had plagued him. All the years of guilt because he had had to spend time away, all the pain was over now.

CHAPTER 2

My entertainment when dad was away consisted mostly of watching the world pass by out of the big living room window. Directly across the street lived an elderly British widow whom dad had nicknamed the Duchess. Her home was a miniature Victorian complete with witches cap. It was a house right out of one of my children's books and had been placed there especially for me. It leaned like the Tower of Pizza and was weathered grey by the wind, rain and salt sea air. On Halloween Eve the Duchess, as she was now called, as much because of her fine fur wraps and stylish hats, as for the majestic way she carried herself when she walked down the road banged an old iron washtub. She claimed that this frightened the evil spirits away. I was mighty pleased to know this and although the other children on the block said she was a witch, or worse, crazy I was positive that the Duchess was no less than royalty. I spent many hours standing at that window hoping to catch sight of the Duchess making a grand exit from her little mansion; or more importantly my daddy coming up the walk.

It was at around this time in my life (I was five years old) that dad invented the Easy Lynn jar opener. It was all very exciting, what with the reporter from the local newspaper interviewing dad and the photographer there to take pictures. It's just the three of us in the picture. Dad my sister, and myself and she got to hold the jar opener. That venture never paid off however and soon dad went away again. Whether he went away because he was sad or because he had to go out of town again to work on heavy equipment, I don't recall, or perhaps I never did know. The story has always been that the invention was stolen and the principle used to operate the thing used in industry.

I was back to the window now. With dad gone there was no one to take us to the park or out to throw a ball, or build beautiful houses with my plastic snap together blocks. Beautiful houses like the one dad said he was going to get for us one day.

Well next door to the Duchess lived the lady from France, Miss Robert. Her exits from the very ordinary house she shared with her elderly parents were not grand like that of the Duchess. Miss Roberts was a rather sad figure. Miss Roberts didn't make me feel happy at all.

Every morning she left the house carrying a large shopping bag in each hand. The kind of paper bag you got if you put a nickel in the slot when you entered the big front doors at the department store.

Every evening she returned with the same bags, only they must have been heavier at night I thought, because she walked a lot more slowly coming than going. Her arms extended their full length, she grasped the handles one in each hand and as she tottered along she rolled from one foot to the other. The bags looked like heavy weights and I decided that the weights were what kept her from losing her balance.

Miss Roberts worked as a housekeeper for a prominent doctor and although Grand said that she was in her early thirties she seemed to be older than the happy Duchess. With her head down and her shoulders slumped, she trudged back and forth to work and church on Sundays, and spent all of her free time working in her little garden.

Grand said that Miss Roberts took special notice of who went to confession on Saturday nights (she had told Grand so) and she went to communion on Sunday mornings. Grand said that she ought to have pulled herself together after her sister ran off with her boyfriend and found another one. Dad just referred to her as the old maid.

The minister is starting to speak. Something he's reading from the bible, about believing. The gift of faith, faith in the afterlife. Faith in God. Reminds me of what dad said. Said it all the time. "Optimistic. You've got to be an optimist. Keep trying and things get better. That was it. "Never give up. No percentage in that" Yes that was what he said.

Miss Roberts' father must never have told her that. Miss Roberts' father hadn't invented the snuffo however. I must have been around eight by the time of this invention. He flew off to San Francisco to try to get someone interested in manufacturing the little plastic cone attached to the suction cup. The little device that when you placed a lit cigarette in it, it snuffed it out without bending and breaking it and therefore you could relight it and this would save the smoker untold amounts of cash. I'm not sure what happened to that either. I was too young to make sense of patents etc. All I know is that dad went away again and we moved into my grandmother's house for a time.

Grand was friends with the Chinese grocer. He had one small stall when she met him and she made a practice of saving her egg cartons and paper bags and returning these to him for reuse. They were recycling long before it became chic. Grand gave him as much business as she could and Sam brought her Chinese tea and ginger at Christmas. He also extended her credit, so that she was able to feed her growing brood of grandchildren.

I was nine years old now and dad was working somewhere up near Alaska. He changed the tires on the big logging trucks in a lumber camp. It was bad he told us years later. Bad being away from his kids. Bad sleeping in a bunkhouse. He didn't drink or play cards so he turned his attention to building things. One particular piece I recall vividly was the cedar chest. It was a beautiful job, a chest carved out of a single piece of cedar. He brought it home to mum as a present one spring. He only had two weeks off every six months. Two weeks to try and fill six months of time with three children before he had to leave again.

March and August was when he came home. Very seldom at Christmas was he around. When he was home he took us out a lot however. He was always trying to teach us something. How to ride a horse, skate, fish whatever he could afford to do at the time I suppose. I remember him keeping just enough money back for his necessities at the camp that first year and when he arrived home asking mum to release some money to him. There was a big fight about that; she had wanted to save everything. He sat at the table and cried. His hands were all stained and cut up from the work he did. He said he couldn't always wear gloves in that kind of work, even when it was cold.

After that he held on to enough money to be able to afford to take us places and buy us clothes. Clothes that weren't hand me downs from our cousins. "One good suit of clothes, a spit shine and a smile and you're first class you know." He had tried to put a positive spin on whatever had happened and yet children know, I did. I knew what Grand had meant when I had overheard her tell mum that no-one could be expected to do nothing but be a work horse, as she called it for someone else. "He loves his children" I heard her say: "He deserves, and so do they to be able to go and have a little fun with the short time they have together".

Short time together. The years passed so quickly. I was just ten years old a moment ago. "Life is a gift. The greatest gift. Do you know that? You can't sit around. You have to get out there. You have to do, see great things. You never know how long you've got." He was right of course. Grand knew that he was right. She said that she should have Kick-started mum many years earlier. Mum, well this day isn't about her is it? He never did say anything negative about her. Never said anything but how he had thought she was so beautiful and so talented.

CHAPTER 3

When he ran off to the city as a young Man, dad earned five dollars a week as a garage laborer and paid three dollars of that to his voice coach. His teacher Mr. Harris had done all he could to help him. That was before Mr. Harris left Mossbank to enlist in the air force in England, his home country. After Mr. Harris left, dad ran off and found work for room and board at a local Mossbank farmers. "No one had any cash to pay for help, but they had lots of food. I'd never seen so much food. I felt pretty darned smart to have talked my way into the Larsens. I could never get over being able to have seconds at meal time. It was unreal. Hell we didn't get firsts a lot of the time at home you know. You don't know what it is like to be hungry. Terrible thing. when you're hungry nothin else matters. Nothin. all you can think about is getting something to eat. That's why they introduced the lunch programs in schools. Well somebody had a smart idea for once."

The hymns are being sung now. I can't sing. I can't try.

They were over thirty when they married. She'd been a concert pianist, but never turned her talent to work for her, teaching or anything. Grand said it was because she was disturbed.

Apparently they had gone to Hollywood musicals every chance they got throughout the war years. They met while performing in amateur operettas and then dad joined the navy. Grand said that they ought to have been single-minded in pursuing careers, or got on with it. "Day dreams don't put food on the table darling." Well that's what she told me and often.

Mum had been offered a job with a radio station when I was about five months old but had turned it down. Occasionally we three children were lined up on the sofa and told to listen while mum played the piano and she and dad sang. We were told that they were teaching us an appreciation of good music. We were never allowed, much less encouraged to participate. We were a captive audience, I think. This was really the only times they got along together. They talked to and treated each other differently then and I suspect we could have snuck away without being noticed if we hadn't been too fascinated by their pleasant behavior to want to sit and watch.

Once a year Grand's sisters would visit from California, and then while mum and dad sang the three old ladies would nod and smile and cry and it was difficult trying to decide who to watch.

Well when we were small we heard a lot of excuses as to why mum and dad had not found successful careers as singers, but I guess the bottom line is simply that neither had the confidence to get out and try. I never did believe that their failure to realize their dreams was due to the fact that they had three children to care for. They were after all past their thirty-third birthdays when I, the first came along.

When dads inventions failed and his marriage was all but non-existent he turned his attentions to my brother. My brother, dad said was going to be a great man one day. And to this end he focused his attention and the wealth he would finally realize, losing in the bargain two subsequent wives, the understanding of friends and family and finally the will to carry on.

Jimmy was a beautiful little boy. He had large blue eyes, a head of thick dark blonde hair and a sprinkling of freckles across his nose. His little face often harbored a pensive expression and though sometimes teary-eyed he'd always work to force a smile. In the early years he possessed an empathy that extended even to his gold fish. Tears rolling down his cheeks he sprinkled more and more food into the bowl, all the while begging the dead fish to start swimming. He would suffer many more losses.

The day I left home for good, he walked in as I was packing and shyly, his hand outstretched, he offered me a present. Neatly wrapped, in a salvaged piece of Christmas paper, I found a rabbit's foot. "For luck" he said with tears in his eyes and hugged me good bye.

Another hymn. Dad used to sing this. Amazing grace. He did believe that there was as he put it, an omnipotent being. He finished high school at nights after working all day at the garage when I was a baby. Mum accused him of seeing another woman and after he got his high school diploma he didn't go any further. The same thing happened when he joined a choir.

Poverty affects people one of two ways I imagine. Some strive to better themselves, others accept fifes crumbs. Dad had lots of faults, I suppose we all do, but to his credit he taught us to never accept defeat. "Sunk before you start, you know, you do that. If one thing doesn't work you try something different."

The minister is speaking again. Talking about dad having accepted his departure from this life. As far as I know it's the only time he ever accepted anything without a fight.

That strawberry roan hadn't belonged to him when he was a boy. I realized as I grew older that that had been a wonderful story made up for a little girl who loved horses. Marie had belonged to the Belvederes. They were the black family who had been forced to sit on the opposite side of the school room. Their mum had been good to the ragged little white boy. She'd invited him in and fed him on occasion and talked to him very kindly he said. Those days children were seen and not heard, or that was what they were told was the way it was to be. I've always had the impression that poor kids were not even supposed to be seen, never mind heard.

The Belvederes were well-off compared to dad and his family. They had food and even shoes, and eventually all of old lady Belvedere's grandchildren would become professional people.

Dad took us to visit old Mrs. Belvedere when I was in my early teens. He said he wanted us to know that there were good people everywhere and that it didn't matter what a person looked like, that it was how they treated others that counted.

"My you make yourself look ugly when you cry. Your face will stay that way you know. Not that it makes any difference. None of my children are as lovely as I was, and this one is so little like me I can't believe she is my daughter. Look at her mother. She doesn't have the gumption to defend herself either." Her expression was defiant, her mouth contorted in an ugly grimace. "She's like him. Sits there, won't react."

Doesn't want to fight you mean. But then who in their right mind would require another human being to defend their looks?"

Then Grand turned to me and said: "Darling, we're all born with the face God gave us and we make the best of what we have. And incidentally Emma, she is no less attractive because she is different." I looked so much like dad.

Late at night huddled in my closet, I wrote dad letters begging him to come home. My flashlight grasped firmly in my left hand, a cheap writing tablet balanced on my knees, in my childish scrawl I ended each letter with; I love you round the world and back.

CHAPTER 4

He always wrote back and he'd enclose stamps and a little money for emergencies. And when he came home in the spring he loaded us in his old second hand car and took us to visit botanical gardens. That was the first place he wanted to visit after spending all that time in the barren north and the cold.

The service is over now. The chapel director and the minister are descending the stairs to the floor. The minister is reaching for the little wooden box, the chapel director the blanket of flowers.

"I wish to be cremated," he had written on the back of an old grocery receipt. No frills, nothing fancy. Have Rose Garden chapel make the arrangements. Divide whatever is left in my account between my three children." Three names and addresses listed.

This little note had been found in the worn briefcase he'd carried with him since the days he and our stepmom had begun the little lumberyard. Those days had been the happiest of his life and ours, as those ten years had been the only years we had ever known the luxury of being able to visit parents who lived in a real home and enjoyed a normal life. She'd been gone now for almost twenty years. She's with him now however, he with her. The two men are turning toward the door. It's time for us to follow.

Is he watching? We three are making our way to the limousine. Did he listen to my son give the eulogy? The part Lenny had added about grandpa being responsible for the fact that he was now a teacher? The part about grandpa teaching him the times tables? How when Lenny was eight or nine he taught him how to drive the forklift and paid him to move wood that didn't need moving, just so he would learn the value of hard work? Did he hear that?

I hope so. I hope he heard all the wonderful things that were said. All true and sadly, many taken for granted. The limousine is on its way to the little church now. The little church built by grandma Eva's father. It is one of the stopping places on what is now known as the (drive).The last time I followed the drive I accompanied dad. It had been a beautiful spring day much like this day. He had met me the day before at the Greyhound stop at the little convenience store just blocks from his apartment. It was my forty-fifth birthday and he had a lovely card waiting on the front seat of his car. The vehicle he drove was no longer a shiny white Cadillac, but a beat up old station wagon. True to form, he praised the old boat, claiming that they didn't make cars like that anymore.

The Cadillac. He been so proud of finally succeeding. He'd driven it to Mossbank especially to show it off. The locals understood. The locals knew of his past. The locals, his people, were happy for him. They didn't mind the bragging, and showing off. They were happy for him.

Farm country. Pastures, trees, barns and everyone in the limousine talking, talking; I'm not listening, I don't want to hear. I just want to remember.

The drive. We visited the old school house. One room. Desks and benches that seated two. An old wood burning stove still sat in the corner and the children's scrawl was yet visible on the worn slate blackboard at the front of the room.

The clearing that his childhood home had once stood upon. A clearing not as big as the average living room, the living room in the home he'd once owned. He looks sad. He sees things I cannot see. I try, and I listed, and I think I understand. I think. He has the same sad look that comes across every year at Christmas He always watches A Christmas Carol, and when the spirit pulls his robe back to expose the two children he always starts to cry. The same look. That same look. And I said something like "Let's go now, and visit the church before it gets too late".

We're almost there. The limousine is approaching the entrance to the church yard. There's Great-grandpa's headstone. It's almost time to say goodbye.

And we visited the graveyard, dad and I. And he did a little dance and he asked me if it made me a little nervous to see the family name on a headstone. And I said no. And he showed me that there were two plots available, should two more Witcombs want them. And I said I wasn't afraid and that I intended to be cremated. And he said: "Well that's a good idea, so the worms don't eat at you" and then more introspectively he said: "Yes, that's a good idea." And I said: "Let's go now to the farm for a visit; it's getting dark." And he said: "What makes you so smart anyway? You know I love to go there. Happy, lovely, people there." And we walked toward the car. And he did a little dance. And we had a happy day.

Everyone is gathering round now. We three are at the front of the group, closest to his resting place. His resting place atop that of Grandfather Whitcomb. The chapel director has stepped behind Grandfather's headstone. He's holding the blanket of roses. The minister has placed the small wooden box beside the hole and as I begin to wipe my eyes the director glances toward me and then instructs the minister to place the box in the hole. That's better. Now the minister is saying a few final words of comfort and the director places the blanket of roses beside the grave. Such a small pile of dirt. Small, everything seems less now. Diminished. We are offered a rose. I hesitate. We ought to leave as many roses as we can there. What would dad advise? "Take the rose and leave," he'd say that. "Take the rose and leave; I'm not in that damned hole anyway. You know that don't you?" I know.

"There's power in nature. We're all a part of it." We were standing on volcanic ash at a beach in Hawaii. "The force of nature, it's unreal, you have to respect that You know that don't you? Some power created all this. God, it's great; the whole world, great, incredible, you know that."

I know.

CHAPTER 5

He had tried all of his life to define himself in relation to the rest of the world. "Different. We were always different. No-one else, none of the other kids around had a mother who ran off. No one else was poor like us. Lots of poor people around, but not like us. Didn't even have an outhouse. Do you believe that? Didn't even have an outhouse. I did alright didn't I? Built a business, a house, travelled, seen a lot of the world. I did alright didn't I?"

Yes dad, you did alright.

People are milling round, talking, offering their condolences. I'm walking with a cousin and she is walking me over to visit her father's grave. It's her way of comforting me, I know this. Good people and kind, very kind. You did alright dad, and you came full circle. You came home. You gave most of everything away when you decided the time had come and now you are home.

It's time to leave. Everyone begins to walk toward their cars. We enter the limousine now on our way to the hall to sip coffee and nibble at sandwiches and talk about the man who did alright. They don't know about the depression he suffered, the mood swings that came on for no apparent reason, the lifelong battles that he fought. Battles fought in his head. The trips to the therapists, the counselors, the guilt he felt because he had had to spend time away, "To get better so that I can go to work and make things better." They couldn't know that he did more than alright.

My last trip here and he is in the nursing home. He won't talk and I know he can talk.

"You were depressed, dad.

He nodded yes.

"So depressed."

He nods his head yes.

"You can talk; I think you've just decided you don't want to. Am I right?"

"Yes. You know. Yes you're right."

I tell him that my son has told me what he'd said, their conversation before I arrived. "Grandpa, don't you want to feel better again?"

"No. I'm tired, I just want to leave." He says, "That's right."

"I can't do anything? Say anything, be there more often, anything to change your mind?"

"No" he tells me. "I'm old, I'm tired, I just want to leave."

"You're not afraid".

"No. I was, but I'm not anymore."

"Remember yesterday? I told you that I want you to know that we know you love us. I know that you always worried about that. We Know. You understand?"

"Yes, and now I'm not afraid anymore."

"You know we love you, I love you. You did your best for us, I know that. We know that. It's important you understand that we know that".

"I do know that, and now I'm not afraid."

I rush off to get him more coffee and when I return he has moved to a chair closer to the window. He's pointing at a small tree close to the window. "The tree is beginning to bud, dad. It's spring our favorite time of year. They've told me that I can take you out to the farm, dad, once you feel stronger. You'd like that wouldn't you?"

He shrugs a bit and says "Sure".

Another day and I arrive at the home early, eight o'clock and he's still sleeping and I walk over to his bed and say "Dad, it's me Hedy".

He opens his eyes and smiles and I tell him that I've brought him more clothes, his better clothes, hats, gloves, his warm jacket so that he'll be ready to go out when he wants to. And he just smiles and I tell him I've brought him a bag of his favorite chocolate bars and he grins and puts out his hand. I hang all his clothes and tell him that he'll look first class. "That's what you always told me, right? First class?" And he smiles. I put the quilt his surrogate mum Mrs. Larsen had sewn years ago over him and he sits up and running his hand over the quilt says, "Oh God, that's great, that's just great. You did great."

He's up now, dressed and we walk a bit before breakfast. We stop at the entrance to the front doors of the home and he stops. He's looking at the board with all the residents' names and room numbers on it and I ask him if he's looking for his name and he nods yes. I point to his name and he nods again and smiles. He asks me what the date of the month is and the time of day quite often and I take it as a hopeful sign that he might not want to leave, not yet.

We have our meals together in the cafeteria and I remember the day I left the table in the co-op cafeteria and walking back from the bathroom watched him sitting alone at the table waiting for me and thought; it's alright today because he knows I'll be back in a few minutes but what of all the other days? And I feel like crying and I can't let that happen because he never wanted us to cry.

His eyes are bad. No operation, glasses, nothing can cure his sight. I hold a Readers Digest out to him and ask him to tell me the smallest size print that he can now see to read. He points to the largest letters on the front cover. "There's nothing you want me to bring? No photo albums, no world atlas?"

"No, it's no good" he tells me. The world atlas with the pages worn and falling apart. He liked to study the atlas and could name the most obscure rivers and towns; liked to quiz us, said it was important to know where everything was and that way you knew where you were in relation to everything else on the planet.

I hold his hands and ask him if he'd let me manicure his nails and he smiles enthusiastically. I work on one hand while he holds his cigarette in the other and I remember he has stipulated cremation after his death and I ask God to please allow me the time to manicure his nails again and again. He's looking out the window and that's good, because he never liked to see us cry.

His hands aren't stained and cut and rough from work now; no, they're smooth and thin and bluish because of poor circulation. Cold, cold hands warm heart I think. "I read once that it's better to try to accomplish something spectacular, even when plagued by defeat and fate, than to live in the twilight zone between success and failure. You believe that?"

"Yes" I'd said and now I said: "You did well dad, you worked so hard, you did well." And he smiled.

The hall is emptying and we are walking toward the limousine. The limousine; dad would have said "What? Oh, why did you blow money on that?" Or would he have said, laughing, "Well hell, that's first class, you know how to go first class. That's good."

We're pulling out of the drive now and passing close to the grave site. They're all talking and I feel quiet with my thoughts and I am grateful for and comforted by my belief that dad is enjoying his garden in another place. I recall something I had read a short time ago though I don't know who wrote it and I silently repeat it.

"What if you slept,
And what if in your sleep you dreamed?
And what if, in your dream, you went to heaven
And there plucked a strange and beautiful flower?
And what if when you awoke, you held the flower in your hand?
What then?"

MRS. JOB AND THE DESERT DEVILS

This is a Las Vegas story and true in every sense of the word. I have changed the names only to protect myself from the guilty.

I will begin this tale with my return to the valley of the damned on October twentieth of the year two thousand and two. I returned after a two year absence to care for the Broker's property in return for free lodging. For those of you who are unfamiliar with my earlier writings, I assure you that this move was nothing short of courageous and in the end proved to be foolhardy indeed. I was however, or so I believed at the time, in financial straits and looking for a leg up as it were. Little did I realize that within one year I would be fortunate to escape with legs, let alone money.

I arrived owing approximately six thousand to various credit card companies, but with a stout heart, great optimism and needless to say, misplaced trust. The night I arrived all went well. Baby (my cat) settled in nicely, not having forgotten the place nor the master. I toured the house with Broker, reminiscing, sharing new stories of travel experiences and all the usual pleasantries shared by two who had parted somewhat acrimoniously and yet decide after an interval of a few years that the other may not have been such a bad sort after all. At any rate the first six weeks went well. I enjoyed the yard work, watering, looking after the greenhouse plants and his poor old cat. All this on days off and before and after work, as well as the laundry, dishes and cleaning.

Just like old times, although this time I was not being compensated with food, wage, car, insurance. Nevertheless, I was happy for the opportunity to recover financially and the assurance of a good job reference. So the days perked along, peacefully enough with me finding a job working in the men's department at Dillard's department store and looking forward to the day I would begin work with the school board and move into my new apartment.

The time arrived when Broker made an agreement to purchase yet another second house, another home away from home, love nest, vacation home, call it what you will it was the fourth such house in six years. This time however it would not be yours truly helping him set the nest to rights. He had a new love as he called it and she was waiting for him at her daddy's trailer in northern California. The pick-up was loaded with various and sundry items necessary to begin life anew (at least part time) and Broker drove off one morning at sunrise only to return four weeks later with the hooker from hell. And so my story begins.

I arrived home from work at around ten p.m. Friday December the first, to find Broker sitting alone in front of the television. She - we'll call her Tush (a slight variation on her name) had, he told me gone straight to bed. The drive had apparently done her in. Had nothing to do with the fact that she had left the most foul messages on his machine claiming they were her jealous reaction to me being there, as she was so much in love with Broker. At any rate, I reasoned that she needed a good night's sleep in order to face the following day. Next morning I awoke at four a.m. to the sounds of the television and the MTV channel. There she sat in the dark, a hand raised even with each side of her face, fingers snapping and head weaving back and forth. I introduced myself, walked into the kitchen to make coffee and returned to sit in the Broker's big living room chair.

I switched the lamp beside the chair on and commented that she must have got up very early as she had her make-up on already to which she replied, "Oh no, this is all tattoo work; I worked nights and had to look good at all hours." Interesting.

She spoke in a little child's voice telling me that she hoped to find a Christmas dress the color of her finger nails, at which time she displayed long green talons for my approval. Lovely. Mercifully I had to work that day and so excused myself, wished her a lovely day and closing my bedroom door prayed Baby would be safe until I returned home that night.

I arrived home late from work and again Broker was sitting alone in his chair in front of the television. She had (made him) he said, take her to a revivalist church that evening and decided to go straight to bed. "I didn't know she was a church going person", he said. As we will see there was method to her madness.

Sunday. Well it was the Christmas season and we were all working ten and twelve hour shifts and six and seven days a week, but we closed at six on Sundays and so I arrived home to find Baby running round the house and her collar gone. I looked everywhere and then Tush found it in, of all places, the first place I had hunted, the cushions in the kitchen nook. This woman was a real heroine, or perhaps she just thought twice about tossing my cat away.

The following day I finally had a day off and this would prove to be a most unforgettable day. Broker left early, seven thirty, to play tennis and had asked Tush to take his truck to be serviced that morning - he had made an eight-thirty appointment. I left to run errands and returned home to find crazy lady wrapped in a towel and cutting her toe nails in the living room, the nails left in the carpet in front of his chair, perhaps as a welcome home present. It was ten a.m. and this would be one of the longest days of my life. She kept running to and from the bedroom, each time sporting a new personality. I kept working round the house and she kept doing whatever, meanwhile changing clothes from one set of hooker rags to the next. Crazier with each change.

Then at about one in the afternoon and still no Broker, there was a knock at the door and I answered it to find three little Philippino people, two women, and one man asking to see Tush. I called to her and she emerged dressed in a long red dress and wedge sandals, perfectly made up, hair combed and of calm demeanor and as she approached the door she claimed she could not imagine who knew that she was there. Then the little people smiled as I invited them in and thanked her for calling them over. As it turned out they were only too glad to have been invited over by Tush to pray for my full recovery from drug abuse. They spotted my typewriter on the kitchen table and wished her well with the book she was writing, at which time I, having had enough, told them the typewriter was mine and that I had no idea Tush was a writer as well. She now asked them to step outside and as I decided to step outside the door after a few minutes interval I overheard her tell the little people about all the thousands of people she had helped in her work as a psychologist (with an eighth grade education?) and how it had paid off, because after her mansion in the bay area burned she had met the Broker and fallen madly in love and he was now saving her from financial destruction, or words to that effect. The little people took their leave and the hooker emerged. Wild-eyed, she told me that I had stepped on her toes and that now I was going to pay. First however, nothing would do but yet another beer; she had been drinking beer since about ten that morning. Then she changed into her snot green shirt, a long oversized men's shirt that had seen better days and proceeded to call her brother. All the while using the sleeve of said shirt to wipe her nose.

"You know I don't need this shit," said the church-goer. "I can get any man" she told bro and giggled. "You know I've been on the street since I was fifteen. I hate these kinds of people. Education, big deal. Who the fuck is this bitch? I don't need this. And this is nothing but an old shit. What do I need this shit for?" Well bro must have impressed upon her the need for the rich old Broker because after what seemed an interminable length of time she hung up and grabbing the truck keys in one green taloned fist and half a dozen beers in the other, she waved the keys at me, giggled the crazy giggle, and informed me that she could drive, drink, do whatever she wanted to do and I was to just watch what happened.

I called the police and we combed the grounds. It is an acre full of palm trees and thousands of shrubs, plants and all sorts of garages and sheds to hide round, and she hid well because we did not find her, but the truck having been blocked by the police cruiser had not been moved either. Broker returned just after dark that day - long time for tennis? She grabbed him before he made it to the house and impressed upon him how badly she had been treated by me all day. Well, as the old German told me "He's pussy whipped." you will meet her shortly. He, the Broker, told me that while he believed me and knew that Tush was a liar and a con artist, he just wanted her around for a year for fun. And so dear reader I was forced to leave, yes pack up, load my car and Baby and I drove away at about nine that very evening.

THE GERMAN WAR BRIDE

"It's alright, Baby" I said as we drove away. I knew in my heart that I had been set up by Broker. He had stayed away far too long that day and being a vindictive man, aligned with a psycho pathetic woman and one desperate to do anything for him for money, had enjoyed some vindication for my having abandoned ship in Malibu. Well here we were, Baby and I once again looking for a place to stay, and fortunately we had been invited by the German widow only a few days earlier. She, a recent widow and alone with two big dogs, was in need of someone to caretake the house and dogs, while she flew to New Mexico to enjoy Christmas with her daughter and grandsons.

I would never have imagined that I would find myself living in what the Broker's wealthy old client had referred to as the house of love. Well we would see I thought.

My room was wonderful. The whole top floor of a home high in the hills, with a beautiful view of Las Vegas. The walk-in closet was the size of most bedrooms, huge bath and a bedroom that you could easily fit the average size living room in to. Such luxury, and the old woman seemed to be much nicer than I had remembered. well we would see.

Now the old woman was not actually the widow of the wealthy old client of Broker's. She was however, the longtime girlfriend, fifteen years long. Nevada not being a state that recognized common law relationships could have meant that she may have been left in sorry straits indeed had it not been for the generosity of the old man, who, had left her the house on the hill, two hundred and sixty five thousand, a new van, twenty thousand and a fifty thousand dollar bank trust, as well as five hundred thousand dollars in cash. Yet greed being what it is, the old woman was angry at not having been left to hear her tell it "nearly enough."

Actually, the old man had inherited her when her husband had died fifteen years prior. She and Teddy had been renting the house when Teddy expired, brain tumor. Left her with nothing but twenty dollars to her name and the rent owing. At any rate as it turned out the old client asked her one day approximately two weeks after Teddy's demise if she accompany him on a trip to Jamaica, a cruise, and having accepted the kind offer of a trip to cheer her up, she stayed on in the house and a new love was born-or something.

Her daughter now called every day, a new development since the old man's death as said daughter had not wished much contact with mom until coincidentally, the old man died and left a tidy sum. Not as tidy as they would have wished of course, him having been worth some twenty million at last count.

The old woman much depressed at not having been left enough to really feel appreciated, proceeded to drink even more than was her usual bent, which meant that she bent the elbow often enough to cause severe inebriation by about three each afternoon and may enjoy the experience so much that sobering up and having another go at getting cross-eyed drunk was not out of the question at least five out of seven week days. Weekends she spend at the neighborhood casino, offering nice crisp bills to the greedy slot machines and as the machines sucked the money up, she partook of the free libations and amazingly, drove home by dinner time without killing herself or anyone else.

I spent time with the dogs and took to my room early every evening. They must have been lonely before my arrival and often I would sneak down at least once if not twice to give them extra treats, and pats before retiring for the night.

If the old woman was not in a mean belligerent frame of mind I would sit in the old man's living room chair and the dogs would snuggle up to me and I would stay as long as I could tolerate her company, otherwise I moved to the kitchen and again sitting in what had been the old man's chair, the dogs would come to rest by me one on either side and I with a hand on each head. I felt as though an unseen force was encouraging me to act as protector and sorry that I was not in a position to spirit all three of us away.

Well the days marched on and as we neared Christmas day I was invited to a party by one of the twins. You may recall them from the Key Largo story, the two from Chicago. Inherited the trusts, penny pinching, saloon owners, the kind of men who invite you over for dinner and suggest a dish for each to bring to contribute, so that in the end all they have furnished is a seat at table in the mansion and some cheap wine. Well platonic twin called and I accepted the invitation to attend a Christmas party with him and two old cronies of his from the Chicago days. It turned out he wanted an invitation into the old lady's house as he had spotted her unused van parked one day and hoped he smelled a deal.

Christmas Eve arrived and he called me to tell me that he had made a great deal with her to buy the van for two thousand dollars. I responded that she had offered it to me for one thousand and the foul language began. He even told me in the worst sounding man voice, by that I mean his heroes, the old Chicago hit men types, that he was going to get me, ruin me. Well that was only the beginning of a lot of trouble for me, financially and every other way and all because an old woman sold me something under the guise of doing me a favor, that turned out to be something ready for the scrap heap. Of course her behavior had not deteriorated until she had my money and I had spent my income paying down debts, rather than hanging on to my cash for the rainy days that were to follow.

Christmas Eve, I hung the phone up and spent my time with the dogs, taking breaks to run upstairs to say hello to Baby. I had driven the old woman to the airport and she had flown off to New Mexico to visit her newly-loving daughter earlier in the day. I was determined to enjoy my evening and Christmas day as much as possible under the circumstances. The circumstances were such that I found myself alone with the pets and I decided at least no one around to make me miserable, so I enjoyed a lovely Turkey TV dinner and a bottle of Piesporter wine, gave the dogs a pat, a treat and headed off to bed.

Christmas day I could have hemmed the duck pants Mr. Chicago gave me to hem as a favor to him the night of the Christmas party but decided to toss them in the charity bag instead. He had bragged that he had found them at a thrift store in Florida for fifty cents when he had been down visiting his brother for Thanksgiving, so it was a terrible loss indeed for him. I did not expect to ever hear from him again, but some people have unimaginable reserves of gall and after the new year he appeared one Sunday hollering outside the front door, "My pants, I want my pants". Yes, there he was clutching the bars on the locked alcove gate, knuckles white hollering for his pants. I admit they were an unusual pair with the little mallard ducks embroidered from waist to cuff all round. I peeked out the upstairs window when the hollering started and watched as he scribbled down my license plate number.

Mr. Chicago kept calling. He called when I was away at work and by the time I returned home at night the old lady was beside herself with aggravation and gin soaked as usual. I finally drove over to the nearest police precinct and filed a harassment complaint and after that the phone calls to the old lady began to subside, though not before he threatened to ruin me. Little did he realize that by purchasing the van (from the old German woman, who, began to brag to me about having been raised a Nazi youth in Hamburg during the second world war, and then began to taunt me that if my ancestors had not immigrated to the United States I would have been made a lamp shade by her people) I was financially ruined. I called the Broker to ask him to convince Mr. Chicago to leave me alone and he told me that Mr. Chicago had always been the greediest person he had ever known and had wanted to make money by reselling the van. Now this may not sound to you to be anything all that devastating, but consider the fact that Mr. Chicago had masqueraded as a friend for years, knew of all my troubles and yet was capable of such viciousness. Greed. A good thing in this instance because it exposed this pathetic old gambler for who he was.

The old woman had always told me that she did not like living in the house alone and that she would be happy if I could find a position in a school close to home so that I might go on living in the upstairs until she sold the house.

The way things turned out however, would set me on a course to financial ruin, from which I would not be able to salvage the credit rating I had worked so hard to build after leaving the broker. You see as soon as the estate attorney informed the old woman that her five hundred thousand dollar inheritance was going to be released within a week and the house put in her name, she went out and picked up a few of those little rental magazines you see in boxes all over Vegas, free.

She presented them to me when I arrived home from work one afternoon and when I reminded her that I had told her that I had put a deposit on an apartment one week prior and was to move in three weeks, she told me that it was not soon enough because she was getting her money and getting rid of the house ASAP.

I had to pack up and move into one of those expensive weeklies within a few days and the expense was so great that I could not then afford to take possession of my apartment and lost my deposit. At the same time I received my first pay check from the school district and found that I was being paid five dollars less per hour than assured. Now don't suppose for a moment that I did not enjoy the executive studio and the fact that I no longer arrived home from a hard day's work to the verbal abuse of a drunken old woman, or that I did not appreciate working at the school, it's just that I was heading toward financial hell, through hard work and sacrifice.

I kept making the credit card payments and then the van began to need repairs. Brakes, yes she had sold me a vehicle that had virtually no brakes on the front and the rear brakes were nearly non-existent. The mechanic turned as white as a sheet when he told me and then showed me the condition of the van. The axels would need to be replaced very soon, within a month he said, and then after I had spent close to seven hundred dollars on various repairs I stalled on the way home from the school one afternoon and had to pay to be towed to my mechanic and was told that I would have to spend another five hundred dollars soon to keep the engine from dying. I won't bore you with the details, trust me I was going down fast. I took the van to one of those men who advertise that they will buy any vehicle and even he did not want it. Sure, you say I ought to have had everything checked out before I handed over one thousand dollars, but remember, this old woman had been the long-time girlfriend of broker's best client, was inheriting lots of money and as we often judge others by ourselves, I foolishly believed that I could trust her.

Well now I began to spend weekends looking for another vehicle. The advertisements said 0 down and we finance everyone. You know the kind. Good credit, bad credit, no credit, bankruptcy. Well I still had decent credit, but I was a woman walking in alone as well and so one after another five dealerships in all, I scoured the city for a little car I could afford to make payments on.

When all was said and done I ended up with an over-priced two year old vehicle that was going to cost two hundred and forty four dollars a month over seven years and that brought my little car, that I agreed to purchase for just under ten thousand dollars to a grand total of seventeen thousand and change.

All of this debt took time to accrue however and it was now summer and I was not going to get paid a stipend through the vacation break because I had not been with the school district for six months. I called Dillard's department store and felt sure that having worked so hard, and given two weeks' notice, though it is not required in the state of Nevada that they would surely have me back for the summer. Silly me. I found that Dillard's claimed they had fired me. Fact was they told me to not work my two weeks, something about scheduling, but fired me? What for?. This now showed up on background checks and for the life of me I could not find another summer' job. I say another because Seven-11 had hired me for weekends, but even I could not live on fourteen hours a week at seven dollars an hour. I was off to my son's with my new little car and would have to borrow money to return to Vegas and my job as assistant to the SEC teacher in an elementary school. Now my troubles would begin in earnest.

LEAVING THE DEVIL'S DESERT

My final trip out of what had for me become a hell on earth. Too dramatic? Hell no. You would have had to have lived it. I would not wish it on anyone, however. As I drove out of Las Vegas for what would be the very last time I reflected on some of the major instances of the past year there. The little ADHD children were paramount in my thoughts to be sure and I had promised myself that I would do everything in my power to bring their story to the attention of the public.

It is approximately a fourteen hour drive from Las Vegas to Great Falls Montana, and then only another two to where my son and his little family live in Taber Alberta. On this occasion it would take a bit longer however, as the snow had begun to fall just as I reached Great Falls and so I stopped for the night. I admit that I was not looking forward to crossing the border. I don't particularly like Canada, but I would have to have somewhere to stay until I published and found enough money to be able to settle elsewhere. With that goal, the prospect of returning to a warm climate and living independent of the desert devils, I pushed forward.

My years long friend, the young man who had helped me return home to Florida from South Korea, had sent me one thousand dollars so that I could take advantage of the recent school assignment. Now I owed him as well as my son almost the same amount and where was I? I was sitting in a cheap motel in the cold in Great Falls Montana, out of work, in debt and thoroughly disgusted with myself for trusting those I had considered friends and a school district as corrupt as any casino operation or strip club.

Well here I was. Forget for a moment the financial aspect and consider the heartache of being powerless to rescue children from an abusive classroom situation. Ah yes and there were the dogs that the old woman professed to love.

Angie, weak, her sense of smell all but non-existent, cataracts blurring her vision and she sitting rubbing her poor old eyes trying to clear them and the old bitch laughing at her all the while through her gin fog. Buddy, the gentle pit bull slept with the old girl, and though he was ostensibly her favorite, she allowed his nails to grow as uncomfortably long as Angie's and could not have cared less had his food and water ran out, which is the reason I had hung on as long as I did and much to my detriment, because should I have left that horrid house earlier oh well - shoulda, woulda, coulda, they say. What's the point? If I have learned anything it is that in order to be in a position to help anyone or anything, you must first help yourself.

I can look in the mirror. I protected, fed, watered and showered love and attention on the dogs and children and did my best to meet my financial obligations, yet in the end it was all too much for one woman alone. Those people whom I had considered friends for many years in Las Vegas turned their backs on me when I was in grave danger of homelessness and hunger and those who did not, cursed and cheated me financially.

At last I am free of it all and I pray that the publication of my story will free others.

I returned to Las Vegas with two hundred and fifty dollars in my pocket book, yet I had what I believed at the time to be a decent paying job to start with and the promise of furthering my education through what was known as the alternate route program. This would enable me to work and while earning my living take classes at night to earn my education degree. As things stood I had only a BA and various and sundry certificates and diplomas, eleven in all.

The first few nights I spent in a cheap motel, a twenty minute drive from the school. It was bad, the temperature was still in the nineties and there was no air conditioning. I didn't think that there was anywhere left in Vegas that could live without it in this day and age, but then I was about to discover a great many things that I had not imagined possible in this day and age. I was charged forty dollars a night for the privilege of staying in this filthy dump and tired from the long drive back, had checked in Thursday in the late afternoon, after wearing myself out looking for the most affordable place to rest until the weekend. Friday morning I was due at the school for what I had been told would be orientation.

I entered the classroom and introduced myself to Mia. Young, almost six feet tall, husky and she told me twenty-nine years old. She was a young black woman from Ohio and she wasted no time letting me know that she was not looking forward to the school year ahead.

THE LITTLE ROOM OF HORRORS

Mia had returned to Las Vegas from her summer in Ohio on Wednesday, just two days prior to our meeting she told me. For this reason the room was not yet decorated and she asked me if I was an organized person, because she said she had no idea where to put anything and hated the idea of being there anyway, but that she had to fulfill her contract. Her contract consisted of three years' service to the Clark County School District, payment for the cost of the Master's degree program which she had just completed and for which the district had paid. She had two years left to work in the special education program to, as she said, free herself from her commitment. "Two more years of hell. You'll see what these kids are like. My hair even started to fall out last year I got so stressed. I really hate teaching, but I got me a free education so I have to live through this hell. We got three kids to start, but they will likely give us two or three more. Don't know nothin' bout 'em, just that they'll be no better than the kids last year. ADHD monsters. Isn't that bad to say? Well you'll see anyway."

So this was my introduction to the teacher I would be working with. An angry young woman who disliked the children she had not yet met.

I spent the day with her organizing book shelves and the cabinet that would hold all the toys, games and candy that she would purchase on a credit card given her by the district. Jelly babies and very few tinker toy cars were given out over the following two months. She did buy tins of vanilla icing and jars of peanut butter, rice cakes and a variety of soda crackers however and holed up in her room at lunch, never eating in the teachers' lounge or venturing out of the room unless absolutely necessary.

On many occasions I was sent to the copy room and virtually every time I returned from making hundreds of copies, ninety-nine percent of which were never used, I found the room in chaos, with one of the children having been relegated to the corner and perhaps another throwing a tantrum.

I am getting ahead of myself, however. Let me return to the first day of classes. I am told that we will be meeting three little ADHD children at the bus. They are seven years of age and have been assessed as being slightly retarded. I walk to the bus with Mia. We stand there waiting for the school bus to arrive. Each of us have been issued with a two way radio. I turn as I realize someone is approaching and recognize the principal, vice-principal and two of the office workers, two of four office workers, who, I am told have been trained to be part of what is known as the intervention team. I would very soon dub them THE SWAT TEAM.

Well there we all stood. Six adults, armed with two-way radios, the principal, vice-principal, nervously talking about how to handle their three new charges. I stood there incredulous, thinking they sounded like three cops discussing the apprehension of three hardened criminals, rather than three educators discussing how to assist three damaged little souls transition into a strange new environment.

The bus finally arrived and three frightened little people tentatively stepped down the stairs and nervously looked around. I smiled and walked over to greet them and as I did Mia in a harsh voice, the sort reserved for new army recruits, barked at them to line up over by the wall and not to speak or make a sound. One little guy, Shakur, kept looking down at his shoes, and I saw that they were new and complimented him on how good he looked. His big sad brown eyes looked up at me and a huge smile spread across his face.

"Never mind the shoes" Mia said. "We got rules here and I'm gonna make you memorize them. And you gonna behave like you in the army. I don't put up with nothin, so you listen up and behave and we gonna get along".

Stace, not fragile, nor as frightened looking as Shakur, nevertheless stuck the two middle fingers of his right hand into his mouth and looked at the ground. Eric, who, it would become apparent was not at all prone to tantrums, but simply slow, and who loved to draw and print his name over and over, just stood looking around as if he had just landed on another planet. Well that made two of us.

Well there we were, all lined up and marching to our new room. They had to measure an arm's length between each other, and were not allowed to say one word all the way to the class. Mia made them start over three times. Back and forth we went until they were not one step out of line and did not make one peep. By the time we arrived at the classroom door I was exhausted and a bit angry myself. You can only imagine how badly these three little guys must have felt.

Their little backpacks were hung on the hooks inside the door and they were ordered to take their seats. Mia then walked to the front of the room, wrote their names on the board and informed them that they would have check marks placed after their names every time they broke one of her rules.

One check mark meant a warning, two meant time out, three and you were not allowed to eat lunch in the lunch room and would lose the privilege of playing outside after lunch. On and on it went and all assuming the worst. The ultimate insult, as far as I could see, was when she brought her dictatorship to the point of abuse by telling them that they would be penalized for laughing without first raising their hand.

One did not have to be trained in a Master's program centered on attention deficit disorder to know that the very term suggests that the child has the attention span of a cat and that many of these hard and fast rules were going to be broken.

This was not the army. This was supposed to be a special education class. This was an abusive, and mean-spirited young woman who had no business interacting with children. My heart sank. Because of budget cuts, the school that I had been employed at when I had first joined the district had cut me from their program. I was then forced to find another school and because the change had meant a slight raise in pay and status, my probationary period had been set back six months. Now I was starting all over again, which meant that I did not have a leg to stand on when it came to voicing an opinion. In other words, look the wrong way and you could be let go at a moment's notice with no recourse. Sound unbelievable? Well as we get farther along you will realize what I was up against. At this time, early in the school year I had hoped that if worst came to worst and I was unable to appeal to Mia's sense of right and wrong, or even just some spark of humanity, I would be at the very least able to appeal to the principal. Surely after twenty some years in the field of education she had some sense of compassion and cared about the children? Foolish me. Pension, status, control. These were the principal's motivators and when she referred to, or even looked at these poor little souls it was with derision, and contempt. For the life of me I could not understand Mia however. She was African American and all five of the children were African American. I would have thought that she might feel protective of them and even more inclined to care for them. Then an incident took place that shed light on the fact that on the contrary, she not only did not feel for the children, she found them an offence to her and her race and said as much.

One afternoon I walked into the class after my lunch break and found her standing close to the door, just watching the children. She had a look upon her face that is difficult to describe, sort of a mixture of disgust and sadness. I asked what the matter was and without moving she quickly responded, "Look at them; all African American and I'm African American, they're over-represented." I had the sense that she felt they were an embarrassment to her and in the weeks to come I would feel certain that this was so.

I asked her again about their backgrounds and she said she didn't know, hadn't had time to read their histories and added: "Who cares anyway?" I told her that it might help to further our understanding of each child's particular needs if we had a sense of what their circumstances were, health, family etc. She then told me that she would get their folders for me to read and I could then fill her in. "I'm not spending any of my free time readin' up on 'em" she said.

The following morning Mia produced the folders and I read through them every chance I found a spare moment throughout the day. The next morning I attempted to fill her in as she put it.

Little Shakur was living, as he had since birth with his grandmother. He had two younger siblings who were learning disabled as he was. He had been born cocaine, alcohol and heroine addicted and with a heart problem. At the age of four he had been assessed as slightly retarded and a picture of him taken at the time of that assessment shows a frightened child with a frozen look on his face; attempting to smile?

Apparently so. The psychologist wrote that Shakur did not possess the capacity to react with expression appropriate to his emotion. He did not appear able to distinguish between a smile, look of anger, sadness and so on. The little face in that picture will remain with me to my dying day. I had never seen anything like that little face. He had come a very long way in the three years since and I believed that if Mia, who had told me that this particular child was the one she hated to have the most, would look at the picture and allow me to tell her about his struggles, that I could bring her around to feeling some compassion. It was not the case. This little guy who now was very expressive, loved to laugh, talk and worked to write his name as perfectly as possible, even crying when he made a mistake with a letter and insisting upon doing it over to until he felt proud of it. This little guy, very frail physically and despite his heart condition put on strong medication, so strong that he seemed dazed at times, sick to his stomach and with an appetite so small he would have eaten nothing had I not bribed and encouraged his efforts to eat just one more spoonful, had come a long way.

Yet when I told Mia everything I had learned, she looked at me with contempt and told me that I had better just follow her lead, that Shakur reminded her of the child she had had last year and that he wasn't getting any special treatment. This was a lie however, because she began to show him very special treatment indeed. She had singled him out to vent her anger upon; no-one was safe, but Shakur would need the most protection.

Shakur wanted a little tinker toy car so much and the only way for him to get one was to win it by behaving.

Keep in mind the fact that these children have extremely short attention spans and that for Shakur to force himself to remember to raise his hand every time he had a question, or to hold himself in his seat when he felt the urge to jump up and talk to another child and to keep this up until lunch time was nothing short of miraculous. He accomplished this however and when lunch arrived he was told that now he had to wait until it was time to leave for the day. He made it and you could see the exhaustion, pride, and anticipation on his little face. A huge grin spread across his face and his eyes lit up as he put his backpack on and took his place in line. Then when Mia offered nothing more than an "order hands to your sides, not a word" and so on, he raised his hand to remind her of his reward for being good all day and she told him that he was not getting the car because he had asked. His knees buckled and he fell to the floor in tears. I moved toward him and she told me to leave him alone, that now she was going to write a report to his grandmother telling her about how he was behaving at this moment and that he was going to get a whopping when he got home. If this was not severe emotional and mental abuse of the worst kind then pray God I did not know what was and that only days later I would be told by the principal that this was acceptable behavior by an sec teacher, frightened me, horrified me and thank God I was not fool enough to swallow any of it.

One behavior that illustrated the way the children felt about that room was the way they would jump up and run to the door any time anyone knocked. Invariably every child asked if they could leave with the person. Another was the fact that they would tell Mia she could leave now when we entered another room for say physical education, music etc. This did not endear me to her as you can imagine and she was always terribly disappointed when the children received glowing reports from the other teachers and myself regarding their behavior. Most often she would say to me and in front of the children. "You tell me the truth. You not supposed to be here to protec 'em." I am quoting Mia verbatim. This is a woman who is supposed to be university educated, a Master's degree no less and who spoke like someone who had not managed to get through the third grade. Two of the children, Isiah and Stace used more advanced diction and pronunciation than this special education teacher.

Still determined to win his car, Shakur whispered to me as soon as he got off the bus that he was going to be perfect all day long. I told him that I knew he could do just that and a huge grin spread across his face as his eyes sparkled in anticipation of winning that sixty cent tinker toy. We entered the room and without a word Shakur hung his backpack on its hook and smiling at me conspiratorially he quickly took his seat at his desk and began coloring the picture that had been placed there for him.

Mia began walking toward the back of the room and as she did she began passing out candies to each child and praising them for coloring their pictures. Then as she came to Shakur she stopped, looked down at him and resumed walking without giving him his reward as she had the others. This is an attention deficit hyperactive child remember and at this he suddenly burst into tears and pushed his desk over. She smiled and told him that now he certainly was not going to win any car. Thus began a siege that would last the better part of the day and leave this poor little soul a sobbing, shaking and hopeless little one by the end of the day.

The other children were adversely affected of course. As always happened, when one became upset, the others reacted. Some would tear up whatever they were working on, others cry, throw their own desk and it always ended with the crises team, or as I had dubbed them, the swat team, having to be radioed to assist.

This looked like something out of a B movie. The principal, vice-principal and a couple of office workers running into the room and grabbing onto a fragile little child. One on each arm, leg, then turning the child so that he was face down on the carpet and pinning him there until he was worn out from the struggle. After this the child would be sat in a chair, the adult sitting in a chair behind him, his arms crossed over his chest, his hands pinned to his shoulders by the attending adult. I had watched Mia cause a child to react this way so often in the first two weeks of school that I began to wonder if she were not purposely causing the child to react and now I had my answer. A few days after the incident with Shakur we were sitting at a table with the children and they were all quietly drawing, and talking together, when Mia suddenly looked at the clock. "Only one thirty" she said. "Two more hours to go. Last year I used to hope that one of 'em would do somethin' just to break the boredom." So now I had my answer. This was really the junior version of one flew over the cuckoo's nest I had thought at the time.

The fact is, the crises team should not have had to be called even once a day, let alone five and six times a day. These children are extremely sensitive, very affectionate and aware of rewards for good behavior. Most often all that was necessary was that I give a child a pat on the back, a little candy and a smile, while I reminded them of how proud I was of them for behaving so well and the child would settle down.

Stace with his two middle fingers (of whatever hand was free at the time) did not need to be told by Mia one afternoon when he was feeling particularly restless, that if he did not stop sucking his fingers she would cut them off. This happened on at least three occasions in my presence. Little Ridge stood at her desk one afternoon and asked her what the ring of keys she was holding were for to which she replied: "To cut your throat with if you not good." His eyes grew large, his thumb was shoved quickly into his mouth and he replied: "Teacher, I be good. I raise my hand to ask a question. I do all my work. I clean for you."

Ridge is about the size of a three year old and is afflicted with Obsessive Compulsive Disorder, or OCD. If you asked Ridge to tidy his desk, he will begin there and if not stopped will continue tidying every desk, book shelf and then start on the sinks, counters, tables, anything that is possible to clean, until his little hands are wizened from soap and water. A perfectionist, even the items in his pockets and backpack were neatly arranged. And though he did not know how to tie his shoes, his socks were pulled up and his laces neatly tucked in the sides of his sneakers, so obsessive was he about the laces that he stopped at least four times to arrange them within a three minute time span.

Ridge is a sociable little guy. Ridge loves to talk and he loves to make you laugh. If he had the answer to a question he would forget to raise his hand at least ninety nine percent of the time, yet he would always apologize when he caught himself making a mistake and he was always ready to assist the other children with their work. He had learned as much as many so-called average seven year old children and yet had been assessed slightly retarded only three years earlier. I never did understand this, but then I had been advised to just do as I was told, and not question, by both the principal and Mia. At any rate to give you an idea of how Mia handled a little person like Ridge we will look back to the afternoon, a Friday afternoon and all five children happily lined up at the classroom door ready to walk to the bus. Ridge suddenly bolted out the door, but sprinted back in just as quickly as he had disappeared, a twinkle in his eye, he was laughing. As soon as he was back in, he turned on a dime, arms by his sides and stock still, as were all the others. Suddenly Mia grabbed him by his left hand, so forcefully that he was pulled off his feet; shocked, he gasped. His backpack on, he was unable to right himself and she continued, dragging him down the hall.

He now began to screech as anyone would and when I attempted to take him from her she told me to look after the others and one of the swat team by this time walking down the hall ran and grabbed his other arm. Just assuming that he had been causing a problem, she went along and poor Ridge was dragged to the bus and turned over to the driver, who later told me that he was shocked, as to his knowledge Ridge was never a problem. "Just a great little guy". All five children were basically great little guys.

However, anyone, you, I, the so-called normal, or average child down the street, would be hard pressed to keep up great little guy behavior while under the supervision of a whole team of people who seemed bent on exacerbating every situation, exaggerating every behavior, and in essence keeping you under a microscope every second of every day.

Isiah was another bright child. He had a vocabulary that exceeded his seven years and was possessed of great compassion for others, even Mia. One morning he overheard her telling me that she had not done anything over the weekend any differently than she ever did. "I don't do anything but sit home alone; I don't go anywhere. Some life".

Isiah piped up to say, "Oh you should get out and see things, do things and enjoy your life you know. It isn't good for you to be sad alone."

Isiah was a bit taller than the average seven year old, but had to have weighed more than one hundred pounds. He was in appearance the miniature version of a Sumo wrestler. He was always thirsty and had to urinate at least once an hour. Unfortunately at least fifty percent of the time he used his extra bathroom breaks to run off and it was to the office that he ran. This was true of all of the children.

Isiah lived with an aunt. He had been a ward of the court, a foster child, since birth and had just recently moved in with the aunt, who, he said, would not answer him when he asked her why his parents were in prison, but would send him to his room for asking. I told the principal about this and her answer was that these children lied all the time. I responded that I knew that his parents were in prison because I had read his history and that I believed he needed help to deal with his feelings. He had issues I told her and she told me once again that he was lucky the aunt took him, that no-one wanted these kids and to just return to the class and not worry about them. "They won't be learning anything much anyway. It's just somewhere to put them; they have to be stuck somewhere".

Isiah one morning was sitting at the large table with Mia playing a game when suddenly he jumped up and bursting into tears, shouted "I am not a looser. Don't call me a looser. I hate myself. I'm fat and everyone hates me too." Then he climbed up on the table and kept hollering that he wanted to die. "I am going to kill myself" he hollered it over and over, all the while crying uncontrollably. Mia did nothing but tell him that now he was going to lose his recess that day. Things escalated until the swat team had to be called and I took the other children outside to keep them from becoming upset. So Mia was not bored that day.

I kept writing reports regarding his behavior so that his aunt would realize how very disturbed he was and hopefully get him help. When he complained of having headaches Mia told him that she had never heard of a seven year old having a headache and that if he did not quit complaining she would put another check mark beside his name on the board and he would lose his recess. I was sure he was suffering from diabetes and yet no-one appeared concerned. Indeed the vice-principal would walk right up to Mia and tell her to have me do something, as though I were invisible. She would pass me in the hall, or walk into the class and never acknowledge my presence. This behavior became more pronounced after I went to the principal's office to ask about their knowledge regarding the children's physical treatment.

One lunch hour in the cafeteria Shakur lost control and began using foul language, hollering that it did not matter if he were good or not anyway and that he wanted to just kill everyone. I simply picked him up and as I carried him in my arms back to the class and away from the others I heard my name called and the vice-principal chasing after me. No, I was not to pick him up; it was against the rules. She had me put him down, then grabbed his left arm and turned it behind his back, then a swat team member came along and grabbed the other arm. I watched as these two women dragged this emaciated little guy down the hall, his arms twisted behind his back and him hollering for help.

The day following this lunch room incident Mia decided to supervise lunch along with me. How sad. While I had been quite successful at lunch with the children, now I was forced to listen to her tell them that they had ten minutes to eat everything, or it was going in the garbage, and admonish me for helping them open their packages. Then she sent me to the room to retrieve something for her and when I returned I found that she had taken the food from Shakur. His whole lunch had been placed in front of Isiah and Shakur was left with nothing but a small piece of chicken strip on a napkin. His desert was given to Stace. His big eyes filling with tears, he looked up at me and told me that he could not eat that fast. So thin you could almost see the veins in the sides of his head, so weak, and nauseated by the medication, was Shakur. I looked at Mia and asked her point blank what she was doing. She did not answer, but when I turned to leave the room, appeared shocked, and upset and asked me where I was going. I suspect she was afraid that I was finally going to report her behavior in earnest. This would eventually happen.

Later that day she complained again that she thought more of her hair was falling out and that she thought she should go to a doctor and get, "Prozac or something for my nerves." I asked her why she could not just enjoy helping the children and talk to them, ask them what was bothering them, pat them on the back, anything, a bit of kindness to keep them from becoming upset. She did not answer. She did not have to. She hated the whole situation and the young victims of circumstance would pay for her unhappiness.

The following week Mia told me that she was completing her Teacher's assessment of my work. I had only been at this school for three weeks by this time, so that an assessment was unusual. I had been with the district for six months however by this time. I was told that the vice-principal would call me down for an interview after Mia handed in the assessment of me. I read the document and signed it as requested, yet was refused my copy. I was told that I would receive my copy after I had spoken with Sherry. Now I walked down to Sherry's office, sat in a chair outside her door, and waited. One half hour later I was shown in. I was told by Sherry that although I had been given a good assessment she wanted me to know that if I did not like working there that this would be the perfect time for me to quit. "Why would I quit?" I asked "I had been willing to begin the six months probationary period all over again and was working at a salary far short of what I had been promised. I had travelled one thousand miles to return to the job. Why would I quit?" She turned beet red and answered that she just wanted to be sure I would be there through the school year for the sake of the children. I knew better. I had seen too much and the fact that Sherry was supervising Mia and had shown no concern regarding Mia's behavior toward the children did not bode well for Sherry.

Interview concluded I now asked for my copy of the assessment and Sherry told me that they had made a mistake in assessing me, for although I had been in the system for six months, I had only been at this particular school and position for a little over three weeks, so the assessment meant nothing and she refused me a copy a second time. In short, the assessment was nothing more than a pretense to get me to the office, feel me out regarding the job and impress me that Mia really liked me working with her. I imagine they felt some relief now. They had convinced themselves that I was no threat.

Little Ridge had a problem which I had brought to the attention of one of the specialists who visited the school on a regular basis. A tall, quiet spoken lady in her mid-thirties, she was obviously concerned with the well-being of the children and they intuited that and loved her visits.

I had asked her to watch him when she visited, as I was concerned with the fact that he kept fashioning penises out of the clay and could not keep his hands out of his pants. Whenever a tape was played he also gyrated to a fast-paced beat as if simulating a sex act. All of these behaviors combined with the things he verbalized to me had convinced me that he was being abused at home.

He told me one day out on the playground that a brother liked to put pepper in his bootie. As calmly as I could I asked him what he did when that happened and he replied "I don't do anything, just lie there on the bed." I was Broken-hearted for this little fellow and told Mia as soon as I returned to class with the children. Her response was something in the area of "That's awful but what can we do about it?"

"We can find someone to report to" I told her, and she said "Yea, and then the family gets mad and comes after me. That's dangerous. It not our fault. We not his social worker. Just keep notes. I'll go and talk to the school Counselor".

One week passed and the counselor never approached the class, nor did she ask to speak to me. I asked Mia and she told me that she had indeed spoken with her. Then I happened to be retrieving the mail from our cubby hole outside the teachers' lounge a few days later, asked about her thoughts regarding Ridge and found that she had no idea what I was talking about. A few more days passed and this counselor knocked at the door and asked Ridge to go down to her office with her. I looked at the clock, ten twenty. He returned at ten thirty. I asked him what the counselor had wanted and he said happily, "Oh nothing. she check my leg, then my arm, then say how I am." And laughing, his attention diverted by one of the other children he stuck his thumb in his mouth and wandered across the room.

Not good enough I thought. I talked to Bonnie the specialist again and she told me that after her first observation she went home that night and described Ridge's behaviors to her fiancé and a couple of friends and without any prompting they all said almost in unison - he is being sexually abused. Now the next step, she warned me, could cause me to lose my job.

"I almost lost my job with the district one time about two years ago for saying I wanted to report this sort of discovery to child protective Services".

I asked her the outcome and all she would respond was that she had obviously kept her job, but she would not say more about it. I told her that I found this outrageous. We were supposed to be caring for these children; was I going to just let this go? Would I sleep at night? What kind of people were in charge here? And perhaps it was time we found out. Well to her credit she got CPS on the phone, called me down to the teachers' lounge and together we told them all we had observed and been told by little Ridge.

Our complaint was taken and an investigator was assigned to Ridge's case. Just days after the phone call made to CPS Ridge was absent from school. A big shock because he never missed school and seemed unhappy when Friday arrived and it meant that he would not be at school for the next two days.

That morning, as the children lined up against the wall, I asked Mia if she had heard anything about Ridge and she angrily replied that she had not, and couldn't care less. "One less to bother with today and that good."

The following day Ridge was back and on this particular morning Mia decided that the children were not walking down the hall in a straight enough line, so they were put through their paces not once, twice, three times, but on the fourth time I took Ridge by one hand, Shakur by the other and walked ahead to the room, the others following behind me, not perfect, but we had all had enough and I had come to realize that I no longer cared what anyone thought. I knew I was on my way out by virtue of the fact that I was now going to begin to more actively defend these children. The principal had given me the devil for asking her opinion regarding Mia and the way the children were being antagonized.

Mia had even taped heavy colored cardboard to the long narrow window in our classroom door and told me that she didn't want anyone looking in. Anything and everything that goes on in here is private and you don't need to talk to any of the others about what goes on either. This is a special private room and no one needs to know about us in here. Frightening? I believe so, as on the day she sat in a chair, Isiah held in a chair in front of her, his arms crossed in front of him and when I asked her how she kept him sitting there for such a long period, she answered with a laugh, "Just give him a good pinch every so often and he don't move till I'm ready".

Eric is the only child you have not met yet. Eric is a light skinned African American child and the only one of the five children that had not been labeled slightly retarded. Eric did not know his own age and could not remember just which day of the week it was, but Eric was quiet, liked to draw, fashion figures out of clay and print his name over and over. Eric was never at risk of being activated, as the principal had referred to what Mia did to cause a child to become uncontrollably upset. Eric was fine until he drew a lady with green eyes and long blond hair, and said "look teacher, I drew Miss Wiliker because she's pretty and she's nice".

Eric soon found himself sitting in time out crying because he had, according to teacher, been drawing when he should have been cleaning his desk.

These were babies. It does not matter their chronological age. These were children who had not matured emotionally past the

Pre-kindergarten level and who nevertheless were being punished for not being able to conform to the sort of behaviors required of army cadets. I felt like throwing myself on the floor at times and could wholeheartedly empathize with them.

The days passed, each day as emotionally charged and unhappy as the day before. A check mark beside a name for laughing out loud, for jumping up from a seat, perhaps to give a crayon to another student, for not wanting to complete coloring a paper. Threats. No lunch in the cafeteria. No play time. No music. Desks were tossed. Mia's desk was cleared many times. The swat team was called, five, six times a day. Children ran from the room, hoping to get some special attention from someone. I was ordered to leave a child alone when I attempted to talk to or pat him on the back to calm him. Then the day arrived when I too was grabbed by the arm and pushed aside.

Stace had been so well-behaved all day, but you cannot force a seven year old with a learning disability to sit in a desk hour after hour with little relief and expect him not to rebel. It was close to the end of the day and he told Mia that he was finished with his picture. He began to whimper and pleaded to be let alone to do nothing. I walked over to him and as I had done many times in the past, put my hand upon his back. He looked up and smiled and as I began to tell him how good I thought he had been all day Mia approached, grabbed my arm and said, "Get away from him; I'll handle this." Oh she handled it by threatening to write an unfavorable report to his parents. This was the threat that would bring every child to tears and Stace and Shakur always had a violent physical reaction to this threat.

He pushed his desk over and Mia walked to her desk and picking up the dreaded report form, waved it at him, threatening again to write his parents. Now the desk next to his was tossed and the next and the next, until there was not a desk standing and the top of Mia's desk was cleared as well. He hollered threats, he was going to kill all of us he laughed. Bring a gun, blow the school up, and on it went until, you guessed it, the swat team came down and Stace who had been the model student all day was reduced to a writhing, crying, hollering bundle being held down, face down on the floor by four adults, one holding each limb. He was then dragged to the bus, down the hall, out the door, past all the other students and out through the gate to be shoved up the steps, and into his seat. All so unnecessary and all so sad.

Shakur tossed his desk and effectively cleared the room including Mia's desk on my next to last day there. Then calmed down remarkably quickly and began picking up the contents of her desk as ordered. Suddenly he stopped and having happened upon a math paper began working the problems. I motioned Mia to look, thinking that it would enlighten her as to his condition and all I got for a response from her was, "So who cares? He better get picking that stuff up and I want it all in order."

My last day of class involved another sad incident with Stace. It was a Friday and he had told me when he stepped off of the bus in the morning that he was feeling sick to his stomach. His mother had told him to ask for a soda cracker if he felt that way and to be still. He seemed fine until we were walking back to the room after I had taken the class out for an extra bit of time in the playground near the end of the day. He told me he felt sick and I told him to run ahead to the room. Five minutes later as we approached the class room door I heard him crying and when I opened the door found him being held down by three of the swat team.

"Oh miss Wiliker" he cried. "help me."

I said "My God what has happened to him? He was wonderful all day. I let him run ahead because he felt sick to his stomach."

Then I heard Mia's voice say, "Well he run in the door and I told him to go out and walk in properly and he refused."

As we walked the children to the bus later she told me to be early on Monday because she wanted to talk to me. I recall telling her that as it was I was coming in at least a half and three quarters of an hour early. I was and I was not getting paid a bit extra. "Oh well" she said. "Come straight to the room".

And where else would I go I thought. Never had I received a thank you for being early, or staying late. I had been admonished however, for eating too many of the crackers she kept along with all her other junk food one day. One of those days that had been so hectic that I once again had not taken my lunch.

Monday arrived and I decided to approach the principal and ask her to be present at this meeting that Mia had requested. I knocked on her door and as I entered she glared at me, asking what I wanted. Her behavior was not even civil, let alone professional.

"What do you want now?" she snapped.

"Just to talk with you regarding a meeting Mia has asked me to have with her this morning". I continued that in light of the fact of being grabbed and shoved by her myself, I wanted someone else present. At this Linda began to shake and her voice level now almost a holler she ordered me to sit down. "Those are serious charges." I went to speak and she ordered me not to say a word. Her face red, hands shaking she turned to her computer and typed out a memo, then ordered me to sign it. This was a Monday morning and the memo (which I have kept) asked that a union representative meet with myself, Mia and Linda the following Friday. Union rules state that whenever a problem of this magnitude surfaces it is dealt with as soon as possible. However Linda, almost hollering again, told me that she was busy and that Friday would be the earliest she was prepared to BOTHER with me.

She now called Mia in and Mia, refusing to meet my eyes told Linda that she did not remember touching me. I did manage to say and above protest, that I had been supportive of Mia, but that there were issues that had to be dealt with.

"You make me sick", Linda had said while we waited for Mia to arrive. "This is the second time you have come in here. Mia is your superior and you have no business coming to me. "What you need is an education."

I simply sat watching her. After this last statement she caught herself, shocked it appeared at her own words. "Oh I forgot, you are educated. Well Mia is the best sec teacher I have ever seen and she has had lots of aids, dozens, and they never complained."

Dozens of aids? And she had taught for only one year prior to the present. I made no comment. I knew that I had witnessed more than they would have liked and that they were upset that I was not an insecure kid that was going to keep quiet regarding the abusive treatment of myself or the children.

She ordered me out of the office and told me to decide to return to the class, or leave. I reiterated what I knew of the union rules and she repeated that she did not have time to deal with anything until Friday, but that she was really disgusted with me and wanted me not to forget that. She now told me to go to the office manager's office and decide what I wanted to do. I went down there, and the office manager told me to go to the teacher's lounge and call personnel regarding the problem. When I returned to the office manager, she stopped me before I had time to enter the door and told me that in the interim, Linda had told her that she was to tell me when I returned to leave the building. So they had gotten rid of me, but they could not silence me.

I called Legal Aid and spent two weeks making and receiving calls to a woman named Violet there. At one point she told me that she was sure there was abuse going on in the system, but that no-one was coming forward, she believed out of fear. She said that they had a child advocate there, then told me that the advocate was out of town. Then she told me days later that a parent had to be the one to complain. How, I asked, can a parent complain if they are not aware of the situation? She did not know. Those were the rules however.

Into the second week Violet told me that she would try to have a Legal Aid attorney take my case. I was out of work and had been told by the support staff supervisor that I would not get another job and indeed I had not. The children were still at risk and I was in danger of becoming homeless. I had all those bills to pay and simply surviving was becoming nearly impossible.

Her request for some assistance for me fell on deaf ears. "It's all very political here" she told me.

"Then I am ruined and the children will continue to be abused" I responded. "And we live in a city where we have no recourse when something of this nature occurs".

"I tried" she told me and added, "good luck".

I had made calls to the specialist Bonnie and never received a reply. I called Child Protective Services, and spoke with Michelle, the investigator who had been assigned to investigate Ridge's situation. I told her that I had lost my job because I attempted to help the children, but that I was concerned about Ridge.

Michelle assured me that Ridge was being monitored. He was safe and would be protected. Well it had not all been for nothing. She was shocked about what had happened to me, losing the job, the abuse. Who would have believed that even sin city could have a school district that cold?

I was unable to find an attorney to represent me pro bono and had not found another job. I was defeated.

I have kept everything, all the memos, proof of what has taken place. Lastly, I have the memory of those little children, their big sad eyes questioning, trapped, victimized before they had left the womb.

I was forced to return to the school to collect my final pay check. Two of the office workers were especially friendly, most nodded and looked away. Cathy, the head custodian came over to the counter to talk while I waited for the check to be found. Her eyes were shinny; she said "We miss you". She asked how I was. She had quite often stopped to keep an eye on the children in the lunch room when I ran to retrieve something for them. She had been kind to the children and me. She cared.

I asked her if the children were alright. She said they have a new one in there now. She's big and has a powerful voice. When she says something, well, they are under control. My eyes feel moist. Do I look as sad as she? She pats my arm. "Good Luck" she croaks.

"God bless" I whisper and I am gone.

Lightning Source UK Ltd.
Milton Keynes UK
UKHW03n2101020718
325058UK00001BA/16/P

9 781786 231741